THE MYSTIC THEATER OF DOCTOR XOCTARIUS: VOL. 1-2

Dominic R Daniels & Doug K Owen

ISBN: 0692376240
ISBN 13: 9780692376249

Dedicated to
Phil & Mary Daniels
Richard Martin Spalding

PROLOGUE

The fog over London was particularly dense that night. From the rooftops, it would be difficult to tell if there was even a world beneath. The scent of smoky ash laid heavy, and old soot layered the buildings like freshly fallen snowflakes. The year was 1859. The city was alive as two friends were traversing through the streets of London, their only guide the scant light of the candle lamps. They were both close to the age of 22. The autumn breeze carried a chill that passed through their thick—and expensive— coats.

"How much farther is it?" George asked Robert. He held up a hand to shield his bright blue eyes from the bitter wind. The other man, with his light blonde hair tied back, pointed down the street into the wall of fog.

"Not much farther. My flat is two more blocks down and then three to the right," he replied. The first man groaned; he started to wonder if they would even make it to his friend's home without freezing to death. But the promise of cheerful warmth and delightful comforts to be found there drove him on. Soon they would be free of the cold: safe and encapsulated in comfort.

The sound of their footsteps on the cobblestone sidewalk echoed off the russet brick walls of the nearby apartments and offices. The farther they walked through the mist, the more the world around them moved into view, if only for a little. It was enough to give them a scope of the sheer size of the buildings around them, towering several meters above them, looking down upon them like giants.

From out of the gloom, something else could be heard: a sound that was almost lost in the clicking of their boots on the ground. George stopped Robert quickly, just to be able to hear.

"...Amazing and spectacular!"

It was coming from up the street, just in the direction they were headed. The two friends looked at each other inquisitively, and proceeded. Surely neither of them could have expected anything amazing or spectacular on their way home after a long day in the law firm's office, where they worked as clerks.

And then, slowly rising out of the mist, it towering above them as they watched.

The structure was massive, certainly taller and more grandiose than any of its neighboring buildings. It lurched out of the fog like a galleon coming to port, one that had a metallic, disjointed hulk, certainly every bit different from the orderly, organized facades of its neighbor buildings with their red brick walls and whitewashed window frames. This place was windowless, a monolithic cube of metal, with vents, parapets, and alcoves stuck on random parts. Two chimneys bellowed out thick plumes of black, oily smoke into the night sky.

In front of the titanic structure was a single man wearing two large clapboards draped on his front and back. His mustached face was turning bright pink from all the noise he was making. The boards he was wearing were emblazoned in gold: "Enter the Mystic Theater of Doctor Xoctarious!"

"See the machinations of the great Doctor Xoctarious! Visions of the past and future! Tales to astound! Tales to terrify! Sights and sounds that shall remain with you for all time! All who enter here are guaranteed wonder and the highest inspiration!"

The two friends were puzzled. How did something like this escape their prior attention? There was nothing advertised in the local gazette about any theater exhibitions. And how did such a place as this go completely unnoticed until now?

"Did you know about this place?" asked the Robert to his friend, who stood paralyzed in awe at the size and complexity of the structure.

"I've never seen anything like it before," George whispered.

"But you just said that you live in this area!" Robert stammered. "How could you have never known about this until now?"

"I'm telling you, I never saw this!" George replied. "Maybe it was just recently built."

"'Recently built?' Are you mad?"

"Either that, or we both are. There's only one way to know for certain."

Together they approached the announcer, whose voice carried louder than ever, clearing his throat through his bullhorn, such that the blue-eyed friend had to cover his ears.

"Visions of worlds far beyond our own! Beauty unparalleled, never again to be seen! All are welcome to the Mystic Theater!"

"Excuse me?"

"WONDERFUL AND MAJESTIC—can I help you, good sir?"

"Er, how long has this theater been open?"

"The doctor has been operating this theater for many years now."

"Well, this is the first I've ever seen it, and I live not too far from here."

"He's only just arrived from abroad, you see. His theater travels with him as far as Bombay, Shanghai, Istanbul, and now London."

"How much is admission? I'm afraid I don't have much."

"Just a penny is all."

Robert checked his pocket and heard the jangle of loose change; surely he had enough for his admission and his friend's. He handed the man the coins.

"Thank you, sir."

"Most welcome. Enter, and enjoy the show."

Robert turned to his friend. "Fancy a show tonight?"

George shook his head. "I'd much rather be having meself an ale with Marie, that lovely nymph at Marley's; her beauty makes me soul jump."

"Oh, come now! There's time to be a dullard later; let's have a bit of fun tonight!"

George looked up at the theater and was still having difficulty calling it that. From here, he could see a myriad of gears constantly spinning, pistons hammering, and even entire sections of walls pushing in and out, like a mechanized heartbeat.

In the grand foyer of this fantastic entry way were waves of rows with performers on platforms among the crowd: String musicians of both high esteem and low, jugglers, tricksters, and venetian-masked fools, perfumed tambourine dancing ladies, and beautiful women with Egyptian-painted eyes and lovely limbs: graces of mystery, these beauties— esoteric, indeed.

There were magicians on raised platforms, performing sleight of hand with tarot cards and conjurations of evocation, illusions of sweet-scented flowers: there were birds of paradise appearing from blue and white flames, and wisps of the color jade, transforming into the flesh, bone, and blood of birds; the crowd was in awe. Some were fearful, but the wise men drew back with the flick of their wrists, their living exhibit disappeared to dust in their hands. What strange manner of Heaven was this?

The two friends were shocked and amazed. It all looked so pleasant, yet quite nightmarish— overall, it seemed but a humble show of elegance.

A voice shot through the vast crowd just as the sound of thunder cracked, and instantly all the performers slowed their motions to a slow crawl. The fast, rhythmic dancers continued their moves but at a much slower pace, and their hands pointed to the main stage in the back. The conjurers on the platforms, whose hands were frantically waving around, suddenly moved with a controlled, slower motion, and they, too, were all gesturing and pointing to the stage. The audience took this as a cue to proceed into the main auditorium.

The main theater was no less a mystery in its design than its exterior. Every column was built of rough, corrugated iron, adorned with wildly spinning cogs of brass. The seats, to the relief of the audience members, were richly cushioned with red velvet and thick padding. As everyone found their seats, the lights illuminating the halls went dim and petered into darkness. Then, in an instant, the lights crept back on again. All of the performers and magicians that populated the halls vanished.

Before them, the stage began to glow, and from out of the ornate red curtains emerged a man. He stumbled out onto the empty stage on a silver walking stick. He was a tall, slender fellow, dressed in finery. His dapper top hat and coat were spotless and black, and his shirt was pearly-white, adorned with gold-trimmed lace. A shimmering emerald ring glinted on the hand carrying the walking stick. Despite his vigorous-looking face, the rest of his body looked disproportionately frail, as if he were an old man wearing a younger man's mask.

The two friends, seated in the center of the audience, were every bit as confused as everyone else. After what they have seen in the foyer, could this strange man be their host? Could this be the much-touted Doctor Xoctarious?

The man cleared his wet throat loudly, the sound of phlegm echoing alarmingly. Most audience members shut their eyes in disgust.

"Ah, there we are," spoke the man onstage. His voice was surprisingly lighter than an old man 's. "Welcome, my friends! Welcome to my Mystic Theater. As I'm sure you may have guessed, I am Doctor Xoctarious: inventor, storyteller, and your host for this evening. I invite you all, if only for tonight, to leave behind your every care and burden. Put away your sorrows and troubles, for they will only hinder you in reaching true inspiration! Together, we shall journey into worlds far beyond your own, across the plains of time in both ways: past, future, and everything in-between! Together, we shall delve deeply into the very mystery of creation, marvel at the fantastical, and confront the macabre!"

An older gentleman in the audience curled his upper lip in disbelief. The doctor onstage caught his gesture and turned toward him.

"I see that there are some among you who do not yet believe," said the doctor. "Be assured that what I have to offer tonight is unlike anything you have ever known in your lifetimes. More than an opera, more than a play, what you will see tonight is of my own design. Tonight, the world around you will disappear, and in its place will be the world of my stories. Let it embrace you, let it encompass you, and may you in turn embrace it to yourselves! Behold!"

Instantly, the lights in the auditorium dimmed to darkness; then, white light blinded them. The bizarre theater that was once around them was gone, and the audience found themselves under blue skies with a boiling sun overhead. The audience was suddenly in the middle of a street, but it was unlike any street to be found in London.

The ground was a rough, dark-gray collection of tiny stones, and lining the streets were smooth paths on which scores of people walked by. The shops had large windows showing off an eccentric collection of wares: low-cut dresses, boxes with brightly-colored logos, all of which were proclaimed by bright signs hanging in the windows, their colors vivid. The people looked around themselves in disbelief, questioning everything around them. What happened to the weather? How long had they been in the theater, since it was suddenly midday? What part of the city were they in? What is wrong with those people walking by with such scandalous clothes? And why is there a box overhead with a red light? And why did it just turn to green?

Their puzzlement turned to terror as a multitude of machines sped towards them. Those machines, in various shapes, sizes, and colors, roared toward the audience furiously. The audience shrieked in horror as those alien devices continued their single-minded race directly in their path. Faster and faster they came, until they could plainly see people trapped inside the machines, each of those occupants completely oblivious to the onlookers in danger.

The metallic monsters sped closer yet, close enough that an audience member could potentially reach out and touch their smooth, shining, and burning-hot surfaces. Panic gripped the audience, fearing the fate of being crushed by the unyielding machines or their unknowing hostages. Everyone who was once seated comfortably in the theater shut their eyes and readied themselves for the inevitable impact.

But that moment never came. The sun overhead dimmed away, and everything went black. The monolithic buildings, the peculiar clothes, the bright signage and the speeding machines: they were all gone. The people looked around frantically, looking for any sign of what happened.

The theater returned to life all around them, the same theater they were at before. Doctor Xoctarious was still onstage, leaning on his walking stick, smiling.

"What the hell was that?!" demanded an audience member. "What is this, a trick?"

"You almost killed us!" shouted another one from the audience. "What were those things?"

From amid the din, Doctor Xoctarious held out a hand to calm everyone down. The shouts only grew louder and angrier.

"Please, ladies and gentlemen, please. I assure you that at no point will any harm ever come to any of you in my theater. I did tell you beforehand that the world around you would disappear and be replaced within the worlds that I weave for my tales. That is merely a taste of what you can expect. Its exact workings remain a mystery even to me, but what I can tell you is that you have all borne witness to a far-flung time and place. In your case, that would be the United States in the year nineteen-hundred and ninety-eight."

The audience was stunned.

"That's right, my friends. You have glimpsed a hundred and forty years into the future, where people travel in automatic vehicles without the need for horses. It is a time in which the world has grown smaller, in that even the slightest whisper can be caught by the public and pored over for years to come.

"But, for now, let us travel slightly closer to our own time. Most of you may very well be alive to see this unfold in reality, , though for others it will be more likely exist for your grandchildren or great-grandchildren.

"Much of what I have to offer may seem strange and unimaginable to you, so I shall be here as your guide and narrator. I will do my utmost to impart, for your delight, stories of heroes and villains, of changing worlds, lives, and souls. Every word that is spoken, every action conducted, will serve the greatest good of illuminating those darkest corners of the heart and spirit.

"When we take our steps into those future worlds that I conjure for you, my friends, please bear in mind that these are only possible futures, ones in which their participants, those who shaped them, have yet even to be born. Who knows? In nineteen-hundred and ninety-eight, the world may be entirely different from what I have shown you. Even *I* can be wrong from time to time." He chuckled softly, making some attendees very nervous. What if he was wrong about his reassurances that no harm would come to anyone?

"And now, we begin with our first tale for this evening, which I call 'Circus of Skin.'"

CIRCUS OF SKIN

by
Dominic R. Daniels

1

THE ARRIVAL INTO NEW ORLEANS

There was a strange but friendly tingle of hoodoo magic in the bayou air; the humid April springtime air moved among the fireflies and weeping willows, and the heat was sweltering more than ever, making sweat flow down the brows of passersby, and they tasted its sweet bitterness mixed with the smell white wine and honey.

Among the bright lights of the wildness and revelries of Dixieland's "Crescent City" was New Orleans, the city of dreams and wonders, for dreamers and dream-makers. These were the pioneering days when the Tin Pan Alley jazz & blues legends such as John Robichaux, Freddie Keppard, and eventually the masters Louie Armstrong, Johnny Dodds, and Robert Johnson, the soul-selling, crossroads bluesman who would grow the music into a phenomenon that the world had never seen before.

The billowing smoky coal-trains rode in from Kentucky down to Georgia, carrying their precious cargo of tamed wild animals, side-show freaks of oddity, and the old-time flair of the whiskey-filled loud mouths, fiery-tempered ring leader showmen, all in a circus caravan of amazing performers, traveling as a carnival that had just came into town, arriving in this jazz festival Mecca of vice and vanities: New Orleans. It was a daring temptation to the masses with diversions and fantastic flights of fancy, a once-a-year auspicious spectacle known as Mardi Gras.

The cuisine was world class, the girls' skirts were shorter, and music was the best of the ol' Mississippi. It was 1910, and the celebration was in full-swing with candle-lit vigil processions combed with mischievous-costumed devils, scantily-clad cabaret girls, and black-tie vaudeville tap dancers, filled with ecstasy and jubilation among the crowds.

There were also just-married brides and grooms out from the churches who were caught in the chaotic but wonderfully intoxicating jamboree of a traditional Fat Tuesday celebration. Included in this massive assembly were Pentecostal ministers and spirituals, along with the essence of the ether spirits of Catholic Saints and the many Voodoo Loa, who danced with violent, steamy passion in the pitch-black starry skies, among the mass crowds and pageantry of confetti blasting and colorful, flower-filled parade floats. It was beautiful— they didn't have to go to France to experience the love of the mother French Orléans; the American south brought it to them.

At the historic and well-known Congo Square in the Tremé neighborhood, just across from Rampart Street and north of the French Quarter, was the carnival, with a dash of spice and mystique. Traveling all the way through seven continents was Ireland's greatest sensation: "Shamus McGrogans World Famous Circus of the Bizarre and Strange!"

Among the glorious madness of this nocturnal wonderland on the fairgrounds came all types of people, moving in droves from the inner city to see this delightful venue: renowned and rich southern aristocrats and industrialists, stockbrokers, corrupt businessmen, gangsters, gamblers, smugglers, doctors, lawyers, pretty prostitutes, working-class tradesman, musicians, and large families dressed in fine wool, tailored suits, and upscale dresses, with their little boys and girls dressed in refined clothing, carrying assorted red and blue balloons, and their soda pop bottles filled with cherry- and lime-flavored fizzes, with the smell of fresh-roasted peanuts and buttery popcorn open air. There was even rumor that President Howard Taft had come into town to see the traveling show, but no one knew for sure.

One young man in particular was a freckled and thin but handsome teenage youth, with blue eyes and dirty brown hair, by the name of Danny Weller, age 16 and already an adept in the art of swindling and pick pocketing. He was a tall and nimble brat. His poor Catholic Irish mother and his Jewish Lithuanian father who came from a lineage of shoe makers and leather workers in the Midwest, were both long dead, and he had learned from a very early age how to survive on the mean streets of Chicago by himself. He had just arrived in New Orleans, as a stowaway on the box-car lines.

He lived by the code of the grafter and tramp with only an 8th grade education, but he had the cleverness of a thief and was a talented self-taught piano-player also. Trouble was not uncommon for this mischievous boy, including incidents with the local authorities, and when the business of thievery was slow, he would participate in local amateur fights in town hall boxing matches to earn a few extra dollars each week. But no promoter would take him on because of his past juvenile criminal record, despite their knowledge of his good right hook.

To grind out a regular living, he would play on the dusty musical keyboards at liquor-filled saloon lounges where the local chiselers and card-players would spend their nights, and in the ashy cigar smoke-laden pubs were young and curvaceous hookers with their pimps, hustling the game of the right for the price for flesh.

Payment for Danny's night's work was a small pint of stout with a cold ham sandwich and five dollars, just barely enough to rent a small room to sleep for a night. It was a hard life, but to him, there was also a sense of care-free and romantic adventure like he remembered in childhood reading the tales and other works of Mark Twain and Jules Verne.

Danny had set his eyes on New Orleans with the hope of joining a jazz band and finding stable employment. His plans were, after establishing himself as a professional successful musician, to settle down with a home of his own and perhaps, if time allowed it, to continue his education in High Adult School and maybe even attend a university in order to continue his love of music, and, with luck— if one day the future permitted it— he'd become a famous conductor with his own jazz orchestra at Carnegie Hall in New York.

But those dreams had to wait. He had to face reality first. Living in the south was more affordable than the bustling cities of Illinois. However, he lacked the necessary funds to find lodgings, and he had no desire to sleep under the filthy rafter floor-boards of the Creole whore-houses in the city.

He also was hungry and tired. The four-day ride from upstate to Louisiana had tightened the skin over his bone-rippled chest to near starvation. With little food and no money in his pockets, he had not eaten much for three days, except for a green sour apple and some day-old rye bread that he was given as an act of charity by a kind, wrinkly old peddler woman near the train yard where he train-hopped to begin his travels.

Seeing that the fair grounds were filled with food stalls and merchants selling all types of various wares, he planned on trying to con one of them and snag a free meal; he also planned to find a place to rest and decided it would be more cost effective to sleep at the fairgrounds in one of the empty caravan wagons. Sometimes the traveling circus would have one or two to be used for the storage of costumes and props in large steamer trunks. He planned that if his little operation turned out in his favor, he could get a few hours rest after midnight when everyone had gone home during the wee hours of the morning; then, an hour before sunrise, he could depart and head into city to look for work.

However, he also noticed the favorable shining gold pocket watches of some of the wealthy gentlemen, and the glittering ruby rings on the hands of fair young ladies in the square, and he suddenly had a change of heart: mugging seemed more profitable, and there were no patrolmen in sight. "This is my lucky night; a bunch of sweet smelling fancy pants," he said to himself, confidently in his thoughts.

Cocky as ever, the opportunist within him beckoned him to go for the chance of scoring some easy cash - after all, with fine loot like that, he could work the large crowd and walk away at the end of the night with enough money to last him a month. During these days of criminality, he carried on his person several useful items: a small razor-sharp pin knife to cut the out pockets of his victims from the outside, and a pair of lock picks in his inner right coat pocket.

He also carried a deck of Madame Le Belle playing cards and a set of loaded dice, should he have the occasion to cheat in a game of chance. Ready for action, he quickly went to work, brushing against the crowds and slowly picking their pockets, clean and very subtle; like a chameleon in their midst, he robbed them of nickel and coin, paper money in ladies pockets, and a few gentlemen's silver silk handkerchiefs from their back pockets, and to top it off, he pocketed a shiny silver pill-box containing snuff with a pinch of opium from one of the drunken suspendered codgers in the nearby area. He was fast and careful.

In a few years' time, if he chose, he could have become a true professional thief for the street gangs, but crime did not appeal to his nature all the time. It was only a necessary means to make a fast dollar in a pinch; that was all. Within a half hour he had about $50 in cash. He then backed off, knowing his limits, and he stopped before anyone noticed anything, stuffing his knapsack with his booty. Satisfied with his pickings, he purchased a hot dog with relish and mustard, a soda pop, and some cotton candy from one of the venders, and he ate in bliss. His grinding stomach was filled, and he felt satisfied for the moment.

He then turned his curiosity to the distractions set up for the crowds and went to see with the rest of the on-lookers what was taking place within the center of the square. Just before the entrance of the big top stood a large display of fireworks in the opening ceremony of the circus with elaborate dancing jugglers and face-painted fire breathers who spouted an inferno of bright balls of flame from their mouths into the air. At the center of a raised platform stood a tall and menacing man of about 40 years; his hair was grayish black with a set of distinct, curled black eyebrows, and a short black goatee on his chin. His eyes burned reddish-brown like Satan, and he was dressed in a expensive scarlet velvet long coat with tails and gold brass buttons, with black leather pantaloons and charcoal-gray German-made long boots. He had a stern smile on his face and a black leather whip in his right hand, and in his left hand, he held his yellow boa constrictor named Aradia, who hissed hideously at the audience. The rest of the large reptile was wrapped around his neck, gingerly holding him in a loving embrace in her coils. He gently kissed his pet on the head to calm her.

He was a notorious but intriguing man. Professor Shamus McGrogan was a man of great substance and a self-proclaimed magus priest, an apothecary of herbal drugs, a chemist, a lion-tamer, and a playwright. There were with rumors that he was a former member of the magical organization in England on Queen Street, and its sub chapters in Ireland were known as The Order of the Illuminates of Thoth. He was also a 33rd degree Freemason whose reputation as a showman left a hypnotic but cruel mark on the souls of his audience.

It was alleged that he would combine stage magic with the dark forces of black magic. Some people said he was trained in the black arts by the Order's founder Sir Samson Martyus Medina. McGrogan was said to have summoned demon and angelic spirits before a live audience, sometimes even conjuring deceased human souls as he evoked them to physical appearance and commanded them to bow to his will. If these wild stories were indeed true, the infernal spirits of Baal and Asmodeus themselves would have been proud. He was more twisted and corrupt than the infamous Boss Tweed in New York, but he was smart and just as crafty as P.T. Barnum.

Everyone loved him and hated him at the same time for his impressive abilities as an entertainer. The newspapers called him "A Ghastly Wicked Showman whose desire to raise Hell would make Heaven cringe." But the moral decorum of the times though played it as merely a theatrical act. He never used his so-called occult powers to harm another. He was charismatic but and vilely twisted: that was the best way to describe old Shamus, as he introduced himself to the audience in the square.

"Welcome, ladies and gentleman to the greatest show on the face of earth. Spirits, spells, deformities, and abominations of all nature are what you will see here in this tent tonight. See the great Cat Man Jargas! Is he man or beast? See the sultry flying acrobatic albino twins, Emily and Irene! Are these sisters, sirens or angels from the ethereal plane? See Helga the Fat Lady; her beauty is matched by her sweet plumpness! Her appetite knows no limits! Don't worry, young sirs; there is plenty of flab and flesh to go around." The young men laughed in the audience at Shamus's wit.

"And our grand master of mysticism and seer ship, the Immortal Cornelius Metaphis! He knows the past, present, and future of ages to come. Nothing but the absolute truth! Legend has it he is over a thousand years old! The last of the living great Yogi Maharajas of India! Enter to see our depraved world of Heaven and Hades!" He continued to roar to the crowds with a sinister but comical wickedness in his thick Scottish accent.

The crowd was enticed and eagerly entered the big top tent, along with the devious boy Danny caught in the mix. Taking their seats, they noticed the old candle spot lights lit up the big top with an array of wild tiger acts, with Shamus taking center stage, keeping these monstrous felines at bay with the pierce crack of his whip, as they reluctantly jumped on platforms to obey his charges.

There was a large performing rag tag group of troubadours playing in the background, building up the suspense. He rewarded the great cats, including the lioness that jumped through a series of kerosene burning hoops, with a large living giraffe that they brought in the show, led in by the animal handlers, tied with ropes. *This was different, indeed. What was about to happen?* Danny thought, and he had a terrible feeling of butterflies in his belly; something felt very wrong.

His heart was beating like a war drum, preparing for the moment as if he was at his own execution. It was disturbingly horrifying as McGrogan let these wild beasts terrorize and shred the animal limb from limb in a bloody massacre of torn flesh and bone; the carnivorous cats ripped apart the young giraffe live in front the audience. Blood spurted all over the center ring, soaking in a large pool of dark crimson and puddles of bile from the animal's intestines, as the poor giraffe screeched its last breath of life.

The crowd was shocked by the sheer devastation of this disgusting display of unholy carnage. But McGrogan seemed to enjoy it! The crowd was quiet at first, and some of the children cried; a few people left, but then Danny saw, to his own amazement, the crowd rose like in pews at a church, spewing cheers of morbid joy! They loved it! The promised terror of this hideous man was true! He was a bloody monster!

The raging madness of the blood-lusting crowd was as if the time of witnessing matches of gladiator combat in ancient Rome. It was breathtaking. Surely this was a circus from the pit of Hell itself! They all cheered in amazement.

Then, the lunatic beasts began to turn on their cruel taskmaster, and he signaled for help to be brought in to subdue the situation. Flying down from one of the wooden trapeze rafters above the center ring was a winged feline man; he actually had flapping wings on his back! And there was no wire to support this fur filled humanoid being. Could this being be a true theramorph? Danny was stunned.

The man touched down to the ground and, with a furious indignant rage, he wrestled with the three great cats, like some men wrestle alligators in the swamps of the local bayou. Throwing the heavy cats off of him, they piled onto each other, the weight of each of the beast on each other; this must be Jargas, Danny thought.

This mysterious creature began to speak to the cats in their feline language; it sounded something like a mix between the screeches and gruff roars, almost human! The beasts bowed to the crowd with Jargas in the center of them. The crowd cheered; this man beast was the master of the cats and led the tigers and lionesses off back to the cages, away from the bloody center ring. "Now then, ladies and gentlemen; I shall bring back to life the giraffe that you have seen before you, that was killed by these wild animals,"

He began to chant incantations of blasphemy in a indistinct language, "Spectra, achiati, levy, heiulio, nehuch! Va tasti, shadai, el zaduk! Arise! Arise! Blood and flame; pierce the night with the soul of this one slain! Bring back the life which these cats took; restore to me this child of the animals, of flesh, burden, and soot!" Casting his spells, a strange aura of energy emitted from his body, its piercing light was bright as a thousand stars, then the light shot back into his own body, and out of his mouth came a black mist and his eyes glowed demonic red with fire as he levitated.

Five feet off the ground, he was sending his spiritual energy into a whirlwind of smoke, and he sent his current of energy to flood the arena with dark fog; it enveloped the bloody corpse of the deceased giraffe, and there appeared a pentagram with red satanic light under the body as green and blue flames shot from the pentagram on the ground, encapsulating the dead animal. This mysterious fire burned the animal up, covering the remains; then the fire began to die down, and out of the flame stepped young giraffe colt. It had been reborn and was completely unharmed! The pentagram vanished along with the blood on the ground, and young giraffe colt was perfectly sound.

It bowed to its master in respect, for this man was a true magus; he had resurrected this animal that was sacrificed in order to show a display of fantastic power. The creature was alive as if it had never died. The crowd cheered with amazement.

Shamus floated back to the ground and ran to the giraffe and petted him on the head, with the giraffe licked his human owner's face. It was almost touching. This man had the gift of true magic! Danny was in awe; out of the bloodshed came rebirth, like a phoenix rising from the ashes of the old and coming into the new life. If only he could play in an expedition show like this, he would become world-famous! That night, the world was never the same for him.

Over the next few days while hanging near the circus grounds among the street performers and clowns, Danny mustered up the courage to speak to professor McGrogan about getting a job with the carnival. Around noon, before the carnival had officially opened for the day, he spoke to the old master himself.

The professor was in his caravan office with the door opened; it was sloppy with old beat-up furniture layered wall to wall with stacks of records and other special documents in haphazard disarray. But it had its quaintness, filled with interesting arrangements of green and black bottles filled with strange insects and liquid potions of unknown origin, like the workshop of an alchemist.

Among his shelves was some aspirin, a bottle of chloroform, herbal tonics filled with? sage and mint; there were also was two medicine bottles with cocaine and morphine, and a sealed cork jar filled with dried Egyptian Blue Lotus leaves, mixed with English smoking tobacco, and a few additional grams of brown hashish. Although perfectly legal in England, at the present time, it was as far back as 1875 when the United States had passed its first anti–drug laws; it was quite illegal but still enjoyable to purchase and dabble in narcotics, even around the turn of the century in North America. The law turned a blind eye here and there for the right price. This was New Orleans, after all: a modern bohemia for all to savor. The professor was busy sitting at his desk on a rickety tall wooden stool chair, writing with his large raven feather quill, and dipping its tip into an inkwell bottle of black India ink mixed with human blood, going over scrolls filled with handwritten informa-tion of accounts on the admissions that the carnival had made the nights before.

He began to scrawl on his scrolls, adding the new accounts as he pressed down with right hand and let the tarry ink begin to bleed into the dry parchment, he was pleased; a glare of satisfaction was in his middle-aged eyes and a sinister smug ran across his lips, and although he was slightly tired from the last evening's show, he was pleased with his businesses profits.

He opened a small green bottle on his lower shelf and a small drinking glass, and he poured himself a sip of French Absinthe, and took down his Japanese long pipe that was hanging by a small twine rope on the wall, and filled it with a small bit of blended can-nabis hemp that he had in his jewelry box on this desk. He took out a wooden match and lit his pipe taking in a few cleansing puffs. Suddenly, he heard a small knock on the side of the door, and he turned his attention to the young lad who stood before him and cleared his throat.

"Boy, leave me be! Let a man be left to his work in peace!" He was annoyed by the sight of this whelp.

But Danny was determined to get work at any cost.

"Professor Shamus, please hear me out, sir," pleaded Danny.

Setting his pipe down, the professor relented.

"All right, son; you have two minutes. My time is exceedingly precious. What do you want?" he insisted.

"My name is Daniel Weller, and I'm a traveling musician, and I thought maybe you would be hiring at this time," said Danny confidently.

"I am not, and I will definitely not hire a young thief such as you!" spat the professor in disgust.

How could he have known? There was no one watching Danny when he ripped off his victims the night before.

"I haven't done anything!" lied Danny. He was surprised at the perception of this strange man.

"I saw you in the crowd; you picked nearly every pocket you could last night. Why should I not call the police? Unless, of course, you would do something for me in return," said the professor.

"You don't have any proof!" protested Danny.

"There in your pouch, my little trickster. That's my proof. You think me a sucker! I don't have to guess. I know!" said the professor.

"Want to bet on it?" challenged Danny. Wits would be his best weapon in this situation.

This impressed Shamus. He knew the boy was guilty as sin, but the young man had spark.

"I like you, son! You've got spirit!"

"Want to play a game, then? Does bit of gambling run up your alley?" said Danny slickly.

Shamus had a feeling in his spirit, a six sense of intuition about this young man. But he let his over-inflated ego get the best of him.

"Name your game, son," said the professor.

"Dice or cards?"

"Dice is fine," said the odious Professor.

"Name your wager, old timer," said Danny.

"Alright you rascal pup. If I win, you turn over all you have in your pockets to me," said the professor. He had no problem taking stolen goods for his own purposes.

"And if I win, what will you trade?"

"A paid position, sleeping quarters and three square meals a day, my boy. Do you fancy that?" said the professor.

"Yes sir, Mr. McGrogan; I would appreciate it," said Danny, smiling; the prospect of paid work made his spirits lift.

"Make your play, my boy," said the professor pulling out from his desk draw his own set of red dice.

Pulling out the loaded dice from his pocket, he dumped his treasure trove on the ground with a thud that clanked with the coins and shiny pretties that spilled out from the pouch like an old penny arcade slot machine. You could almost hear the sound of a rusty cash register, making that fresh sale sound: *Cha-ching!*

The eager young man began to roll a few lucky sevens, although luck had nothing to do with it. And the professor also rolled his dice. Amazingly, he too had rolls of seven. It was tied to the finish line, but who would win this bet? One more roll was all that would be needed to win. Winner take all.

But Shamus stopped him on the roll; he was suspicious. "Why not use my dice this time?" he said, handing them over to Danny.

Now the young boy was in a real pickle, because if he lost the bet using the professor's dice, he would be right back where he started, and he even might be turned over the local police for prosecution, but Danny had no intention of being sent off to the workhouses or even jail despite his teenage years. He already had a long record with the law, and he did not wish to face incarceration again.

Two years earlier, he had spent 3 months locked up in Chicago for fighting with another boy, breaking his nose in a skirmish. The other boy was the one who started the fight, trying to bully Danny, but Danny, defending himself, took to fight too far and severely injured the other boy on purpose; besides breaking his nose, he also broke his ribs with a pair of brass knuckles he kept on him at the time. The court had looked in favor of the other boy and made Danny do time in reform school. He had no plans to go back to that old life, no matter how short the stay was for him. He was lucky enough to be released later on good behavior.

So with a look of determination in his eyes, grasping a sparkle of hope, he took the dice and let them rip; gingerly he flung them to the dusty ground, with the dice spinning on their edges, the anticipation building in each of the players until the dice landed on their sides.

Seven! The professor's jaw dropped, and then both them let out long but jovial laugh. Danny had won the match. The goddess Fortuna, Lady Luck, must have blessed the boy, for it was a rarity for the professor to lose in a game of chance, much less to keep his fierce temper in check when he would lose.

"I know you cheated, son, but since you won honestly with the last roll, I will not report you the police. "

Danny's gut sank with shock. The professor knew the whole time.

"Darn it!" said Danny, frustrated. "Can I still have job, please?" begged Danny, blushing and embarrassed.

The professor smiled. "You have a job, son, but let me have your silk handkerchiefs, and we'll call it even, my young friend,"

The teen delinquent immediately handed over the silk handkerchiefs from his stash and gave them to the professor. They shook hands in agreement, and the pact was made.

"Now then fine, young fellow; what instrument do you play?" enquired the professor.

"I play the piano," replied Danny, calmer now.

"Splendid," said the professor smiling. He took a liking to the boy immediately.

"Would you like to hear me play a tune for you?" asked Danny, a little nervous.

"Absolutely, but just to let you know, you will not be playing on a piano tonight. Do you have any experience with a pipe organ or calliope? Our last organist quit over a dispute. I will tell you your pay in advance, but it's not much; $15.00 a week. Is that a problem?" asked the professor, seriously. Just because he liked the boy did not mean he would put up with shoddy showmanship.

"No, that's fine; I've have played the organ for the preachers when the revivalists have come into town back home,." he said smiling.

"Good. Just do your job and do it well. No sassing and no funny business; you get me, lad?" the professor said sternly.

"Yes, sir!" said Danny, attentive like a little soldier ready to do his duty.

"Come with me, son," said the professor as he brought the boy to a steam pipe organ at the big top entrance to test his young employee's skill set.

"Here we are. This steam organ has been in my family for generations, as such with the all the McGrogans. I'd decided to keep it for the business. Call it a passion of mine for old heirlooms, I guess. Now, what type of music would you like to play for me?"

"I can play jazz," said Danny, smiling.

"Not that damn Dixieland trash! It makes me sick!" said the professor in disappointment. "Can you play anything else?"

"The classics: Mozart, Beethoven, Bach; is that enough? I can also read sheet music," said Danny.

The professor's frown turned to a sinister grin. The immortals of music were much more to his liking. He lived, in his mind, within a time without the new automobiles and modern conveniences of life, and he enjoyed it that way within the eccentricities of his character. One thing was for sure, if Shamus did not get his way at all times, he would explode with fury. Childish— some could say— but he was much more domineering than a child.

"That's better. If you're going to work in show business, you should learn your craft from the best, and the best was the original masters; the old composers were like gods," said the professor, with an appreciation of their work in his black heart.

Getting down to business, he handed the young man a piece of sheet music from Beethoven's 9th symphony. Danny, feeling timid but determined, sat at the steam organ which the professor turned on, and he cranked up its piston-like engine to get the rusted machine working, this arcane device, and it started to warm up.

As Danny began to play, it was like all time around him ceased to exist. As he closed his eyes and imagined himself at Carnegie Hall in New York, he saw himself as a pianist on the stage dressed in a fine black and white tuxedo with a golden candelabra lit to perfection with romantic and beautiful elaboration sitting on top of the grand piano; the spotlights were on him, a young star, and the massive crowd in the hall listened to him playing his music as they watched in awe and grace at the sheer beautiful talent of this young man; the music he played, although not his own, was so heavenly, one might think that it was the original Beethoven playing his own masterpiece.

Danny kept on playing as he drifted back to the present, and a large crowd had gathered was around him, and they were listening to him play. As the boy opened his eyes after finishing the musical piece, applause broke out around him that seemed to make the universe shake; it was breathtaking. The crowd cheered in exaltation and clapped with passion. They loved him! He was a born pianist.

The professor was very impressed indeed. Surely this kid would be a gold mine to him, and he promised himself in his heart to never let the boy out of his sight. Never!

But to Danny, he felt appreciated and reveled in the moment. Tonight would be a night of music, wonders, and enchantment, and the excitement was enough to give him goose pimples.

As the hours passed like grains of sand through an hourglass, the sun began to set in the distance, and warm air in the atmosphere began to cool down a little; the rest of the fairgrounds began to open for another evening of pleasurable, red-hot hellish delights. Who knew what mischief a young rebellious-minded boy could get into, to have fun and even get paid for his services? The temptation of fulfillment beyond admiration called him to soon give his first performance to a large audience.

It was the first show he would ever play outside the low-life bars and pool hustling halls; this would be a true challenge.

2

A NEW LIFE

A t a quarter past five in the early evening, the crowds began to enter the big top tent and find their seating for the show. A hand-cranked loud speaker by the promoters pierced its blasting sounds like a whirlwind through the musty air with urgent news: "Ten minutes, ladies and gentleman! Ten minutes 'til show-time. Kindly, please take your seats and get ready for the thrill of a life-time! It's all coming to you in just ten minutes' time; thank you."

The performers were finishing getting ready in their dressing rooms among the candle lit mirrors with makeup artisans preparing them before they went on stage. Among the attendants were harlequin dancers dressed in sets of black and red diamonds; there were clowns of every silly shape and size, dressed in oversized red flat-sole shoes and polka dot shirts with yellow buttons and puffed up bow ties, all covered with an interesting display of face paint and red bulb noses.

There were also pin jugglers, fire dancers, fire eaters, and a colorful display of Chinese Dragon dancers. Vinchenzo Barinni the Famous Human Canon Ball was there, and Master Kenai De Shant and his well known Ethiopian tribal drummers. The main attractions beside the animal acts themselves were The Death Defying Flying Acrobats and the seductive busty twins, Emily and Irene Desmond; there was Helga Clarington the Fat Woman, Jargas

Remo the Cat Man, and the mythic fortune teller and rumored shape-shifter Cornelius Metaphis.

Professor Shamus signaled to Danny, curling his right index finger for Danny to come to him near the changing rooms to meet his new co-workers for the show, and he did so, lining up to meet his new colleagues. "Danny boy, come here. I'd you to meet the rest of our circus family. You will be working with them in the shows and behind the scenes," said the professor happily. "My children, this is our new organ player; his name is Daniel Weller, who just came in from the Midwest, treat him right and make him feel welcome," instructed the professor.

Jargas greeted the impetuous youth with a friendly smile, his fangs showing a little under his cheetah like spots and whiskers.

"Nice to meet you Daniel; you will like working here," said Jargas.

He shook the boy's hand with his furry paws, and his long fingernails were claws, very sharp, but he was polite and would never harm the boy. He was a gentleman of a monster indeed. Danny was a little stunned at the sight of this being. Was he really a creature of legend or a man in a costume?

"Don't be afraid; I assure you, I will not harm you," said Jargas calmly.

"Are you really a Cat Man, or it is make up?" asked Danny, curious, just like a little boy in a museum.

"I am what I am and that is all need be known," said Jargas, snickering.

Danny was shy but felt warmed by this introduction. The tender, loving, and chubby Venus known as Helga shook Danny's hand with her dainty right hand, and she had a lollypop in her left.

"Pleasure to you meet you. Oh, how and sweet and scrumptious you look," said Helga teasing him.

"Oh, please don't eat me, Madam. I am too young to die," he said, a little intimidated.

Helga laughed with jolliness in her heart.

"How sweet you are; here, have a lollypop," she said, giving him the tart candy in her hand.

"Thank you; you are very kind," said Danny, surprised, taking the gift from her with gratitude. He put the candy stick in his upper shirt pocket to save later for a treat.

"You're quite welcome, young man. You remind me of my youngest son, Clarence, before he passed away. My dear Clarence, always sweet and reckless. You know, Shamus has told us of your wager with him," said Helga.

Danny blushed again.

"It was dumb luck that I won," he said. The group laughed together.

Next, he met the enchanting Desmond sisters, who were albinos dressed in purple and golden glittering leotards detailed with patterns of stars. They wore purple high heels on their lovely legs, and white and blue face paint on their eyes and rosy cheeks. Their lips where painted with pink and red lipstick. Their skin was pale as bleached bones and surprisingly cold like reptiles. Their eyes pierced through human souls, as they were both green and yellow with a hint of black pearl. These women were bewitching in nature.

Their nails were long and sharp as razors. They were very fair and very beautiful. They could have any man they desired but were always too busy arguing with each other about everything. As identical twins, they were very intriguing but sometimes a little insane. They had magnetic personalities almost split in mind, sometimes; they were friends and sometimes enemies, they were also quite scandalous and enjoyed to be pleasured by both men and women alike in the bedroom when they got the chance. They were a strange duet, those two, as only two sinful seductresses could be.

"Hello little creature, tasty little man; do you want to play?" said Irene. Danny felt nervous as if he might faint, but thin his loins began to bulge.

"Hi," he gulped.

"Irene, he is only a boy; you should not say things like that to him. He's too young for that and has no experience," said Emily equally teasing him yet correcting her liberally lecherous sister.

"What would you know, Emily; always playing mind games with young gentleman," snapped Irene.

"Come now, ladies; please, behave yourselves," said Cornelius the Great. The two girls smiled and backed off from their antics. It was all good but dirty fun.

The old fortune teller hobbled to Danny on his walking stick, dressed in an acetic Hindu monk's robe with large black prayer beads around his neck. His eyes were blue but nearly transparent from age, yet they glistened and glowed like diamonds in the rough. His mustache was white as death itself; his skin was dark as ebony but smooth as silk; he was nearly blind and half deaf, and he was skinny and crippled but full of wisdom and great patience.

He wore a traditional home spun Indian white washed turban with a blue feather in his wrap, and he wore a topaz amulet of Shiva around his neck to protect himself from the forces of darkness. He was a man of peace and deep insight. It was said that he had great powers of healing and could exorcize legions of demonic entities with a mere gesture; he was a remarkable elderly man.

"I sense a sadness about you, child you have a troubled past. You have been on the run for quite some time," said Cornelius.

Danny felt uncomfortable. The old life was not something he even thought about. But he remembered to be respectful to the elderly and did not wish to be rude to the old mystic.

"Yes, life has been hard for a long time, but I am happy to meet you all," he said trying to hide his shame of being a thief and street urchin.

"You will do fine, child; listen to the professor, and be sure that you do not anger him," said Cornelius cautiously, though the professor was within earshot.

"Never mind that old fool!" spouted The professor.

He knew that Cornelius could see into his soul. He was afraid of the old fortune teller, but he would never admit it.

"What are we standing around for? Come on, everyone! Get to your places: the show is about to start!" commanded the professor.

The whole circus troupe and other performers got to their positions as Danny got to his in the organist box and began to play on the main calliope the introduction music to start the show.

3

SHOWTIME!

Professor Shamus signaled the gaffer men to the turn on the spotlights, while Danny continued to play alongside with the flagged trumpeters whose burst of sound and dance were like a royal assembly of kings and queens were present. The spotlight turned onto the professor introducing the evening's production, "Welcome, ladies and gentleman! Boys and girls of all ages! Welcome to most to magical show you have seen on the face of the Earth!" touted the professor proudly. "If I may direct your attention to the center ring high above the rafters: behold, the Flying Desmond Twins, who will perform The Deadly Double Duel Swing Dive without the safety of a net!"

Some of the crowd was stunned with a sense of dread; some of the children covered their eyes with fear.

"I assure you, ladies and gentlemen, that the risk is very real; kindly remain in your seats during this dangerous performance! One wrong move or any distractions for our starlets could mean certain death," he said.

The drums boomed like the rhythm of a heart beat, and the twins took off like a flash of lighting, building momentum in speed as they swung back and forth preparing to back flip twice in mid air just like birds taking off for flight, and they jumped, flying to each other in slow motion; as time slowed, their every bit of concentration was set on pushing to each other and catching each other, surging spiritual energy through them.

"And now, ladies and gentlemen, it is time for the Magic! Here they go! " bellowed Professor Shamus filled with joyful madness.

A violent tornado of black flames enveloped and wrapped itself lovingly around the twins as they spun with it in the form of a perfect circle, yet floating in the air, spinning faster and faster. The sound was as if Ezekiel's Wheel was churning, raising the angelic power of the Cherubim themselves.

The burning circle spun faster and faster like a table top, the centrifugal force began to blast air like a hurricane, blowing top hats off the gentlemen and ladies' bonnets in the seats. In a relentless force, sparks of lightning and electricity shot from the twins' bodies until they pushed off, exploding into twin orbs of light!

As the large orbs split, they transformed into two giant birds, the most beautiful beings any human could have seen. There was a great blue eagle with three women's faces; each had white hot eyes brighter than the sun, and light spread from this creature with beauty, a light so glorious that the sounds of angels were speaking to the crowds, and the music of the heavens was singing, rising with glittering light and fairy dust of dreams and fantasy.

The second bird was even more dazzling than the first, an ethereal orange and strange beast; she had the head of a female lion but with human female features, the body of a woman, and the legs of a Roc bird. She had eight wings and was thus a goddess.

Out of her mouth came hot coals and embers of sacred flame, and her eyes turned golden as she roared with terror and authority. The two birds began to fight with one another in a duel of strength and magic in mid air.

In a show of spiritual swordsmanship, they circled each other in the air, waiting for a chance to pounce and strike, clawing at each other, then backing off again. They were trying to pin each other like wrestlers until the vanquished foe would tap, but neither would give up. They continued to fight and began to shred each other, clawing off feathers, similar to roosters fighting in a death match.

The professor, signaled them to stop, or they surely would have killed one another. Even in these forms, the sisters were still competitive, just as they were in their natural states. Seeing their master's signal, they disappeared and turned back into the human sisters as before as they floated down to the center ring, gracefully touching the ground like skilled pixies. It was marvelous! The two sisters bowed with grace and ease. The crowd went wild; it was as if heaven had sent these beings to them. The sisters bowed again and blew kisses to the men in the audience, smiling, and they skipped off the stage.

"Not bad, my friends, for a starter, are they!" said the professor, clapping for the twins, and he was very pleased.

"And now, my friends, dear ladies and gentlemen, I will show a wonder to satisfy your appetites! Are you hungry for some treats? Food, that is! Raise your voices; don't be shy. Raise your voices so it shall rain abundance upon you!" shouted the professor with charisma.

The crowd thought it was a gag, but having fun with it, they began to cheer, one drunken man even yelled out, heckling. "Give us some food, you old Devil!"

The professor bowed at the audience's demand, signaling for Helga the Fat Lady. Helga walked to the right side ring with the spotlight on her. Heavy as she was, she was not a slow walker. "Oh, my dumplings of love! Let me give you sweeties and tasty things!" said Helga with love and joy, her appearance changed from a large beautiful woman into a even larger woman, sprouting high in height miraculously like a tree would grow in a time-lapse. She grew and grew and grew until she was so big, she was a giant!

The audience screamed with terror when they thought this monster would devour them whole because it was just as the tales of old had said. But surprisingly, she did not, and instead, she created in her hands a large silver platter covered by a silver tray cover and set it down in the empty center ring. She lifted off the cover lid, and it vaporized in her hand. Appearing before them was a gigantic frosted and strawberry-covered chocolate cake with candles on it, and they were already lit!

Then she disappeared right before their eyes and reappeared as a normal woman in the side ring just as before and delicately bowed. The audience clapped with happiness.

"On this special night, my dear friends, from our circus family to yours, we would like you to celebrate with us our 150th birthday!" said the professor. Naturally, he was lying; his circus had been only in operation for merely 90 years, but this was good public relations, and the crowd loved it.

"Now, who wants some cake!" he vouched. The audience started raving it up. With a snap of his fingers, pieces of cake appeared on plates right before the audience's hands, each with small lit candle on it and a fork. The giant cake in the middle of the ring disappeared and the center ring appeared empty.

Now, the audience was really having fun! This place was heaven! No circus in the entire world was like it. Danny played with his piano with passion and was happy as ever. Shamus went over to the boy and told him, "Play it to them, son, one hell of a happy birthday song," Danny smiled, and he began to play the classic birthday song which all generations knew by heart.

"Now, make a wish, ladies and gentlemen, and it will come true by tomorrow morning, but be warned. Be careful what you wish for because you really might just get it. Either good or evil," warned the professor.

The whole audience obeyed and blew out their candles, making their magical wishes.

The crowd ate and was merry! Danny was beside himself as even some cake appeared for him too while he played at his organ. He was having so much fun. He thought of his childhood dreams with his head in clouds and how he had daydreamed about fantastic worlds and places, and it had came true. He never wanted to leave this place. He had found his own personal paradise.

While everyone enjoyed themselves, up next came various acts: Feathered dancers in risqué clothing, lions and bears being controlled by Jargas the Cat Man, an array of pyrotechnics and small fire work effects with Chinese Dragon dancers with blast of humor and oriental magnificence; it was like the lunar parades in San Francisco with a combination of theater and ancient dance. There were also clowns in silly acts who vaulted on winged blue horses, and jesters juggling exploding balls of multi colored confetti in the air.

As the show was soon coming to a close, the professor spoke and darkened the entire big top, and Danny stopped playing any music for final act of the evening until only one spotlight was on him.

"And ladies and gentlemen, I bring to you our final attraction for the evening. A vision of the future that may yet happen, behold: Cornelius the Great.," said the professor in a serious and chilling voice.

Danny knew what he had to do and began to play a more somber and stern piece in his musical arrangement.

A strange sense of foreboding fell over the big top tent as a single spotlight shone down on the old prophet and mage. Standing before a braise of hot coals, he poured grains of special powders in them and incense mixes of frankincense, jasmine, and oil of turmeric, and he closed his eyes in meditation and clasped his hands in prayer. His aura became visible to the crowd and changed from yellow to a pure aqua blue and violent purple, his eyes glowing with pure mysterious light.

He dipped his hands into the smoke from the hot coals and took in the scents to calm his spirit, and then he began to speak to the crowds his prophecy to come. He created before them a vision of pure terror out of the smoke which was like a projector would shine a silent film on a screen. "My spirit races with time; great change is soon to come to America, and in ten years' time, the county will explode with wealth and power, but there will also be sorrows as well," and as the old seer had said this, the crowd saw in the vision a cloud of with images in it, people coming and going in the year that was to be 1914 to 1920, with New York City vast in its lavish parties for the elite crowds, and it showed moral decay and less restriction, indulgences to the masses just as if it was New Years Eve every day. And then, the darkness fell, showing the events of death and destruction also to come.

"A World War will spread throughout Europe, and it will be horrendous, and thousands will be killed in the attacks on cities; men, women and even young children," he said.

As the vision continued, it showed the abomination of European cities bombed and families destroyed. The people in the crowds were now getting nervous; Shamus did not like this one bit, as he did not want to have spread panic among his patrons, and he signaled the old sage to stop, but he did not.

He continued to prophesy the future, how the world was about to change and these people needed to know how to prepare for the changes to come. For the sake of their families and future generations, it was necessary to survive and to listen.

"Economic collapse will also come and a Second World War in 1939 will follow, and the United States will fight to prevent Germany from conquering Europe. Be warned that great evil will come from Germany. A man of power and hate shall rise, and he will be loved by many of his people, but he speak lies and deceit, and the many of the Divine's holy people shall be put to death. Pray, my friends, for the world, whomever your gods may be. Pray to Heaven for the deliverance of the earth and the seas," he said.

As he spoke, the crowd saw in the vision the rise of the evil man the seer spoke of, dressed in iron crosses and wearing the mark of a swastika with red lace, dressed in uniform, the mark of Lucifer in flesh and blood that would cause so much inhuman suffering; he would be hated and seen as an ambassador of evil, a wanton of violence. Adolf Hitler, a shameful mark in history forever, saluting and hailing his millions of followers in military parades, playing political and propaganda music, the march of pain.

"I say again my children, pray! Pray! Pray to God in Heaven so that you, your children, and your grandchildren will survive the hell that is to come!" warned the old prophet ominously.

By now Shamus was furious. He did not want a riot of paranoid customers. The crowd was horrified with fear. Then the old seer stopped as a flash of lighting struck his body, and with a blast of thunder, he was gone and had disappeared. The lights went dark with the music dying down, and then the lights came back on and the members of the circus bowed, with the audience relieved that the prophecy was ended. Shamus sent a harsh look toward Cornelius but bowed with the rest of the circus to the audience.

The audience rose and clapped for a show well done, and then they dispersed. It was a fantastic performance, but the message of the end would stay in their minds for years to come, and some would listen, while others did not. The passage of time would reveal all things in the end. But tonight, for the young Danny Weller, he had proven himself and found a new life: the circus life.

4

A CHANGE OF EVENTS

Over the next six months, Danny was finally able to settle into his new life, and money was coming in with a steady paycheck. He was happy with his living arrangements, and he was becoming close friends with his associates whom he worked the main show with and those who worked on the midway grounds.

As for Professor Shamus, he was happy that his profits were flying high like shooting stars, thanks to the hard work of his employees and his newest little maestro.

But the professor was not happy about one of his workers, and that was the mystic Cornelius. The old man's health was rapidly deteriorating as the days went on, he was approaching his 1,002nd birthday, and the professor was beginning to believe that his use for the old monk was running out and was thinking that he would retire him soon from circus life.

At dinner one warm Sunday night, under a medium-sized cabana tent, Danny and his companions from the sideshow sat at a relaxing feast at a large grand oak table with decorated and wood carved chairs and bottles of champagne poured into tall crystal glasses, and a toast was given.

"I must say, my children, that your hard efforts have been paying off just fine, so we will celebrate this evening. I have decided that you all deserve a day off, so rest and enjoy yourselves in any way you desire," said Shamus raising his glass pridefully.

Jargas, the Twins, and the other performers lifted theirs and sat down to drink, and Helga brought out a hot roasted turkey stuffed with spices and breadcrumbs on a rollaway server cart to her friends, and a side dish of mashed potatoes with rich brown gravy, and a platter of steamed carrots cooked in Irish whiskey and sweet red onions, including cranberry sauce and cornbread. To finish it off, for dessert there was a large cherry pie.

But Cornelius was not present for the meal; he was sick in bed with a high fever, his body weak and exhausted from his work, and his energy drained.

"Now then, my lovelies; it's supper time! Let us eat," said Helga as she walked over to the table wearing her oven mittens and her rose flower pattern apron, and she set the food in the middle to serve. As much as she loved to eat, she also loved to cook, and Sunday dinner meant the most to her.

"Oh, this reminds me of the days when my father, William Clarington the First, would come home from his work at his office. He was a fine physician, of course, and my mother and I as a young girl would prepare a bountiful meal like this," she reflected, reminiscing.

"My dear Helga you never cease to amaze me," said Jargas, impressed.

"I suppose I should bring you a saucer of milk, you conceited old cat," said Helga joking.

Jargas chuckled along with the others present.

"This is wonderful; I feel so alive," said Danny happily.

"Haven't you ever sat down to a family dinner?" asked Irene curiously.

"No, not for a very long time, "said Danny quietly.

"I take it they died," said Emily insensitively.

"Emily, please, dear sister; let us play nicely with the little mouse," said Irene in return.

"Never mind them, my young friend," said Shamus as he carved the turkey and served himself first and then his friends.

"Where is Cornelius?" asked Danny surprised that he was not there with them.

"The old buzzard is in his room sleeping, sick with the fever; I would pay for a doctor, but my expertise in medicine is good enough for that old fart," said Shamus, annoyed.

"You should not say things like that about Cornelius. Shamus, he is a good man," said Helga, turned off by her employer's comment. Shamus indulged himself in swig of brandy on the side, a little bit drunk and annoyed.

"The old man needs to retire; he causes an uproar in the shows," complained Shamus.

"He is just telling the truth, boss," said Jargas, defending Cornelius.

"The old coot's prophecies are starting to scare our customers, and I don't like to see our audience leave here worrying about the future. Why bother with that when it has not yet arrived," said Shamus, eating some of his mash with his spoon.

"You do know, Professor, that his predictions are never wrong, " said Jargas.

"I know, and he predicted a year ago that a great fire would take place here in the States, and when it happened, we got letters and had our faces in the tabloids calling us prophets of doom. Well, I don't care for that type of press," said Shamus, irritated.

"There were other reports, positive ones; remember when he said six months ago that China would end slavery, and then they did," said Helga, serving herself some cranberry sauce.

"Regardless, that old man's predictions are stirring up too much trouble for this circus company in the newspapers, and if he has to predict something, let it only be good news," said Shamus arrogantly.

"You don't think a World War will come, Professor?" asked Irene, concerned.

"Rubbish," replied the professor.

"Maybe if we all blow each other up, then there would be some decent change," asked Irene sarcastically.

"Doubtful, my dear; Regardless, Cornelius has been with this company ever since my grandfather ran it; I think it's time that the old windbag stepped down, "said Shamus.

"It would not be right to put him in a home, Shamus. He's too old, and you know that," said Jargas.

"What I say, Jargas, goes. Either that decrepit stargazer goes into a home, or he goes on the street! I will not have us lose profits for a crippled and delusional old man," said Shamus harshly, getting more drunk by the moment.

"Boy, he is in a rotten mood tonight," muttered Emily to Irene under her breath.

"I heard that, you little bitch! Close that pretty mouth of yours, or you won't be having a pretty smile so soon," said the professor cruelly.

The others just went quiet; Danny did not like this, and he was starting to feel as if he had made a terrible mistake in taking employment with the professor.

"Sorry, everyone; my stomach is bothering me. Excuse me, please," lied Danny, excusing himself.

He left the cabana and went to check on Cornelius, feeling sorry for the poor old soul. Danny went to the kitchen next door and prepared a fresh plate of food from the extra servings that Helga had cooked earlier, then he went to Cornelius's tent next door with the plate of food and a bottle of sweet wine he stole from the kitchen's wine shelf and brought it to the ill man.

Entering the ancient seer's dwelling, he set down the food and wine on the night stand next to Cornelius's bed. He turned up the dim lit oil lamp in the tent. The old monk awoke, gently opening his eyes and yawning a little, and then he noticed Danny in the tent.

"Hello Daniel, " he coughed a little. Danny checked Cornelius's forehead; his fever had gone done a bit, and he was feeling slightly better.

"Your fever is subsiding, which is good," said Danny.

"Thank you, son. Why did you come to see a sick old man? You should try to enjoy yourself tonight; I am sure the moon is out," said Cornelius, still tired.

"That's okay, Mr. Metaphis; I just wanted to bring you some food, and there is also some wine. I thought you might get hungry later," said Danny respectfully.

"That is very nice of you, but I am afraid I'm not the best company for a good young man like yourself," said Cornelius.

"I'm not that good; I am a thief who took this job out of desperation to survive. Does a good man have to be a crook to eat?" said Danny, ashamed of his past.

"My son, you have a loving heart; don't be so hard on yourself," said Cornelius, feeling supportive. "How do you like working in the circus?" he asked, interested in the boy.

"I like it, but there is something, I want to talk to you about," said Danny; his conscience was bothering him about what the professor had said earlier, but he was debating whether to tell the old man what he heard at the dinner table. It broke him to pieces; he just could not bring himself to hurt the old man's feelings. In a way, he felt sorry for him.

"Is something the matter?" asked Cornelius. He had a feeling that the boy was hiding something from him, but he could not point his finger on it.

"It's nothing; why don't you try to get some more rest. I'll bring some fresh cold water for you to drink, later," said Danny filled with a tender sympathy for the man.

"Why don't you stay a bit and tell me about your life, my son; I get very lonely in my years, and I don't have that much company," said Cornelius.

"You have the others," said Danny encouragingly.

"Yes, I do, but I like to keep to myself at times, the centuries have been long for me," said Cornielus in deep contemplation.

"Centuries? You mean you really are over 1,000 years old?" asked Danny.

"My son, this life and circus both are major mysteries; we have all come from distant days and ages long past, and it's a long story. I will tell you sometime about it, but not tonight because these old bones ache with pain. Your company though gives me great solace," said Cornelius, enjoying the young man's visit.

"Oh please tell me, I would love to know how it all happened," pleaded Danny.

"With youth brings the lesson for patience, my son," said Cornelius.

"Alright," said Danny softly.

"Stay for a bit and pray with me, for I am going to die very soon," said Cornelius, who knew he was beyond his twilight years and the time to leave this world was close at hand, and he would travel the long path where all holy men go to reunite and commune with the Eternal God, the Creator.

Danny stopped dead in his tracks hearing this; he liked the old prophet for he spoke truth and had a kind spirit.

"You won't die, Cornelius; I know that even though the professor doesn't appreciate you, the rest of us do, and the others have told me that you've been like a grandfather to them. They would hate to see anything horrible happen to you," said Danny compassionately.

"Yes, I love them too. It's good having a family; we've all been together for so many years. I remember seeing the twins when they were but children, and their father was also part of this circus; he too was an acrobat, and their mother, but they were killed when they attempted to do the same swing dive you saw the twins perform those months back when you joined us. It's a very dangerous stunt, and very difficult to achieve. Many trapeze artists are too afraid to take such risk.

"The reason you see the sisters argue so much is that they hold a great deal of guilt for about their parents' deaths, and you see it was them who begged their mother and father to show them how to do that trick. They were little girls when it happened. It was so devastating for them both, and they had meant no harm. So I took care of them after that for a long time, and they respected me greatly, twin white witches that they are. As the years passed, they came to hate each other, always blaming each other for their mother and father's death. That's why they are the way they are," said Cornelius with sorrow.

"That is very sad. Were their mother and father also witches?" said Danny.

"Yes, they were; great wise ones, when the world was young. They were guardians and priests of the ancient world, long ago," said Cornelius.

"What about Jargas and Helga?" asked Danny.

"Jargas is very old, my son; just like me, but even older; his family bloodline comes from the pharaohs of ancient Egypt. He was once a great prince who ruled the over the lands of the Nile in the Valley of the Kings, and some say he was cursed by his wife, a beautiful princess, for having an affair with the high priestess of Bastet, the cat goddess. For his transgression, Jargas was transformed to become neither a man nor a beast but of two worlds, and so it has been for all this time," said Cornelius coughing to clear his dry throat, and Danny poured him a goblet of the wine and the old man sipped it gently.

"Thank you, my son," said Cornelius in appreciation.

"Is it true? The story, I mean," asked Danny

"I believe so, but I don't know for sure," said Cornelius.

"What of Helga?" asked Danny.

"Oh, dearest Helga. She is a very intriguing woman and very talented in many areas of expertise," said Cornelius.

"Well, who is she?" asked Danny.

"I am not sure if you would believe me, son, and you have already seen many strange things that most human beings rarely if ever see in a lifetime," said Cornelius

"Nothing surprises me these days," said Danny smiling a little.

"Helga is a descendant of the great spirit Gigantia, a legendary massive fat goddess who was worshipped at the megalithic temples of the island of Gozo, close to Malta, and there is not much else I know about her, but she brags to me of that is where here great heritage comes from, so who knows," said Cornelius, not sure himself.

"So all of you are supernatural beings, aren't you?" asked Danny, surprised.

"It's not something we like to openly talk about, my boy; we merely play our parts for the circus," said Cornelius smiling.

"But I heard that the professor said that you were immortal," said Danny.

"Young man, never trust a showman. They are certified liars most of the time. Shamus likes to mix half truths and half lies, something I never do— be warned. He is not to be trusted, and he sold his soul long ago," said Cornelius.

"So the magic is real then?" asked Danny.

"Yes it is, but the power he calls upon is not from the Divine but from the forces of darkness. He is a duplicitous, evil man, and I pray that you leave this place soon. His greed for wealth is insatiable, and his hunger for power is endless. He will use you just as he has used us to get what he wants, " warned the old Seer.

"What about your gifts?" asked Danny.

"My gifts are from heaven, though the whole monk routine is a gimmick, son; a bit more theatrical on my part,"

"Who are you, really?" Asked Danny.

"A wondering old soul who was charged to preach the Divine's messages until my time is done. Soon, I will go home and be at peace for eternity. I need you to promise me, though, that you will leave here; I am worried for your safety," said Cornelius, and he truly did worry about the boy, as did his fellow companions.

"What do you mean?" asked Danny.

"We are all the professor's slaves, my son; we have been for a long time. Do not think that we ourselves have not tried to escape from him. He made a deal with the Prince of Demons, Beelzebub. Beelzebub himself would make Shamus the most famous showman in the cosmos if he would gladly serve the Demon Prince and his court for all eternity. So Shamus made his deal and it was done.

"Shamus found us over the years and imprisoned us with his power, which is the reason we are forced to remain with him. He was cruel to us; he tortured us and starved us, maimed us and defiled our flesh with sickness and hexes. The only reason we have not tried to attack him was that he has always been too powerful to defeat, so we gave up hope and tried to make the best of our circumstances, and after many years, it became normal, and the old devil did not need to beat us or starve us. We simply obeyed him, and he let us be. We made him and his wretched family the wealth of a king, but it was never enough, for his lust for gold and plunder is insatiable. I am sure that he spent most of the fortunes on lavish living because he left us with barely anything. That is our mystery and our curse, so now you know, my son," said Cornelius. So it was that the terrors of this foul circus were exposed, and it was no paradise; no, this was hell.

5

LOCKED UP

Suddenly, Shamus came into the tent, overhearing the truth told about his demonic deeds. His lion whip in hand and a pistol in the other, already in a drunken stupor, he wanted to kill the boy and the old man. His secret was exposed!

"So the old man told you the truth! I'll carve your flesh from your bones and eat it in a stew if you dare tell anyone what you have discovered!" threatened the professor.

"You filthy bastard! You don't scare me!" spat Danny, not afraid of the professor.

"You ungrateful child! I took you in and gave you a home, so how dare you to insult my authority! I'll teach you a lesson !" raising his whip and slashing his whip at Danny, the whip cutting into the boy's face, a fresh open wound as scarlet blood seeped out, knocking Danny on the ground. Cornelius jumped out of bed in his night gown attempting to stop the attack, but McGrogan pulled out his pistol and shot the old prophet in chest, killing him instantly. His prophecy of his own death had came true.

"Noooo!" screamed Danny in shock. "You killed him!" shouted Danny.

The rest of the sideshow performers heard the clamor and rushed inside the tent to see what had happened. Shamus raised his pistol now at Danny.

"Don't make a move, you fools, or I kill the boy!" yelled Shamus in rage.

"You fiend! How could you do this to him; the old seer served you better than any of us!" said Helga hysterically.

"Shut up, you fat sow! His time is done. Go back to your rooms and say nothing of this to the other performers; you and they all know the penalty for disloyalty," raged Shamus.

"One day, you will fall from your throne, you evil man, and I will love it when that day comes!" roared Jargas, in hate.

"Don't even think it about it, you mangy flea bag. Or I'll kill him, I swear," said Shamus, ready to pull the trigger.

Jargas and others backed off and left.

Danny cringed with fear, now truly afraid that the professor was going to kill him, but he did not; he continued to whip Danny mercilessly, and as that stinging spiked whip cut through the boy's clothes, leaving him raw, his thin body slashed to ribbons with tidbits of shredded hanging skin and blood-soaked flesh, the boy passed out, and he fell to ground.

The professor stopped his attack, putting his pistol away, back into his holster and picked up the unconscious boy, carrying him in his arms and putting him in a nearby cage to be his prisoner. The rest of the circus performers were too afraid to challenge Shamus as they saw the wounded minor, and the professor slammed those cold iron bars shut and locked Danny up with a padlock.

Then he went back to the dead seer's room and had his animal handlers remove Cornelius's body and dump it around midnight into the river, weighed down and heavy-chained so that it would sink to the bottom of the cold murky water, to be eaten by the river crabs in the pitch dark waters of the swamp's abyss.

Shamus closed down the grounds, and the rest of the circus performers were informed by whispers of the beating and Cornelius's death, too afraid to challenge their ring master, so they sadly went to their rooms to grieve.

With the weight of the killing on their minds, they did not have the boldness to challenge him. When past attempts in escapes were made, this modern Marquis de Sade resorted to sucking the souls out his workers and feeding their bodies to the lions, a barbarous but an effective form of cruel dominance that worked all but too well.

About an hour before dawn, one of the professor's guards, a middle-aged, red-bearded man with red suspenders and vertical black-striped pants wearing a bowery hat, got up to break from his watch over Danny's cage. He looked in to check on the lad with his oil lantern, as he tried to warm himself by a small bon fire that was kept to burn all night, and he felt sorry for the boy. He was big as a buffalo but kind as a harmless doe.

He opened the cage and removed the young man's bloody shirt and cleaned the boy's wounds with his handkerchief and dipped it with some brandy that he had on him. Danny awoke in pain and was disorientated, and he backed up on the ground, fearful that the guard would hurt him, but he did not.

"Easy, boy; the professor's asleep," said the guard.

"What did you do to me?" asked Danny, afraid.

"Just cleaned your wounds is all I did. It will be about sunrise in an hour. I'll come back later and bring you some scrambled eggs and sausage; you should try to get some more sleep," said the guard kindly.

"Thanks. What is your name?" asked Danny.

"My name is Gibbons," said Gibbons.

"He held you prisoner, too?" asked Danny.

"All of us son, that black-hearted devil," said Gibbons.

"How long have you been here?" asked Danny.

"Long enough. Now go back to sleep, and I'll see you in a little while," said Gibbons. Danny closed his eyes and drifted back to sleep.

As he opened his eyes, a strange mist was wrapped around him, and he was in the dreamscape where all dreamers go. In this place, he found himself floating in a ball of water, shrouded in white mist, and traveling amidst a large ball of light as he flew like sparrows above the sea of glass; the water of the ocean below him was indeed clear as glass, and he could see every size of strange sea creatures below him, and some were so hideous that a person would faint at their mere sight. Others' beauty was beyond heavenly, and he could not describe such forbidden beings.

He saw lightning and heard thunder, and he saw strange faces of angels and demons whom he saw floating around him as they whispered to him in his ear. They had cold, icy, and apocalyptically beautiful features, somewhere beyond glorious height, dressed in silk blue robes covered with pink and violet light, their eyes burning with the brightness of a thousand suns, and the cool air around them was like the moons of Jupiter. Some of these beings had blond hair and eyes of transparent jasper, with sets of twelve wings on their backs, the others were hideous creatures, their ugliness too horrible to describe, who had multiple horns and black wing feathers; some had twenty red and black eyes that burned with hell fire, and they had six arms with small claws and cloven hoofs for feet. Their four tongues were long, and they had fangs long as tusks.

Both good and evil forces both were present; these creatures had tired of the professor. His contract was cancelled. He had displeased them. The forces of light and darkness both wanted to claim him for judgment.

"Defeat him! We will aid thee," they said to Danny in unison, their voices chiming in strange peculiarity.

"How can I? He almost killed me," asked Danny.

"Friendship and love can defeat any evil, and a blaze of hope will light your way," they said together.

Danny saw flashes of his mother and father before him, their spirits holding him as child and as a baby. He looked into their eyes and remembered what love was then; he opened his eyes, and in a flash of purple light, he awoke.

The sun had come up; Danny was greeted by Gibbons, who was holding a hot breakfast plate of food for him. He had also brought a brass pot of fresh-roasted, steaming Arabic coffee with a cup of milk and a cube of sugar. It was still strong, but after the night that everyone had, it was needed.

Gibbons opened the cage and let the boy out to eat. He handed Danny the plate with a fork and small copper cup filled with the coffee to drink. Danny was so hungry, he began to gorge himself on the food eating quickly with the appetite of an elephant. "Easy does it, now; you'll get a stomach ache if you inhale it like that," said Gibbons.

"The professor wants me to keep a close watch on ya, so you'll need to get yourself cleaned up and get to work. You'll be cleaning the animal stalls today," said Gibbons reluctantly.

Danny saw he was a prisoner, and the circus was under the tyranny of the professor. He so desired his freedom. But he felt sorrier for his friends in the sideshow and the rest of the performers in the circus. They were all trapped together with him in the same fix.

Not saying anything, he went to the shower stalls and cleaned himself up; the warm water was refreshing and cleansing on his wounds. Then he dried off with an old towel and got dressed in a pair of fresh clean clothes, and he went to work cleaning the horse stalls and giraffe stalls. He also gave them their feed, and the animals themselves seemed to enjoy his company, and he also noticed scar marks on them as well.

The cruelty of this place was beyond comprehension, he thought, as the animals seemed happy to receive some affection from a human who cared for them. It was love that these poor creatures needed, and Danny was happy to give it to them. They were gentle with him and licked his face, playful but safe. He petted them and went off to do his other assigned chores for the day.

Later that night, he performed under the big top tent, as usual, with the crowds witnessing the show, but this time, the magic of this place had worn off, and he desired more than ever to be far away from this dreadful place, and he could see the same feeling of mutual agreement in his co workers, though they hid their true intentions well for the show. They had to.

Danny remembered from the dream what was said to him by the winged beings, and he planned out in his mind a way to try to find an escape. He was completely through with the so called glamour of circus life, but if he had to escape, it would not be by himself. He wanted to help all of his friends. They were his family and he cared about them just as much as they cared about him. But how would he do it?

6

THE PLAN TO ESCAPE

A few nights later at two in the morning, after the main show had ended for the night and all of the performers had gone to bed, Danny was wide awake in his sleeping tent, dressed in his pajamas as he lay in his hammock, pondering away at trying to find a method of escape.

Suddenly, an epiphany hit him, and he remembered the dream that he had a few days before, after Shamus had brutally whipped him to near death. The piece of the dream that made sense to his scheming was the quote when the angels and demons had given him an important hint, *"a blaze of hope will light your way,"* he remembered, and he came up with a plan to free his friends and himself from the grasp of the hideous McGrogan.

He quickly got out of bed and got dressed, and then he rushed to Jargas's tent and woke him up to tell him what he was up to. Jargas was sound asleep in his bed, purring as he slept, though not the most comforting sound.

"Jargas, wake up! Wake up!" Danny hissed, trying not to be too loud.

"Ah," said Jargas feeling startled.

"Daniel, it's late; go back to sleep," said Jargas, who was tired.

"Jargas, listen to me; I think I found a way for us to escape," said Danny. Jargas rose fast, fully alert. He got out of bed.

"Well, what is it?" asked Jargas.

"We'll set fire to the big top, use me as bait for the professor, and the guards will be too distracted trying to put out the blaze; then, they'll release all the animals from their cages at the same time, and while that is going on the rest of you can make your escape and run, and I'll join you later," said Danny.

"My friend, that is a good idea," agreed Jargas. "But I have something up my sleeve to add to the plan," he continued.

"What is it?" asked Danny.

"Trust me," said Jargas.

Jargas and Danny quickly went and woke Helga and the Desmond twins, including Gibbons and a few other performers and informed them of the plan. Taking careful precautions in the dead of night, they put their strategy into action. It would be a grand final performance.

7

MUTINY

Danny and company quietly snuck to the kerosene cabin, which was used to store fuel for the circus's main lighting equipment during the shows. The grounds were dark, but being a cat, Jargas could see perfectly in the blackness and guided them to the room; there, Danny lit a candle and handed it to Helga, and while he pulled out his lock picks and went to work, he picked the lock open.

Their group entered the cabin and brought out from it a few small barrels of fuel, and there was also some fireworks and gun powder there in storage, which they confiscated to use in their plan.

Sneaking over to the big top tent, they began to spread the gun powder around the tent and then doused the tarp with the kerosene, including other tents and stalls in the nearby vicinity. Emily and Irene grabbed dead branches from the grounds and wrapped them with linen sheets that they stole from the washing stalls, drenching them with the fuel, and lit them, making homemade torches.

Then used these to set fire to the big top tent, which instantly began to burn, and the blaze spread quickly throughout the grounds. Suddenly the sound of shouts woke up the professor in his tent as he heard the noise. "Help! The big top is on fire! We'll be killed!" screamed the animal handlers.

Shamus quickly hopped out of bed, rushing in his red long john pants to the scene as the fire was spreading throughout the whole carnival; the heat was intense and the smoke was rising with burning embers flowing up into the pitch-black sky.

The sounds of sirens approached as an old horse-drawn fire truck with fire fighters arrived on the scene, trying to help put out the blaze, but the twins did not allow it as they began to mutter together spells of binding and protection as a wave of translucent energy flowed in front of the fire fighters; a cloud of energy blocked their path, and they could not move, and they fell down to the ground as if they were dead

Shamus was enraged. "My circus! My dreams! I'm ruined!" he screamed with hate.

He caught sight of Danny who was also lighting other tents on fire with a torch and grabbed the boy, with gritted teeth ready to tear him apart with own hands.

"You little bastard! You did this to me! Now I will kill you as should have done before!" He seized the boy by the throat with his strong hands, ready to strangle him, but Danny pushed the burning torch in the professor's eyes, blinding him with the fire.

"AAHHHHHHHH!!" he screamed in agony, letting go of Danny as he hobbled around helpless as a child. His were hands on his face, trying to deal with the sensation of pain, and his sight was gone; he was blind as a bat and helpless.

"Help me! I can't see! Someone, please help me!" he screeched like a banshee.

Jargas, Helga, the twins, and the other performers surrounded the professor, encircling him with Danny on the sidelines.

"Now we'll show you who the real beast is!" said Jargas with green fire in his eyes as he transformed into a large cat: no longer a cat-man but a great leopard!

The twins transformed also into two large white tigers, their eyes though different in color with green and yellow, and Helga also changed into a large fat centipede creature, and her face still had the resemblance of her human form but was much more de-monic in appearance: her eyes burned red as lava, her teeth were all fangs filed down to fine points, and she grew in size by ten feet in length.

Gibbons backed up, afraid, holding his arms around the boy the protect them both as they witnessed these monsters tear the profes-sor apart, as they ripped open his jugular, while blood spewed and flesh was torn, with the professor screaming curses and regrets as they ate him alive, chewing off in sheer madness and bloodlust his arms and legs.

His chest was bitten open and the beasts were eating his bloody heart, his lungs and liver until finally they pulled off his head sepa-rating it his body, and the creatures' faces were smeared with blood and malice, and they looked as if they were going to kill both Danny and Gibbons.

But they stopped as they looked into the eyes of their young friend who had saved them, and instead they ran off into the dark-ness. Shamus was dead.

"Let's get out of here, Daniel," said Gibbons.

The two fled from the circus fairgrounds as the police were in the area with a coach and horses to see what was happening, but Danny, Gibbons, and the rest of the remaining performers had abandoned the inferno. Gibbons managed to prepare a wagon and some horses an hour before, so he and Danny and him quickly mounted the wagon and took off into the night, far from the fair-grounds, and by sun up they had entered into the city.

EPILOGUE

As Gibbons and Danny were riding on the city street, Danny had noticed in the wagon, there were seven large burlap sacks, and the weight of the cart was starting to pull down on the horses and make them tired, so they stopped to rest.

"Hey Gibbons, there are some sacks back here. What's in them?" asked Danny.

"I don't know; maybe horse feed," said Gibbons.

"Let's take a look," said Danny as he got down from the cart with Gibbons, they opened the sacks to find copious amounts of gold coins and multiple folds of cash.

"Well, I'll be damned," said Gibbons.

"Where did it come from?" said Danny. Looking inside the treasure- filled sacks, they also found a note, which Gibbons picked out and handed to his young friend. Opening it with enthusiasm, he read the letter out loud. "We thank you our dearest friend for setting us free, and this is the fortune that the professor hid from us all these years; take it and be on your way. Your friends from the Circus of Skin," read Danny. Cornelius was wrong. Shamus's own greed kept him from ever sharing or spending a single penny.

Gibbons and Danny smiled and rode into the morning dawn.

Sometime later, Daniel Weller and James S. Gibbons purchased a large plantation house near the outskirts of New Orleans, were they remained for many years as close friends; Daniel eventually became the jazz musician he always dreamed of becoming, and he grew in fame and success for a long career that would last him a lifetime.

He never saw the shape shifting cat man Jargas again, or the whimsical giantess Helga, or even the mad Albino twins Irene and Emily, but he always remembered that wondrous spring of 1910, which he had spent with them at the circus, long ago, and he never forgot them; to him, they would always be his friends in his heart, and people's true character is not what they look like, but it is what is underneath the skin.

The plantation field disappeared in an instant, as if the entire scene around them was made of smoke that got stirred up in the wind. Where the green fields and majestic manor once stood, there were the thick columns and spinning cogs of the Mystic Theater. The audience looked around themselves, trying to get their bearings back.

Some audience members felt disoriented after the sudden change of setting, and neither Robert nor George could blame them for their discomfort. The scenes of hideous beasts, brutal torture, nightmarish sorcery and revenge were far beyond anything George could have possibly imagined. Whoever this Doctor Xoctarious person was, he must have had the sickest mind in all of humanity to be conjuring up such hellish imagery.

The doctor took the stage and was lit from beneath by an array of candles. He could clearly see the looks of dismay and horror all around him in the theater hall. He frowned slightly as some members of his audience screamed. At least one lady in the audience was passed out. He made a hand gesture off to the left side of the theater, and a black-suited attendant rushed to the unconscious lady. The man held a small vial near her nose, and the lady jolted back to consciousness in an instant.

"I warned you all beforehand that within my Mystic Theater, there would be adventures beyond all imagining. Also, I did make known that no harm shall befall any of you. Despite everything that you may see or hear within these visions, they are all simply players in a story of my design.

"The Circus of Skin stands as an everlasting warning against dealing with forces that lie beyond the understanding and control of any mortal. What keeps a man such as McGrogan alive, that he uses these creatures and machinations for his own gain? And what of the poor creatures destined to be his servants? That, my friends, is a discussion to be held among you. Were there ever any true monsters to behold in the circus?"

Silence hung over the audience of the Mystic Theater. A chill crept up George's spine and his skin broke out in goose bumps. His breath came out in slow, labored gasps. Around him, others were feeling just as uncomfortable as he was. Sitting next to him, Robert clutched his chest tightly, shutting his eyes and gritting his teeth. A vein was bulging on the side of his forehead.

"Robert?" asked George to his friend. "Are you alright?"

Robert said nothing, instead trying to slow down his strained breathing. He inhaled and exhaled sharply, over and over, trying to steady himself. When he finally became stable, he slouched in his seat and sighed.

"How did I ever let you drag me into this?" Robert griped.

"I thought it was your idea," George asserted.

Robert opened his mouth to speak, but the deep clang of a bell cut him off abruptly. The unseen bell tolled six times, reverberating through the auditorium. Onstage, Doctor Xoctarious resumed his role when the last tolling finished its low, chilling echo through the hall. The gears and rotors on the columns continued churning without pause, and all eyes were on the doctor in the middle of the stage, wondering what more he could possibly offer, and if it would be as terrible and tragic as those stories that came before. Many people in the hall were beginning to yearn for some respite from the morbid scenarios that they endured.

"I see that some of you are starting to grow weary, and in all honesty, I cannot blame you," said the doctor. *Even after presenting such horrifying imagery,* George thought to himself, *how could he still be keeping such a calm, cheerful demeanor?*

"I know full well that my tales are not for everyone. There are many among you now who may wish I'd use my Theater or my talents to present other things. A field of flowers, perhaps? Or a sunset over a mountain? Such things, I will consider, but that is for another time.

"You may find yourselves asking, why am I showing you these things? Why have I gone to such herculean efforts to build this place, spin life into its every cog and gear, if I meant to curdle your blood and chill your hearts? Surely, there would be easier and far less extravagant means to do that, would there not?"

George nodded. After all, he was made to endure over the course of several hours, and even he had reached a limit. He found himself questioning why he ever had such a fascination for ghost stories, if it led to him patronizing places like this.

"The truth is this: every one of these tales holds a deeper meaning. If the only thing I sought to do was to scare you to your wits' end, what would there to be gained from that? Well, aside from a trip to the insane asylum, anyway. Look carefully, my friends, past the danger and death, and see what can be learned from these stories. Who knows? You may even find a little of yourself in this *dramatis personae.*

"However, I think a change of pace is in order," announced Doctor Xoctarious. "A little respite from the macabre, and we'll let the deathly chills be cast away...for now."With a wave of his gloved hand, the theater once again disappeared, a sensation that the audience was well-adjusted to by now.

Where the ornate columns and crimson curtain once stood, there was a massive tapestry of color that exploded above the audience's heads. Against a field of blue, streaks of pink, purple, red, and yellow unfolded in ethereal, formless shapes. A warm breeze caressed their brows, carrying a faint smell of salt and earth.

The sun was setting over an ocean, and the audience found themselves seated on a flat, grass-laden field that came to a stop over a cliff wall some fifty feet down, leading to the sea. The edge of the cliff was far enough forward that nobody felt to be in any immediate danger from where they sat. The light wind was soothing, the aromas were pleasant, and the distant roll of the waves was almost hypnotic in its repetition. George relaxed in his seat and smiled. Suddenly, all those nightmarish stories felt distant to him, and all his other assorted worries were going away as well. The doctor made good on his promise to deliver respite, and he conjured a midsummer's sunset for their enjoyment.

Beneath George's feet, the grass was a deep, vibrant green. He looked around him, and took off his boots, setting them neatly underneath his seat. He let his bare feet sink deeply into the ground, feeling the grass between his toes, soft and comforting. The sensation made him quiver with happiness, and he let out a great exhale, releasing his every tension. How that doctor was able to perform such acts as transporting everyone from an odd, eclectic theater hall to a distant hilltop in perfect weather, all in the blink of an eye, was a wonder far beyond him. If it was all an illusion, then this excursion made it all worthwhile. Perhaps the doctor was not such a heartless monster after all, if even he could find it in him to grant his audience a moment of peace. Under a bright, multihued sky, the breeze blanketed the audience in tranquil warmth. The ocean waved beneath them continued to cascade against the cliff wall in their never-ending cycle.

"Comfortable?" asked a certain jovial, light-hearted voice. George was almost too lost in the moment to have heard it, but it was Doctor Xoctarious standing directly on the edge of the precipice. His coat fluttered in the breeze that blew behind him, as if the wind was deliberately trying to nudge him off the edge. Several heads in the audience nodded to him, wholly content with this new vision they were given.

"Good," the doctor noted. "If your pulses are all slowed and your spirits renewed, there is another tale I would like to impart to you. This one concerns everyone who had ever held fast to the belief in a power higher than themselves. For what being there may be in the world beyond our own, does He not look with fondness over the whole of Creation? Does He not care for the meekest every bit as much as the strongest? And what would be the only thing that this distant deity would require of his people? Would any deity, who lives far beyond the understanding of mortal men, require very much to keep notice of the affairs of mortals?

"Let us investigate these questions by paying visit to the coast of Italy, in the year fourteen-hundred and eighty-nine in a tale I call: 'CARPE NOCTEM.'"

The scene changed once again, but not by much. The sunset grew to a deeper shade of indigo, and the colors caught in the clouds lost some of their vibrancy. The breeze that once enveloped the audience in the face was now at their backs, and the sound of the rolling ocean waves felt more distant. George looked around; they were in the same general area, but only several yards away from where they started. Faced with this realization, he looked under his seat for his boots that he'd taken off to savor the grass beneath his feet. His boots, thankfully, were still under his seat. He hurriedly put them back on, just in time to watch the scene unfold before his eyes…

CARPE NOCTEM

Story by Doug Owen & Dominic R. Daniels
Written by Doug Owen

To the far west of the Kingdom of Naples was the small, sleepy village of Prete. On a hill overlooking the sea, rows of small wooden houses were lined up against a dirt road. Following the road past the homesteads and occasional tavern led down a slope and onto the beach, where the larger buildings were all roughly-hewn wooden ports and brick-built trade offices. Only one ship was docked, her crew working tirelessly to unload various crates onto a nearby horse-drawn cart. The captain of the ship, whose coat was longer and more well-kept than his crew's sweat-stained white shirts, barked orders to keep everyone moving.

"Più veloce!" he commanded. "Faster, you dogs!"

The crewmen grunted and strained to lift the heavy crates into the cart. The four large horses attached to the cart, all with dark brown pelts, looked less than pleased with the load they were made to carry. The captain then turned to the trade official, a shorter man with graying hair and a wrinkled complexion.

"So, that was five hundred florins for the unloading, and how many more was it to transport by land?"

"Er, that would be ten percent for land transit, Captain," replied the trade official. "I'm sorry if that seems a bit much, but we really need the money."

"Ten percent?!" the captain roared. "This is extortion!"

"You'll forgive me for saying so, but land transit from here to Potenza would be your best option. Either that, or you'd have to sail around Sicily to get there."

The captain grumbled, and stuck a hand into his pocket. "Alright, fine. Take it."

With that, he shoved a handful of golden coins into the officer's hand, and walked over the faded wooden planks back to his crew.

"*Spostare!*" he barked at the crewmen. "We need the cargo moved before dusk!"

As the sun dipped beneath the horizon, the cart and the ship went their separate ways over the dusty road and the wavy sea. The trade officer, satisfied with the gold in his pocket, locked up the trade office on the wharf and headed up the road to the rows of houses. Candle lights flickered in each of the windows, lighting his way home.

His house was not too much different in build from any other in Prete, if not for a slightly larger size and more windows, as well as a barn in the back and various tools scattered in the front yard. The official scowled as he tripped over a fishing pole on the way to his front door.

"*Mannaggia!*" he griped as he regained his balance and hit his shoulder against the front door of his home. "I thought I told him to put that thing away!"

The door opened, and a woman with long black hair, a petite form, and a cheery smile greeted him.

"How was your day, Lorenzo?" asked the lady who helped the officer into the house.

"Long, miserable. Those bastard seafarers kept arguing about the transit rates."

Together, they headed into a well-lit dining room. On a wooden table, a set of candles in a silver candelabra on all alight, casting the room in a bright orange glow. Lorenzo took one of the chairs around the table and sat down, easing himself.

"The ones we had to raise just to make ends meet?" asked the woman.

"*Si*, Isadora. They've never let me hear the end of it. But at least we got fifty extra florins for that linen shipment that went through today."

"*Va bene,*" Isadora replied. "I just finished making dinner, and Gavino's in his room as usual."

"How was his catch today?" asked Lorenzo, stroking his short, gray beard.

"He didn't say. I don't know if he even went out at all."

Lorenzo scowled and got up from the table. "Gavino, that *porcellino!*"

He stormed out of the room just as Isadora was setting the table. Her expression was clearly worried. Across the house, she heard banging on a door, and shouting.

"Gavino!" Lorenzo roared, pounding sharply on a closed door with his clenched fist. "Gavino, open this door right now!"

Slowly, the door opened, revealing a young man with close-cropped hair. His leather vest had a patch missing, and his shirt and pants were stained with grass and dirt.

"Gavino Santorini, what in God's name have you been doing all day?" Lorenzo demanded sternly, towering over his son. "You were supposed to be at the docks!"

"I know, Father. I was on my way over, but I fell on the road on my way over. Almost got stampeded by a carriage."

Lorenzo stared distrustfully at his son. "You *fell?* Is that the best excuse you have?"

Gavino sighed. "Alright, I was taking a carriage out of town and got thrown out when they found me on there. I thought I could make it to Forlí before daybreak."

Lorenzo slammed his hand on the door in frustration, giving Gavino a sudden shock. "You mean to tell me you shirked your job?!" he growled through clenched teeth.

"I've never been any good at fishing! You know that!" Gavino shot back.

"That stunt of yours could've cost us several hundred florins, boy! If we lose the contract with the fishermen, we'll be ruined!"

"So focus on the crop yield—we could make some money off of that when it's time to harvest!"

"And how long is that going to be?" Lorenzo retorted. "Weeks? Months? We can't wait that long! We need every florin we can get!"

"Father, I'm not going to stay around here forever," Gavino contended. Lorenzo held up a hand to shush him.

"I don't want to hear it," he growled. "From now on, you are going to that dock every day, starting at dawn tomorrow, and you will catch all the fish there are! You're twenty-three years old, and you know basic responsibility by now! Is that clear?"

Gavino folded his arms and said nothing.

"Gavino, you know perfectly well that we need you here! As long as you're under our roof, you will work with the rest of the family. I've been in the office dealing with *bastardo* captains all day, your mother has been tailoring, and your siblings are all at the very least conducting business for us and for the community. And what have *you* been doing all this time?"

"Studies," Gavino replied confidently. "I've read about what's happening in the north, all those scholars and scientists and inventors, it's amazing! I have to get up there and join them!"

"And leave your family to poverty? Is that really what you want, boy?" Lorenzo shot back. "The Commandments clearly state that you shall honor your father and mother."

Without another word, Lorenzo slammed the door to the bedroom, leaving Gavino alone in the cramped space. The single candle on his nightstand was flickering, illuminating a room with only a bed, table, and a heavy wooden trunk. Gavino opened the trunk and pored over several stacks of paper.

His eyes filled with tears as he read over the stories about the new learning and discoveries coming out of Venezia and Firenze, way to the north of Napoli, where Prete merely took up useless space. Time and again, Gavino hungered to be a part of the revolutions happening so far away. Hidden away in his cedar? chest were copies of *The Decameron*, which was a collection of tales from Firenze; *The History of the Florentine Peoples*; and works from Giovanni Pico della Mirandola (a particular favorite of his) and other authors that gave him a sense of hope. Through those writings, he felt that there would be no limit to what he could accomplish. He could become a scientist, a diplomat, an artist, or a poet. Or maybe even everything all at once; he would certainly find a way to balance all those roles. Those were his dreams, his passions, and they were the only things that gave him some hope for the future.

It would be a future away from the drudges of Prete and his family, forcing him into a business that he despised just to raise some extra money. There was hardly anything worthwhile in Prete; no libraries, no schools, no laboratories. It was only just houses and trading posts, people grinding away at their own mundane lives just for the sake of making it to the next day. Gavino swore to himself that he would not end up like his father: a money-loving snob who drove his own family like slaves.

There was a soft knock on the door, and it opened to reveal a man older than Gavino but younger than Lorenzo. His tunic was dirtier than Gavino's own clothes, and he was shaved bald. He carried a tray with some bread, a cup of water, and an envelope.

"Master Gavino, some food for you, and a letter from Remo," said the man. "Just arrived this afternoon."

"*Grazie,* Lino," Gavino remarked. "You may leave now."

Lino was the family's indentured servant, the only one they had. Lino lived in a smaller house on the family's property, and he tended to the family's needs whenever they arose. Lino was paid a token fee for his services, and soon he would buy his own freedom and move away. There were times Gavino felt envious of Lino, being able to move away from the Santorini homestead as soon as he was ready to do so. Lino did his job without complaint, and he kept what now may be a sizable income for safekeeping until he could take it to seek his fortune elsewhere, just as Gavino yearned to do for himself someday.

Gavino opened the letter and munched on some bread. It was from his old childhood friend, Remo Uberti. He lived down the road from Gavino, and throughout most of their lives, they were inseparable friends who would explore the beaches and cliffs surrounding the community (much to the chagrin of Lorenzo, who preferred Gavino to be at work).

> *"My dear Gavino,*
>
> *Weeks have passed, and I am missing your company greatly. You crossed my mind recently, and I could not help but feel happy. I remembered all those nights we spent prowling the beach and exploring the caves underneath the cliff. I wonder if you also remember that lone hill off to the east, in the middle of that grassy field. It was the one you used to call 'Solo Terra,' since it was so far from everything, far as we knew.*
>
> *I know how badly you want to be free from this tiny spit of a town. I know how desperately you want to study the emergent sciences. All I can say is take heart, for I know your luck will change sooner than any of us may believe.*
> *With kindest regards,*
> *-Remo."*

Days passed in their usual course. The sun rose and set over Prete, the land to the east, and the sea to the west. Gavino continued to go about his labors, filling his father's coffer with as many florins as he could muster from the daily hauls of fishes. He despised fishing; it meant long days on the docks with large, sweaty, belligerent men who were much more adept at getting the fish to come to them. Gavino never had any luck at all with the fish; the instant he'd cast his net, the fish would scatter in the water.

Gavino trudged down a short, steep slope to a dock against the smaller cliff side near the beach where the wharf had another ship making an arrival. Gavino hauled a wicker basket and a net over to a corner of the dock, where some of the other fishermen were already hauling in nets filled with fish. The smell of dead fish and sea water was making Gavino gag, but this was his job, much as he hated it.

His net was tossed neatly into the water, and when Gavino tugged on the rope, there was definitely something weighing it down. Another pull and the net broke the water's surface. Dozens of glassy fish-eyes stared up at him from beneath the net. One more pull on the heavy net, and the cord snapped just as the net came onto the dock. Several of the large, gray fish spilled out onto the dock, flopping madly. Gavino grumbled and picked them up off the ground one by one, tossing them into the basket. Behind him, one of the burly veteran fishermen laughed at him.

"Hey, *stupido!*" one of the fishermen called to him when he was in the midst of grabbing fish from the broken net. "Finally found the need for a new net? Or maybe the fish are trying to escape you!"

Gavino said nothing as the other fishermen laughed at him. He picked up a particularly large fish, held it by its thin, flimsy tail, and slapped the fisherman across the face with the fish. The slap was loud, and the fisherman gripped his reddened face in shock.

"Go die in a hole, you *merda!*" Gavino shouted at him, and then he went back to his work. Most of the fish finally stopped flopping around on the deck. The fisherman, after recovering from the slap, angrily shoved Gavino off of the deck and into the water. Gavino splashed around awkwardly, and then pulled himself back onto the deck. The fisherman spat on the ground near him and left. His cohorts followed, leaving Gavino alone on the deck with nothing but a wicker basket and a pile of dead fish. He was completely drenched and shivering. In a rage, he kicked the mound of fish back into the water. He stood there breathing heavily, trying to steady his mind from the anger that gripped him.

As he walked up the slope from the dock, he saw a crowd of people standing by the road. It was not uncommon in Prete for everyone to know everyone else, but there was never anything announced that Gavino knew about to warrant a large crowd, so his anger was quickly replaced with curiosity. He walked to the edge of the crowd, peering between peoples' shoulders to see what was going on. Most of the people around him looked either suspicious or at the very least inconvenienced.

Several large carriages were rolling by in a grand procession. Pulled by large horses with long, flowing manes, these ornately-painted vehicles carried people that nobody in Prete ever knew. They were dressed in fine linens and silks, smiling and waving at the citizens like dignitaries in a parade. Gavino noticed that many of the carriages were painted with the same emblem: a long oval shape with an eye in the center. What it meant, he had no idea. It was an insignia he had never seen before.

The procession came to a stop near the docks, and the entire throng of people followed them there. Lorenzo's office was the first building they arrived at, and Lorenzo hurried out of the building to confront the massive group that took up space in front of his office.

"What's going on here?" he asked. On cue, the first carriage opened, and out of it stepped a man as old as Lorenzo himself. He was thin and clad entirely in black with a lacey cravat. He walked on a long walking stick with a shiny silver top. He ran a finger through his short silvery beard and smiled at Lorenzo.

"I take it you are a man of stature around here?" asked the strange gentleman. Lorenzo nodded, raising an eyebrow.

"Most delighted to meet you, my good sir! Jacopo Vicente, at your service."

He vigorously shook hands with Lorenzo, who looked uncomfortable. Lorenzo looked past Jacopo and saw other people climbing out of their carriages. They were all kinds of people; young, old, men, women, and children. Most of them were also clad in black, and all of them looked excited. They all looked around at the people crowding around them, and kept to themselves. Nobody from the caravan was actually talking with anyone else.

"What brings you here to Prete, Signor Vicente?" asked Lorenzo.

"Opportunity, of course!" answered Jacopo enthusiastically. "We have traveled across all of Europe in search of opportunity! All of us, the Covent of Visum!"

"What?" asked Lorenzo.

"The Covent of Visum: those who have the Sight!"

"THE SIGHT!" shouted all of the people from the carriages in unison. The sudden, perfectly conducted response shocked Gavino slightly, who was watching from among the crowd. Jacopo turned from Lorenzo to address the crowd.

"My friends, we have traveled long and far to reach a town that would be suitable, and here we are at last! With your blessings, we would like to help transform this fair town of yours into the greatest economic center in all of Napoli! We have money, we have resources, we have skills, and we have connections! All of us seek to establish a new commune here, and if you, the good people of Prete will cooperate, there will be wonderful things in store for all of you!"

"What can you offer?" asked one of the citizens from the crowd to the large group in black.

"Hope, my good sir! We offer you hope, and Prete is long overdue for it! We have attracted the finest talents from across Italia, from the northern city-states of Venezia, Firenze, Forlí, and beyond!"

That alone piqued Gavino's interest. If these people were connected with the great scholars in the north, then maybe he wouldn't have to travel as far to learn everything that they were learning up there.

"Be assured, my friends, the Covent of Visum is a peaceful fellowship, and together, we shall bring wealth and business to Prete beyond all counting!"

Some of Prete's citizens clapped warmly for this proclamation, but Lorenzo, still standing behind Jacopo, looked suspicious. From across the crowd, Gavino could see the look his father wore, and suspicion was returned to him. Why would Lorenzo Santorini, of all people, be distrusting of someone who intended to bring businesses to the community?

That question was on his mind as he went back to the dock to finish hauling the last of the fish, and take them to the trading post. He left the small, cluttered shack with only twenty-five gold coins. It would not nearly be enough to satisfy his father.

"I take it you saw those people?" asked Lorenzo to his family at dinnertime. Gavino sat between his two older brothers, Aldo and Gino, and his one younger sister, Maria. Having the entire family in the kitchen made the space quite cramped. The children all took one side of the table, and Lorenzo and Isadora took the opposite side, nearest the wall. Lorenzo leaned backwards in his chair, reclining right against the wall. Gavino said nothing, only going back to his meat and bread set before him.

"That Covent group?" asked Aldo, whose deep voice matched his muscular frame. "I didn't see them arrive, but I heard there were hundreds of them coming."

"I was there when they arrived the other day," Gino chimed in. "Couldn't have been any more than fifty of them. Families, children, and how far have they been traveling? And why come here, of all places?"

"Maybe they're looking to invest; who knows?" Maria added. She brushed away some of her long blonde hair out of her face and took a long sip of water from a pewter cup from the table.

Lorenzo scoffed. "They're against the Church; they have to be! They way they all talked about 'sight' and being peaceful, what nonsense! And those images on their carriages— what else could those be besides the very scrawls of the Devil?"

"Lorenzo!" Isadora scolded him. "They are guests in our town! Have some respect."

"They're a nest of vipers, and they've come right to our very doorstep! It's just as it was taught in Scripture! 'For false Christs and false prophets will rise up, and they will present signs and wonders...'"

"Lorenzo Santorini!" Isadora snapped, interrupting Lorenzo's sermon. "All this while you've been working every one of us to bring money in for the family. Well, now we have people who can help us with that! You heard what that man said: he can bring wealthy patrons to the town! Who are you to deny them their help when you could benefit the most from it?"

Lorenzo was speechless, and went back to his eating. Gavino looked across the table, wondering about his father. Did he adore God more than money, or the other way around?

A month passed since the arrival of the Covent of Visum. Their carriages were all parked in the fields far to the eastern edge of the town, and they had since begun to build houses with wood cut from nearby forests and bricks molded from the ground. Rarely ever did Gavino even notice any Covent members among his peers in the community, aside from maybe a Covent family in the trading post, or a Covent fisherman at the dock where he usually worked. As far as he knew, the Covent had not yet actually done anything for the community.

The sun was setting by the time Gavino was nearly finished on the fishing dock. He had barely caught anything today, and he was not looking forward to the lecturing he would be sure to receive from his father.

"Been a while, Gavino!"

The sight of Remo Uberti on the dock made Gavino smile instantly. Remo was slightly shorter and chubbier than Gavino, with wavy black hair and a small scar on his chin. His emerald-green shirt was freshly cleaned and slightly stiff in the arms and shoulders, so Remo did not look too comfortable wearing it.

Gavino promptly embraced Remo, smiling and laughing. "Been too long, my friend. I really miss seeing you. I still have your letter as well."

As he hugged Remo, Gavino noticed someone standing behind Remo, near the slope that led back up into town. From the look of his colorless garb and unfamiliar expression, Gavino guessed it had to have been one of the Visum.

"Can I help you?" asked Gavino, letting go of Remo and turning to the stranger. The strange man bowed his head and pressed the tips of his fingers together to form a triangle shape with his hands.

"May understanding be yours always," whispered the stranger in a deep, airy voice. "I am known as Severo of the Covent."

"Er, nice to meet you, Severo of the Covent," Gavino replied awkwardly. Severo stopped making the strange gesture and stood upright. His posture was near perfect.

Remo placed a hand on Gavino's shoulder. "I've been talking with Severo here for a while. He's been telling me about his travels. He's been to Venezia; can you believe that?"

"You have?" asked Gavino excitedly. "What's it like up there? Did you see the libraries? The scholars? What are they like?"

"It was a city of interest, that much I can say," said Severo. "But it is getting late, and I need to return home for conclave."

"Conclave?" Gavino wondered.

"It is a sacred observance, like your feast days. Forgive me, but I must be going."

As Severo turned to leave, Gavino tried to stop him. "Wait, Severo. I'm sorry I didn't get to know you very well. Perhaps we can meet again soon? I'd like to know more about your, er, Covent."

Severo turned to Gavino with a serious expression, as if Gavino had just insulted him.

"It is not for the outside peoples to see, or know."

Without another word, he left.

"Better this way, Gavino," said Remo to his friend. "Take my word for it."

"What do you know about them?" asked Gavino.

"I overheard two of them talking earlier today. They mentioned something about a man dying at one of those conclaves."

"God grant him peace," Gavino instinctively responded.

"Well, I don't think it was an accident," Remo added. "The way Severo described it, you'd think he was enjoying it. He said the way the blood was flowing, you would think he was writing poetry about it or something. It was horrible.

"That's what I came down here to tell you; I don't trust these people, and you might do well not to either."

"I understand, Remo. But if they're like that, then what motive would they have to be spreading their wealth all over the town?"

"Or maybe it's a ruse of some kind," Remo interjected.

"I don't know, but I think we'll need to take a closer look."

Gavino soon found himself regretting those words, as he and Remo snuck out of their homes late that night. Remo was sporting a black cloak with a hood that nearly covered his head, and offered a similar one to Gavino, who took it without question. Together, they moved among the unlit streets into the night. All the homes had their lights out, so the only light by which they could see came from the waning moon overhead.

They pressed on to the eastern field, where the Covent settled. Several campfires were reduced to embers that glowed orange, providing just enough light that Gavino could get a bearing on where he was. He had never before been to the Covent's area, and the ground was littered with various gardening and smithing tools that they had to carefully walk over. Off in the distance, they could hear voices shouting and chanting. What they actually said, Gavino could not distinguish.

"Where's that coming from?" whispered Gavino. Remo looked around and pointed.

"*Solo Terra*. That way."

Gavino instantly remembered *Solo Terra*, the lone hill that Remo mentioned in his letter. It used to be a favorite hideout spot of theirs when they were growing up; it was far enough from Prete that their parents would find it difficult to hunt for them if they were ever in trouble.

Gavino and Remo crawled on the sloping, grassy ground when they approached the lone hill, which stood only a few feet in the middle of a valley surrounded by sloped-up land, like a crater. Together, they peered over the edge of the slope and promptly averted their eyes from the extremely bright fire in the center of the valley. The hill of *Solo Terra* stood in front of the fire, and all around the hill and fire, Visum members stood at attention, all staring at the top of the hill.

An altar was erected at the hilltop, upon which a woman was laid down, shackled by her wrists and ankles and clad in only a few scraps of linen. She writhed and struggled against her bonds desperately. Gavino did not recognize who she was.

Standing above her, wearing a flowing, regal robe of crimson, was Jacopo Vicente, brandishing a long, thin sword that glowed menacingly in the firelight.

The crowd of Visum members cheered as Jacopo stood over the woman on the altar. From the edge of the valley, Gavino could see everyone from the caravan reveling and cheering. Old and young men, women, and even small children. All of them were there, cheering wildly. Gavino felt a chill sensation crawl into the pit of his stomach.

Jacopo raised the sword directly over the woman, who recoiled in fear. Her eyes were wide, and she was mouthing desperate words that Gavino could not hear over the roar of the crowd. Jacopo pointed the sword down over her, and a hush fell over the crowd. All eyes were on him in palpable anticipation. Then with a sudden, swift motion, the sword plunged into the woman's chest. Her scream was loud and filled with agony, a scream that was drowned out by the sounds of jubilance from the crowd. They cheered more and more, louder and louder, as Jacopo kept stabbing the woman, who convulsed and shrieked helplessly with each stab into her tender flesh. Blood cascaded from her open wounds down the altar, and pooled up at the base of the hill. Several Covent members took to dancing wildly in the blood pool, splashing and waving around maniacally.

Gavino could hardly believe what he was seeing. Their leader, Jacopo Vicente, had committed a clear act of murder in front of his entire congregation, and they adored him for it. It was madness such as which Gavino never would have thought possible: to celebrate the brutal slaying of an innocent person, to drown out her desperate pleas in bloodthirsty jeering, and her dying screams in partying. Murder in and of itself was bad enough, but to consider it as so wonderful a thing, and to happily celebrate while it was happening right before them—Gavino felt ill, and Remo next to him turned to a side and retched the contents of his stomach onto the grass.

"The woman has been Subjected!" Jacopo declared triumphantly as his prey stopped moving. The Covent's cheering reached a crescendo. Jacopo held his bloodstained sword on high, waving it around in circular motions and letting small drops of blood fly off of it and onto his audience. Several people were flecked with the blood, and they danced joyously.

"With enough Subjections, the Portal will open wide to all of us!"

"THE PORTAL!" the congregation chanted energetically in unison.

"Yes, the Portal!" Jacopo sermonized. "For I have received a vision years ago in the wilderness, that a great Portal existed deep underground, and when it is fed with enough lives, it shall open wide and thank those who sustained it with power beyond all imagining!"

"POWER!" came the response from the Covent.

"Yes, power! We shall all be transfigured! We shall all have power! Power over nature! Over life! And over death! The Portal shall open!"

"THE PORTAL SHALL OPEN!"

Gavino had heard enough. He grabbed Remo's arm and pulled him to his feet. "Come on!" Gavino hissed, and together they fled from *Solo Terra*, through the Covent settlement, and back to Prete. With fear as his fuel, Gavino bolted into his home, locking the door, and staying out of sight. He covered himself in a thick wool blanket and stayed there until his heart rate slowed down to almost normal. He knew that Remo would be back at his home doing the same thing.

He tried to sleep, tried to get back to normal now that he was back in his safe and familiar home, but much as he tried, he could not will himself to sleep. The image replayed over and over in his mind: the young woman desperately crying on the pedestal as the leering, merciless Jacopo drove the sword into her body again and again. He could still hear the perverted shouts of the congregation cheering for blood.

Who was that woman? Why did Jacopo kill her? How could anyone possibly take this much delight in the death of another? What was the mysterious Portal that Jacopo mentioned, and why would it want the deaths of people to yield whatever fantastical powers it promised?

Gavino's eyes were still wide open by the time the sun rose.

Aldo Santorini was usually the first of the siblings to wake up in the morning. He fancied himself the most industrious, most robust of all the family. He prided himself on his routines that he knew worked with maximum efficiency for himself and for his family. In the bedroom, he scoffed at his brother and sister still dozing. The sun was already spilling bright beams of light through the window. In the corner of the room, he saw a large pile of blankets. Aldo raised an eyebrow; who could have been so thoughtless as to leave their blankets bunched up in the corner instead of neatly put away.

He got up and pulled away the blanket, revealing Gavino underneath, who looked pale and haggard. His hair was unkempt and his eyes were bloodshot. Gavino let out a curt, sharp yell upon being discovered. The rest of the family stirred slightly, but they were still asleep.

"Gavino?" Aldo inquired. "What happened? You look like you've seen a *fantasma*."

Without warning, Gavino got up and hugged Aldo tightly, breathing heavily all the while. Aldo was surprised at this sudden act of fraternal tenderness, but he was not heartless. Aldo patted his brother's back gently as Gavino held his tight grip around Aldo's body.

"What's going on?" asked Aldo.

"I—I can't—it's just—I—oh God!"

"Take your time, Gavino. What happened?"

It would be several hours and the support of his entire family before Gavino was able to let out a single intelligible word, let alone state in full what he had seen last night. Lorenzo, Isadora, Aldo, Gino and Maria were all there as Gavino recalled what happened.

"Are you sure that's what you saw?" asked Lorenzo. Gavino nodded. After a moment, Lorenzo crossed his arms and exhaled. *"Pazzesco,"* he scoffed. Gavino stood up, furious, balling up his fists. Gino and Maria had to hold him back as he took a step towards his father.

"You don't believe me?!" he yelled. "I was there! I saw it all!"

"Are you trying to besmirch their good name? Look at everything they've done for us!" Lorenzo pointed at a fine new rug on the clay floor, new silver goblets on the table, and a chest in the living room that was overflowing with coins. "The family is richer than ever, and the whole town is prospering! We've had more ships coming here to port than ever! And it's all thanks to the Covent!"

"But Father—!"

"Not another word!" Lorenzo interrupted him. "Get it through your head; you simply had a bad dream about them, that's all! There is simply no way that they could have done anything like this! *Impossibile!"*

Gavino was in foul spirits when he walked outside. it was true that the town was benefitting greatly in the past few months. Houses and office buildings suddenly became larger, and more people were walking the streets. There were sailors and tradesmen from abroad, and families selling wares from carts on the side of the street. Every so often, Gavino could also see a Visum member among the people going about their businesses.

At one small shop on the wharf, he saw a Prete citizen named Alfonso, who was once Gavino's old teacher, being turned away because he did not have enough money to buy a new jacket. A moment later, a Visum member had come up and bought the jacket for them man, and he gave the shopkeeper some extra coins as a token of generosity. The sight of it all made Gavino ache inside. Knowing what he knew about the Covent, the murderous cult that they were, and seeing them in broad daylight among all the people he had ever known, outdoing and outshining everyone, was enough to make him seethe with rage.

He turned on the dirt road back to the neighborhood, and he slammed his fists on the Uberti family's door. Thankfully, Remo was there to answer the door.

"Gavino, you idiot; why are you out here? They'll see you!"

"I tried warning my family, they didn't believe me. I don't think anyone will."

Remo hastily pulled his friend inside and locked the door. Looking around, Gavino noticed that Remo's house was not much different than his own, only that the wood paneling that formed the walls was a smoother texture than his own walls, and the room was slightly smaller. Gavino sat on a wooden bench against the wall, trying to collect his thoughts. Remo peered outside a window, looking at everyone who passed by. Few of them were Visum.

"Did you tell anyone?" asked Gavino. Remo shook his head.

"If I did, then they'd know. Covent members are everywhere these days."

"My family is under their spell right now. My father can't say a word against them, not as long as they keep filling his coffer. I can't trust anyone now."

"You can trust me," Remo corrected him. "I despise those Covent snakes more than anything else in the world. They have to go!"

"Well, there has to be some way to convince people about this!" Gavino protested.

"There should be," said Remo. "If what Jacopo and even Severo said was true, then this can't be the first time they've killed someone. We have to find something that proves they did it. Maybe find the bodies somewhere, or we'll find the sword he used."

"Or get one of them to confess!" Gavino growled. "Every one of them was there when that woman was killed!"

"No; then the rest of the entire group would descend upon us!" Remo stopped him. "We have to be discreet with this."

It was late by the time Gavino and Remo were ready to make their move. Another conclave was soon to be happening at *Solo Terra*, so they had to be careful when moving around the Convent's settlement. The area was just as cluttered with tools to sneak around as their own neighborhood, and only a few Convent members were still in their homes. The sun was setting, so there was enough light to see by, but it was already fading fast. Gavino and Remo stuck close to the ground and darted underneath parked carriages to avoid detection. A single Convent member, an older man, stood by idly as the two young men slipped behind him unseen, moving carefully and silently towards a large structure in the center of the settlement.

By the size and grandeur of the place, Gavino guessed this had to be Jacopo's mansion. *In the relatively short time that the Covent of Visum made their home in Prete, how could they have found the time to build such a place as large and ostentatious as this?* Gavino wondered. The house was two stories tall, set with Roman-style columns and wooden framing upon cream-colored plaster. Several Covent members walked by the carriage under which Gavino and Remo were hiding, heading to the front door. Jacopo, in his scarlet robe, was there to answer the door.

"Master, the time has come," said one Covent member.

"That it has. I'm ready."

Together, the group walked away over to *Solo Terra*. The sun had already dipped below the horizon, and the last vestiges of light were fading fast.

"How do we get in?" asked Remo rhetorically. Gavino looked around the place from where he was perched, and he noticed something off to the left side of the house. He pointed in that area.

"Looks like a side door over there. Let's go."

Gavino's suspicion was right; a side door to the house led directly into Jacopo's study. The walls of the tiled room were taken by well-stocked bookshelves, all of which held books with obscure and foreign titles. Gavino had no time to savor all the grand opulence of the room, with its cozy-looking velvet chairs and deep, plush rugs.

Against the left wall was a desk, and atop the desk was a ledger that Remo opened. Together, they rifled through its contents, marveling at the secrets it held.

> "Alberto,
>
> The families of Santorini, Auditore, and Pazzi are starting to inquire too much of us. We cannot risk letting them get too close, nor can we immediately choose any of them for Subjection. Give them each as many florins as it would take to keep them loyal to us and convince them further of our cause. If we keep our hosts satisfied, they will not be a problem to us any longer.
> Yours in confidence,
> -Jacopo Vicente."

"No wonder my father trusted them so much," Gavino realized in a whisper. "He bribed him!"

Remo kept going through the ledger, and more horrifying truths were revealed.

NAME	WORTHINESS	SUBJECTION
Caterina	8/10 Gutted by sword	By vote from Covent
Alonzo	5/10 Castrated, bled out	Refused to serve Covent.
Padre Simono	9/10 Oiled, set alight	Spoke out against Covent.

These words were almost unbearable for Gavino to read. Aside from "Worthiness," which was measured in ways he could not hope to understand, the names were people he knew, and the "Subjections" they faced were too terrible to imagine. Also, every bit as frightening was the way they were chosen for these fates, either by having wronged the Covent in some way, or they were chosen by the entire Covent. They were systematically killing anyone who crossed them, adding more bodies to their insatiable bloodlust in the name of some mythical Portal.

"What are you doing here?" demanded a voice right behind them, jolting them both out of their disbelief. Gavino and Remo spun around to come face-to-face with two towering Covent members armed with long knives.

"Sneaking into the Master's study carries a harsh penalty. We shall see if the Portal will be satisfied with your deaths."

As the two guards reached out to grab them, Gavino ducked and rolled on the ground off to a side, avoiding them.

"Remo, *run!*" Gavino hollered. Remo was grabbed by the guards and struggled bitterly against them. In their tight grip on his forearms, he elbowed one of his captors in the stomach and grabbed the ledger from the desk, trying to use it to slap at the other guard. The guard slapped the book from Remo's hand, and stabbed him in the ribs.

"REMO!"

Remo fell to the tiled floor, clutching his chest. The guards stood over him scornfully, and then turned to Gavino, readying their weapons. Gavino had no other choice but to dash for the door, leaving Remo and the ledger.

Once again, Gavino was carried by terror as he fled. This time, however, the darkness robbed him of his sense of direction, and he ran toward *Solo Terra*, where another conclave was under way. A large metallic spike was mounted on the altar, and Jacopo was standing around it on the hilltop, waving his hands around and conducting every motion of the congregation as they eagerly awaited a new victim to be Subjected. The fire in the pit was just getting set, and the flames were starting to rise. In the flickers of light, Gavino's eyes met with those of Severo, who stood right in front of him among the crowd of Visum members.

"I told you, this is not for you to see or know," Severo said grimly. "When the Portal opens to us, you will be left out."

"You're insane!" Gavino shot back. "You're killing innocent people for a lie!"

From his perch on the hill, Jacopo saw him as well, and pointed at him.

"Heretic!" he yelled at Gavino. "Blasphemer and liar!"

Gavino had never run so far or so fast in all his life. The entire Covent of Visum was in pursuit of him through the night, screaming at him and running to catch him. Gavino pressed on ahead, fearful of what machinations they could subject him to, and desperate to save his own life. It would not be long before he reached Prete and his home, where he would be safe.

But as soon as he crossed the threshold into his neighborhood, the marauding Covent behind him did not give up the pursuit. They ran through the roads and among his neighbor's houses, looking among the shadows for their prey. Gavino stumbled into the safety of his house, locking the door behind him and blowing out a candle, burying the room in darkness. He waited by a window for the bands of Covent members to pass him by, then he would have to plan his next move.

Behind him was a faint rasping sound and a click. Someone had lit some tinder. Gavino spun around to find his mother, Isadora, re-lighting the candle. Once again, the room was bathed in the orange glow, and Isadora's figure could be seen as well. She wore a flowing white nightgown that contrasted with her black hair.

"Mother, we have to hide! The Covent!"

"I know, Gavino," Isadora replied, her tone sounding reassuring. "Everything will be fine; trust me."

"But they'll find me here! Put out the candle!" Gavino begged, but she refused to move.

"We need you to fulfill your duty to the family, my son," said Isadora. Gavino was perplexed; how could she be talking about business when his life was in danger?

"What are you talking about?" demanded Gavino.

"The Portal will open soon, but it can't open without enough blood. We will all be changed by it, and we need you to bleed for it."

"It'll be an honor!" said his father, coming up from behind him. "The Santorinis will be the ones who provided enough blood for the Portal to open and yield its power to us all!"

"Father, no!" Gavino begged. *"Et tu?"*

His parents grinned maliciously as they took hold of Gavino. Even his siblings, emerging from the bedroom, leered at him scornfully as they dragged him out of the house.

"He's here!" Lorenzo shouted to the Convent members in the darkness. "Take him! Kill him!"

"NO!"

Gavino pulled himself from his parents' grasp and darted into the shadows. The Visum members closed in on him as he ran among the narrow spaces between houses and offices. When a Covent member blocked his path, he made a sudden turn for the next alley and continued running. It seemed everywhere he turned, there was another enemy in his way for him to avoid. Every place that ever seemed familiar and inviting to him— his entire world— was reshaped in the Covent's twisted image. His own family, the flesh of his flesh, had turned against him and fell victim to Jacopo's evil teachings.

Gavino ducked in the shadows and stayed out of sight. The Covent was now beginning to set torches alight, looking for him. He carried on throughout the town, of single mind to stay undetected and stay alive. There would be no house, no office, no place anywhere that would offer him sanctuary. Every single living person in the entire town was after him, driven by the Covent of Visum.

"Come out, Gavino!" called out a voice in the night. "Come out! You can't stay hidden forever!" It was the voice of Severo, hollering with the same steely, stern voice as he ever spoke with. It seemed to Gavino to be getting louder every time; he was drawing closer with his blazing torch in hand, and the shadows that were Gavino's only saving grace were starting to disappear quickly as he approached. Severo waved his torch around as he walked calmly through the alleyway between houses, his eyes darting all around in his search for Gavino.

He had always figured Gavino had been suspicious of his family and his commune ever since they first met, even after giving him and Remo their customary greeting: "May Understanding be yours always." Clearly, Understanding was never his to have, and he would pay for that mistake by being next in line to die for the Portal to open. Severo grinned slightly, thinking of how beautiful it would be to watch Gavino die on the hill, and what mighty secrets the Portal would yield to him and his family once it finally opened.

Severo was running out of alleys in this part of the town to scan, though the night was still young. Sooner or later, he'd find the fugitive Gavino.

The church had not been opened in several weeks. The air was thick with dust, which made it bothersome to breathe. It smelled of stale wood, which bit at Gavino's nostrils. However, the large, open space of the church included plenty of wooden pews and a large block of an altar to hide behind. With the entire town out in full force searching for him, it seemed the most likely place where he could remain for some time undetected.

There, in the presence of a long-forgotten God, Gavino Santorini stood, a man who once only wanted to travel to the northern countries and join the intellectual revolutions happening there, leaving behind his mundane life of serving his money-hungry father day after day.

Now, his entire world had been consumed by the blood-hungry Covent, who wanted nothing more than to capture Gavino and ritualistically kill him in ways he could scarcely imagine. He remembered the woman on the pedestal, and the names and descriptions of those others who were "Subjected," and vowed that their fates will not be his. As soon as dawn broke, he would hijack the nearest carriage and flee from Prete, as far away as possible, where the

Covent would never find him. The more distance he could place between himself and anyone even so much as remotely connected with the Covent, the better for him.

Or would he really need to do that? Would he really need to flee just yet? He remembered his own father, and how, before the Covent came to their village, the only thing he ever wanted of Gavino was to serve his family and the community. The community needed him desperately, and everyone, no matter who they were or what they did, had an impact in this tiny town. No matter how menial the task, everyone had a hand in building up the community before the Covent had arrived and corrupted everything. Perhaps there would be a way he could make a difference in Prete after all.

Remo was still alive, but for how much longer, he couldn't say. The knife from the Visum guard had dug deep past his ribs. The pain was excruciating, and his wound was slick with blood and continued to seep through the cloths he held to it. He could feel his strength slipping away and was finding it harder to even keep his eyes open and maintain focus, as if he were falling into a deep sleep. The room in Jacopo's lair was empty; every single Covent member was out in full force looking for Gavino, leaving Remo for dead.

He could not move, and he could not call for help. He realized that this is where he was to die, and nothing was going to change that. Alone, mortally wounded, and in the middle of an unfamiliar place, he was another anonymous victim of the Covent of Visum's lust for blood.

To his right, the door to the outside courtyard opened. He could just barely feel the rush of cold air that seeped into the study, and he could almost discern a single shape that emerged from the door. The shape stopped suddenly when it saw Remo lying there against the wall next to the desk.

Then, he could almost hear weeping.

"Remo, I'm so sorry! I never should have left you!"

"*Va bene*, Gavino. It was not any fault of yours."

Gavino stooped down by his friend's side, and a single tear fell from his cheek and into a small puddle of blood from Remo's wound. More tears followed, and Gavino had nothing to say. Every sound that escaped his constricted throat was a desperate, mournful sob.

"Gavino, it's up to you now," Remo whispered. "Take the ledger and get as far away from Prete as you can. Bring it to the *polizia*, anywhere the Covent is not. Make them pay, Gavino."

"I will," Gavino whispered, taking the ledger from the desk. With that, Remo shut his eyes, and they remained shut. He went rigid, and his breath completely stopped.

The flat, leather-bound book was in Gavino's hands, the only weapon he had against the Covent. Soon, all their secrets would be revealed, and once he was clear of Prete, he would take it to the nearest officer or magistrate in whatever city-state he would come across, and with luck, he would bring an armed force to Prete to quell the Covent permanently. Jacopo Vicente would die, and the Covent would be well and truly disbanded.

"You wanted me to serve the community, Father," Gavino said to himself. "This is the only way to do it."

"Or you could die for the Portal, boy!" said the voice of his father, right behind him. Gavino spun around quickly and beheld his own mother and father in the room with him. They grinned maliciously as they closed in on their prize fugitive. Gavino's heart sank; his own parents were still kept under the Covent's evil hold.

Solo Terra looked much bigger than Gavino remembered it in his youth, as well as a much more forbidding place at night, illuminated by fire light, and filled with cheering, dancing, frenzied Covent members. He was kept in a tight hold by his own parents, forced atop the hill where the sacrificial spike was mounted on the pedestal. Around the spike, in full regalia, Jacopo was dancing. He circled around the spike with fluid, harried movements, and some members of his congregation mimicked his every move. Gavino would have found it amusing, watching some Covent members bump into each other, oblivious to each other and caught up in their quasi-religious ecstasy. But the only thing he could feel, if ever he could even feel anything, was the crushing, defeating dread of his own impending doom.

"The Portal is a lie!" Gavino screamed over the din of the crowd, his voice hoarse and cracking. "He's been using you all your lives!"

"*Silencio,* boy!" Lorenzo snapped at him. Even after everything that transpired, he still saw Gavino as an unruly child, and this time that child was going to die by Lorenzo's own wishing.

"Father, don't do this!" Gavino begged. "Listen to your son! What kind of man would let his own son die like this?"

"You always were a disappointment, boy. We'll see if the Portal even wants so much as a drop of your blood!"

The only thing Gavino could respond with was this: "Beware of false prophets, which come to you in sheep's clothing, but inwardly they are ravening wolves, Father."

Lorenzo lowered his gaze at Gavino, looking at him as if he were a worm. Nearby, Jacopo had finished his crazed dance and was motioning for Lorenzo and Isadora to bring forth Gavino. They did so without hesitation, pulling him by his arms near the spike and holding him over it with two strong hands pressed on his back. Gavino was bent over the spike, feeling it coming closer to his chest. He pushed back with all his strength, but it would not be enough to break through the grasps of his own parents. All around him, the crowd waited in anticipation.

"*Morte,*" one Covent member started whispering. "*Morte, Morte, Morte, Morte…*"

More whispering followed from the congregation, slow and rhythmic. More voices joined in the choir, becoming a tapestry of frantic, single-minded will. All eyes were on the top of the hill, willing Gavino to finally be impaled and bring an end to his meddling. Soon the mystic Portal would open somewhere in the valley, and they would all be changed by it. Jacopo, Severo, and the Santorini family conjured up daydreams and visions of what would happen when it finally opened. What power would they all possess to crush everyone who opposed them? What command of the elements, of life and death, would they all wield?

In one final struggle, Gavino steered his body off to a side of the spike just as his parents pushed down on him, and they doubled over behind him. Gavino hopped to his feet, and stormed towards Jacopo, who stood dumbfounded. Gavino reached out and grabbed Jacopo's throat, squeezing it tightly. Jacopo gasped as his eyes went wide in disbelief. Gavino steered Jacopo around the spike with his hands firmly clasped around Jacopo's neck. His parents got up from the gassy ground, and tried to stop him. But they were too late.

Gavino shoved Jacopo, who lost his balance and fell backwards onto the spike. The silvery blade, now tinged with streaks of red, popped up through Jacopo's stomach and propped him up side-ways. Jacopo's head was upside down, his last vision being his con-gregation stood frozen in shock. Rivers of crimson flowed from his lifeless body, spilling to the ground at the base of *Solo Terra*.

"Listen to me!" Gavino screamed. "All this time, you've all been killing people—GOOD people—just because he told you to! He's been lying all along to all of you! There is no Portal, and there nev-er was! You were all tricked into believing it just because he's been shoving money in your pockets and made all those false promises to you! Well, what are you going to believe now?! Tell me, Covent! All of you, tell me right now what you believe in!"

His only response was silence. The people stood around him motionless and unbelieving. Even his parents behind him were un-sure of what do to. They would never again be certain of anything.

The biting cold of the night disappeared, and the blazing infer-no that lit the scene vanished as the Mystic Theater materialized around the audience once again. Many in the audience could feel the same sense of disillusionment as the Covent of Visum had, while others felt a sense of righteous purpose that had carried Gavino Santorini through the night.

"Whom can you say was correct, my friends?" asked Doctor Xoctarious. "The young man who fought so passionately for his life and the fragile sense of community that his world was built upon? Or the clandestine Covent of Visum, and their promises of power at the expense of human lives?

Look yourselves over; do you not see yourselves similar to one or the other? Know that there are those wayward souls out in the larger world, wielding great influence and transforming even the mildest of hearts into their own image. Corrupted abominations are these people whose hearts have long been replaced with stones. Evil can easily consume anyone, but only if it is allowed to do so. Guard yourselves well, my friends."

As the Mystic Theater fully materialized once again, the lights turned back on, and the bell tolled seven times. Doctor Xoctarious, upon the stage, removed his hat and gestured to the back of the theater hall.

"You may take this moment to refresh yourselves if you feel the need to do so," announced the doctor. "We shall resume in a half hour's time."

Hearing that brought needed relief to George and Robert, as well as most of the entire audience. They got up on wobbly legs and stumbled towards the door, back to the main entrance hall.

Tables were set against the walls, each one well-stocked with bottles of chilled wine, and plenty of glasses. Platters of meats and cheeses were also on hand for the guests' delight. As the guests helped themselves to refreshments, Robert walked through a door marked "WC," a place to relieve himself. Minutes passed before he rejoined George in the foyer for refreshments. George took an especially large piece of Brie cheese and some sliced sausage, the taste of which was far more intense than he ever knew. After all the frightening adventures that he embarked upon with Doctor Xoctarious, he had almost forgotten he had an appetite.

"Enjoying yourself, George?" asked Robert. George nodded.

"I've never seen anything like it in my life," George replied, swallowing his food. "I've no blessed idea how he does it, but that doctor is a genius!"

"I always knew you had a predilection for morbid tales, George," said Robert. "Did you ever read or hear anything like that before? All that torment and death? Is this really the stuff that fascinates you?"

There was nothing George could say to that. Beyond the façade of characters in dangerous and deadly situations, he could see some higher meaning to each of the tales. He could learn things from their situations in a sort of distant way. The bloodshed and fantastical acts were not really of importance; what was important was what happened to the players in the shows. Did they emerge from their tribulations, and how did they do so? What became of them by the time the Mystic Theater returned in place?

The bell tolled again, and by command, the guests returned to their seats in the Mystic Theater. When the last guest entered, the heavy iron doors slammed shut behind them, pushed by unseen forces. It frightened the last few guests to enter.

Doctor Xoctarious took the stage again, delighted that his guests found his refreshments satisfying. He cleared his throat quietly and presented the next tale.

"Are there any among you who have loved another? Have you ever felt that indescribable yet immutable bond between yourself and another, which you could dread to imagine your life without your lover? This is a tale of just such a thing: a love that was so strong and pure, that a young man risked everything to safeguard that love, even at the expense of his most valuable asset. There are some lengths that man was never intended to go— some truths that have remained hidden from the sight of mortals— and for very good reason. May I now present a tale of love, loss, and mystery, that I call 'Love Kills.'"

LOVE KILLS

Story by Dominic R. Daniels
Written by Dominic R. Daniels

The year was 1941, at the time of the greatest conflict in human history, the Second World War. It was the age of man's hatred over his fellow man, filled with genocide and indiscriminate acts of atrocities, due to be of difference of economic class, race, heritage, education, and philosophical religious background.

It was a cold and bleak October on the 1st day, the eve of Yom Kippur in Reichkommissariat Ostland, Germany, in the city of Vilnius's ghetto, which would be an evening of rape and the robbing of human dignity when the massacre of 3,900 Jews took place under the iron fist of the Nazi regime.

Lined up in rows and shackled in heavy iron chains, bearing the yellow patch of the Star of David on their clothes, were men, women, both the young and old, fathers and mothers, grandfathers and grandmothers, even little children and babes, who froze in the icy chilling winds They were formerly rich or poor, middle class or underclass, and it did not make a difference anymore. They came from all walks of life: rabbis, doctors, lawyers, butchers, tradesmen, occupations of all kinds, and they stood like cattle on the road to the slaughterhouse with no hope of deliverance from the power of the invincible Fuhrer who had torn their world apart.

Half-starved and penniless, this sad little community faced their doom quietly, and some of the prisoners struggled with the Gestapo guards and screamed at God all sorts of rotting blasphemies, cursing Him that He should burn in His own Hell for abandoning them in their final hour, while others prayed and worshiped the Almighty with faith and reverence in Yiddish as they made their peace, looking forward to the new life as they would soon cross over into Abraham's Bosom were souls go. Others did not care; to some, Sheol was better off than this man made Hell, as watery salt-filled tears ran down the faces of dirty soot covered children who held onto their mothers and fathers breast as their parents cradled them in protection.

The gray helmeted and red-draped fascists raised their machine guns and Lugers, as blonde and blue glassy-eyed Hitler-Youth drummers, dressed in traditional beige, buttoned, collared shirt uniforms, bearing the mark of the Axis, and wearing black-suspendered latter hose shorts alongside them, as they beat their drums with the heaviness of destruction in equal rhythm and tone.

In charge of the firing squad was the menacing SS Commander Johansen Christophe Ives, a tall, stiff, and pale faced man adorned with various medals on his uniform; he donned a silver monocle on his left eye and a fine lit marble cigarette-holder held in the canines of his teeth as he puffed and smiled with a gleeful grit savagery.

He was 52 years old, clean shaven and bald, ruthless and intellectual. Killing people made his day; he savored the sweet suffering of others, especially the Jews. He hated them as much as he hated humanity itself, deep in the recesses of his jaded, warped mind. However, he was a true loyalist to Hitler's vision of a master Arian race. He was the perfect enforcer. Ives was versed in all methods of sadistic torture and belligerent cruelty; he was backed by the teachings and a lower head Templar member of the Nazi, Thule Occult Society, against the so called Protocols of Zion, as Ives barked orders to the soldiers and his dogs.

"Prepare to open fire; dirty swine like this are fortunate to receive such mercy," said Ives ruthlessly.

His German accent was thick and deep. He signaled his executioners with a conductor-like gesture of his right hand, which bore a silver ring with the insignia of a skull and the swastika.

The little children shook with fear in their family's arms, shutting their eyes tightly, terrified with anticipation for the impact of the bullets that would soon split through their flesh to pieces and kill them as they listened in horror. They heard the sounds of the soldiers' MP40s, cocking their triggers, the claps on their automatic rifles clicking clean with pristine accuracy, then silence that lasted for less than a second but felt like an eternity. They were trapped with no way out.

"Damn you, Kraut devils! May God destroy you all!" screamed one of the Jewish prisoners, a young man clasping tightly his wife and infant daughter in his arms. He would rather have himself shot shielding them than to see his family annihilated.

Ives just chuckled hideously with stone in his heart.

"If your God exists, then let him receive you!" challenged Ives cold- bloodedly.

Mothers and children began to weep; men had looks of desolation. . They were going to die by the German Invader who took their lives, freedom, and futures, and there was nothing they could do to stop it. Now was the moment of the crossing, when souls go to be judged— good or evil, right or wrong. The world went dark. Where was God? Where was God? Where was God?

"Shoot them!" raved Ives smiling, no remorse, and no guilt.

The soldiers aimed and squeezed back the triggers on their weapons. In unison, the blasts of the machine guns erupted with hellish fire and smoke containing the scent of freshly lit sulfur with each shot. The noise was like a thousand bombs falling as repeated rounds of ammunition spouted from the chambers of the guns. The look of doom on the Jewish prisoners who were guilty of no crime was frozen on every face as the bullets riddled their weakened bodies. Their flesh was sliced to pieces, ripped raw like bits of meat. The scene was rife with blood, shattered bones, eyes blown out of sockets, brains splattered, necks severed, and stomachs bursting in fountains of crimson. The death squads continued relentlessly cutting through them like a knife through hot butter. The people dropped like flies to the ground, destroyed. The stone streets were painted red in blood, a sacrificial river of life taken flowing from their decimated bodies and pouring into the sewers. On this day, evil prevailed.

As the gun-powder-perfumed air wrapped itself in the nostrils of the soldiers, the oceans of smoke cleared like a fog in the wind, with all the condemned lying on the ground dead, and Ives felt pleased with his brutality and work; he raised right arm in military salute to the unholy god of flesh, Baphomet in human form.

"Hail, Hitler!"

It was the same in the other ghettos in Vilnius, including other cities such as Odessa, Luxemburg, Stanislawow, and many other parts of Nazi occupied Europe. The German invaders continued to march on and destroy all life in its path.

Back in Berlin, in the Capital of the Fatherland and head quarters to High Chancellor Adolf Hitler, was an SS medical and high-ranking military Nazi officer, by the name of Hans Sebastian Gruber, age 34, a prominent half-breed German and Jewish doctor and biologist. He was a close friend of Emil Maurice who was Hitler's personal body guard, and both of the men had good relations with the High Chancellor himself, which drew a deep resentment from Hitler's top execution leaders such as the enigmatic Heinrich Himmler and others.

They hated both men with equal jealously and desired to remove them as soon as possible, but the Chancellor would not allow it, and he respected both men greatly and kept a close friendship with them over many years, despite of the men's Hebrew ancestry.

Hitler cared little about that, and made his best efforts to keep Hans and his bodyguard's racial heritage a secret, playing favorites. As for the rest of the Jews in Germany, in Amsterdam, Poland, Austria, and the rest of the Nazi-occupied regions of Europe, he would be not be so merciful and continued to order the ethnic cleansing until his vision of a New World Order controlled by the Third Reich was completed as Supreme Divine Emperor of the whole earth. The Nazi spiritual and racial belief was to infect global society with the bloody ideological and theosophical mystical and occult Teutonic teachings of H. P. Blavatsky with her book *The Mysterious History of Racial Evolution*. Other influences included Rudolph Hess and other mystery schools of thought for the creation of the super human and other various esoteric beliefs to be ruled by one race only, the master race: the Germans.

In the later months of December 1941, Hans had discovered that his beloved wife Evita was ill as she laid in the Beelitz-Heilstatten hospital in Brandenburg, and she was transferred from Berlin with the doctors trying diagnose her aliment, and her condition not seen before; she had injured herself by accident in the medical wards where she worked as a nurse, discarding some dirty needles, and she had been contaminated by them. Her immune system had begun to weaken, and no medicines or vitamins were helping her recover, which worried Hans greatly.

Hans himself, despite being in service to the SS, was secretly a devout Jew raised by his Jewish mother, a school teacher, and his German Catholic Christian father, a prolific novelist of many successful books and a composer of many symphonies in popular modern European culture.

He was born on December 24th, 1907, in Hamburg, Germany. His parents had divorced when he was 12, and young Hans was left to be raised by his uncle, in Berlin, Otto Van Gruber, who was a colonel in the German Imperial Army, and his aunt Felicia, a housewife and the owner of a hat shop, and she was also a mother of six boys and three girls.

Life in his uncle's home was strict but not always unpleasant. His uncle had come to love and admire his nephew even more than his own children, and Otto quickly became an ideal role model for Hans, and the young boy desired in time to enlist in the German Army with the hope that one day he would become like his uncle, a prestigious and high-ranking military officer.

He dreamed that in his later years, he would write novels like his father about the wars and military conflicts that he would serve in.

At the age of 18, he enlisted in the army, and as the years progressed, he found promise as a soldier and later attended University at Cambridge in England, with a doctorate degree years later in medical science, and he entered back into the German-armed services to fulfill his dream.

In his early thirties, he was introduced to the politics of the Nationalist German Socialist Workers party at the Beer Halls where they spouted anti-Semitic propaganda by a young ambitious former German corporeal officer, who had been awarded the medal of the iron cross, by the name of Adolf Hitler.

Hans secretly disliked the Nazis beliefs but joined in the organization with Hitler and Emil Maurice in order to prevent persecution to protect his wife, also a Hebrew half breed, and their young four-year-old daughter, Agatha.

After Hitler rose to power as High Chancellor of Germany, Hans was brought into Hitler's most trusted circle. In his weakness, he had betrayed his true spiritual roots and religious faith, and he was ashamed but he did not want his family to be killed by the SS, so he killed his own people after gaining influence and some close military relations when Hitler had became Chancellor, but Hans in his heart never enjoyed the killing. He hated it, and as a medical practitioner and scientist, he was assigned to also work in the concentration camps and was forced to perform inhumane acts of devastation with teams of fellow Nazi scientists, putting his own people in the gas chambers and using eugenic genome experiments on them for his leaders' debased plans of war.

These heinous and mind-numbing operations dulled Hans's spirit, and he began to lose his own faith in the Lord of all Life, Jehovah the Divine. Hans desperately yearned for personal supernatural forgiveness and the deliverance of his people from the German horde, and his friendship with Hitler was a farce, and there were was nothing more that he desired than to personally kill the Fuhrer and avenge his fellow Israelites.

On a bone-chilling winter night, December 20, 1941, the snow fell with blankets of the great white flooding the city's of Berlitz streets with ice and sleet; it was 11:00 in the evening, and Hans had been given time off from active duty and went to his wife's room on the second floor in small wing of the hospital that was at his disposal, to check on her progress.

Evita was awake in her bed, comfortable, as she read the evening newspaper by a lit lamp on her nightstand that brought this dreary place some peaceful luminance. She heard a small knock on her door that was already slightly ajar.

"Who is it?" she asked.

"It's Hans, my love,"

"Come in, dear,"

Hans walked in the room, dressed in his black SS uniform. He closed the door behind him and removed his officer's hat and went over to Evita and smiled a little with gentle tenderness in his heart, and he kissed her on the forehead.

She smiled back with love.

"How are you feeling, my sweet?"

"Tired, but with enough strength to walk today; I've missed you," she said calmly.

"I've missed you too; the doctors are still trying to find out what is the matter, "said Hans concerned.

"It's probably nothing but the flu, I should be coming home in a few weeks," she said confidently, with gentleness.

"I am not sure about that; you're getting worse each day, and if you don't get better soon, they are going to take you for serum treatment in the sanitarium," said Hans.

"Why don't you call in Father Gorstein; he has great healing gifts," suggested Evita.

"No, I will not subject you to holy fools and charlatans; they cannot help you, just as we can't help our own people," said Hans sadly.

"Don't say that. One day our people will be free from German rule, and our country will be not a place of bigotry and hatred but of democracy," said Evita with faith.

"I wish I could believe that, my love, but I am ashamed at the torment that the Fuhrer puts on our people, and I chose to join them," said Hans, deep with regret.

"I'm sure God would understand; you did it to save us. Does that make it right that you are forced to do what you do? No, but we have to choose the lesser of two evils," said Evita reluctantly.

"I can't even go to pray at the Synagogue, out fear that we may be watched by the Gestapo," said Hans. "I am tired of hiding behind a mask of false patriotism, for what this nation has become, we have lost our way Evita. We have lost our way," said Hans, filled with grief.

"God will forgive you if you ask Him," said Evita with hope.

"God will never forgive me; I am a monster just like them. I poison our own people in the camps, I burn them with hot irons searing their flesh, and I'm forced to starve them for weeks at a time until they die of hunger and their skin peels off and rots from skin diseases and no sanitation," said Hans near sick himself at his guilt. "How, in this entire world, could the Lord of all Hosts forgive people like us; I deserve to die and our people deserve to live," said Hans, devastated.

"What else could we have done? Surrender? Go and die with our brothers and sisters in the camps or be gunned down in the ghettos. You heard what had happened at Ponary and Vilnus," said Evita in defense.

"Yes. We should have chosen to die with honor with our people, not live as dogs for a tyrant master," said Hans with self hatred.

"This war won't last forever, dear," said Evita

"Yes, but the memories for us will. I hear their screams in my dreams at night; I see all their shriveled and burnt faces in my nightmares, calling me, "Traitor!" May God forgive me, may God forgive me," he said ashamed, as tears rolled down his hot cheeks.

He collapsed on the floor, his legs spread open on the floor near his wife's bedside and he wept. She held him and he held her, they knew what they had done was wrong, or worse. It was evil.

Evita knew her husband spoke the truth. They lived in safety and security under Hitler's protection while the rest of their fellow Jewish kinsmen were being purged by the Great Beast Himself, the Antichrist in flesh and blood. It bothered her consciousness to no end, but she tried to bury the ugly truth deep down in her soul.

"Don't cry, Hans; please don't cry. Otherwise, you will make me cry," said Evita.

Hans got off from the floor and regained his composure, wiping his tears off his face to be sensible.

Evita calmed.

"How is our little Agatha?" she asked, worried for their daughter.

"She cries to me in the middle of the night, wondering if her mother will ever come home, and she does not understand," said Hans.

"Just tell her the doctors are our giving me some more treatment, and that I will be home soon," said Evita.

"I already have; I sent her to stay with her cousins in Cuxhaven, and she will be safe there for now," said Hans.

"My dear, don't trouble yourself with me; I love you, so go back to the inn and rest, and come back and see me again tomorrow when you are feeling better," said Evita sadly.

"Alright," he said nodding his head, still shaken up.

"I love you," he said, kissing his wife on the lips.

"I love you too," she said.

Hans put his officers' hat back on his head and went home back to The Green Rooster, the name of the inn where he was staying. In his private sitting room upstairs in the inn, he had set up a small laboratory, filled with a Bunsen burner and an arrangement of test tubes of all kinds of chemicals while he tested samples of his wife's blood to find out what was the problem in her body, and he frantically looked through his microscope.

A brass crucifix of Christ was on the wall next to his small bed looking down at him, and there was a bottle of brandy that he kept on his end table. The room had a small fire place that was lit with a few pieces of red hot coals to bring him some warmth, as the blankets he slept under were paper thin.

Hours passed like leaves blowing in the wind, and the remorseful SS officer checked glass slide after slide, trying to find an answer, and three days later while at work in his sitting room, Doctor Hans Gruber came with a theory that this aliment must be a new form of disease. It was a debilitating disease not yet known too much in the world. He saw his wives antibodies destroy themselves under the glass.

"My God; its living death," said Hans in shock.

In a private meeting that day at 10 o'clock in the morning, on December 16, 1941, he filed a report to the Government Ministry of Public Health to address the issue and had discovered that similar cases were occurring in different parts of Europe and even in Asia. He also discovered that this new disease was killing its victims rapidly; there was no cure to its deadly outbreak. The cause was unknown, but he suspected that poor sanitation in hospitals and city slums were of the causes. But medical science was not able to solve this problem; a vaccine was not developed, and two days later back at the hospital, Hans received the worst news that any husband should ever have to hear.

"I am sorry, Commander Gruber, but your wife is dying, and she will not live but another six weeks at the most; her immune system is killing her from within," said the hospital's chief physician. Carl Van Franks.

"There must be something you can do for her!" pleaded Hans.

"I am sorry Commander, there is nothing that we can do to save her," said the doctor.

Hans was not going to lose the love of his life without a fight, so taking his wife's previous advice, he contacted Father Elijah S. Gorstein, a well known Polish mystic and astrologer who was said to have served in Russia in the same monastery where the legendary and infamous mad monk Rasputin had studied and began his work as a faith healer, then later served the Romanov Czars of Russia.

A week later, Gorstein arrived. He was dressed in a traditional Greek Orthodox monk robe with strange symbols on his priestly vestments and garb, equipped in his feeble hands with a set of rosary prayer beads; he was a dry old bastard of a man but man of deep conviction and pious nature nonetheless. At age 62, he had a receding white hair line and a beard longer than Father Christmas. Under the close supervision of Commander Gruber and his secondary SS Officers present in the hospital wing, the old spiritualist healer began his work in attempt to physically heal Evita's nervous system and purify her blood and soul to prevent her from dying a premature death at the age of 28. Taking out a vial of consecrated olive oil mixed with basil and sea salt he anointed the young woman's forehead in shape of cross and began to pray in a deep spiritual language.

"*Espata, esperin, nu ata, le mori ai;* Divine God of the Universe, I pray to thee. Creator of light and darkness, by your Holy and Blessed Power I beg you, O Holy Adonai, please take pity on this poor child, and do not look on her sins, but on her past good deeds," prayed Gorstein.

As Father Gorstein continued to pray over the woman, he heard in his spirit a voice speak to him.

"The answer is no; her husband's evil is an abomination in my sight," said the holy voice. Then it left.

"I understand," said Father Gorstein in reply.

Gorstein turn to speak with Commander Gruber.

Evita passed out in her bed.

"There is nothing I can do for her; I am sorry," said Gorstien.

Gruber erupted with anger. "You damn holy fool! I was told that you had the power to heal anyone of their aliment, if they had faith," he said.

"Indeed I am equipped with such spiritual power, but that power is not of my own, but of God's, and your evil deeds have cut you off from His help;   this is not my answer, but judgment from the Lord," protested Gorstein.

Gruber's eyes became a deadly stare, silent but filled with hate. He then knew surely that he was forsaken, and a cold hardness formed in his soul.

"Execute him, "ordered Gruber to his men.

The two other SS soldiers immediately seized the old holy man by his arms, with him struggling.

"What are you doing to me? You can't do this; I'm a human being, and this is not civilized!" protested Father Gorstein in shock.

"You're an enemy of the state. Under the powers bestowed to me by the high Fuhrer himself, I am charged to cleanse you of your fanatical doctrine! Since your God will not serve man, then let man never serve your God! " said Gruber cruelly.

"Blasphemer! This is sacrilege!" shouted Father Gorstein.

"Take him to the detention camps and kill him," mocked Gruber.

"May Hell have mercy on your damned soul, because Heaven will not!" screamed Gorstein.

Gruber had made his final choice; he truly had become the enemy of everything he chose to be against. If his wife would die at the hands of the God that he felt was an All Powerful Divine Tyrant who refused to heal her, than he would destroy everything that Christianity held sacred and would kill anyone who chose not to serve Nazi Germany. He would no longer feel grief for his fellow Jews. He would slaughter anyone who did not serve the rulers of the state, and he would enjoy them all. He was no longer his former self, but a true beast.

The SS guards knocked out Gorstein and dragged him out of the room.

Five days later, back at the Inn in the conference room, Gruber received word from his head assistant that his wife was dead; her body had lesions and her eyes turned pure black. As soon as he heard this, he went mad with rage, shooting his own assistant in the head, and his assistant's brains splattered with blood and fragments of cranium all over the walls of Gruber's room. Gruber's face smeared with blood and the scent of death. He had his guards clean up the mess and burn the body. If they spoke about the matter to anyone, he would kill them just the same.

Gruber became a soulless man, and he joined the SS Templers in the Thule Occult Society at a private sanctuary in East Germany, and was initiated into the order under name Brother Alpheus Libras over a period of several months in a dark room, and he locked himself away from the rest of world.

The jet-black room contained five lit torch-stands on the floor and he sat in the middle of them in the shape of an inverted pentagram with a Universal Circle around the pentagram, and the room contained silver and gold framed black mirrors surrounding every wall of the room.

Gruber was dressed in a dark robe decorated with various sigils made of gold embroidery. He carried a ceremonial short sword and a pouch containing mixtures of various herbs and drugs to enter into a shamanistic state.

He would meditate there for hours at time and fast in silence, and he would read for hours on in about the dark arts from a vast collection of various infernal books, becoming adept in the arts of astrology, crystal gazing, geomancy, and spell casting in the Left Hand Path spiritual traditions of necromancy and death magic. His training in the occult sciences also included developing clairvoyance and other psychic abilities in practice the art of levitation and various Hindu yoga techniques.

"If God will not restore my wife to me, then I will sell my very soul to the spirits of death and reincarnation, and let the masters of darkness possesses my life to return my love to me," he vowed.

With a blood-inked book bound in the dried human skin of slaughtered infants, the Book of Shethamhoth\ was a small but powerful 16th century Enochian and Kabalistic spell book that contained dark incantations with passages of power to summon all forms of spirits, gods of the ancients, and angels, and it also included lists of demon kings and dukes from the shadows, and he would accomplish this evil deed of absolute power relying upon the practice of Solomonic Magic.

However, there would be costs, so if one as a practicing necromancer and magician could control such spirits and dark gods, it would be indeed possible to actually resurrect the dead back to life, though the cost of doing so was extremely dangerous. Only a handful of successful sorcerers in the society had ever attempted to perform such degrading acts of blood sorcery and had succeeded.

The risk of pulling spirits from human bodies either alive or dead was pure insanity and suicide. Many magicians could not handle the demonic energies that would fully take over their systems, and the infectious spiritual blight of death itself would enshroud the magician, at times slowing killing them, which included shutting down the organs in the body and draining of internal fluids, causing periods of mass dehydration, blacking out, and in some instances, states of possession.

These malevolent spirits would come to gain full control of their human hosts; some would never leave and would even try to kill other occultist members in the Thule organization. If the necromancy rituals should fail, the magician conducting them would be killed by the demons. Hans was warned not meddle with such deadly magical operations, but he informed his brothers in the order that he completely understood the risk and would not stop until his goal was achieved. Like others before him, such as the famous Dr. John Dee and black magician Edward Kelly, he was fully prepared to raise all the spirits of Heaven and Hell if it be needed.

He was even willing to sacrifice his own life for the safe return of his precious Evita; he loved her and would die for her with no regrets. He became infested with pure evil and madness and was a mockery of mankind: a psychopath.

In order to complete a powerful feat of arcane black magic such as this, it was best to perform the necessary rites on a day were the spirit world would meld with the human physical plane; it would be on the eve of May Day, known as *Walpurgisnacht,* one of the most satanic holidays for diabolists, so Gruber made his arrangements and kept to his studies for period of months in the dark room which he seldom left except to either eat, sleep, or defecate. Over that time, it was on the day of the ritual that he would perform the resurrection operation, he received news from the outer order that his daughter, too, had died.

He read the telegram that came to the Thule Society's head quarters a few days before the first eve of May, after he got dressed in a traditional business suit and had a glass of whiskey, sipping it as he read the notice; he sat at his desk in his sleeping quarters and read by candlelight.

> *Brother Alpheus Libras,*
> *It is the Order's deepest regret to inform you as one of the finest commanders of the Fuehrer that your child, Agatha Gruber, has passed away; the doctors have confirmed that the cause of death was an infection of tuberculosis in her left leg. The doctors treated her for the last few months with various methods, with some signs of improvement, but it was not enough to save her. She died this morning at approximately 8'o clock in her bed. The head nurse reported the incident to our chief of staff, when she came to bring breakfast to the child's room. We mourn for your loss, and we give you our deepest condolences.*
> *Highest Respect and Sympathies,*
> *Commander J. Ives*
> *May 1st, 1942*

"AAAHHHHHHHH!!! Damn them! I will kill them all; curse the day that I was born!" he raged as he shook his fist to Heaven spewing indecorous hatred.

He meant in these fierce words, the rest of the Christians and Jews of Europe. He sent word that same day for his soldiers to ransack the local Jewish Synagogues and Temples, including burning Christian churches and openly massacring all who opposed him, torturing prisoners, forcing them to renounce God; some did and they lived, while the others didn't and they were burned alive in crematoriums.

He also had his followers participate in book burnings of religious, poetic, scientific and philosophical nature, and he had his men tear down crosses in church squares and urinate and spit on Bibles, desecrating statues of saints and of the Immaculate Conception the Virgin Mother Mary. The only god Gruber now worshipped was hate. Hitler had no complaints and was pleased with Gruber's' orders and openly encouraged his high commander for these additional exterminations to continue. The Nazis were drunk on the human elixir of madness.

Later that night at around 11:30, Gruber entered into the dark ritual chamber where he conducted months of study and magical practice in secrecy; Brother Alpheus Libras, dressed in a ceremonial purple and black robe with a gold crown on his head and a protective consecrated amulet in shape of the Pentagram of Solomon, began the necromantic operation of resurrection.

He would have no assistance in this working and be left to his own peril if he failed. In the ritual chamber was an illuminated stone altar with various candles in red and black color and shape with strangely carved Norse runes that were hand chiseled by a master mason into the altar.

On the top of the altar contained the body of his dead wife, dressed in a red laced gown and decorated with various blood-painted sigils and talisman jewelry on her legs, neck, face, feet, and hands. Her body was decomposing, her skin peeling and turned frostbite blue, though she still held her delicate features and beauty even in death. Her eyes still retained their beauty and her lips were still lovely.

He had her body preserved with various flowers and spices' including natural herbal extracts instead of using traditional embalming methods; she had been buried in his home town in Hamburg. In the days prior to performing the ritual, Evita's body had been exhumed and shipped in a red oak coffin to the Thule Society's headquarters.

Though eager to perform the ritual, he had suffered bouts of severe depression at the loss of his daughter Agatha and began to drink heavily, but he stopped in time and began to fast for a few days in advance to prepare his mind for this exotic work of the occult because if he failed he would surely be killed. If he succeeded, he was not quite sure what the results would be, and the only way to find out was to carry out this magical experiment and document it by a scientific approach in his diary.

The black mirrors were still in the room hanging on the all sides of the walls; Gruber took out from a wooden chest in the corner of the room and retrieved a tapestry knit perfectly with the Circle of Solomon in attempt to conjure both spirits good and evil for his working.

He laid the Circle of Solomon in the center of the room before the altar and sat down in the middle star where the magus is supposed to be. The Circle on the sides of the tapestry contained the elements in signs and symbols of the elements of Fire, Earth, Air, Water, and the Ether.

He was ready and took out the Book of Shethamhoth from his pocket, and began to recite the spells to begin the ritual.

"*Astrious, Vakarata, esatani, de morva, dii! Astanata, varea, de may angento satani!* Spirits and gods of the ether come by the dark realms of flame and light; open thy gates to Lucifer's sight. Angels and demons I call; hear me! I conjure thee to astral form in this material plane. Come forth, I evoke thee! Hecate, queen of Darkness: come to me! Azazel, maker of War and Destruction, come forth! Murmur, demon of resurrection cometh to me! I call you all forth; bring me your master, the angel of the bottomless pit, Heosphoros! Satan!

His infernal Majesty! Be quick! I evoke thee! I evoke thee! I evoke thee!"

As Gruber finished the spell, beams of light and shadow erupted from the mirrors all round him in the room as they shattered to pieces on the floor, and the candle flames began to change color as reds and blues, and the air turn stagnant and dense as if a presence or multiple presences were in the room with him.

He froze as the room turned bone cold in temperature, and his breath became as mist, while the room began to vibrate and shake as the spirits came forth around him; as three shadowy phantoms appeared from the symbols around the magic circle, he saw that they were made of light and shadow, yet they were burning with fire.

Their forms turned to different guises: the first spirit was the human form of a beautiful woman with violent red hair that burned as red fire, and her eyes were blood shot red, her face purple and fair as lavender, and her lips were scented like roses. Her body was stunning. She had gold bracelets on her arms and rings with symbols on them, her hands were as talons, and she had the most beautiful purple angelic wings on her back with blaring eyes the color of rubies. This was the Goddess of Witchcraft, Queen Hecate, worshipped by the cults of Ancient Greece long ago.

"We have come; what do you wish of us, magician?" asked Hecate.

"Where is the other three? I do not see them." said Gruber.

"Here were are," said the second spirit who took the form of a hideous creature. He had ten horns on his brow like that of a bull, and he had three eyes in the center of his forehead with the body of a man but the legs of goat; his arms and hands were that of a man.

"Who are you, O Spirit?" questioned Gruber.

"I am Azazel, the Prince of War and Weapons, the General of the Fallen Hosts," said Azazel

"Where is your duke, Murmur?" asked Gruber.

"I am here, foolish human; how dare you summon us for the love of a woman?" said the third spirit Murmur, taking from of a centaur with the head of a vulture.

"I need not give an explanation, demon! I am the master of the Highest Ascent. You obey me!" said Gruber proudly.

"Murmur, that is enough!" commanded the forth spirit who took the form of a handsome man dressed in a suit, holding a golden cane in his hands. His face was of the most beautiful of beings, hair of golden color and eyes of white light, and his skin was smooth and his tongue was that of a serpent, and he had four large black wings on his back.

"Lucifer: how fitting that you are here," said Gruber.

"Do not play games with me vain and foolish human. I know already what you will ask," said Lucifer.

"Restore to me then the life of my wife and daughter, and let it be so, and for this I will exchange my immortal soul," bargained Gruber.

"You stupid human, don't you realize that you already belong to us?" said Lucifer smiling.

Gruber was dumbstruck.

"You sided with us from the very day you first spilt innocent blood, just like your Fuhrer, and he will join us soon, in time," said Lucifer.

"That's not my concern. I don't care what you do with him; just let me have my wife and child back! You have the power!" said Gruber.

"Very well; a contract of good measure is needed here. But know this: you will regret the choice you have just made, for one day we shall come and collect you, one way or the other," said Lucifer.

"If I am hell-bound, then I am bound tightly; the Creator who made us both betrayed me, and I would rather serve the darkness for a thousand years than to be His slave," said Gruber.

"He did not betray you. You betrayed Him," said Lucifer.

"Give me the contract, you old snake, or I will send you all back to the abyss!" threatened Gruber.

"Your pride is unacceptable. Agreed then the choice has been made. I will grant you your request, and your wife shall be brought back to life, but your child I cannot bring back," said Lucifer.

"Why?" said Gruber.

"Her soul is not my property but God's," said Lucifer.

"No!" said Gruber.

"Take it or leave, my friend; that is the deal," said Lucifer.

"I agree to the terms," said Gruber.

"Excellent," said Lucifer, as he conjured out of a black mist a contract inked in the blood of a thousand humans slain. He pulled a large red feather, as he telekinetically passed the damned document to his human client.

"Pierce your heart with the tip of the pen, and sign the contract with your blood," instructed Lucifer.

Gruber obeyed. A carved sigil of Satan in the flesh of his chest cut into his robe and carved his flesh. The sigil hardened into a scar, the mark of the devil whose is the number of a man; three scores six hundred and sixty-six, which is the mark of the beast. He then signed the contract with the feather quill that the Devil had given him and gave it back to his master.

"Let it be known among these witnesses of the damned that the contract is set. You will have your wife back, but she will never remember who you were," said Lucifer as he and the other fallen spirits shot forth electricity and red lighting into Gruber's body, transforming him into a hideous creature worse than a million heresies, and he was beyond demonic: he had thirty horns on his head and twenty eyes, and he had four arms and hands that were of bird talons, and his face was no longer that of man but of a wolf, and his speech left him as he fell inside the circle, it's protective force disappearing and leaving him open for full possession.

The pain was that of white fire surging into his body and soul, relentless agony, and time ceased completely, as he fell to the ground unconscious. Lucifer laughed with evil and shot green mists of energy along with his demonic allies into Evita's corpse, resurrecting her lifeless body back to its previous human beauty, her skin returned to it fair pinkish color, her eyes blue as opals, her lips red as bloody roses.

But she was no longer a human but that of a night breed creature, a hybrid fallen angel and human. She appeared human but not ever to be a human again, and she would have no memory of her past about her husband nor her lovely daughter.

Gruber awoke and screamed in violent agony. His wife was lost even though she was now alive, and he would never have her again.

"Foolish mortal, don't you know I always keep my word," said Lucifer laughing and disappearing with the rest of his satanic hosts. They left the newly transformed Evita with the transformed demon that was once her husband.

She screamed at the horrifying sight of her husband going insane.

The rest of the Thule Society brethren broke through the door hearing the scream, and, seeing the beast come out of his trance, they believed the monster killed their noble brother Alpheus. One of them unsheathed his ceremonial sword and plunged the sword through the demon's heart, killing the creature to save the woman from him.

At that moment, Evita's body begun once more to decompose and die as it turned into dust like of a mummified corpse exploding in a blast of flame and ash. Both lovers were dead and their souls were destroyed, lost to Hell for all time.

The old saying was true. You always hurt the ones you love, and for these two souls it was their love for each other that killed them.

The bell chimed six more times, and the theater darkened once again. George and Robert readied themselves for what other tales the doctor was sure to bring them. What more could Doctor Xoctarious put them through? They had already seen visions of torture, despair, and death; how much more could he expect his audience in their fragile minds to stand?

"And now, my friends," spoke the doctor in his lighthearted tone. "Let us journey for now to a time slightly more like home. But at the same time, unlike your time—if that makes any sense. It will all become clear in a moment.

"What you will see is an alternate version of modern times, an age of high discovery and inventiveness. What if the most imaginative, the most intellectual, were given far more of a share of society than they have now? What would the world be like if those free-radicals were given more of a chance to reshape the world? And what would progress be in that day and age? Together, I invite you to delve deep into this offshoot of history, to what may very well be Scotland in eighteen-hundred and sixty, in this story that I like to call 'Within the Deep.'"

Once again, the Mystic Theater disappeared, and a new scene took its place...

WITHIN THE DEEP

Story by Dominic R. Daniels
Written by Doug Owen

The audience found themselves flying through a storm, as if their seats were levitating and being jostled about by the icy winds and sheets of frigid, stinging rain. They soared through massive black clouds that completely enveloped them, obscuring their vision.

In the midst of the darkness and wetness, a flash of lightning ignited right before their eyes, accompanied by the loud boom of thunder. George held with white knuckles onto the armrests of his seat, terrified of falling from the now-floating theater seat and into the tempestuous oblivion beneath him, with only a simple chair as his saving grace. But somehow, he could feel himself weighted down on the chair, as if held by invisible forces. The audience continued its trek through the storm, and as George wiped away rain from his face, he remembered Doctor Xoctarious's repeated assurances that no harm would befall them. If that was the case, then why was he sending his audience several hundred feet through a storm with the almost certain danger of falling?

Something in his mind suggested taking the doctor at his word. He could feel the movement of the chair begin to lessen and slow down, and he let out a breath of relief. He may as well enjoy the experience, as the doctor would have intended him to. So far, there have not yet been anything popping out and threatening his life, so the doctor must have something in control.

Soon, the audience found its way through the cloud cover and down to a rocky stretch of land where a large, rectangular warehouse built of brick and iron stood stalwartly against the storm. Nearby on an outcropping was a lighthouse, where a bright beam of light rotated around methodically, piercing the relentless stormy night with a reassuring presence.

Inside the warehouse was a cacophony of strange devices littering the walls and floor. Miscellaneous tools were scattered in a heap against one corner. Rotating brass and copper machines whirred and buzzed on a workbench. Hulking steel boxes were alive with flashing lights and buzzing noises. What took up most of the space was a remarkable vehicle forged of brass and wood framing, which gave it a slightly aesthetic appeal. Its bottom was a boat-sized pod, large enough for several people to sit comfortably on fine velvet couches mounted inside, or to take control of a metal panel with a steering wheel and various levers. Suspended above it was a taut textile sack that was large enough to envelop the entire vehicle.

Over in the lighthouse, the place was no less as cramped as the warehouse. In the narrow, circular-shaped chamber, a machine was in full operation. Bunsen burners spat bright blue flames, wheels spun on wire tracks, and a large glass chemical vial tipped over, spilling an amber liquid into a tea cup held by a man, who took a long sip of the newly-brewed tea from his spectacular— if not impractical— tea-brewing device.

The man was Dr. Jonathan Morgan. Despite his youthful frame and light-brown hair, he felt weighed down by enough pressure for an older, more experienced man to handle. Every waking hour of the day was spent either at his laboratory in the lighthouse, or building the vehicle in the warehouse. Tonight, he pored over his notes and calculations, trying to unlock the secret for a certain fuel source for his vehicle.

"Hmm, if I use petrol or other fossil-based oils, the combustion chambers would not be able to handle the heat and pressure, so I can't use those. Steam power would require large amounts of water and a means to evaporate it. If only there was a way to compact a fuel source and have it run indefinitely... Perhaps a stabilized chemical structure..."

His work was his life, and it was apparent. If ever he did go home, it was only for a few hours at a time simply to eat or sleep. So, his appearance was usually haggard and unkempt. His coat was wrinkled, and his shirt was stained from oil and sweat.

Outside, the storm continued to pound mercilessly against the outside wall of the lighthouse. The sound of the waves crashing against the rocks sounded closer and more violent every time. But Jonathan knew he was safe inside the lighthouse, which had stood for years against far worse weather. Still, it made him feel no less uncomfortable.

He looked up from his desk and stood up, stretching his back and neck. His body felt sore from staying seated for too long, and his eyes were beginning to hurt. The glow of the oil lamps that provided light around the room were starting to go dim; they needed refueling.

Jonathan turned to a nearby window that overlooked the coast. Behind the glass pane, he was safe from the torrential rain and lightning. He wiped away some condensation from the glass and took a look outside. He could see the waves impacting boldly against the rocks, the rain collecting in small pools among the jagged stones, and—there, a body.

Jonathan was taken aback. Who could possibly be outside at this time, on a night like this? Without a second thought, Jonathan threw on a hooded cloak and raced out into the storm, carrying a small iron lantern.

The rain bombarded Jonathan, and he stopped among the jagged rocks to wipe away the water from his glasses. When he put them back on, his vision cleared, he beheld a person lying facedown on the rocks. A woman was lying unconscious as a wave poured over her in a shallow tide pool. Jonathan raised an eyebrow in suspicion, but also was a bit embarrassed; the woman was completely naked. He stepped in closer to the small tide pool where the woman lay, the light from his lantern sparkling in the water droplets that covered her, revealing her graceful, slender form. Fear crept in up Jonathan's stomach as he inched closer. Was she dead? If so, then how?

He reached out a hand to touch her lightly on the left shoulder; there was no response from her. Jonathan stepped back and took another look. He could see small bubbles forming around where her mouth would be, and her back heaved up and down slightly. She was still breathing.

As the rain was beginning to lessen, Jonathan pulled the woman upright. Her head hung down as he placed her in a sitting position in the shallow pool. He put his lantern on the ground, removed his cloak, and draped it over her for her own protection. Then he hoisted her onto his shoulders and took the lantern back in his free hand. The rain was becoming less of a problem as he walked to his home nearby.

Jonathan Morgan lived in a modest house at the edge of a sea-side neighborhood. His home of brick and wooden framing was the very first house on the street, so nobody was there to ask about him carrying an unconscious person over his shoulders in the middle of a stormy night.

Inside Jonathan's home was a large velvet couch and a polished wooden table, and most of the walls were taken by fully-stocked bookshelves. Jonathan placed her on the couch and proceeded to light the room with a series of gas-powered lamps, and he built a fire in the hearth. The room was bathed in peaceful, inviting light as Jonathan took some blankets from a nearby closet for his guest. After placing the blankets in a stack next to the couch, he went into the kitchen to start some water boiling in a tea kettle on a black iron stove.

The woman started to stir in her sleep as Jonathan placed a thick woolen blanket over her. Jonathan recoiled back as she opened her eyes, which glowed a brilliant emerald color in the light of the fire. Her eyes went wide, and her expression was one of confusion and fright. She looked around the room, then at Jonathan, who stood near the fireplace with his hands out to show her that she had nothing to fear from him. She looked under her own covers, and gasped. Jonathan went red-faced; hopefully she wasn't thinking of the situation in the wrong way. The woman then sat upright and got up from beneath the covers on the couch.

Jonathan stood by as she wandered around the study, looking inquisitively at his possessions. She eyed the spines of the books on the shelves, running slender, graceful fingers over their leather surfaces. She stopped to stare at an oil painting on the wall of a ship at sea. She lightly touched the rough canvas surface and the small, smooth flecks where the paint had long since dried. Her mouth moved, but no sound came out.

Jonathan went into the kitchen as the tea kettle started making its high-pitched screeching sound. He took the kettle off the stove burner and prepared two cups of strong herbal tea. The woman was still looking around by the time Jonathan came back to the study, setting the teas on the table. He invited her to sit down with him, and reluctantly she did so, sniffing at the earthy aroma of the tea.

"I made some tea for you," said Jonathan. "Would you like some?"

The woman said nothing, instead sitting next to Jonathan and staring at the small ceramic teacup sitting on a saucer, as if the very notion of tea was something new to her. Jonathan took his cup of the steaming amber liquid, blew on it lightly so that the steam dissipated, and took a small sip. His guest tried to mimic him by taking her cup and blowing on it more forcefully. The scattered tea flecked onto the table and the tiled floor.

"Gently," Jonathan told her calmly.

The woman tried again, blowing less forcefully on the tea and letting the ribbons of steam dance in her breath.

"When it's cooled off enough, you can drink it."

The woman took a slight sip, letting the tea touch her lips. Quickly and instinctively, she pulled the cup away from her lips and set it down on the table. She clasped her hands over her lips, her eyes wide with fear.

"Was the tea too hot?" asked Jonathan. "I'm sorry. Let me get you something else."

It was not long before Jonathan prepared a glass of cold water for his guest. She took it and pressed it to her lips, savoring the cooling sensation. Jonathan sat next to his guest and wondered about her. Who was she, and where did she come from? How did she end up unconscious and unsheltered among the rocks in the middle of a storm?

Jonathan also considered the duration of his guest's stay with him. His research and construction was too important and precious to him to allow anything to keep him from it. He sat back and looked at she started to drink from the glass, quickly consuming every drop of water there was. Jonathan kept his hands at a distance from her; he felt strange about having a naked woman staying in his house. He summoned up all of his willpower to not stare at her exposed body. As graceful and beautiful as her form was, he did not intend to embarrass his guest, especially given her quiet inquisitiveness, like that of a child.

Gradually, she began to feel sluggish. Jonathan suggested perhaps she get some rest, and she nestled up underneath the blankets. The fire in the hearth was petering out, and Jonathan extinguished it with the leftover tea, letting the flames die out in a cloud of smoke. He then turned off the lamps, and he went upstairs to his bedroom.

The same questions that were on Jonathan's mind continued to haunt him. Was this girl to be his responsibility for a while to come? Why was she completely unable to speak, or even know how to drink tea? Perhaps she has some sort of debilitating condition, or lost her memory. What if someone would want to find her, someone who would instantly come to conclusions about the state she was in, naked and mute, and assume the worst happened to her?

Morning came faster than Jonathan would have wanted it to. His guest was still sleeping soundly by the time he went outside to take his brisk morning walk through the neighborhood. The rain had stopped thankfully, but the biting chill of the wind forced Jonathan to turn up the collar of his long coat. The cobblestone roads of Aberdeen were slick with rainwater. There were very few people outside at this hour, given the weather. The only ones Jonathan saw were the constable, the cart drivers, and a child selling newspapers on the corner. For a penny, Jonathan bought a paper, his eyes scanning the headline story.

"May 28, 1860—STORM SINKS 100 SHIPS."

Apparently, the storm last night was far worse than Jonathan knew. The death toll from the shipwrecks, far as anyone could tell, was at least 40 sailors. Jonathan sighed as he read the story, lowering his head slightly in respect for those lost. A thought crossed his mind: what if his mysterious guest was a survivor from one of those lost ships? After all, the docks were not that far from where he lived and worked, so it may be plausible that she was adrift from one of the wrecks before she washed up ashore.

"Jonathan?" asked a lady's voice behind him. Instantly he spun around to behold a woman with light blonde hair, wearing an expensive white silk dress. Her powdered, rouge-laden cheeks were curled up in a smile at Jonathan.

"Wendy?" Jonathan stammered, looking every bit surprised.

"It's been a long time, hasn't it, Jonathan? Four years, at least."

"Er, yes, it has," Jonathan meekly replied. Wendy looked at the paper in Jonathan's quivering hand, and held a gasp.

"Oh, I've heard of that as well," she said. "Such a shame. One of those ships was carrying a parcel for me. I imported a new set of shoes from Italy."

"Dear, that's enough," said a voice behind Wendy, belonging to a gruff, bearded gentleman. His beard was as red as the vest he wore beneath his black coat. He was balding, and a single drop of rain patted the hairless part of his head.

"Your husband?" asked Jonathan.

"Yes, that would be me," said the gentleman aggressively. "Lord William Hennisburg. I assume you must be the one who had Wendy before?"

"For a time," Jonathan replied simply. "Probably for the best that it happened."

"Indeed so," William agreed with a nod. "I provide the young lady with comfort and security, and you go back to that ramshackle place of yours with your little toys. What good will those do anyone?"

"Begging your pardon, sir, but I'm sure people will benefit greatly from my inventions," Jonathan asserted. Both William and Wendy looked down at him as if he was two feet tall, but Jonathan was unfazed.

"I am on the verge of a breakthrough, an airship capable of flight for sustained, indefinite periods. It can take any passengers anywhere they wish. I've already worked on different permutations for the fuel samples. It would rival the works of Giffard and Dr. Bland!"

"You don't need to sermonize me, son," William interrupted. "I've seen airships before."

"But never anything like this!" Jonathan implored.

"What of that other junk in your collection? Can it ever be practical?"

"That depends on what you mean by 'practical,' Lord Hennisburg."

William placed a hand on Jonathan's shoulder. Jonathan shivered with his touch.

"You see, word has reached me that a war is brewing in the United States. The old colonies are splitting themselves apart. What they rightfully deserve for having broken away from us so soon."

"What's that to do with me?" asked Jonathan. "I've never even been to America before."

"What this has to do with you is simple: my company could place you on commission to design and manufacture weapons for the Americans. Nothing brings in the riches faster than an arms race, wouldn't you say?"

Jonathan brushed his hand away. "I'm sorry, but I would much rather be content to help humanity rather than harm it."

William frowned, and turned to Wendy, who nodded slightly. As they turned to leave, William uttered a dire warning to Jonathan: "You'll regret this, Dr. Morgan."

Jonathan was in foul spirits when he stumbled home. His mysterious, beautiful guest was awake, and Jonathan instantly forgot his troubles.

"Did you sleep well?" asked Jonathan. The woman made no sound, but she nodded assertively. Remembering something, Jonathan went to his closet and brought out an old dress with a pattern of flowers against a faded white background. The laces were yellow and fraying. The woman looked at him with a small sense of surprise.

"Oh, it's just, I don't usually keep things like this around my home. It belonged to someone from a long time ago. I think this might be a good fit for you."

His guest climbed out from beneath the covers, again exposing her naked form, and again Jonathan found himself trying to avert his gaze. The woman slipped into the dress neatly; the skirt was slightly short for her and higher off the ground than usual, but she was perfectly covered. She smiled, admiring herself in a nearby mirror on the wall. She ran her hand over the dress, trying to smooth away some errant wrinkles while Jonathan was in the kitchen.

The iron stove burned brightly, and the aroma of sizzling bacon and fresh coffee filled the air. The woman sniffed at the air, and let out a slight gasp. From the kitchen, Jonathan saw her reaction and wondered even more about his guest. Surely she could not have always been in such a state.

The next hour was spent at the breakfast table. Remembering the incident last night with the heated tea, Jonathan instead offered his guest a cup of water with her breakfast. He allowed her eggs, black pudding, and bacon to sit and cool off slightly as an added precaution. The woman tried to mimic Jonathan in his own movements as he ate. Watching Jonathan pick up a slice of bacon and bite it slightly, she grabbed her bacon in a tight grip, crumbling the crispy piece, and chomped down on it viciously. She then chewed on it in an exaggerated motion with her mouth wide open, and tried swallowing it. She was left choking and gasping. The puzzled look Jonathan gave made her embarrassed, and then she picked up her fork when she saw what Jonathan did with it.

"Just take small pieces, stick them with the end, and gently bring it up to your mouth, like this," said Jonathan demonstrating with his own plate of fried eggs. She took the fork in her own hand, and used very slow and calculated motions to take a bite of some of the egg white. Jonathan smiled as she completed the bite, as did his guest smile when she swallowed and savored the warm, smooth taste. She then proceeded to the black pudding, savoring tiny bites of the blood-based sausage.

After breakfast, Jonathan took a small tablet and a piece of chalk from a desk against the far wall of the living room, and he brought his guest to the couch.

"Can you speak at all?" asked Jonathan. She shook her head.

"Can you write?" he asked, to the same reaction.

"Then I shall teach you."

Jonathan wrote a series of words on the tablet in white chalk, things that were already in the room, such as "couch," "table," "picture," "desk" and "mirror." He spoke each word aloud, sounding out each individual letter sound slowly and delicately.

"C...C...Co-u-ch," she uttered. Jonathan smiled, and continued the lesson. It would not be long before his guest began speaking with more confidence, and they started going over words that represented abstractions, such as "happy," "love," "hope," among other things. Jonathan was surprised with the ease by which his guest was able to speak more fluidly. Jonathan wiped away some of the words from the tablet with his bare hand, and cleaned the chalk dust with a rag draped over the right armrest of the couch.

Finally, Jonathan wrote his own name on the tablet. The woman stared at the name with the same inquisitive look.

"That is my name, Jonathan. Sorry that it's a bit longer than the other words that I've taught you. That is what people call me, what I am known by. When people say 'Jonathan,' they are talking about me."

"J...J...Jon-a-than," said the woman.

"Yes, Jonathan. That's my name. What is yours?"

The woman stared at the tablet, and Jonathan realized that may not have been the best thing to ask his guest. She took the chalk in her hand, and placed it to the tablet. Jonathan almost expected her to scribble with it, but instead she wrote, in embellished cursive, one single name: "Angelica."

"An...Ang...Angel...Angelica."

"Angelica," Jonathan repeated. "That's a beautiful name."

"Beautiful name?" asked Angelica.

"I certainly think so," Jonathan replied. "I am delighted to meet you, Angelica."

Jonathan extended a hand to her, and they politely shook hands.

Hennisburg Manor was a stark contrast to Jonathan's modest home. Where Jonathan only had enough furnishings for himself and his guest, Lord William Hennisburg filled every available room with large, smooth, spotless couches and intricately carved and finely polished wooden tables. Where Jonathan only had a painting and a mirror on the walls, Lord William surrounded himself with ornate tapestries, life-sized portraits and a coat-of-arms over his fireplace. Two crossed swords set in the meticulously-molded metal emblem gleamed in the glow of the light from a roaring fire in the hearth. The hearth itself was much larger than Jonathan's own fireplace; this was almost large enough for a grown person to walk into.

Lord William sat comfortably in a leather armchair that faced the fire. He swirled a glass of cognac in his hand and gulped it all at once. Behind him, seated on some of the other couches, was his wife and several of his business associates. The petite, blond Wendy looked out of place among the group of burly men with sour expressions.

"Don't you have any idea what this means, Lord William?" asked one of the men, a tall man with a slightly round face and combed-back brown hair, wearing a fine leather vest and a spotless suit to match. "If tensions keep rising, the United States will be split into two factions. And only one of them will keep supplying our textiles."

"So, the United States won't be united for very long," Lord William mused. "Is your offer still open, Mr. Waits?"

"I just got back from there myself," Mr. Waits replied. "My associates all agree that if we want those cotton shipments to keep coming, we need to invest in the breakaway faction."

Lord William got up from his seat and stared down at his associates. All of them returned his hostile gaze. He walked over to a small table against the wall to pour himself another glass of liquor. He held out a full glass among the people, but they all shook their heads and refused. So Lord William drank it himself.

"All I can offer," Lord William coolly replied, "is simply the tools for the Americans to fight each other with. I will not directly fund any side unless I know with absolute certainty that my investment will be returned."

"If you invest enough, you'll have your return when they win," replied Mr. Waits. "It's that simple, William. They wouldn't forget your contributions."

Lord William lowered his gaze at Mr. Waits, insulted by his lack of a proper title. "Assuming, of course, that they do win. Money can only go so far in times of war—beyond that, it's a different matter."

"So, what can you offer?" asked Mr. Waits.

"An old acquaintance of mine happens to be a local inventor. A brilliant mind, but misguided. He told me this morning about an airship that he is in the midst of designing, with new and previously unseen means of propulsion. If we learn more about it, there may be all kinds of applications for their needs."

"Such as?" Mr. Waits cut in, much to his host's displeasure.

"Perhaps a faster method of transporting soldiers? Or a new form of weaponry? If you want those, I suggest you start showing me the proper respect as Lordship.

"To acquire the knowledge itself," Lord William continued. "That would be a simple operation. You may find that overpowering and convincing Dr. Morgan will not be difficult for any of your men."

The lock on the heavy door was no match for the expert lock smith that Mr. Waits employed. When the iron padlock fell to the ground, his associates undid the chain around the heavy door's handles and pulled them wide open. Mr. Waits looked around the desolate warehouse with a lantern, the light going over various devices that were silent and unmoving.

A steel antenna nearly hit Mr. Waits on the head as he walked by, and he quickly ducked under it. To his left was a pile of miscellaneous scraps of metal, some of which were fashioned into the shapes of cylinders or riveted sheets. To his right was an off-putting vehicle of brass and wood, with a large, empty sack suspended right above it.

"Sir?" whispered one of his comrades behind him. "What now?"

"We find the blueprints for that thing."

"And the doctor?"

"Kill him if you find him. Let's get to work."

The spies swarmed around the room, going through the drawers in every desk, opening every cabinet, rifling through papers, looking for anything that would resemble the device in the center of the room. One man, a lean and muscled raider, touched a protruding dynamo and instantly recoiled his hand in pain from the sudden electrical shock. In rage, he kicked the machine. The sound of his boot against the machine echoed through the warehouse.

"Quiet!" Mr. Waits commanded in a harsh whisper.

The raider who made the noise lowered his head and took a step back from the machine. In the darkness all around him, he heard a faint sound of breeze. He looked around, seeing nothing among the gadgetry that cluttered the room.

In a motion just as sudden as him recoiling from the machine that zapped him, he was pulled into the shadows. He tried to scream, but was quickly cut off by silence. Not a moment later, another spy was yanked into the shadows by some unseen assailant. Their screams barely had a chance to escape to alert Mr. Waits, who was still poring over a stack of papers that was taken from a nearby desk.

He was looking over such things as chemical compound formulas and hastily-scrawled notes. Most of it was completely foreign to him, and there was no sign anywhere of any blueprints, not even so much as a sketch of the airship. The thought soon came to him: if they could not find the blueprints, why not simply take the entire device with them? Surely his men would be up to the challenge of hefting it out of the warehouse and hitching it to a carriage.

But the complete lack of sounds around him was unsettling. Though it wasn't that long ago that he ordered his men to stay quiet after the brief mishap, surely he would still be able to hear boot steps or ruffling through things.

"Where is everyone?" he asked, hearing no response. He held the lantern aloft, letting the light flow over the airship and the other machinery around the room. He moved the lantern around to all sides, the shadows rising on the brick walls, becoming more pointed and menacing. His hand holding the lantern was quivering, and his pulse quickened. He reached into his pocket, withdrawing a revolver.

"What's going on?" Mr. Waits asked. From out of the darkness, he heard one single sound, someone breathing heavily. Rounding a corner around the airship, he could distinguish among the machinery the shape of a body. He held his lantern up, and found one of his men lying in a heap on the ground. Mr. Waits approached quickly, then recoiled back in fear; the man on the ground was covered in ragged, bloody gashes. He gasped for air desperately, his face contorted in horror as he looked up at Mr. Waits.

"Sir," the man gasped. "Something's here...!"

As if on cue, some massive shape descended onto the wounded man, and his loud, agonized screams were cut off by gurgling. Mr. Waits dropped his lantern and rushed out of the warehouse, darting for his carriage and spurring the horses into action. He took off as quickly as he could, leaving the warehouse far behind him.

Lord William was definitely going to hear about this setback. Overpowering Dr. Morgan was more difficult than he thought.

"Good morning, Jonathan!" Angelica called out cheerfully. Jonathan smiled as he walked downstairs to see her awake and about. She was learning so quickly, or perhaps her memory was returning after that fateful night. He figured now would be a good time for Angelica to see his life's work. He knew that he could trust her around the delicate, expensive, and potentially dangerous machinery.

"Angelica, would you like to come with me?" asked Jonathan, taking his coat. "There's something I'd like to show you."

The waves continued to splash against the rocks near the warehouse, and the lighthouse was still aglow at the top, its beam slicing through the mist. Angelica clung to Jonathan's arm to stay warm in the bitter chill, as well as to avoid getting too close to the rocks.

"Sorry," Angelica whispered. "I don't like it down there."

"I don't blame you," Jonathan admitted. "Do you still not remember anything?"

Angelica shook her head. "Not a thing," she whispered.

"I'm sure it'll come back to you," said Jonathan. "You've shown a lot of resilience already."

As they approached the warehouse, Jonathan noticed something, and he clapped a hand to his forehead in exasperation.

"God damn!" he cursed. "The lock's undone!"

Angelica stepped back in worry as Jonathan pulled the doors open and looked around. Some papers were scattered about near

DOMINIC R DANIELS & DOUG K OWEN

his desk, and some cabinets were pulled open. Jonathan ran over to those areas and checked the stacks of paper and other miscellaneous notes. He let out a sigh of relief when he figured out that nothing was taken.

He then hastily checked over the vehicle in the center of the room, with Angelica standing by idly, looking all around at the machines. Again, Jonathan sighed with relief, knowing that nothing was damaged or missing.

"Good; nothing's out of place," Jonathan declared. "But why? Someone's clearly been in here, but why would they have gone to the trouble to break in if they didn't take anything? Hmm, maybe they mistook this place for something else."

"Jonathan?" asked Angelica. "What's that?"

She pointed at the craft in the center of the room, which Jonathan had just recently exited.

"Ah, that is my life's work," Jonathan explained. "I was working on a fueling system for it the night I, well, found you."

"What is it?" she asked.

"It's an airship. It's a device that people can sit in, and it lets them fly over the ground, faster than walking, faster than horses, faster than anything else."

"Fly?" she asked. "Like, in the air?"

"Exactly," Jonathan explained, rubbing the cool brass exterior of the ship. "I call it *The Nymph*, named after the elemental spirits of ancient Greece."

"Elemental spirits?"

"Figures from mythology; they're not exactly real. Anyway, once I get the fuel loaded, we can fly on *The Nymph*'s maiden voyage together. Would you like that?"

"I'd love to," she said happily.

Alone in the warehouse, Jonathan figured this would be an opportune time to ask Angelica something important, something that was on his mind ever since she arrived.

"Angelica, are you sure you don't remember anything at all?"

Angelica touched the shiny, smooth, cool surface of *The Nymph* and closed her eyes. "Not that much; I'm sorry. All I remember was the cold, and the water all around me. I remember falling onto the rocks, they really hurt when I hit them. Then I found you."

"Begging your pardon, but I think I was the one who did the finding," Jonathan interjected. "It was the night of the storm, I saw you from the lighthouse when you came ashore. You were unconscious, submerged, and, well..."

He trailed off, trying to stall having to say it.

"You were completely exposed."

"I know," she replied. "Thank you for the dress, though."

"You're welcome. But is there anything else? Do you have a family? Friends? Lover? Where did you come from? There's so much I need to know."

"Jonathan, I don't remember anything, but I believe it will come back to me. You've already taught me plenty, and I remembered my name."

"Yes, that's a start," Jonathan concurred.

Hennisburg Manor became a stressful place that day. Lord William was furious, and Mr. Waits was trying in vain to placate him. The baron threw a cognac-filled glass at Mr. Waits, which shattered against the wooden panel of the far wall, staining it a darker shade of brown.

"What happened?!" Lord William demanded. "You were supposed to take the blueprints and overpower Dr. Morgan! How could you have possibly slipped up?!"

"I told you, something was in there with us!" Mr. Waits tried to explain. "It killed all of my men! I barely made it out of there!"

"Impossible!" Lord William bellowed. "Jonathan Morgan is a gutless bottom-feeder! There's no way he would kill anyone! It's absurd!"

"Well, I'm telling you...!"

"I don't want to hear your excuses!" Lord William roared, slamming his fist against the table. "You're going back there with more men, you'll be fully armed, and whatever it was that killed those people, you bring it to me! My clients are getting impatient, and I will bring them weapons!"

"You want those blueprints so badly, why don't you get them? And try getting a look at the thing that killed my people?" Mr. Waits snarled at him.

"Don't you dare tell me how to do my job!" Lord William shot back.

In the midst of the shouting match, Wendy Hennisburg silently entered the room, raising a hand to get her husband's attention.

"William?"

"WHAT?!" William screamed as Wendy stood stoically.

"If I visit Jonathan directly, would that make things easier for you?"

"What are you talking about?" asked Mr. Waits bitterly. "You want to get killed in there too?"

"Don't talk to my wife that way!" Lord William yelled at Mr. Waits, and then turned to his wife. "If you do, find out what he's keeping in there. If there's any chance we can capture it, the Americans would pay a fortune for it."

Jonathan was coming home after a long day at the laboratory in the lighthouse. Angelica had decided to spend the day reading at his home to leave Jonathan to his own devices. Jonathan felt a sense of accomplishment as he walked the narrow cobblestone path from the lighthouse to his home. Tonight was a very fruitful night; he had finally unlocked the secret of *The Nymph* 's fuel supply. He decided to use compressed gas in the textile sack, and superheat it as much as it can withstand. The resulting reaction would make the gas light enough to provide the necessary lift for *The Nymph* to fly. It would not be very long now before *The Nymph* maiden voyage, and he was every bit excited to get it flying.

As he walked to his doorstep, a figure crossed his path from out of the shadows. By the light of a nearby oil lamp on the side of the street, Jonathan could see it was a woman, but it was not Angelica.

"Wendy?" Jonathan stammered. "What are you doing here?"

"I just wanted to see you again, alone," Wendy replied. "For old time's sake."

"I've known you too long, Wendy. What are you hiding?"

"Fine, I just wanted to make sure you were okay is all."

"Why wouldn't I be?" asked Jonathan.

"Well, you've been alone for a long time. Just you and your work for all those years."

Jonathan instinctively grabbed the handle of his front door, pulling it to ensure that Angelica would not inopportunely come out.

"To be honest, I don't think I'd have it any other way than this. I can work without distraction."

Wendy was offended. "Was I a distraction to you?"

"Er, no; not at all," Jonathan quickly replied. "I tried to make time for you. God knows, I tried."

"And you never managed to sell a single thing from your stack of inventions, did you, Jonathan?"

"I had everything in order to sell the steam generators to Boulton and Watt years ago. That firm would've paid me a fortune!"

"But you didn't, did you?"

"Well, I..." Jonathan trailed off, then sighed. Wendy stood before him with her arms akimbo.

"I'm sorry, Wendy," Jonathan whispered. "I'm sorry it all fell apart. I'm sorry about me, and I'm sorry about everything."

Jonathan turned his gaze down, tears forming in his eyes. Wendy put a hand to Jonathan's cheek to hold his head up. He looked directly into her eyes through the tears.

"Jonathan, it's me who should be apologizing. I was so focused on money and security that I barely had any time at all to realize how special you were. Marrying William was the biggest mistake I've ever made. He drinks, he fights, and he surrounds himself with those charlatans from America."

"William," Jonathan repeated with a scoff. "I wouldn't be surprised if it was that bastard who broke into my warehouse."

"What?"

"This morning I found the padlock broken. Nothing was taken or destroyed, thank God, but if I could just prove that it was him…"

"Don't worry about it, Jonathan. I'll talk to him and make sure he never even so much as comes to this corner of town again."

"All this talk from him about weapons and war in America; I can't take any of that," Jonathan complained. "My work is meant to be peaceful, to bring people together. I just want to make a difference in life, that's all I ever want. Maybe I'll take *The Nymph* and everything else to England, closer to the firms that would pay for them and use them respectfully."

"I'm sure you will, dear," Wendy muttered.

A moment passed with Jonathan looking into Wendy's eyes, seeing the regret and wistfulness. Did Wendy still have feelings for him after all this time?

The only thing that broke the moment was the door opening wide, with Angelica smiling at Jonathan and then noticing Wendy with surprise. Every bit as much surprised as Jonathan, Wendy was deeply offended.

"Who is that?" Wendy demanded. "And why is she wearing MY dress?"

"You left it here when you ran off with William."

Angelica stood innocently in the doorway while Wendy stormed off without another word. She disappeared into the gloom, leaving Jonathan standing outside. He thought about walking after her to explain the situation, but not in front of Angelica, who would almost certainly follow. Besides, it was not that long ago when the divorce was finalized.

"Who was that, Jonathan?" asked Angelica.

"Her name is Wendy," Jonathan answered. "She was my wife, once."

"But not anymore?"

"No, not anymore. We divorced three years ago."

"Why?" she asked.

"It just… it just didn't work as well as I'd have hoped," Jonathan confessed, but then he remembered his breakthrough, and his sense of excitement promptly came back. "Come with me, I'm about to ready *The Nymph* for flight. We're going to fly tonight!"

Angelica embraced Jonathan tightly. Jonathan was taken aback when she squeezed out of him, but he returned the gesture kindly. Together, they walked over to the lighthouse, where the fuel cells were ready to be installed for *The Nymph*. From out of the shadows nearby, Wendy was watching with jealousy, but then she remembered her mission.

Jonathan rolled *The Nymph* out of the warehouse on a small set of wheels built into the underside of the vehicle. The air sack above the car was already beginning to expand, so he had to hurry before it completely expanded inside the warehouse. If that happened, he would have had to cut away the entire roof in order to be able to fly. Angelica stood by the wall of the warehouse, tying to a metal loop a rope that was attached to *The Nymph's* fuselage.

It was not long before the sack expanded to its capacity, and *The Nymph* was beginning to float. Jonathan quickly climbed into the car and invited Angelica aboard. She sat in one of the comfortable couches lining the car as Jonathan untied the rope attached to the warehouse. The rope fell to the ground, and *The Nymph* was several feet off the grassy field. With a twist of a knob on the control deck, *The Nymph* veered east over the waters, soaring higher and higher until the cliffs started looking tiny in the distance. Angelica laughed with delight as Jonathan steered the craft even higher, breaking through the cloud cover and into the night.

Jonathan looked around after leveling *The Nymph's* altitude. From here, the clouds seemed to be the ground, and the stars and the crescent moon seemed closer and brighter than ever. The air was still cold, but it was not windy. Oil lamps were alight in the vehicle, turning *The Nymph* into the only thing that gave off a golden glow among the silvery moonlight on the cloud tops. Jonathan was too intoxicated by the splendor and majesty of the scene around him to even feel the cold. Angelica raised her hand out over the railing, and waved it through a cloud. It scattered like smoke upon her touch and left some water dripping off her fingers.

"Angelica," said Jonathan, turning on a phonograph near the control deck. "May I have this dance?"

A moment later, the harmonious sounds of violins poured from the phonograph. Angelica squealed with delight at the music.

"Antonio Vivaldi," Jonathan explained. "Spring concerto. It's always been my favorite."

As the violins continued their euphonious, lighthearted melody, the two danced in the space aboard *The Nymph*, high above the world. Every step was in tune; every motion was graceful. Jonathan felt a joy such as which he never knew before: his life's work was coming to fruition, and at long last he had someone special with whom to share the moment. Among the silver-laced clouds in the golden glow of *The Nymph*, he felt as close to Heaven as ever he felt himself likely to get.

He leaned in close to Angelica, and they kissed.

Far below him, down at the warehouse where *The Nymph*'s home was, Wendy Hennisburg slipped through the open doors and looked around. Even without *The Nymph* taking up space in the middle of the chamber, it was still far too cluttered for her taste. Some of the lamps were still burning, filling the room with light. Jonathan had forgotten to extinguish them.

Ahead of her was a desk that was buried underneath mountains of papers. She figured that Mr. Waits had already checked this area, and she went off to the right side, an area that would have been inaccessible with *The Nymph* parked there. There, in a wooden cabinet, was a folded scrap of paper scrawled with *The Nymph* 's dimensions and specifications.

"The blueprints!" Wendy whispered with excitement. Her husband was about to get his prize after all. She turned to leave the warehouse when something caught her eye in a corner. Among the piles of brass and iron, there was something stacked against a corner, something that looked out of place. She moved in closer to investigate, and instantly stepped back in fear, running out of the warehouse.

A human skeleton lay against the wall, striped with dried blood.

The horrific image stuck with her as she stumbled into the living room of Hennisburg Manor, delivering the folded paper to her husband. He took it gladly, and smiled devilishly as he unfolded it and read over *The Nymph*'s construction plans.

"Well done, my dear," William proclaimed. "The investors will be well pleased with these designs."

"William, there's something you need to know," said Wendy.

"And what might that be?"

Wendy tried to find the right words, as the image continued to burn into her mind. "There was a— there was... something there, in the warehouse."

"What?" asked William.

"A skeleton," she breathed. Lord William raised an eyebrow, and placed his hands on her shoulders.

"Was it one of Mr. Waits's men?" asked William.

"I don't know. It was leering at me, covered in blood! It was horrible!"

William held on tightly to her shoulders. She held her head down, trying to forget the gruesome sight that she saw.

"Listen to me," said William. "I'll take care of this. Once I find that Dr. Morgan, I'll make him answer for those murders. And I'll make sure that he stays behind bars for the rest of his days, and I'll even invent some charges against him. Perhaps conspiracy against the Empire, or maybe he wanted to sell his inventions to those insurgents in the Far East..."

"What's that?" Wendy interrupted him, pointing at the window. Lord William looked outside, finding only clouds and a waning moon, but Wendy was pointing at something distinct in the sky. Looking closer, William found a large balloon-like craft flying in the sky. He then turned to the blueprints, and compared them to the floating vehicle.

"He finally did it," William uttered with contempt. "I'll see to this myself."

Jonathan wished he had more time to fly with Angelica on *The Nymph*, but it was getting late and the fuel cells were beginning to weaken. The balloon was starting to lose altitude, and no matter how much extra heat Jonathan added from the control deck, *The Nymph* was gradually starting to fall. He had no choice but to alter course back to the warehouse on the coast. Still, the past few hours with Angelica was the most delightful time he ever knew in his entire life. What gave him hope was the notion that there could be even more times like this in the future, and with improved fuel cells to keep *The Nymph* aloft longer.

He landed the craft down next to the open warehouse and stepped out, tying off the rope to the warehouse door to keep it anchored. Angelica stepped out of the craft, and after getting their bearings on solid ground, they embraced and kissed.

"That was the most beautiful experience I've ever had," Angelica remarked.

"The same can be said for me, my dear," Jonathan replied, hugging her tightly. He closed his eyes and savored the moment, a moment of perfect serenity and the truest love. The only thing that could have spoiled it all was the sound of a click, and a man's gruff voice behind him.

"Dr. Jonathan Morgan?" asked the voice. Jonathan loosened his grip on Angelica and turned around to behold several people standing behind him. Among them were Wendy and Lord William, also several burly-looking strangers and a police officer with a drawn revolver pointed directly at Jonathan's head.

"What's going on?" asked Jonathan.

"I'm arresting you on suspicion of the murder of three men on the 30th of May," said the officer, who had the voice that disrupted Jonathan's serene moment. "Two witnesses here claim that the murders took place on your property."

"Impossible!" Jonathan rebutted. "I don't know of any such thing!"

"Don't even think about denying it!" William shot back. "My wife and Mr. Waits here can attest to the bodies that were found in your warehouse, Dr. Morgan!"

"So you did break in to my warehouse!"

"That's beside the point!" William roared. "Inspector, you'll find the bodies inside the place! Do your duty!"

As the inspector walked toward the warehouse, Jonathan tried to step forward to stop him, but he was quickly halted by Mr. Waits and his cohorts with their guns drawn. Jonathan and Angelica stood petrified. A moment later, there was a yelp of exclamation coming from the warehouse, and then the inspector ran out of the doors toward Jonathan.

"There's three skeletons in there!" the inspector yelled. "What kind of devilry is going on here?"

"Sir, I swear I have no idea what is going on!" Jonathan stuttered in fear. "I've never seen any skeletons in there!"

"Nevertheless, they were found on your premises, making you responsible for the crime!" William asserted. "Arrest him!"

The officer flashed William a foul look, then proceeded to place Jonathan in shackles.

"What will happen to my property?" asked Jonathan as he was hauled over to a carriage with iron bars in the windows.

"It'll all be foreclosed and sold off, as usual."

"Sold off to me, as it were," William added behind his back.

Jonathan struggled viciously against the shackles and the grip of the officer. "NO!" he yelled bitterly. "You can't!"

"Watch me," William replied with a smirk, with Wendy at his side.

As Jonathan was hauled away, Angelica was trembling violently. She fell to her knees, sobbing and seething with rage. Curious, William walked over to Angelica and looked down on her like a frightened child. She jerked her head up at him and William stumbled back in terror. Her face was absolutely nothing like the innocent-looking face that she had before.

What was once Angelica was now something else entirely. Her skin turned from a rosy tint to a slimy pale gray. Her arms and fingers elongated, and her legs conjoined into one massive limb beneath her waist. Her feet flattened and turned to their sides, forming a flipper for a tail. Her eyes turned larger, rounder, and completely black, and her mouth was filled with rows of sharpened teeth, like a shark.

The thing that was once Angelica swiped at William with long, sharp claws that were once fingernails. William screamed and fell to the ground as blood gushed from the three slash marks on his right shoulder beneath his torn coat. The creature then turned its gaze to Mr. Waits, who was fumbling for his gun. It pounced upon him and bit right into his throat, pulling away flesh from his neck and leaving him to die gurgling on his own blood. One by one the other men fell victim to the creature. Some tried to fight back, but their shots went wild and completely missed. All of them were viciously, relentlessly torn apart with its killer claws.

William staggered to his feet, still gripping his bleeding shoulder, and hefted a rifle from one of the killed members of Mr. Waits's gang. He steadied himself, and when the creature spotted him and lunged for him, he fired off a single shot, loud and powerful, which impacted against the monster's bare chest. A gash exploded with dark fluids in its gray, slimy abdomen, and it fell off the edge of the cliff into the sea. William looked down and found no trace of the creature beneath.

"Take Dr. Morgan to my manor and lock him in the basement!" William commanded the few who survived the attack. "Destroy the airship and burn everything to the ground!"

First, there was pain in her chest. A sharp, hot and intense agony such as which she had never known before. Then there was cold. The water completely enveloped her, and her gills sucked at it hungrily. The land creature attacked her with a powerful, alien weapon, and the pain was far too much for her to bear.

Even worse than the pain that wracked her body was another kind of pain, which attacked her heart. It was a pain that was unfamiliar to her, but it still wounded her every bit as much, of not more, than the strange projectile that was launched into her body. It was a thought. A simple thought that caused her this terrible anguish. The thought of having lost Jonathan after all that he had ever done for her, and everything that she felt for him.

Land creatures had a word for this sensation: love. They claimed that love was a powerful thing, repeating time and again from a poet's words how love was "light from Heaven." She never understood those words until now. She remembered those times spent with Jonathan. When even her memories were gone, those moments of learning and discovering came flooding back to her mind. What she wanted most was to be alive, if only just to be able to be with Jonathan again. Using this as her power, she willed herself to heal from the physical wound, and return to the surface. The wound in her chest gradually began to close, and she could feel her strength return.

The cellar of Hennisburg Manor was dark and empty, exactly what Jonathan felt within. The heavy oaken door at the top of a staircase was sealed shut, and there was nothing but locked trunks and stacked crates that were nailed shut. It would not be worth Jonathan's time or effort to try and look for anything among the crates that could be useful to escape; the guards posted at the door were heavily armed.

He remembered when he was hauled into the cellar by those two black-clad, muscular thugs armed with shotguns, as Lord William kept demanding time and again for him to start working on a new craft like *The Nymph*, one that would be exclusively a combat vehicle for wartime. All those times, Jonathan staunchly refused, and he was thrown down the stairs into the cellar, landing on a hard wooden floor, the fall impacting his hands and knees. In the gloom of the cellar, he rubbed his agonized knees and tried to make sense of everything that transpired.

His the beloved airship *The Nymph* was destroyed. His warehouse and laboratory were burned to the ground. Most especially strange in the midst of his losses was the woman he came to love: Angelica. Apparently, she was far more than an innocent young amnesiac; he watched from afar as she transfigured into some creature that mauled several people. How did Angelica hide that from him? What kind of creature was she to begin with? Most especially, how did Jonathan never know about it until now? Whatever she was, Jonathan chose only to remember the charming, innocent girl that he cared for, danced with, and in the depths of his heart had come to love.

Now she was gone, and everything that Jonathan had ever strived for was destroyed by the avaricious husband of his bitter former wife. He had nothing left to live for and no other way to recover from such terrible, massive losses.

He closed his eyes and slouched against the wall, wishing vehemently for death. He imagined someone coming down those steps and pointing a shotgun to his head, ending all of his misery. Surely what afterlife awaited him could be no worse than that which he was made to endure over the past few hours.

From among the waves, a creature with gray, mottled skin crawled out onto a beach. Clumps of sand stuck to its moistened flesh, and it looked around at a cluster of nearby houses on a grassy hill up from the beach. It staggered on its long arms and massive single limb of a leg towards the houses.

A villager, Kenneth, walked out his door that night to find out the source of the orange glow that he saw outside his window. Whatever it was, it was keeping him from sleep. From outside, he could see the old warehouse and lighthouse off near the rocky coast both set ablaze. He wondered how such a thing would happen; he had always assumed that those places were long since abandoned. Out of habit, he said a small prayer and placed the sign of the cross on himself, out of respect for whoever may have been involved in the fire, if there was anyone.

Before he could go back inside, something crawled out of the shadows and held him by his neck, something with long, sharp claws and slimy skin. It looked at him with dark amphibian eyes.

"Where is the carriage with iron bars?" it demanded in a low, raspy voice.

Kenneth was too terrified to speak. His mind was reeling at the monster that was holding him, and now was tightening its grip on his neck.

"*Where is it?*" it hissed viciously. Thinking quickly, Kenneth pointed a finger down the road, away from the burning buildings.

"It went that way, toward Hennisburg Manor!" Kenneth sputtered. The creature released Kenneth, who collapsed on the ground in front of his door. He held his throat and tried to catch his breath as the creature sped away into the gloom.

Lord William sat on one of the couches in the living room with Wendy at his side. He took a draft from a glass of brandy, and relaxed in the fine velvet seat.

"I'm sure Dr. Morgan will come to his senses sooner or later," said William.

"Was it really necessary to burn down his lab?" asked Wendy.

William scoffed. "He's an inventor; I'm sure he can make something new."

In an instant, the oil lamps that illuminated the room were extinguished. The roaring fire in the hearth petered out to nothingness. The room was veiled in complete darkness, as was every other room in the house, as William found through the open doors. The guards from Mr. Waits's gang, stationed at every door with loaded weapons, looked around curiously.

"Stay on guard, men!" William commanded as he closed the door. He turned to Wendy and went back to the couch, holding her close.

"Don't worry, my dear," William whispered to his wife. "We'll get those lamps refilled, and get the lights back on soon."

Moments passed while the couple lay silent on the couch in each other's embrace. Lord William almost failed to notice a muffled scream coming from outside the room. Then there came another scream, and the unmistakable sound of gunfire. Alerted, Lord William got up from the couch and drew a revolver from his coat. He gestured for Wendy to stay down, and he went cautiously to the door.

Three long claws pierced through the solid wooden door, sending splinters flying onto the floor. William stepped back in surprise, and the door flew open, revealing the creature that was once Angelica. It took one look at William, and pounced on him in an instant, much faster than William reacted. The creature pinned William to the floor and took the gun from his hand, throwing it into the fireplace among the glowing embers.

"Where is Jonathan?!" the creature screeched.

"Forget about him!" William retorted. "Why would you risk so much for a spineless bookworm who never amounted to anything? Come work for me, whatever you are, and I'll make you a fortune!"

The creature raised a hand to swipe at him, but William kept vainly imploring it. "You're adept at killing; I can see that! Come work for me, and you can kill as many as you want, and be paid for each corpse!"

The creature refused the offer, slicing William's throat with its claws. William hacked and gurgled as blood gushed from his open wound, and he collapsed in a flowing crimson puddle.

Wendy was terrified by the scene that unfolded in front of her, and she tried to run for the door. But the creature stopped her and she fell onto the floor near the pool of blood from her dead husband. The creature stood over her, looking down scornfully at Jonathan's former lover.

"He is a good man!" the creature bellowed at Wendy. "Where is he?"

Wendy pulled herself to her feet and grabbed the first weapon she could find: the crossed swords inside the coat-of-arms emblem over the mantle. But as soon as she pulled the sword off the wall, the rest of the heavy metallic emblem went with it, and she could not pull the sword out. She tried to swing around the entire emblem, hoping that the pointed ends of the crossed swords would still be effective, but it was not. The creature slapped the entire emblem out of her hands and it skidded across the floor, well out of her reach. Cornered by the creature, she had no choice.

"The cellar!" she confessed. "He's alive in there!"

As the creature turned around, Wendy picked up the sword-crossed emblem again, and tried to stab the creature in the back with it. The creature grabbed Wendy's arm, and in a sudden motion it neatly severed Wendy's arm at the elbow, unleashing a torrent of blood and a shriek of pain from Wendy. With the emblem still in the severed arm, the creature stabbed Wendy with the point of a crossed sword and exited the room, leaving Wendy to die.

The sound of the door creaking open shook Jonathan from his abyss of despair. He looked up at the top of the stairs, expecting to see his executioner as William or one of his cohorts. Instead, it was Angelica, as radiant and pure as ever. She was not the amphibious monster that she once was, but instead, she was the same girl with whom Jonathan fell in love.

Angelica flew down the stairs and they embraced tightly, then kissed. All the pain and agony Jonathan felt just a moment ago now seemed like a lifetime ago, taken away by the love of his life.

"I thought I'd never see you again!" Jonathan stammered between kisses.

"I came back for you, Jonathan," said Angelica softly.

"But what are you?" he asked. "How did you hide this from me?"

"I was called many things before. I was called a 'naiad,' or a 'ceasg.' You might call me a mermaid."

"A mermaid?"

"More than that. It's what I tried to remember, and it took this long to come back to me."

Angelica took a step back from Jonathan and pulled in a deep breath. These words would be very difficult for her to say.

"I am the monarch of a realm beneath the sea. I went on a journey to the land to find a mate, someone who is pure of heart, who could share in my dominion. But that night, I was tossed about on the sea, and struck my head on the rocks. I lost my entire memory, but I knew that once I recovered, I would have found the one I was destined for."

She pointed right to Jonathan.

"Will you accept this honor I grant to you, Jonathan?"

Without hesitation, Jonathan nodded, and took Angelica's hand.

It would be several months before *The Nymph II* was deemed worthy to fly. Despite the loss of the original blueprints and notes, the knowledge of the ship's construction and the fuel system was still fresh in Jonathan's mind. With Angelica's help in building the craft, it went much faster and smoother than it did before.

One clear summer's day, as the sun was shining overhead, Jonathan took one last look out over the crashing waves, feeling the warm breeze ruffling his hair. Angelica stood at his side.

"I'm ready to go," said Jonathan.

The Nymph II took off and Jonathan piloted it over the water, low enough that he could see the rough surface of the water churning and waving in every direction. On Angelica's cue, Jonathan steered the ship lower to the sea. He thought the ship would splash down and sink, but Angelica closed her eyes and muttered something low under her breath. The ship descended lower and lower, closer to the ocean, close enough that Jonathan could feel the spray coming off the waves as he piloted the ship.

The Nymph II splashed down, and then it slipped below the surface, but Jonathan was completely dry. The water itself formed a bubble around *The Nymph II*, such that not a drop of water filled it. Jonathan sighed with relief, and then looked around in amazement. Illuminated by the lamps in the ship, he could see schools of tiny fishes swimming freely about, scattered by larger fishes with long, flat dorsal fins.

"So this is what it's like underwater," Jonathan remarked.

"Wait until you see your new home!" said Angelica, pointing ahead. Nothing could have prepared Jonathan for the shock and amazement of what lay before him.

An entire city, larger than any district in Aberdeen, hidden completely beneath the ocean, was laid out in majesty before Jonathan. Graceful structures of stone, metal, and coral were lined up atop the sea floor. As the ship approached these buildings, they felt larger and grander up close. Ahead, a mighty palace decorated with luminous lights greeted them. Jonathan simply had no words for the sensation that overcame him, seeing the colossal palace, with its gracefully curved walls and stalwart towers, all of them lined with a multihued glow that gave the impression of a giant stained glass window. It was completely unlike anything he ever could have imagined.

"Welcome to my domain, and it will be our home together," said Angelica.

The palace and all the other buildings from beneath the sea disappeared into nothingness, and the Mystic Theater took its place once again. George sighed with slight disappointment; the undersea world was so fascinating and so beautiful that he would have loved to spend more time there to discover its myriad secrets.

"Poets and playwrights have long tried to explain the nature of love," said Doctor Xoctarious. "All that we do know is that it can be found in the most unlikely places, and it can happen among the most unlikely people. Is there any among us who by happenstance or fate may yet come to find the one with whom we were destined to share our very lives? Perhaps all one needs to do is look in more places, or simply wait for the right moment. Fate has a way of changing everything in one's life in a single instant."

OF GODS AND MORTALS

Story By
Dominic R. Daniels & Doug K. Owen
Written by
Dominic R. Daniels & Doug K. Owen

1

ANCIENT DAYS

The bell chimed seven more times as the audience in the Mystic Theater was transported back through time and space through the vast burning constellations and star dust to Mother Earth when she was but an innocent maiden, before the dawn of creation itself, and the scenery changed with a new vision to behold just as one would gaze into a black obsidian looking glass, scrying between lucid dreams and reality.

In a cloud of ancient mist held between the skies and firmament was a glorious floating empire where no mortal had ever seen or walked or touched, and in this sacred land were two island kingdoms on a colossal platform, powered by seven golden Vakan orbs, which were awesome mechanized devices of purified liquid energy underneath the heavenly cities, which kept the cities high in atmosphere against the earth's gravitational pull and magnetic fields.

The earth under the seas was uncharted territory except for the human traders on merchant ships and those who lived the off fish from the high seas and conducted business with the many island kingdoms ruled by human kings and nobility. The first sky kingdom was made of molded golden light and crystals, and this was the kingdom of Ymatiais. The second kingdom was a carved mountain fortress but humble city in the green valley regions of Lemuria, and this was the kingdom of Knutos.

It was the age of celestial kings and elemental gods, back to the time of the titans and Grigori, when the mighty heroes of old battled and hunted ravenous creatures of legend and the lost angelic tribes of the cosmos had ruled the universe.

In that great eon, seven millennia before the human birth of Christ, the Son of Man, there were two races who existed, obsessed with gaining the power of secret knowledge and deep wisdom of the hidden mysteries of life, and there were the beautiful but vain angels known as the Y'matas, and the humble but brave angels known as the Knutas, and for thousands of years, they constantly shed blood and warred with one another in the search of spiritual and alchemistic truths of the divine.

Then, one day, after tireless years of battle and killing on the fields of weaved glass and tears of cherubim sorrows, two angelic kings met, their armies behind them waiting for orders to attack.

But a ceasefire was declared on the battlefield. The first king was Ishtock, ruler of Y'matas, who was an old wise king dressed in armament with growths on his body that doubled as armor with brilliant gold and silver, and his purple royal robe caped around his broad shoulders with open slits in back with his four large wings extending out of the cloth and a crown of jewels of rubies and amber with fine sharp points, and his eyes burned with grayish smoke and white auric color.

He sheathed his sword and approached his better half in calmness. Walking up to King Ishtock was a young and noble angelic warrior, who was King Tarak the ruler of the Knutas, and he had fiery red hair and a small beard on his face, a very handsome face, and elegant gilded youth, but he was a strong and wise sovereign too. He was dressed in simpler attire, in leather-sewn armor and hand-crafted gauntlets of armor on his arms and legs, and he too had wings but unlike the king of the Y'matas. Tarak only had two large red wings on his back, and on his chest, he had an iron cast breastplate with the symbol of the Tree of Wisdom. King Ishtock also had this symbol on his armor but the tree on his was the Tree of Knowledge.

The two kings, both the young and the old, stood motionless, looking at one another, their eyes seeing through each other's spirits, a sadness and remorse in both of them. Tears came down their cheeks in unison, for they had had enough of killing and had enough of seeing their men dying, and for what? Wasted delusions of grandeur and power that had brought the divided Empire to utter ruin.

"Tarak, I wish to make peace between both of our kingdoms; do you accept this devout and honorable offer?" asked King Ishtock.

"I do, old king, but on the terms that my people and yours will learn to live in peace and slay each other no more. Second, that our kingdoms share our resources equally so that our people will make the lands prosper and the country will bloom with wisdom and tenderness," rebutted King Tarak.

"I accept your terms, and I thank you, my fellow Lord," said King Ishtock in respect. bowing before the young king. Tarak returned the gesture in bowing to his elder. Embracing each other in friendship, they unsheathed their swords and lifted the up to heaven for all their warriors to see, and they joined the blades together making an oath that would last until all time would be done.

"On this day, my sons of Ymata, your king unites a truce with these brothers in arms! Raise your swords in agreement if you are loyal to your king!" shouted King Ishtock to his army.

Ishtock's army was silent, but one by one they raised their swords in the air and saluted his majesty with exaltation.

"Hail, King Ischtock, Lord of the Y'matas! Hail King Tarak! Our brother and friend of arms!" shouted the army of the Y'matas in one voice.

"They agree," said King Ischtock to his fellow lord.

"Good," said King Tarak.

"Now, have your men do the same," said King Ischtock.

The young king obeyed Ischtock's request.

"Hear me, my soldiers! Do you agree that we should unite with this feeble old bastard and feast tonight with our shining comrades in arms? Or shall we continue to spill blood and go home with dead friends and no bread?" announced King Tarak joking.

"Feast and drink!" they yelled laughing as they raised their sword to honor the truce.

"You heard the verdict! Welcome in ally ship my friend. Tonight we are brothers!" said King Tarak.

The two kings laughed and shook hands. The alliance was made, and there was much merriment and feasting with lovely winged wenches and wine at King Ischtock's castle, but it was a peace that would not last.

Two centuries had passed and the peace that was to be eternal had ceased to exist. War broke out again as the son of King Ischtock, the new ruler— a capricious young Emperor named Ashatoh— fought against the High Prime Minister of the Knuta, who was named Emak.

The Y'matas had broken the truce, and the war had again taken hold of the two kingdoms, and a lust for power and control including a change of government for each of the two kingdoms. A dictatorship had risen in the realm of the Y'matas, and for the Knutas' lands, a Republic had risen, no longer ruled by a leading figure head but a collective of the commoner with their own judges, senators, and a Prime Minister.

One day on the eve of the Summer Solstice at the setting of the sun, the Knuta Senate Elders met in the Hall of the Holy Judges, a great council chamber with grand columns made of emeralds and opals with a separate majestic temple made of polished marble and gold to give worship and homage to the ever living High God, who made both the angelic tribes in the darkness of space, and he had created them from lightning and omnipotent fire.

The senators and Prime Minister of the Knuta were deeply troubled as they conversed on the council floor to discuss their issues.

A young angelic senator named Tyris, who was dressed in robes of priestly Olympian fare with limited silver shoulder guards and copper bracelets on his wrist, appealed to his constitutes for calm.

"Fellow countrymen, elders: lend me your ears! I appeal to the holy senate as a member of this assembly that we recall our troops from Elysista immediately," said Tyris.

Another senator who was older rose from his seat on the third row on the circular hall and spoke. "Senator Tyris, are you proposing that we give up our advantage in battle? Should we risk our people and our conservatories of Elysiatic research to be annihilated by the Y'matas? We have spent countless millennia to gather such precious repositories of knowledge, and it would be a great disaster to lose them," protested Senator Gallas.

"Not at all; our forces are weaker, and our enemies have better weapons and technology at their disposal than we do," said Tyris.

"Then what would you have us do, Senator?" said Gallas.

"What we have, gentlemen, in our collective, is craft and cleverness, so I say simply put: use it. Let us send an ambassador with an armed escort that are filled with finest Turan we have available as a token of tribute so that we can make negations with Emperor Ashatoh, to discuss terms of surrender as both our sides have taken great losses," appealed Tyris.

"Are you mad, Tyris?" said another senator in his seat.

"The last time we met with them in pursuit of treaties, they broke the pact, and nearly destroyed us! We will not let them neither conquer our people nor reign over us with fear and tyranny," protested Senator Gallas.

"I assure you, good senators, that we will not truly surrender to them, but we will discover their plans and use it against them. This strategy will give us a clear advantage in battle, and then we will be able to defeat their forces and end this bloody war once and for all," said Tyris.

"Who should we send on this daring pretense?" said one of the other senators.

"Send out a conscription notice to all the provinces, and gather all the wisest of men in the kingdom to partake in a tournament of a trial, and the chosen of these men will have the character of great insight and courage; the one who is chosen will be of virtue and possess purity of spirit, and whoever of these wise men that passes such a test will be sent to the Emperor as the ambassador," suggested Tyris.

The other senators whispered among themselves, including the Prime Minister Emak, who was also present in the senatorial council, though his seat was not with the other senators but on a high throne on three small steps above the chamber floor. Emak looked deep in his spirit as he prayed in his thoughts to the Ancient One, and he felt a peace come over him.

"Emak, my good servant, listen to your brother for he is wise in these matters," said the High Father.

"But my Lord, we shall surely be destroyed," said Emak with fear in his thoughts.

"Have faith and patience, Prime Minister, for I am with you and your people, so do as Tyris has suggested. I will be with you all," said the High Father.

"But what of our enemies?" asked Emak curiously.

"I have given my other angelic children time to repent, but they will not change their ways; they destroy this precious world which I charged both of your peoples to protect, and they mock and taunt Me, saying 'Let us raise up and overthrow our maker into the endless pit, and then we will be as gods. We have lost our battles to our former brethren, so now we will kill them and our maker!' I have loved them greatly and yet they do not care for the treasures I have given them: eternal life, a fathers' love, material treasures, and everlasting wisdom beyond any creature I have made. Therefore, my heart is deeply broken because of their evil," said the High Father. "Do as I say, my servant,"

"Yes, my Lord; I will obey," said Emak in his spirit. Then he diverted his attention to the senators who spoke openly.

"All in favor of this concept by Senator Tyris, raise your hands in a vote," said Emak.

All the senators in the chamber room raised their hands in agreement.

"Good, my brothers. Prepare the conscriptions immediately; we must find such a man; we shall find us our champion, "said Emak.

The next morning, as soon as the sun rose, the high captains of Knuta sent out conscription notices to all of the provinces in the land of the kingdom to gather every prophet, divine magician, or seer in all the villages, towns, and city-states in order to bring them before the high senate elders in a tournament of miracles so that they would compete in this strange farce. Male and female, no discrimination but equal in power, they were allowed to compete in this contest.

2

THE TOURNAMENT OF MIRACLES

And so they came in numbers thousands to the Prime Minister's mountain palace, and it was a modest large home yet peaceful and full of grace, covered in rich lush green vines and the most gorgeous of flowers lacquered with blue bells, and there were yellow and orange tiger lilies and white roses with pearls and jade gem stone leaves growing from them. This retreat was similar in the design and shape of the ivory towers and temples of the future continents known as Asia and the regions of India.

The skies were filled with tropical blue nimbus clouds as the sun shone through them with vivid colors of pinks and fuchsia, tranquility and love, and in the main courtyard which was the size of a monolith arena, a field of wheat made from the finest thread of silver was trimmed and cut to be walked on with the smoothness of silk under one's feet.

Before the assembled light?, workers in rows that stretched long as far as the endless seas were waiting for the instructions at the high steps of the outer court yard was the main pedestal, where the Prime Minister stood to address the brave men and ever benign womanly angels who had gathered for this contest.

Among the masses of these angelic ministers and prophets was a young angelic monk in his late 20s by the name of Eriad, and he was well-built in physique and fit in beauty, and his eyes were like white diamonds with tints of magenta, and his hair was long and smooth as the softest garments, the color of lavender.

His skin was a light purple, and he also had two large purple wings on his back and wore a silver amulet of a sheppard staff and long sword crossed, a symbol of his clan. He was dressed in a humble monk's robe, his chest partially exposed like a gladiator. He stood with the others, eager to begin. He wanted to be the one, for he deeply loved his people and was devoted to serving his country; he was a patriot of the heavens and a feared servant of the Eternal Deity.

"Most blessed and venerable men and women of Knutos, I honor you all for coming to this challenge today; may the fortune and blessing of the Ancient One smile down upon you by the most righteous power and authority of His Divine Eternal Excellency. Let the tournament begin!" proclaimed Emak as he raised a gold handkerchief in his hand and dropped it to the ground.

The crowds who gathered for this event sat in droves at the courtyard steps for a front row seat to what would be the greatest spectacle in all of creation. The roaring of the crowd grew from the calm that had come before the the storm, and then in it rose as if speaking and humming in one tongue like a place of ordained worship in a thunderous ringing, as if the Holy One spoke with the blast of his voice, echoing throughout the galaxies.

"This trial will be a test of courage and strength, so whoever defeats the creature to descend from the clouds will win the match," declared Emak's advisor to the contestants.

From out of the clouds, a massive shape descended swiftly onto the ground. The Knutas contestants that were lined up on the field looked in terror at the creature that swooped down to face them. Among the crowd, Eriad had never seen anything like it before. Whatever it was, it had the overall body and head of a lion, but the similarities ended there. The creature unfurled four pairs of massive wings adorned with white feathers on its massive, muscular back. It prowled around the field, showing off the two growths on either side of its animal face, and resting atop the lion's head was a golden crown, denoting its venerated nature.

From among its long, golden mane that encircled its head, Eriad found that the strange growths on either side of its face were other faces themselves. One resembled that of a bleating lamb with small eyes and pointed ears, and the other resembled a ram with shiny, golden horns.

The spectators gasped with awe at the creature that prowled the arena's field. On the field itself, the combatants could smell a powerful odor akin to musk and jasmine emanating from the creature's body. Eriad stood in terror and disbelief; what kind of creature is this that the Knutas rulers intended him to confront? What design had the Unknowable intended, that they would risk their lives to fight this holy, deadly entity in the plain view of all their own peers?

The monster let out a loud, ferocious roar that echoed over the arena, chilling the hearts of the prospects that were made to fight it. It then flapped its wings and issued a jet of fire, bright and hot. The blast of flame glowed brightly over the heads of the prospects and the audience. Eriad could feel its intense heat even from a hundred feet away.

He was petrified with complete fear and amazement at the monster that stood before him. Something about this creature, something of reverence and, at the same time, terror of the highest order, combined in his heart. It was a monster that would easily destroy him, but at the same time, it was worthy of the highest admiration.

"Wise men and women of Knutos, prepare to face the Guardian," said Emak to his combatants.

The Guardian faced his opponents without fear, and his eyes became as brilliant neon light with a luster of unlimited power as he roared like thunder.

"Attack me! And meet your maker!" the beast yelled with a human voice, which had a commanding presence of mystery.

The angelic prophets and magicians on the battlefield powered up their energies as blue, red, and golden fire emitted from their bodies, wrapping around them changing their garments and robes to titanium armor and helmets of gold with every different kind of exotic species of bird feathers, and their lower portions into girdles and belts of iron and steel.

Their sandals changed to boots of bronze. In their hands appeared balls of light which transformed into golden shields and swords made of metal unknown to man, that could cut through solid marble without leaving a single scratch on the blade.

But the Guardian stood his ground, calm and collected. He was not the least bit afraid: one guardian against ten thousand angels, and he extended his left clawed paw in the air, and he signaled to them.

"Come get some!" he said.

Emak smiled. "What is a battle without music? Violinist, bowmen, string musicians perform for us a masterpiece of glory!" commanded his orchestra who was seated beneath his steps in the musician's box below on the field though was protected by a wave beam of energy.

And they began to shred on strange stringed instruments of knobs and cords of light, filling this stadium with the speed and hard sound of ecstasy and intense wickedness but with intensity filled with all the force of birth, life, death, and resurrection, known in the far future of humanity as an operatic symphony in exuberant delight.

Springing forth into the stratosphere, the winged warriors shot into the air like a flock of hawks to cut down the great winged cat, who darted in the air to attack; the angels were circling each other in venomous fury, dive bombing in spirals and fancy loops, looking, trying to cut the Guardian with blasting hell fire from the furnace of his fur filled belly, incinerating angels wings to a burn crisp, and as they fell by hundreds to ground like the droppings of a pigeon, their bodies were roasted and no longer retained their angelic powers but became fully mortal.

The Guardian did not even bear a cut on his flesh, and he smiled with charm as he pounced one of the larger male armored angels, ripping open his throat, tasting the sweet blood between his saber teeth, its essence the flavor similar to elderberry wine, and he snapped the angel's neck like a twig with a sharp crack.

"Is that the best you can do? I want to fight a true warrior!" said the Guardian

Eriad in the aerial battle knew where to strike as he flew down. Quickly untying his sash belt, he landed straight on top of the beast on its back and tied his sash around the throat of the beast, strangling. As the Guardian struggled to gasp for air, the rest of the warriors in the air backed away to give Eriad some space, punching the cat repeatedly in the head, incapacitating him as he and the Guardian fell together to the ground landing on the field of bodies with the three-headed lion on top of Eriad. The monsters weighed seven hundred pounds, nearly crushing Eriad, but Eriad summoned up his angelic strength and pushed the holy animal off to his side.

The beast regained his control by dog-piling Eriad, trying to claw at his face and chest, but Eriad, with his massive hands, held the jaws of one of the mouths of the Guardian open, pushing back the weight of its three faces as this thing tried to bite his head off, and as he did it, Eriad saw a holy symbol a mark of kingship on the forehead of the beast, and in his spirit he had a dream about this mark.

It was the mark of the Ancient One. Eriad ripped off the front left fang off the cat, causing the beast to scream with agony, and the lion fell over weeping in pain, his crown falling off from his head, as Eriad quickly got to his feet, unsheathing his sword.

All time and space seemed to freeze and go still like the grave, and Eriad raised his sword to heaven, but he looked into eyes of Guardian, and it began to weep like a child, and tears came out from its eyes, and Eriad was angry, wanting to strike this thing dead that had killed his brothers and sisters, but he just could not.

The crowds rose, cheering him on!

"Slay the monster! Execute it!" they railed.

But Eriad looked with sorrow on the poor wounded creature, and he threw down his sword to the ground, and he knelt down as he comforted the beast, petting his mane and healing him, putting the giant tooth back into the lion's mouth and healing his wound with his powers so it would be made whole again, the pain leaving the holy beast. The Guardian got up and licked Eriads face, kissing him and kneeling in respect to the victor.

Eriad heard the crowd behind him cheer.

"Hail to the merciful one. Hail! The crowd of elementals angels cheered.

"No!" He shouted back to the people.

"Do not cheer for me! My brothers and sisters of Lemuria, do you not realize who this is standing here before us?" shouted back Eriad in anger and conviction.

"What is he speaking about?" said the Prime Minister to his Advisors.

"I don't know," said the advisor curiously.

Eriad knelt down on his knees before the holy cat and placed the golden crown back on his head and fell to the ground to worship him.

"What is he doing?" as the Prime Minister's advisor.

Eriad then did not take notice of the crowd as he worshipped the Guardian in reverence.

"My Lord, forgive me. I did not know! I am so sorry!" said Eriad filled with deep grief; tears flowed desperately from his face as wept in the grass burying his face in his hands before the holy creature.

The Holy Beast spoke with kindness and returned mercy.

"I forgive you, child. I am the one who the High Father will send; I was with him in the beginning and shall be with him in the end and forevermore!"

It was the Eternal One, in this strange disguised form. Though none of the two angelic tribes had ever seen His presence before, even in their creation, they had only heard His voice but did not recognize him in this contest for he spoke to them differently than in his true form.

"I knew you were the one, child; you will be the champion of your people, for you have learned this truth. Courage and strength do not come from a man or an angel's body but from his mercy and compassion of the spirit," said the Eternal One, as he changed into his true form of a man dressed in a white robe with a golden belt around his waist and long hair as white as sheep's wool and eyes that burned with heaven's light with unquenchable holy fire.

The rest of the angels in the whole courtyard were shocked and frightened as they bowed in worship to the God, but the Eternal One did not harm them.

With a single sentence he spoke.

"All angels killed here on this field of death, get up and live again," He said.

As soon as He had said this, every slain angel that was killed in the battle or had lost their wings stood up alive and fully restored, and not one blemish was on their bodies; not one was dead. They were alive again, and they fell and worshiped and gave thanks to the Lord who saved them.

"Well done, my servants," He said. "The choice has been made. You have been given your champion this day! Eriad! He is the one; this angel, Eriad! Give him encouragement and your prayers to me. For this contest has been justly won," said the Eternal One, and then he ascended back into the third heaven, leaving the Knuta in peace.

The battle was over.

"All Hail, Exaltus Platius! Eriad, High Ambassador to the Kingdom of Knutos, our champion!' declared the Prime Minister.

"Eriad, come up here and receive your crown!" commanded the Prime Minister.

Eriad rushed up to the high steps of the Prime Ministers seat and bowed to him in respect.

Emak removed from a jeweled wooden oak box a crowned wreath made of silver ivy and placed the crown on Eriad's head.

Eriad rose and turned to face his people, the victor of this tournament. Tonight would be a night of feasting and praise, but tomorrow the real test to save the kingdom would begin.

3

THE JOURNEY TO YMATIAIS

The next morning, before the Blue Imperial Sloth Macaw, an animal that was born half bird with blue tinged feathered wings with red fur and the body of a tree monkey, had crowed for the sun to rise, Eriad had said goodbye to his mother, father, young sister and the rest of his clan at his home in the inner volcanic caves of the Eastern Winds near the Forrest of Dreams and Rivers of Life Giving Wine, and he had set off, dressed in a standard Knuta military leather-stitched uniform and reed sandals with a burlap satchel of provisions, and he had a pouch of bitter herbs mixed peach sap medicine, a drinking gourd filled with water that never empties, and an enchanted magical spear that he had whittled from his father's favorite long tree that held the memories of thousand years and more.

He did this the night before, after the feast was over, and he set off for the perilous journey that was his to begin and finish, accompanied with an armed escort of three hundred of Knutos bravest warriors who carried within their bodies twenty million pieces of Turan energy. Either he or his small army would save his people from destruction, or they would die in utter failure and loss, but he did not care and chose that to live and fight for his country, and his devotion to personal duty, was adventure enough, and so did his comrades.

On the other side of the shattered realm of the old empire, lay the corrupted house and seat of power of Emperor Ashatoh, the scourge of Lemuria and the most evil of angels, and he ruled over the golden city of Ymatiais with absolute hatred of his fellow kinsmen in his heart.

The young emperor was not as forgiving as his father, the former king, whom he had murdered by stabbing him with an iron dagger in the back during a bloody coup with conspirators by the old king's advisors who became loyal to Ashatoh.

Ashatoh lived in the former Ymata's High Temple of Ancient One, and he had it converted into an illustrious palace filled with every excess, covered in extreme grandeur. There were entire structures decorated in gold and silver and precious stones. Rooms were big and open, and everything was designed and engineered to be pleasing to all the senses.

The Y'matas homes even had their own harems that were well stocked with angelic and succubus women who were kept as sex slaves, and then they were killed and devoured for their energy. The ultimate insult was the main place hall, which was set up with a large marble altar and a large statue of iron and gold that was molded and made into the image of the Emperor himself, who, under penalty of divine and eternal death, subjects worshipped, and those who did not worship the statue would be imprisoned in the palace dungeons, boiled alive in molten gold or have their wings torn off and cast down to the earth to live as humans.

If King Ischtock had still been alive to see the wanton degradation that his son brought on his people, he would have wept with shame.

The elitist faction of the Y'matas believed in containing knowledge for their own ends, and it may even be dangerous if the rest of Lemuria were to know such forbidden secrets.

In comparison to their former brethren, the Knutas believed in sharing free and open knowledge to all people, regardless of their class or state. The Y'matas were beyond beautiful and well-groomed people in physical appearance, but inwardly they had grown vile and corrupt just as the emperor who now ruled over them had.

They presented themselves to each other in the great city, each day wearing copious amounts of gold and jewelry and fine silk robes with laced with perfume; there was feasting and indulging in public orgies, and there were festivals of drunkenness, where people were practicing dark arts of fallen angels and sacrificing their own children to the emperor in exchange for luxurious living and treasures.

The emperor was addicted on the blood of his own people; he would kill the children of the wealthy and drink their blood in the belief that it would increase his spiritual powers tenfold.

In the former Halls of Angelic Studies, Y'mata scholars and aristocrats would meet to discuss theory and the astral occult sciences with the ideology that they only were the worthy ones to rule Lemuria, a political form of meritocracy. The Y'matas used deception and illusions as their weapons of war by implanting visions into enemies, as well as elemental control using fire, water, ice, and the occasional assassination. To them, the end justified the means.

Emperor Ashatoh listened patiently while his emissary brought forth his report. Seated on his luminous throne of molded light in the extravagantly ornate hall, the black-robed and jewelry-wearing ruler sat with a stern countenance.

"Most venerated one; we have received reports of Knutas movement in the wilderness. They would be on course to approach our gates within a fortnight."

"An entire army of Knutas?" asked the emperor curiously. "I didn't think they still had the spine after all these years."

"Most Powerful One, we need to assemble a response before they reach our gates!"

"Do not presume to think for me, you sniveling fool!" the emperor shouted, pointing a ruby-ringed finger at the emissary, who crouched low to the smoothly-paved floor in obedience.

"I pray the forgiveness of your Excellency," whispered the emissary, his voice cracking as his body was trembling in fear.

But the emperor was unmoved and rested his hands on the armrests of his throne. "I shall expect you to show more respect in the future, emissary. You would do well to remember that. As for the Knutas, they will be faced with the full might of our forces. Send a unit of a thousand to intercept them."

"Intercept, my lord?"

"Kill them all," muttered the emperor simply.

The emissary bowed and exited the room. The stern emperor watched from beneath his haughtily lowered eyelieds as the smaller man staggered out of the royal hall. Whatever the Knutas were planning, it would break as easily as their bodies when the Y'matas warriors are finished with them. The Y'matas' durable swords, long spears and rich Aitam would make them all victorious. Inwardly, he recited the Y'matas battle creed, the words which rallied his people against their mortal foes.

My mind is sharp, availed by Aitam who is flowing in my veins. My spirit is indomitable, availed by Utran coursing in my heart. My will is unbreakable, availed by Turan built within me. The energies of my enemies will be mine to take. I shall destroy them.

Even after defeating the Guardian in the sight of all his peers and Exarchs, Eriad still felt uneasy about his task. The Guardian, for all its strength and ferocity, was still just a test designed by people with a specific goal in mind for him. Now, he was at the head of an army of battlers more experienced than himself.

He tried to steady himself as he marched on through the wilderness, knowing that all those hardened fighters were looking to him for guidance. He could feel the weight of his task bearing down on him: to expect every one of his soldiers to carry the Turan within their forms as a prize to the Y'matas. Eriad was carried on only by hope: the hope that every one of his people would survive the trip, the hope that the amount of Turas they carry would be sufficient to satisfy the Y'matas overlords, and the hope that they would not be so swift to attack, as they were most known to do over the years.

The trees in the Úntir Forest, which many called the Forest of Dreams, towered over him and his force. The path between the trees was narrow and sloped over small hills and large tree roots. He heard some soldiers grumbling behind him as they marched in single-file lines through the forest.

The sunlight was nearly completely blocked out from the canopy of leaves overhead, with only a few errant rays of light spilling down over them. Their boots crunched over the thick blanket of dead leaves and twigs on the ground. Eriad himself nearly slipped on a slimy patch of pale green material, but he quickly righted himself and carried on. The soldiers behind him avoided the trap and continued. The armor they wore of thick leather and linen, though it offered freedom of movement and protection from the buzzing insects, retained heat and made every soldier grossly uncomfortable.

Eriad continued with single-mindedness until a hand fell on his right shoulder and squeezed tightly, freezing him in place.

"Be careful, Eriad," whispered the soldier behind him. "I sense their presence nearby."

"Y'matas?" asked Eriad.

"Many of them," came the reply.

Eriad looked around cautiously, counting on the Aitam within him to see the threat that his comrade perceived. He saw nothing among the trees, heard no sounds of rustling or marching. There was only the stillness of the air, the errant buzzing of insects, and the untidy moss and dead leaves littering the ground.

Somewhere in Eriad's mind, he knew something had to have been out there, hidden among the colossal trees, an invisible force that remained unseen until it meant itself to be seen. Something out there had an intention for him and his soldiers, and Eriad, as the leader, was forced to conclude that it had to have been something with malevolent intent.

"On your guard, men!" he commanded. Promptly, the soldiers planted themselves low to the ground and kept a disciplined watch all around them. The Aitam kept them all vigilant.

Something began to move through the brush of the high tree-tops, as leaves began to fall all around Eriad and his men.

"Arm yourselves!" he shouted, as they unsheathed their swords, looking in all directions, huddling close to each other from all sides, ready to strike at their hidden enemies

"Attack!" shouted a voice from above them, as waves of multiple angelic wings extended out from the trees, fully exposed; the Y'matas were camouflaged, dressed in assorted make-up of green and brown war paint to blend in with their surroundings.

Eriad and his men looked up as they saw winged Y'matas warriors descend down on them, landing like thunder, like a plague of locust in rows, all of them armed to the hilt in heavy armor and equipped with two swords a piece for each solider.

It was a standoff.

"Destroy them!" yelled the Y'matas garrison leader.

"I don't think so!" said Eriad.

He pulled a glass smoke ball potion from his knapsack, slamming it to the ground as thick red smoke erupted from the shattered shard spreading its deadly fog all around, blinding the Y'matas' sight, and it stung their eyes as if it were red pepper, bees' venom, and citrus juice infused in the vapor, as they dropped their swords and screamed in pain; the burning was unbearable. Fortunately, the Knuta were not allergic to the concoction and had developed over the years a resistance to the chemical compound that was used in this device's manufacturing.

The Y'mata screamed.

"I can't see!" yelled another.

"Now is our chance!" Eriad lead the charge into battle, and as they rushed into the Y'mata garrison, knocking them down to the ground, they were slicing off heads and the wings off the Y'mata warriors as blood sprayed all over the faces of the fiercely outnumbered Knuta, with the Y'mata regaining their ground, getting up, shaking off the sensation of the poison that blinded them.

Eriad thrust his sword through the garrison leader's chest, and as the blade pushed through, the squishing sound as his metal cut in his enemies flesh right through his back was like butchering a wild boar in a hunt, and the garrison commander was screaming as Eriad pulled out the blade. Blood was shooting all over his armor and face, and he was savoring the bloodlust of the slaughter, and then he pushed the dead angel off his sword and he watched his enemy fall to the ground dead, flat on his face.

Eriad and his men clashed steel against steel as sparks scratched across their blades against their enemies.

One of the Y'mata soldiers behind him grabbed him in a head lock, bashing his skull in with the handle of his sword and knocked him to the ground. The whole world went black. Was he dead or alive?

Time faded into lost memory, and a sense of distortion was all around him, as if Eriad saw himself falling through an endless swirling abyss of light and sound, and his head ringing as if he was hearing fifty temple bells ringing.

Eriad awoke with his head throbbing painfully. As soon as he started moving, the pain began to subside, and he recollected himself. His sword was right where it fell from his hand. Picking it up off the grassy field, he looked around and beheld that he was standing in the middle of a massacre. The bodies of slain soldiers from both sides littered the field, unmoving and silent. Rivulets of luminous blood from the celestial beings flowed freely through the grass, glowing among the bodies. The trees from the Úntir Forest towered above him, indifferent to the slaughter that ensued. Eriad looked around for anyone who survived the attack, but there was no sign of life anywhere in the field.

Nor was there any sign of any Y'matas survivor either. No fluttering of leathery wings, no clicking of their foreign instruments, no raspy curses whispered in the breeze.

Eriad forced himself to walk away from the battlefield and return home. The envoy to Y'matas had failed. All of the treasured Turas was lost, and all the brave warriors were killed. Eriad was completely alone, and the only thing left for him to do, now that the mission was over, was to return home. He hoped that the elders and the Exarchs would be merciful to him.

Following the path away from the battlefield, Eriad came to a clearing among the trees. In this remote place, Eriad stretched his limbs and lay down on the grassy ground, trying to recover his energy. The battle left him drained and weak, and even he came to doubt whether he would make it home alive. *Was this to be my fate?* Eriad wondered. Was he truly intended by the Unknowable to die in the wilderness, so far removed from his home and family, after having led a failed attempt to appease their own mortal enemies? His lack of Utran made his will falter, and the lack of Aitam made his mind cloudy.

But Eriad was nothing if not dedicated. He slowed his breathing, focusing his spirit, and made an appeal to the Unknowable in its distant realm. In prayer he could feel his spirit replenished with a flow of Utran from within. More and more he prayed, until the power was able to carry him further in his journey. This special kind of energy would make his will stronger and would carry him all the distance to his destination.

As he headed down the path, he kept a vigil all around him, and his scientific mind appreciated all the wonders of the forest around him. All around him were secrets, encoded deep within nature itself. Eriad looked up at the mighty trees and wondered how they came to grow so tall, taller than the temples and trading centers of the Knutas. He wondered what energy the trees carried within them; maybe there would yet be a way to tap into its sources of spiritual Utran or focusing Aitan. Eriad liked that idea; the energies flowing throughout Lemuria could be all around him, even in that very valley in the forest, and someday there would be a way for him and his people to unlock those energies and grow further in wisdom.

The immortal forest would be their saving grace, a place for them all to acquire vast if not unlimited amounts of energy. What made this idea even more enticing to Eriad was the notion that the Y'matas would never know about it at all. At last, they would have the upper hand in the constant struggle for knowledge, and their answer was right in front of them all along.

Eriad smoothed out his leather armor and pulled the cowl over his head; insects were starting to develop a taste for his sweaty skin. The armor was very thick and still retained heat, making him feel even hotter, but it offered nearly complete protection from the insects, which made the sacrifice of comfort a fair trade. The supplies bounced around in his knapsack, and the sheathed sword on his belt constantly slapped him on his thigh. Being a warrior for the Knutas, even despite his victory against the Guardian, he knew he was never promised an easy life.

The path snaked to the right past some boulders, and there it was against a massive wall of rough and black-flecked granite. At the base of the mountain, surrounded by tall grass, was a wellspring of clear water. Eriad scrambled down through the grass to find the place where the pool began, and he set down his sack. He took a long drink from the water, and almost instantly he felt an energy flow right into him, along with a renewed sense of acuteness. The water must be rich in Aitam, which sharpened his mind. With every draft from the spring, he could feel more alert and quick. Every last feeling of weakness was left on the battlefield miles back, and Eriad felt like himself again.

The trees of the Úntir Forest were much higher than she thought. From her home in the Y'matas territory, they looked small in their distance, and she thought that flying to their tops would be no problem. Instantly, she found herself regretting that idea; the zenith of the tree offered a dizzying view of the forest and from the thick branches on which she perched, she willed herself not to look down for fear of the height and potentially losing her balance.

Although Eris was an accomplished flyer, there were some heights even she was unprepared to face.

But her masters would not accept her hesitation as any excuse for letting one Knutas escape when they all should have died in the battle. She turned her gaze down, forcing herself not to focus on the trees or the ground down below, but on the single Knutas man crouched over a mysterious pool of water. He was taking samples of the water and dropping a sounding stone into the pool, checking its depth and writing notes in a bound-leather journal. He was deeply distracted with his work, a perfect target for an aerial attack.

She gripped the pendant around her neck and closed her eyes, steadying herself on the tree. Eris placed herself in a state of calm, slowing her heartbeat and her breathing. This is to be the calm before unleashing the storm, as her Y'matas combat masters had taught.

My mind is sharp, availed by Aitam flowing in my veins. My spirit is indomitable, availed by Utran coursing in my heart. My will is unbreakable, availed by Turan built within me. The energies of my enemies will be mine to take. I shall destroy them.

The pool turned out to be much deeper than Eriad could have imagined. Wherever the water was coming from, there must be vast quantities of it down below the ground. The possible benefits could be extremely great; a constant and protected source of Aitam for the Knutas would sustain their population for generations to come. He just had to make certain that it would be safe, but that would be a matter for future testing.

He was so enraptured with the idea of providing a boon to his fellow Knutas that he almost missed the sound of powerful wings above him. The Aitam in his mind told him that something was coming from above. Instinctively and driven by the Aitam, he unsheathed his sword and spun around to behold a Y'matas descending over him. The Y'matas woman, with her wings outstretched and claws out, contorted her face in hatred, ready to strike and destroy.

Eriad struck first with a sideways slice of his sword. The woman abruptly fell, clutching her chest in agony. The sword had sliced right through her finely-detailed scarlet tunic, revealing a red stripe cut into her flesh. The woman clutched her wound, then got back to her feet and scowled bitterly at Eriad. She flapped her wings harshly, sending dust into Eriad's eyes.

He raised a hand over his face to protect himself and ran forward, striking again. His blade connected with the top of the Y'matas's left wing, neatly severing the bony growth and thin flesh. Crimson blood spurted from the wound and splashed onto the grass. The woman screeched, and Eriad forced her down onto the ground, holding the point of his sword at her throat. With his free hand, Eriad channeled his inner Utran and touched the place on her back where her left wing used to be. The blood flow was slowing, and then stopped. He did the same for the wound on her abdomen, all the while keeping her still with the point of his blade poised over her neck.

"You lacked the Aitam to fight me, Y'matas," Eriad coolly hissed at her from above. "I've fought far worse things than you before."

"Let me go, you Knutas scum!" the woman demanded, struggling against Eriad's hold over her.

"Why would I do that?" asked Eriad. "The instant I let you get up, you'll only try to strike at me again. I waste my Aitam on you, and most likely you'll lose your other wing in the fight."

There was nothing that the woman could say as a rebuttal. She exhaled sharply and set her head down on the ground. The sharp pain in her back and chest were starting to subside, but she still fervently hated the Knutas man.

"I've stopped the bleeding," said Eriad. "Never let it be said that we Knutas were without mercy."

Eriad reached into a pocket in his pants, and drew out a silver, cylindrical-shaped device with various prongs coming off it. The woman watched as he pointed the end of the device at her heart, and Eriad noted three glowing lights coming from the body of the device. One glowed bright green, two others in red and blue were very faint.

"It seems you carry much Turan within you, Y'matas," Eriad observed. "The others, not so much though."

"Don't you lecture me, Knutas!" the woman cried out desperately. "We will rip your pathetic hovels out from the ground and toss you into the seas!"

"You may find that difficult to do with only one wing, a sword at your throat, and a man with more power than you."

"Then what are you waiting for? Go ahead and kill me! I'm ready for it!"

Eriad instead only looked at the pendant that she wore around her neck. It was a large circle of gold, emblazoned with an image of a falcon's head and seven crossed swords. Thinking quickly, he withdrew his sword and got up off of the woman, leaving her lying on the grass.

"What is your name? Or would you prefer if I keep calling you Y'matas?"

"Eris," the woman replied simply. Eriad nodded with a slight smile. He liked that name.

"Well, Eris, I think a deal is in order. I will spare your life and let you go back to your home, in exchange for that pendant you wear."

"Never!" Eris shot back, clutching her pendant tightly. Eriad stepped back with his hand on the hilt of his sword.

"Fine, then; perhaps some Turas instead? As much as you're willing to spare, and I'll even let you keep your wing. I hear that Y'matas doctors can reattach them if they're still fresh."

Eris sucked in a breath and shut her eyes, hating everything about the situation. Eventually, she nodded without a word.

"Wonderful!" Eriad proclaimed jovially. "Let's get the transfer over with, so you can be on your way then, shall we?"

Eriad held out his right hand with the palm directly facing her, and she reluctantly held out her hand as well. When their two palms came very close to touching, Eriad focused himself and felt a slight flicker of energy at his hand. He could feel warmth on the skin of his hand emanating from Eris's own hand near his.

A green light began to shine in the small space between their hands when a connection was formed between them. Tiny wisps of bright green energy that curled like strands of smoke started flowing out of the skin of Eris's palm and flowed directly into Eriad's hand. Eriad focused even more, and he could feel the energy seeping into his hand and coursing into his body, in the same way one would eat and feel the food flowing down into one's stomach. Reciprocally, Eris could feel a draining sensation from out of her body.

As soon as the sensation became too much for Eriad, he withdrew his hand and broke the connection. He brought his stiffened arm to rest at his side, and nodded to Eris.

"Thank you for your business, Eris of Y'matas," he said in a friendly tone. "Take your wing with you and be on your way. Let's hope our paths do not cross again soon."

Eris picked up her severed wing and left, humiliated and angry. Eriad packed up his gear and headed back on his journey. The sun was already beginning to set, casting streaks of orange and yellow into the sky. The Úntir trees looked darker and more menacing as the light waned, towering over him the way Eris did when she swooped down upon Eriad not too long ago.

All things considered, today might have been productive after all. Despite the loss of the soldiers and their Turas, as well as the state of war still existing between the two factions, Eriad had found what may be a valuable source of Aitam that the community could easily claim for the benefit of all. The scuffle with the Y'matas assassin Eris had turned in his favor, and he had plenty of Turas of his own to spend. The Turas did weigh him down, as if he had eaten a very large and satisfying meal, paying for it with extra weight on himself. But he was excited to be able to buy some new supplies for his home with the Turas. Hopefully the trading post keeper had some new linen in stock before he closed up shop today.

Along the way home, he also pondered the meaning of the pendant that Eris wore. The image of the eagle's head and seven swords: what could it mean? Some sort of Y'matas code, perhaps? Possible, since he knew full well how warlike the Y'matas fancied themselves. Eagles, he knew, were a very rare species in Lemuria, and from what he knew on the subject, they were fierce and swift hunters. But why seven swords? Who would need that many when man only had two hands to wield them with?

"Yat ütas!" the Chamberlain roared at Eris in the ancient language. "That Knutas filth wounded you, and you let him go?!"

The council of the Y'matas looked down at the wounded Eris in the middle of the circular Grand Hall. The entire hall was made from molded light, an ethereal substance made solid and sturdy, forming the floor on which Eris stood, and the rows of benches above her, which held the black-robed and stern Y'matas overlords.

The walls of light were intricately carved with images of battle scenes extolling the ancient ruler Ishtock. Rubies and emeralds were inlaid into the walls in precisely-calculated patterns. To a casual observer, the scene would look marvelous beyond compare, but to Eris, this would be a scene of extreme danger for her at the hands of her superiors.

"You had every opportunity to eliminate the Knutas man, and you have failed!" barked the Chamberlain, whose robes were inlaid with gold to denote his rank. "You should have struck without hesitation and usurped every last wisp of energy within him!"

"I was there, Chamberlain; you need not remind me," Eris replied bitterly, looking up at the Chamberlain and the other Y'matas around her. "Those Knutas are hesitant to kill, but he seemed every bit prepared to do so."

"Which is every reason why you should have struck first, Eris!" the Chamberlain said sternly. "Those Knutas are starting to gain more knowledge, and we're losing ground on them faster than we're recovering it! We can't afford to let another Knutas escape from us with more knowledge; otherwise, all of Lemuria will be theirs to know! And what do you think that would leave for us?"

"Very little, Chamberlain."

"To say the least, *kút atú!*" the Chamberlain swore in his primal tongue. Eris knew the language well enough to understand certain vulgarities. "As soon as you are made whole again, you will mount a raiding party and attack the Knutas temple in the edge of the wilderness! Bring us every last document from their vaults and capture all their scribes and scholars! We need all their knowledge, and quickly!"

Eris bowed and left the rotunda without a word. Every one of the Y'matas glared at her as she left the room, her single remaining wing twitching.

Eagle's head. Seven swords. What could it possibly mean?

That question stayed on Eriad's mind as he came back to the Knutas city. The sky was completely dark, and the stars were beginning to appear as he crossed through the wooden gate and onto the paved stone path. The buildings in the Knutas city, clearly a stark contrast to the Y'matas' affinity for molded light and ornamentation, were mostly fashioned of square-cut blocks of stone with some wooden beams for extra support.

All around him, his Knutas brothers and sisters were tending to whatever tasks they had left in the day, which would either be setting alight the torches that lined the streets to light his path, or getting inebriated at the local tavern. As he passed the tavern, he could hear the sounds of raucous laughter and boisterous shouting. He wondered how much Turan they were spending in there for drinks that he could very easily brew for himself at home.

Further down the road, past an apothecary with a variety of smells coming from its open window, was Eriad's home. Eriad always loved the rich potpourri of aromas in the apothecary, as it always reminded him of home, and those smells came from herbs that he knew would replenish his mental Aitam energy. Just by breathing in the thick, satisfying aromas, he could feel his mental state sharpen.

As he entered his home, the rest of his family was gathered around an open fire pit in the center of the room, eating meat off the bones of a roasting animal. His father, Katál, a large but fit man with a bald head and sparkling blue eyes, got up from the smooth wooden floor and embraced Eriad tightly.

His mother, the slender and young Amyra, smiled pleasantly and got up to pour some wine from a stone pitcher on a shelf into her cup. Eriad's younger siblings, a sister and two brothers, were also glad to see him return and were laughing and playing in the empty space near the fire.

"Welcome home, my son!" Katál said loudly. "You bring Turan with you, yes?"

"Yes, Father," Eriad replied softly. He had hoped to be able to spend it for himself, but in the interest of his family, he decided to use it a different way. He held out his palm and transferred some of the Turan to his father, who smiled gladly.

"That's quite enough, Eriad; thank you," said Katál. "You wouldn't want me to burst from all that energy, would you?"

Eriad laughed. "No, I think not. You probably should get to spending it as soon as you can."

Amyra looked up at him from down on the floor, after having consumed a fair amount of meat from a bone. "Where did you get the Turan, Eriad?" she asked. Her blonde hair gleamed a bright orange in the light from the fire.

"I was attacked by an Y'matas today," Eriad admitted. Instantly, all of the laughing and chattering stopped, and a deathly silence hung over the room. Every eye was turned to Eriad with disbelief.

"You were attacked?" repeated Katál. "Great Deity, how did you escape?"

"It was no difficulty. I seemed to have more Aitam than she did, and I put it to good use. We did have something of a lively discussion, the kind that usually comes with claws and swords."

"You fought it?" asked Amyra. "You didn't kill it, did you?"

"I had every chance to, but I figured better to make an example of her. I rendered her flightless and bartered her life for the Turan. She had plenty of it stored up, and I don't think even she would miss it."

Katál looked incredulous, and then hugged Eriad again.

"Well done!" Katál said triumphantly. "You've shown compassion to the enemy and turned it to your advantage! Well done!"

"Thank you, Father," said Eriad. "If you please, I need to get my findings about the wellspring to the archives. They'll need it."

"But of course, my son," replied Katál.

Over on the far wall was Eriad's desk, where he kept record of everything that he was sent out to investigate on the Knutas' behalf. His home did not offer much in the way of privacy, so Eriad had to hunch over the desk to keep prying eyes away. It was a simple wooden desk, but it was crammed with parchment scrolls and various trinkets of his journeys.

An amulet was aglow on the side of the desk, giving him some light to work with. He took his journal and transposed every word onto a blank scroll of parchment, writing with a sharpened reed dipped in black ink. Everything he found out about the wellspring in the Úntir Forest was copied over, including its depth, composition, location, and various guesses about what it could mean for the community. He also included a suggestion that the rest of the scholarly guild investigate the spring with more resources.

To his right, fitted directly into the wall, was the opening of a glass tube. Eriad rolled up the parchment and shoved it into the tube, sending the knowledge on a direct route to the Knutas archives. There, it would be pored over and reviewed by his peers.

Once that task was done, he unfurled another sheet of parchment and thought again about Eris's pendant. He drew out a circle and from memory tried to copy the shapes on that gilded trinket: the eagle's head. The seven crossed swords. There was no other part of the ornamentation that he could remember; no script or other pictures. Eriad sat and stared at the picture, drawing off of his vast knowledge for any possible connection to anything of consequence.

Hours passed, and he had no clue, no revelation whatsoever, about the mysterious symbol. His family had long since retired to a corner of the room where they were all nestled in thick fur blankets to sleep. Eriad took a blanket and wrapped himself up in it at his desk to continue his work. There had to be something, and he was prepared to spend all night to crack its code.

He found himself drifting in and out of consciousness. His eyelids started to become heavy, and his sight was fogging up. The Aitam that he called upon to keep his mind focused was beginning to fail him, and he succumbed to sleep right there at his desk.

The stone cavern was massive. Sharp, uneven stalactites hung from the ceiling, and Eriad found it difficult to wander between the long stalagmites that littered the ground. Just ahead of him, the floor dropped away into a deep chasm. A golden glow illuminated the cave from the depths, casting shadows over the rough and rocky surfaces of the cave walls. Eriad would have loved to admire the scene, but he felt something in his heart was greatly amiss. Something was dangerously wrong, and only he was the one to stop it. He did not know why, but he did know that he needed with all certainty to jump into the chasm. Stepping over the stone spikes on the ground, he looked down into the abyss, and without thinking, he jumped.

The fall seemed to last forever. Eriad was weightless, drifting into the nothingness, all the while surrounded by the mysterious golden glow. Nothing could be seen, only felt. The glow then subsided, and while still in freefall, Eriad's sight returned, and he beheld a gigantic cavern opening below him and all around him. He could see seven large golden orbs embedded into stone columns, each one placed around a circular stone platform in the center.

As he continued his descent, the orbs started to change shape. Each one of them suddenly began stretching, as if they were not gold but an amorphous substance. Each one of them stretched out as if held by the invisible hands of a potter. Eriad watched as they shifted shape and stretched more and more, until they started to become flat and pointed. Then he came upon the realization; every one of those orbs had turned into giant swords—and there were seven of them.

From above, something was descending upon Eriad. He turned around and saw something flying fast down upon him, something with the body of a Y'matas, but the head of an eagle. Its piercing yellow eyes looked down at Eriad, and from its beak issued a raspy shriek of bloodlust.

Eriad awoke with a start. Sweat poured from his brow, and he could feel his heart thudding in his chest. The feeling of falling, and the imagery of orbs turning into giant swords, and an eagle-headed monster that bore down upon him, all of it stuck in his mind as he struggled to find rest again. He looked over at his desk and saw the scrawled picture of the pendant still on display. He rolled it up and tossed it to a side. It will not affect his mind any further. *Maybe it was just something out of a Y'matas legend,* he thought to himself. *Maybe some ancient story told around campfires, something simple and innocuous.* He would pay it no more mind, especially if it was going to wreak havoc on his dreams.

The sound of an explosion and an earth-shaking tremor pulled Eriad out of sleep, as well as the rest of his family. Katál was the first to look outside to find out what was going on, and in an instant, he warned everyone to stay down and out of sight. Curious, Eriad walked over to him, but Katál shoved him down with the others.

"Don't look!" he whispered harshly. "Don't get up!"

They all stayed down low to the floor as another explosion echoed outside, accompanied by another violent quake. Between the sounds of destruction, Eriad could hear screaming from people outside. Hastily, he pulled himself to his feet, but his father forced him to come back down, taking hold of his wrist with a tight grip.

"Don't you dare, boy!" warned his father.

"Father, I faced the Y'matas before, and I can face them again!" Eriad shot back. "And since I am still the chosen champion of the Knutas after all I've endured, it is my obligation to go forth and fight!"

Katál was silent, and released his grip on his son's wrist. Amyra looked confused and shocked. Everyone knew what he had to do. Eriad hefted his sword and pulled open the door, sealing it shut on his way out.

The streets that were once so familiar to him had been transformed into a scene from a nightmare. Massive fires engulfed several buildings, and others had been blasted into mounds of rubble. Refugees took to the streets, fleeing from the carnage. Others were flying out on their own wings, only to be cut down by arrows and bolts of energy from below. All the while, the ground beneath him shook with violence such that he had never known before, making it difficult to keep his footing.

Eriad knew this could only be the work of the Y'matas, and he sprinted against the tide of the screaming, wounded refugees to find the aggressors. His Knutas brothers and sisters ran and flew in terror from the unseen menaces behind them. Many of them were bruised and bloodied, and some flying Knutas refugees had crippled wings. The continuing quakes made several people fall, and they would be trampled to death.

From out of the screaming, panicked mob, Eriad could find the source of the chaos. A large contingent of Y'matas fighters, armed with bows, swords, and energy-casting carbines, laid siege to the city. Behind them was a towering monolith of stone, and embedded at its top was a large golden sphere, a stark reminder of that which Eriad had seen in his dream. It was emitting fierce bolts of energy, which blasted against the Knutas' structures and instantly obliterated them.

Eriad readied his sword and sliced his way through several Y'matas raiders, inching closer to the monolithic weapon. He fought with single-mindedness and Aitam-guided acuity, slicing away Y'matas wings and heads. It was not long before he reached the base of the monolith, which was kept on a stone platform on large wheels, pulled by a cabal of slaves.

"You!" called a voice from above him. Eriad looked up, and met with Eris, who tried to attack him once again. Her wings were restored, and she was clad in full armor. Her pendant swung wildly around her neck as she descended down upon him. But once again, Eriad was quicker on defense and struck with the hilt of his sword, knocking her down. Eris, this time, struck back with a swipe of her claws, dealing four deep cuts to Eriad's back and forcing him to the ground.

Eris held him down to the ground and held a clawed hand over him, poised to strike. Among the chaos of battle all around them, the two combatants froze and looked in each other's eyes. Eriad knew his time was about to come, and prepared himself for his assailant to make the plunge. But Eris, after reading her own opponent's face, withdrew and got up from on top of him.

"You could have killed me, and you know that," said Eriad. "Did I leave an impression?"

"You were the only one to have shown me mercy before," admitted Eris. "Come with me."

She extended a clawed hand to Eriad, who was unsure of what to do. Eris was getting impatient, and the golden orb in the tower above them was still spewing forth its rays of killer energy.

"Come on!" she commanded. Eriad had no other choice but to take her hand and get lifted by Eris into the sky. She flew to the north, away from the carnage that her Y'matas countrymen wreaked upon Eriad's community. From above, Eriad could only watch helplessly as the monolithic weapon continued to raze several homes and buildings to the ground. His Knutas friends and family were fleeing while those stragglers were instantly killed. He could feel all their energy going to waste as it slipped into nothingness.

Eris came to rest on a narrow ledge on the side of a mountain that overlooked the community. Eriad fell from her grasp onto the platform jutting from the mountain, and turned to Eris hatefully.

"Is this why you spared me? So I can be left to watch while my city burns?!" Eriad hollered at his captor. She stood silently, holding her pendant tightly.

"This is about more than just your city, Knutas," replied Eris matter-of-factly. "You may be the only one I can trust about this whole thing."

"What's going on?" demanded Eriad. "Why did you bring me here? And what was that thing your people used?"

"Something that we never should have taken," whispered Eris. "Something Unknowable. It is one of seven orbs that have kept all of Lemuria afloat."

"The Vakan?" asked Eriad incredulously. "You took one of the Vakan?"

"It wasn't my idea: it was Ashatoh and his cabal. They should've known better than to tamper with the foundation of Lemuria."

"And you're informing me, alone?" Eriad growled. "Why spare me?"

"It's not for you, and it's certainly not for your people!" Eris shot back. "It's for all of Lemuria. I just figured I'd clear my conscience before the entire country sinks."

"If that's one of the Vakan orbs," Eriad deduced. "And if it's being used in this way, then the Y'matas will have doomed the entire country! Why couldn't you have stopped them?!"

"There IS a way to stop them, Knutas," replied Eris, holding her pendant. "There's only one way to stop this whole thing."

"And what is that?"

"Simple. We marry."

"WHAT?!" Eriad stammered.

"Shut up and listen to me. It came to me in a dream from the High Father. This pendant is a sign of an ancient dynasty that ruled Lemuria before we split into Y'matas and Knutas. They had the entire country under a unified rule, and they kept the flow of energy and knowledge under control. But that dynasty has never been in power for a thousand years, and since then, we've had this entire war."

"And what does this have to do with your idea?"

"The High Father told me in a revelation that I am descended from the dynasty. We were routed and cast down while Ishtock and later Ashatoh usurped the throne. Ashatoh conscripted me into his army hoping that I would die soon in battle, and I wouldn't be able to challenge him! That's why we need to marry, and we need to marry fast!"

"To re-establish the dynasty?"

"Exactly!" Eris decreed. "It's the only way we'll ever get both sides to stop and listen!"

However, in the Knutas capitol city, a different idea altogether was being formed. Prime Minister Emak heard reports from the carnage that overtook the western edge of the Knutas territory. The harried, frenzied reports pouring to him from all sides told of the Y'matas harnessing a powerful new weapon against the people, one that resembled one of the great Vakan spheres from legend. In the modest, stone-carved hall, the aging Prime Minister heard from seven of his closest confidantes about the growing crisis.

An altar in the end of the hall filled the room with smoky incense that scattered with every movement of their hands. The violent surges that shook the ground could be felt here with no less intensity.

"Master, they are using the Vakan itself against us!" one of his advisors shouted desperately. "We need to evacuate now!"

"Impossible!" another advisor cut in. "This was all preordained from above! We must channel all our Utran and pray! Pray for our safety!"

"Pray if you must, advisor," replied Emak. "The threat has come right to our doorstep, and we must prepare to counter it on their terms."

"What do you say?" asked the advisor who had suggested evacuation.

"There are seven orbs of the Vakan, and they have already taken one of them. We shall simply borrow another one of them."

The advisors were all stunned. "You cannot be serious!" shouted the advisor who suggested praying.

"I have never been more serious," Emak returned. "Before the Y'matas breach the capitol area, we shall counter them with a Vakan of our own! Raise as many of our soldiers as possible to slow their progress until we have secured our defense!"

The advisors bowed silently and exited the room. The Prime Minister turned to his altar on the far end of the room and lost himself in prayer. These next few hours would be the most important in all the lives of the Knutas people. Hopefully the Divinity would see fit to side with them.

The cave Eriad found himself in was much larger and more menacing than the one from his dream. The cone-shaped stones that littered the ground made navigating difficult, so he and Eris both opted to fly instead. They soared through the monstrous cavern, past the stone spikes jutting from the floor and hanging from the ceiling, as if traveling between the teeth of a giant monster.

"How long have you known that the Y'matas were doing this?" asked Eriad as they flew.

"I found out not too long ago!" Eris replied, soaring around a stalactite. "They told me that they found the ultimate weapon against your people!"

"And you investigated?"

"I was there when they took it!" said Eris. "I knew that if they breached the sanctum, Lemuria would be destroyed!"

"But they did anyway!" Eriad noted.

"You can't stop fanatics, Knutas! You, of all people, should know that!"

Together they changed course and dove into a crevasse in the cave floor. A strange golden energy was emanating from the place below. Eriad found this scene all too familiar; he had seen this place before in his dream. He knew exactly what was down there.

The main cavern was no less forbidding and massive as it was in Eriad's dream. Where there were seven glowing orbs, there were now six. One of the stone towers had been neatly cleaved, leaving only a jutting stone ruin in its place. The tremors that shook all of Lemuria could be felt here with even more force. Pieces of stone fell from the ceiling, and several cracks were developing in the cave walls. From below, on the central platform surrounded by the six remaining orbs, Eriad could see figures of people facing one of the orbs.

"There!" Eriad yelled, pointing down. He and Eris altered course and sped down to the platform, landing right behind the people who had their gaze turned on one of the orbs.

"Stop!" Eriad shouted. He was not prepared for the people he came face to face with on the platform. All of them were Knutas, and they came armed with energy beams to pull away one of the orbs. Among them was Emak, Prime Minister of the Knutas, and some of his advisors and Exarchs.

These were the very people who made him tackle the Guardian, who marched him on the suicidal mission to the Y'matas stronghold, and they were finally about to pilfer for their own one of the great orbs upon which the very existence of Lemuria depended.

"What are you doing?!" Eriad yelled at his countrymen, with Eris at his side.

"This war has carried on long enough!" declared Emak. "This is the only way to silence the Y'matas permanently!"

"You're tampering with the force that keeps the entire continent alive!" Eris shot back. "Put it back and stop this madness right now!"

"As if you Y'matas had any better an idea?" Emak retorted. "It was you who dared to upset the order of the Vakan for your own ends! The wrath of the divinity shall fall upon you all!"

"If you take that orb, that same wrath will fall upon you and the rest of us!" Eriad implored. "Don't do this!"

"Eriad, you were our champion," Emak said with a hint of pain in his voice. "But I can see that you've thrown in your lot with a Y'matas, and now those scourges are prepared to strike at us all. This is the only way to safeguard our entire future."

"If you take that orb, there will be no future for any of us!"

His words were unheeded. Emak nodded to his advisors, and they began firing beams of concentrated energy directly at the base of one of the orbs. As the bright scarlet beams penetrated the stone pillar that held their prize, Emak held back Eriad and Eris from interfering.

"There's a way to stop all of this!" Eriad complained. "Eris here is descended from—"

But his words were cut off with a massively violent tremor. The instant the orb was dislodged, the cavern shook more than ever, knocking everyone to the ground. The cave walls split open, and rushes of hot air seeped through. The remaining orbs seethed and sizzled with energy, and they all began to crack like pottery. Eriad could only watch helplessly as those ethereal golden spheres shattered and their pieces fell down into the chasm below.

Eriad took Eris's hand, and the two took flight as the stone platform cracked and plummeted down into the depths, taking with it all the misguided Knutas with them.

All around the entire continent of Lemuria, the effects were devastating. Entire mountain ranges turned to avalanches of boulders that consumed the Y'matas kingdom. Their brilliant halls of molded light and precious stones were laid to waste by the rolling boulders, until not one single building was left standing. The Y'matas people fled, only to find no refuge from the disasters that overtook their entire territory. The ground was splitting apart, and thousands of people were swallowed by the depths.

The Knutas fell victim to the exact same disasters in their own territory as well. The earth split and became unstable. Entire buildings sank into the collapsing ground, taking every inhabitant with them. The scholarly halls, the temples to the Divinity, all were completely destroyed. Regardless of their philosophies or beliefs, none were spared. No matter how innocent those beings may have been, or what role they took in the war, no single member of either faction would be alive after this fateful day.

Eriad and Eris flew as far as their wings could allow, away from the entire floating continent, now not so much floating as it was crumbling and plummeting to the world below. Beneath them among the churning waters was an expanse of dry land, which they instantly darted towards. They both collapsed on the dry, smooth sand of the beach and tried to catch their breath. Eriad's heart was thudding madly, and he could barely move any of his limbs.

"Eriad, look!" said Eris, looking behind him. Eriad turned around, and beheld what remained of Lemuria in the sky. Large pieces were falling off of the floating continent and splashed into the ocean in massive explosions of sea foam. More and more chunks of the continent fell loose from the whole, until there was nothing left in the sky to fall. Every last remaining piece of what was once their home and their entire world was lost beneath the waves.

There was nothing left of Lemuria. All their people, all their struggles, all their energy, and all their knowledge was completely lost. The only remainder of what was once the thriving domain was themselves, and the hope that they would find a way to carry on.

Together, those two celestial beings found themselves in a completely foreign world, where energy was scarce and the people were harsh and unrefined. But they still clung to hope that they would fit in this world, and the memory of the lost continent of Lemuria would live through them.

The Mystic Theater rematerialized once again, and the audience felt that familiar sense of disorientation. Doctor Xoctarious stood to the side of the stage, looking pensive while everyone else gasped for air.

"A world completely removed from our own, in every sense," said the doctor. "No one knows to this day whether Lemuria had even existed at all, or where those two survivors could be found. All this while, they were squabbling amongst themselves over the control of knowledge, when they had in their own possession the greatest power that could ever be found, that from mere mortals to celestial beings are beholden to: hope.

"And now, we are reaching the end of our time together, and there is but one last tale to impart to you, my friends. One final sojourn into the morbid and macabre, and it will be over. Your fears will be purged, and your perspectives will be cleared. And at long last, all of your lingering questions will be answered.

"Be warned, though. I have saved this one for last for a very good reason. You have all shown great integrity by enduring all of my tales thus far, and together we have seen worlds beyond reckoning and fantastic scenarios of danger and triumph, but this is far unlike any of the others that came before it. I think you may find that this story may not have such a conclusive end as the others."

" To you, I impart the story of 'Waking Death.'"

WAKING DEATH

Story by Dominic R. Daniels
Written by Dominic R. Daniels

The nightmares started again, and as the portal of thick garish dark water opened, a swirling vortex of green and black pestilence filled the salty seas with millions an underwater phantoms, specters, and shadowy wraiths of all kind.

Sprites and water demons of ugliness, and some were human-like in the forms of wrinkled prune-skinned hags with festering bodies, and their hair was fine as silver, and they had sharp fangs perfect for the taste of mortal flesh; others were beautiful creatures: wicked and sensual women with four breasts and multiple arms, and eyes that burned blue with the majesty of the seraphims and holy light.

There was a young muscular human man, half-naked with only torn pants, and he was trapped in their clutches. His hair was dyed dark red and his eyes were black as night, and he wriggled as these seductive and hellish sirens tore into his flesh.

The ocean filled with waves of crimson attracting sharks of all species, as they sensed the magnetic fields in his body. He screamed in terror as these creatures ate him alive, and he yet he was still living even though he knew he was dead.

"No more! No more! No more!" screamed the young man in the water. He could speak but barely breathe as dirty sea water and bits of seaweed filled his lungs; he was drowning and choking as swirls of bubbles were all around him from violent twisting and churning of the underwater currents, but the sea creatures paid him no mind and continued to rip him apart, clawing his chest and face, and his eyes exploded from his sockets as they began to suck out his soul, which was the color of yellow mist, and his life energy was leaving his mouth, ears, every orifice in his body.

A hot wave red and blue light enclosed his eyes, and the heat was hotter than lava as it seared him and his fellow devourers, until the fire erupted with a blaze, turning the scene to pure darkness.

The young man screamed, awaking in his prison cell. Sweat ran down his cheeks, and his hands were over his eyes, his long hair hiding them.

He was disoriented, brought back from one hell and trapped in another, locked away in solitary confinement.

His name was Elias Burton, 27, a convicted felon and a handsome devil, and he had strange tattoos of Viking markings inked all over his chiseled chest and muscular tight arms.

He was guilty of more crimes and offenses than all the damned put together. He had just been sentenced to be locked up for life with the key thrown away. He was a serial killer with a bloodlust that was unquenchable, and he killed for the exquisite pleasure of killing. Death and hate were all that mattered to him.

If there was ever any love in his heart, he lost it a long time ago. In his earlier years, he was in the biker gangs and worked as a smuggler and drug dealer, the money and power gave him all that he desired: women, sex, violence, and best of all, the freedom to live in wanton excess.

But these fleeting trappings were child's play to his nature; he was not satisfied and began to experiment in unnatural fetishes and sexual role play. One evening in a seedy hotel room, he raped a young girl that he picked up at local pub, and he began to molest her; he ripped off her clothes and cut her body, slashing at her breasts with a knife and forcing his engorged member into her genitalia, stealing her innocence.

Lost between pain, screams, and moans she seemed to like it. He smiled with a sadistic frenzy, and after he had finished ravishing her, he sliced open her throat and let the blood trickle down his palms.

He wrapped his hands, embracing her and kissing her as she choked to death on her own blood and lay still. He experimented in necrophilia having sex with her corpse, and then he bathed her dead body in the bathtub with blood and foamy soap; then he cut open her uterus and removed her ovaries as a disgusting souvenir.

Jack the Ripper would have been proud, yet the time of Elias's era was unlike any other. It was the year 2014, and the city was modern London.

During this uncertain days, man had advanced in all aspects of the human consciousness, in science and medicine, in new forms of social cyber communications of various electronic technology, by this age man had long past discovered the solar system and nearly every frontier of the earth was found. Advancement in genetics and robotics exploded as well as new forms of entertainment in different mediums.

In this time, the lands of the earth were filled with change. It was all about change: the change of mindset, religion, spirituality, controversial, and moral thinking, and it was the most liberal times in all of the millions of years in human existence.

How far humanity would advance in the future remained to be seen, but for the anarchistic Elias, all he had left in the world was time: time in prison to think about what the wicked evils he committed.

When a reporter from the *Daily Gazette* came to visit him in Scotland Yard custody, the reporter asked him in an interview why he killed so many people, and his reply was sick and disturbing, "I did it for the hell of it! For fun!" he said.

The public was appalled and demanded from the courts that his case should be retried, and he should be put to death, but it was refused due to the abolishment of it years ago.

The judge viewed that punishment as too merciful, and suffering in confinement for life would be more fitting for him. Elias would have to live with the consequences of his actions and think about it until he grew old and died, but Elias, incarcerated or not, could not care less, and he kept to himself, busy during the days by reading classical works of fiction in his cell and playing his guitar.

He would also write poetry of sexually explicit and pornographic nature during the long cold evenings, and when he was given the chance to have a brush, he would paint surreal images of morbid design, including the portraits of women that he had killed, their images burned perfectly in the memories of his debauched mind.

This was a form of behavior therapy, and he was surprisingly happy with the arrangement; the solitude was more blissful than a burden. He hated being around people and, from a young age, he enjoyed being a loner. He had only a few friends in childhood but did surprisingly well in his studies at school, and his parents were very loving, but he returned no love to neither his mother or his father; he hated them, and the only thing that he loved at all more than anything was his white cat named Claudius, which he feed small mice and crickets.

Being locked up in solitary also meant that he had no visitors and had little to no contact with the other inmates at the prison. He was more happy being alone than all the other times in his life, and the serenity and quiet was nirvana to him.

The only thing he could not stand was the nightmares, and ever since his arrival at the prison, he could not sleep well and would stay awake for days on end to avoid the dreams, and after a week in his cell whenhe did not sleep at all, drugs of all kinds were given to him by the ward doctors. But he refused to take them as he screamed in convulsions of delusional paranoia. He was over the edge with psychosis setting in; soon, he would not be able to tell the difference between fantasy and reality.

It was 4:00 in the morning when he had awakened, the rest of the cells in the same hall he was located on were quiet. everyone else was fast asleep, dreaming of places, sounds, and colors, but Elias could not fall back asleep. He would spend the rest of the night in silence, and he spoke to himself in his thoughts, his inner voice, which was his only companion in this stoic place.

"Damn it; when will the dreams stop," he said to himself.

He lit a cigarette in his cell and had a few drags to calm his nerves. His eyes were red and bloodshot from lack of proper sleep, and his body was weak, and he felt lightheaded, and for the first moment since his arrival, he began to miss his parents.

He felt no sorrow but just felt sad. Shaking off these emotions, he put out his cigarette and tried to fall asleep once more, and he lay down on the mattress of his black iron framed bed and looked at the ceiling in the darkness. Tossing and turning, he drifted back into sleep and then the dreams came again.

Elias was being chased by red-winged grim reaper spirits of revulsion dressed in shrouds of torn turquoise silk who were after him, and they had no faces.

Elias's body was weightless as he flew through dark purple and gray stormy skies, and there was thunder and pink lightning crashing through the ether. Just over the valley of the bottomless canyon, his soul felt confused and lost as he floated into space, and these shadow spirits of death hung below him like vultures ready to seek and swallow his soul and tear it to pieces.

He floated above them, but they could not see him, and he flew to where he saw his first female victim. She was dressed in a navy blue laced dress, and he saw her leaving with a blonde-haired gentleman dressed in a red-frocked shirt and white angelic wings.

"He is part of the archives of my life," she said, then she flew away sad. Elias began to feel horrible about what he did to her and flew towards a deep stone well which rose high into the clouds that was taller than the tower of Babel, and it was filled with white light, the light sucked him into it, drawing him closer and closer to his doom as he fell into the stone well, falling forever into the black coldness of nowhere, pulled down by demonic invisible hands as they strangled him, killing him for his crimes against man and God.

Elias awoke from his deep slumber screaming into the night, awaking the prisoners near his cell.

"Shut up, you little shit! We are trying to sleep!" they yelled.

He woke up angry and threw one of his books against the door of his cell, cursing them.

"Screw you! I hope you all die!" he raved.

The guard walked down the hall and tapped on Elias's cell with his Paton "Burton, pipe down in there if you know what is good for you," shouted the guard.

"Go to hell!" Elias bellowed.

"All right, you little shit heel; that's it!" shouted the guard, enraged.

He opened the cage and charged at Elias, beating him black and blue, smashing his organs and bruising his body with welts, until blood flowed from Elias's nose, his skull cracked from the pain as the guard continued to pummel him with a beating, cracking his femurs and breaking his hands.

"AAAHHA! Stop please stop! You'll kill me!" pleaded Elias.

"I think not! You didn't stop when you raped and murdered all those women you destroyed!" said the guard. "You deserve worse; now shut your mouth, and don't say another word or I'll come back, and you won't walk for a year," threatened the guard.

"You bastard!" raged Elias.

The guard whacked Elias across the head, the other prisoners applauded and laughed at Elias's cruel punishment, but the night watchman left the cell and slammed the door shut, locking it back into place.

Elias was out cold again and the dreams came back to haunt him, and he found himself in monolith fortress; on the edge of a barren cliffs, the castle was gigantic at five hundred and fifty feet in height and six hundred feet in width.

He was taken by group of dead souls dressed in suits, their faces were of rotting meat with worms and maggots crawling out from the sockets of their eyes and ears, and these shadowy figures were two dead women and men who brought him into the castle to a strange waiting room, and they were fallen angels in human form.

Elias looked at the door behind him as he saw pure black demonic eyes on the door, and he went forth and found himself in the middle of this waiting area.

They told him, "It is time."

He responded, "It's not my time."

"It is time," they insisted. Elias was led through a tall iron door with white light, and he entered into a maze of amethyst and black crystals that was filled with dim light, and he was forced to crawl on his back, his body broken by the angels' grip.

He saw a stained glass window of dark symbols, and finally he took the right passage on a guess, and he escaped from the angels through a trap door shaft, and he fell in the darkness and landed on a ice cold floor in a room trapped by a thick glass wall.

Inside the room, he was trapped in a cube-like cell and saw two demons. One was a pretty girl with green hair who was wearing a black dress, and there was a man who had horns growing out of his cheeks and a hunch-back.

Elias desperately wanted to get out of this room and with intense human strength he was able to pick up a snack vending machine that was in the cell with him, and he used it to smash the window, and the machine broke, and the window barley had a crack.

Finally, after pounding it through, he was able to escape this place. Back in the maze he found himself having a black dagger float to him in mid air, which he grasped in his hand and used it to control the demons to leave him.

In this lucid dream, he created a ring of fire around him which turned into water and then back into fire, to protect him from his enemies.

Suddenly, out of the darkness, was a succubus who approached him, and she resembled another one of his female victims as he lusted after her and had sex with her. A graphic depiction of a male phallus was on her neck and he kissed it then it disappeared and saw that this evil enchantress was head less, and he awoke horrified and disgusted.

But this time he did not wake up in his prison cell but in a large grand hotel conference room in Tokyo, Japan. He found himself dressed and cleaned up in a black tuxedo, attending a large strange dinner party with a room full of strangers; the room was laid out with pink walls, pink flowers on tables, pink dining room tables; it was a reception room, and it was a chemical wedding reception of life and death.

In the center of the room, there are three large rectangular box cakes with pink decorated frosting, white rose flowers in the shapes of human faces on the cakes, and it was black forest chocolate, strawberry, and toffee.

After the dessert cake was finished being served, the party ended, and Elias tried to find a bed to sleep in this open lay away hotel, meaning all the rooms were open to everyone. He found a bed with in all large room with other pink bed covers. He undressed until he was in his boxers and lay down in one of the beds with the pink cover over him.

There was a middle-aged Japanese woman, who was naked beside him. "You're in my bed, " she said.

He responded, "I don't even know why I am here."

The woman did not respond, so he left the bed to find another bed in the same room to sleep in, and this bed was a small bed with gold silk bedding and blankets. He fell asleep in the dream, and he dreamed as hours passed.

He later awake to find everyone screaming, and he was covered in blood; the bedding was drenched in it, with piles of dead female and male corpses all around him. He screamed in terror.

Frighten and disorientated, he did not know what is going on or why this was happening to him. The dream changed with the scenery as he found himself in and interrogation office talking to Scotland Yard in the police station where he was being held as they asked him questions about the crimes he committed, but he denied them.

"Why am I here? I did not kill anyone!" he protested.

"Yes, you did kill someone! You killed plenty; you're a murderer, little Elias. A murderer!" they taunted him with chastisement.

He then woke up in his cell bed with more blood. His bones broken and body bleeding from the cuts he received from the guard's beating, and his muscles were pulverized like tenderized beef from a butcher's mallet.

He began to cry as he for felt for the first time in his life regret.

"I'm sorry! I'm sorry! I'm sorry!" he sobbed. "Let me out of here; Let me out!" he whispered like a little child, lost without his mommy and daddy to save him. But he was trapped in this hell of cell of his own design. He would never be free, and now finally the reality of his situation hit him like a bullet to the head.

He began to think of all the lives he had ruined: friends, families, the women who had children that he killed, and he began to regret everything. He threw away their lives and played with them as if they were dolls to be tossed in the trash, and now he would pay the price.

"When I killed them all, I killed all my potential," he said to himself. "Is this my life? Oh, my God." he said, realizing the hard truth.

Suddenly, a ghastly specter of a woman appeared to him out of nowhere in the cell with him, as he sat up in his blood-stained bed.

This was his wife, whom he had killed a year before and buried her body for her infidelity with another lover, and he cared her, but he was always unfaithful.

"Sarah! Get the fuck out here!" he said.

"I will not, Elias; how does it feel? How does it feel to see us, all of us that you killed? You are a demon!" said the specter.

"This is not happening; you're not here; I am just crazy," he said to himself.

"But I am here, my love, to haunt you for all time; you wanted me forever in life, now you shall have me forever in death," she said cruelly.

"I loved you, and you ruined us. I did what I was supposed to do; what would you have had me do? You think I would just let you walk away? I wanted justice," he defended himself.

"You wanted revenge. That is not justice. You're no different than any of these other killers in this place," said the ghost of his lover.

"I did what I had to," he said.

"No, you kill because it makes you feel good. You are a selfish, cold, and arrogant man, Elias. If you had ever truly loved anyone, you would never have turned out the way you did in life," said Sarah.

"I did love you," said Elias.

"The only person you have ever loved is yourself. You use people like playthings, and you would not care even if your own child died," she said.

"Go away; just go! Go!" said Elias.

"Very well, my love, but I will be seeing you soon; we all will," said the spirit as it left.

He passed back out, and his punishment continued.

In a shield of red mist, he saw before him visions of humanity's past evil, mirroring his own deterioration. The centuries passed like wisps of clouds, time speeding as if through a beam of light, and he saw all the events of history pass before him, including the most recent birth pains of human kind which included images of the Gulf War, the fall of Iraq, the building of nuclear warfare, the corruption of world leaders, the world trade center being destroyed to the recent war in Afghanistan, the battle in Libya within the Middle East, economic collapse of the world, and the other disasters mankind wrought to reflect how the world's evil has brought itself its own destruction.

He woke up finding himself trapped in a mental hospital, strapped up in a padded room. He was rigged up in a white straightjacket in steel chains, and white light was burning the sensitivity of his eyes. He lay on the floor and vomited blood on the floor; the morphine had kicked into his system, but it was not agreeing with him. He had been here all this time: the prison, the nightmares, the police all were illusions… or were they? Elias did not know if it was day or night, summer or winter. He was locked up here in this strange pastel-colored room to prevent hurting himself or others.

"It was just a dream," he laughed at himself. "Just a stupid dream," he laughed manically with foolishness. He sighed in relief. "At least now I can get some peace." He said to himself.

He heard a knock on the door with the door window slit opened, and, getting up from the ground, he tried to gain his balance; it was the doctor who opened the cell door and came in the room to give him his medicine. He was a frail old man who had a strange resemblance of someone familiar to Elias; he had once seen him in a dream, a year ago. He was dressed in a white lab coat and had a stethoscope around his neck, the name printed on his plastic name tag that was clipped to his chest pocket: Dr. Philip Grafton. "Now then, Mr. Burton. How are you feeling to-night?" asked Dr. Grafton.

"Like I've been to Hell and back, Doc," said Elias.

"Oh, I am so sorry to hear that. why don't I give you something, and it will help you sleep," said the doctor as he removed a syringe with fluid in it.

"No, please! No more drugs! I can't take another nightmare!" screamed Elias.

"Oh, my boy, why so irritable? Don't you want to have a nice sleep?" asked Dr. Grafton, smiling in a sinister sense. He approached Elias slowly, readying a syringe with a clear liquid inside. Elias recoiled in fright. the doctor

"Get that away from me!" Elias screamed. But paid the doctor no heed, and took Elias's left shoulder. Elias struggled viciously against the doctor's grip and against the thick straight-jacket holding his arms together. The doctor knelt down and readied his syringe at Elias's neck, trying to aim for his vein. Elias certainly did not make it easy with his constant struggling.

"Elias, please," the doctor protested. "This is for your own good."

"NO!" Elias shrieked. The doctor jerked his shoulder in place and stuck the syringe into his neck in one swift motion, pumping the chemical directly into his jugular vein. He withdrew the needle and placed a gauze patch on his neck. Elias froze momentarily, his breathing and pleading starting to slow down.

"Better now?" asked the doctor. Elias said nothing.

"I've been told of your crimes, Elias," he commented.. "That is for someone more experienced than myself to deal with. My role is simple."

Elias was still trembling and his breath was still coming out in short gasps. "Who are you?" he stuttered as the doctor got up from his side.

"Just a doctor assigned to the prison ward is all," came the reply. But Elias was not having it.

"I've seen you somewhere before!" Elias insisted. "I saw you in a dream!"

"It's possible; we dream of people we may have seen before," said the doctor.

"No, it's not that!" Elias protested. "You weren't a doctor! You were some...THING! Some kind of monster!"

"Of all the people to accuse someone of being a monster..." the doctor trailed off, starting to head for the door.

"It's you!" Elias screamed. "You were in my dream!"

The doctor stood still with his back to Elias. He turned his head around slightly.

"How did I look in your dream?" he asked. "Something like this?"

His eyes turned pure golden, his body transformed to cloaked winged figure with a scythe in his hands, and a youthful face. He was no human.

"What the hell are you?" said Elias in mystified fear.

"I am your worst nightmare," said the angel before him.

This was Death itself in corporeal form. The room vanished to a rotted run down slum of itself, revealing that Elias was hiding out in this old abandoned place the whole time, and the straight-jacket was no longer on him, and he was dressed in his bloody clothes, his bones and body were once again broken, as he wailed in sheer torment.

"Somebody, please wake me up! No! Not again! Not again! Help! AAAHHHHHHH!!" he screamed.

Death smiled in his face as restless spirits of the souls slain by this evil human being in corrupted form began to swarm. Elias's life was filled with death now; death itself came to claim him, and he was the prey.

The angel's face changed again to reveal to the audience a familiar face under the dark robe, the face of an old man with a short white beard. Beneath the robe, he was wearing an eccentrically-styled jacket, which was all too familiar to the audience.

"I am known by many names, but for now I'd prefer to be called Doctor Xoctarious.

"The world is a place of many dreams, good and evil, beautiful or deadly, like heaven or like hell, but you took away these people's hopes and dreams, so now I've come to take yours," said Azrael, placing judgment on the young man, his soul condemned for all eternity.

"No, it's not my time! Please give me another chance! Just one more chance! Have mercy on me!" Elias screamed in cold horror.

"No mercy, my child; judgment shall be your only reprieve. Take him; his soul is yours!" he commanded the spirits of Elias's victims who were with him, among them was his despondent wife's Sarah.

Azrael stepped aside as the lost souls smothered Elias trapping him alive in this boxed configuration of hell, and the room enveloped with darkness as the spirits of this criminal victims dispatched and destroyed Elias's soul, dragging him off to hell forever more.

The visions ceased and the theater returned to its previous form of spinning cogs and pillars with the good doctor leaving a warning to end this tale.

"Death wears many masks and comes in many forms, so be careful how you choose to live, because one day I will come for you knocking on your door," warned Xoctarius.

The audience asked him, "These visions you have shown us. Are they the future? Or are many of many futures that may become reality?"

The old Doctor Xoctarius transformed his appearance to a young man, as two large black wings emerged from his back out of his long tail-coat, and his body and visage disappeared along with the room, and the audience was simply souls of all in the theater in the house of damned, but a door of white light was opened by the doctor to them.

"Are we dead?" one of the members in the audience asked.

"Yes, you're dead. You are all in the station where all souls go before they depart this mortal realm. I promised you would have no harm come to you in this theater, because you are all already dead!" said Xoctarius.

"What is the door of light? Are we going to heaven or hell?" asked George in his seat calling out.

"No, I have been assigned by the Father in Heaven who made you and made me, to give you a second chance. That I leave all up to you."

Burn marks rolled across the movie screen of life's review, as old news footage from the last 100 years of the world's history played forward both the evil and good of mankind. The accomplishments of mankind and the destruction that the world has brought upon itself and the future yet to come to pass was not revealed.

To be continued....

THE NEW TALES OF DOCTOR XOCTARIUS

Written
By
Dominic R. Daniels
&
Doug K. Owen

Dedicated to
Phil & Mary Daniels
Dan Jardanna
Michael Krish Nimsital
Wade "Bob" Harris

PROLOGUE

A spear stood illuminated in a tall glass case. The long wooden pole, worn by thousands of years of use, looked rough and splintery. It ended with an iron triangular spearhead, which had some slight chipping near its tip. The spear stood propped up on a piece of glass inside the case, where it could be seen from all angles.

Gabriel Crowell sat on a wooden bench across from the spear. The rest of the museum around him was dark, aside from some of the other artifacts in cases. Gabriel scratched at the short stubble on his chin and combed his fingers through his dark blond hair. At 35, he wondered why he was still working in the museum, and why his career as an adventure novelist still had yet to blossom. Gabriel dug into the pocket of his long brown coat and drew out his cell phone, reading the text on the bright screen: "Meet me near the Spear of Longinus to discuss your future."

The artifact before him was the only spear in the museum, though Gabriel did not bother to read the plaque at the bottom of the case. All around him in similarly-lit display cases and on the walls, several dim yellow lights shone around different artifacts from times long past.

An old grimoire stood on a polished wooden pedestal under a glass case. On a far wall, several leather pouches were mounted above information plaques under a thick, clear sheet of protective glass. The exhibit on "Mystical Artifacts and Ancient Powers" was not exactly receiving the big draw that the museum was expecting, but it had only just opened, so there was time for word to spread. The summer crowds would be sure to start coming in the next few weeks, and the air conditioners were freshly fixed, so there would be respite from the blistering southern California heat.

Gabriel was starting to feel uneasy. The world-renowned Los Angeles Museum of Natural History had been closed for the past day, and his shift at the gift shop's cashier desk had ended an hour ago. The security guard, a balding and portly fellow named David, had already walked by on his patrol. He saw Gabriel sitting alone in the exhibit hall and nodded at him. Gabriel had known David for several years, and they were on good terms.

Gabriel sighed, knowing that David trusted him enough to leave him alone, even at this hour. Gabriel sat and stared at the spear, and his gaze darted around the other items in the museum. He looked to his right, along the rest of the empty bench, where there were some more ancient tools on display, and then back to the spear. The lights on each of the different artifacts was just enough to see the rest of the museum, but the shadows were still deep enough that it made Gabriel feel nervous.

He looked around again, to his left and then to his right where the other items were on display, and to his surprise there was a figure of a man sitting next to him on the bench. Gabriel recoiled back in shock; he had not heard anyone approach him.

"You're early, Gabriel," said the mysterious person sitting next to him. From the dim lights all around the hall, Gabriel could faintly discern that the man was quite old, with a slightly wrinkled face and a short white beard. The man smiled jovially, quite the contrast to Gabriel's sudden fright. He wore an impeccable business suit and an ascot around his neck.

"You scared the hell out of me!" Gabriel complained. "How did you get in here?"

"My apologies," the man replied simply. "Sometimes I have a way of moving undetected."

"I can see that," said Gabriel, extending out his hand. "I'm Gabriel."

"I know who you are, Mr. Crowell," said the man. "I'm sure you don't remember me; we met in Prague a year ago. My name is Philip Grafton. I am the curator of a new museum."

"Oh yeah, I remember. It was an exhibition we met at, and we wrote letters to each other on your work and my own," said Gabriel.

"Indeed, and as I said before, I am in charge of a new museum here in the city," said Grafton.

"A new one?" asked Gabriel curiously. "Did it just open?"

"Let's just say it's for a limited engagement, as it were," replied Philip. "You fancy yourself a true novelist, yes?"

"Of sorts," muttered Gabriel. "Just something I dabble in, really, just to kill some time. I thought maybe I could get published and make some money, but nobody's taking my work."

"Is that so?" asked Philip.

"I'm just here at this place to pay the bills. They always tell me the same things: 'don't give up,' 'keep going,' 'there's light at the end of the tunnel,' and all that same old self-help nonsense. If I'm going to get a break, better for it to be sooner than later; you know what I mean?"

"I know what you mean, Gabriel," said Philip calmly. "Far be it from me to steer you away from that course, but I have seen some great potential in you."

"How so?" asked Gabriel, raising an eyebrow. The other man smiled and shrugged lightly.

"You've made yourself a lot more apparent than you think, Gabriel," he explained. "I've seen your website and your samples there. I was quite fascinated."

"Well, thanks," Gabriel muttered. "It's good to know that someone thinks so. That is very kind of you,"

"The main reason I am here, Gabriel, is to extend to you an invitation to my exhibition."

"What kind of museum are you running?" asked Gabriel. "Just in case my boss asks me about the competition."

"There will not be any competition, and I would not ask you to do anything that would jeopardize your position. All I ask is for your attendance at my exhibit on September the first, only a few weeks from now."

"Well, my schedule's clear," Gabriel commented. "Where at?"

"I have a small area set up on the outskirts of Downtown Los Angeles, over on Olympic Blvd. There's a small exhibition hall and a theatre there."

"A theatre?" Gabriel wondered. "What kind of stuff are you showing there?"

"It will be unlike anything you have ever experienced in your life, I assure you," said Philip. His calm demeanour never swayed. "Come to the event, and you will never lack for inspiration. I promise,"

"I could always use some inspiration these days," Gabriel replied. "Alright, I'll go. Thank you."

The man nodded, and drew a card from a pocket in his black coat. He handed it to Gabriel with a slightly exaggerated wave of his hand. Gabriel took it and read the finely detailed lettering on the card:

"THE MYSTIC THEATER OF DOCTOR XOCTARIUS— SIGHTS BEYOND WONDER, WORLDS BEYOND IMAGINATION. Now showing for a very limited engagement, September First through Fifth, 2017. Los Angeles, California. Facebook: Mystic Theater. Twitter: @Xoctarius."

When Gabriel looked up from reading the card, the man was gone. Once again, he was completely alone in the museum. He pocketed the card and wondered who that man was, and why he took such an interest in him.

A few weeks later, Gabriel went to the exhibition.

The Metro bus dropped Gabriel off at the corner of Olympic, near a run-down storefront in the early evening hours. A rusted metal gate covered the front door, and there was a fine layer of dust and grime over the plaster walls. The store sign, which was spelled in Korean with bold blue lettering, had a flickering light glowing beneath its chipped plastic shell.

Other stores nearby looked very similar in appearance, and some were worn down with more dust, and some had colourful scrawls of graffiti on their walls, written with stylized letters that Gabriel would not take the time to decipher. A breeze blew by and kicked up some old plastic bags off the sidewalk, making them flutter and fly in the air. All the while, he wondered to himself why Philip would choose such a derelict neighbourhood as this for his museum. This looked like the kind of place where he would expect to get robbed at gunpoint with less than a moment's notice.

As he walked down the sidewalk, thankfully that never happened. Everyone he passed by had their own things to tend to, barely paying Gabriel any notice. An old man was waiting at a bus stop on another corner. A young teenage girl was walking by with both eyes on her smartphone. A middle-aged mother was pushing her young child in a stroller. An older child rolled by on a skateboard, who Gabriel avoided with a step to his side. The skater nodded in thanks to him and skated on down the sidewalk.

Just as Gabriel was about to contact Philip to ask for more specific directions, he crossed the street and found something that stood out very much from the ordinary from the desolate urban structures. Whatever that massive, looming building was, it captivated Gabriel's attention and lured him in. Where the other buildings around it were small, squat buildings of plaster and brick with grimy front walls, this mammoth structure looked much older, and yet at the same time far more advanced.

The entire façade of the building was corrugated and rough metal, lined with thousands of rivets. The sun was setting, casting the giant building in an ominous shadow. On the higher floors of the metal structure, there were spinning gears and whirring pistons, as if the entire building was one giant machine for some unexplained purpose.

Three video screens were erected near the main entrance, hovering over the sidewalk. On those giant LED screens was a computer-generated image of a man wearing two wooden boards on his front and back, which reminded Gabriel of a town-crier type from Victorian times. The boards that the character wore were emblazoned with words in an old-fashioned lettering style, advertising "The Mystic Theater of Doctor Xoctarius: Magic! Monstrosities! Mystery!" Other images flashed on the screens: circus sideshow freaks and leering, shadow-like monsters.

Gabriel stood in wonder at the bizarre mechanical building. How long was it here? How did Gabriel never know about this place until now? All these questions and more swirled in his mind as he approached the main entrance, mesmerized by the grandeur of the structure and the advertisements playing on the screens. He was not alone in this sense of awe; others too were drawn from their usual routines to investigate the strange place that was suddenly in plain view.

Past the riveted steel threshold, Gabriel stepped with the crowds into a large exhibition hall. Gabriel noticed that nobody charged him for admission or even checked for his name. Was the whole event free of charge? Or would he have to go back and pay a quick fee if he missed something?

From among the crowds, he did not see anyone in uniform or with nametags, so if there were any staff around, they were not mentioning anything about a cover charge. That idea gnawed at Gabriel and almost prevented him from enjoying himself in the exhibition space.

What awaited him in the grand hall was a very different experience than the exterior. The walls were pure white and carved with flowing, curvy patterns and illuminated with bright, multicoloured spotlights. The floor was covered with deep and very soft crimson carpeting for which Gabriel was thankful; the long walk to this place was taking a toll on his feet. Around him were displays that were every bit different than those esoteric artifacts on display at his museum. People were crowding around to see the bizarre items kept in glass cases.

Gabriel walked by one of the tall glass cases, which contained a large bone from an ancient skeleton. A brass plaque proclaimed that this bone was from a dragon, and it dated to at least 3000 BC.

Gabriel paused in disbelief that this exhibit took dragons seriously enough to show something to prove their existence.

Nearby, something was emitting a ghostly blue glow. Gabriel walked over to find in another case the contents of a cloud of blue energy, like the ghost of a firefly. It flew in random patterns all through its glass prison, radiating a bright azure glow. Its plaque proclaimed that this was a real will-'o-the-wisp, captured in Northern Ireland in 2012.

Another exhibit in the center of the room, standing on a pedestal above the heads of the attendees, was a complete skeleton of a very large human being, at least fifteen feet from the top of its yellow, cone-like, Cro-Magnon skull to its toes. The plaque beneath it claimed it was the skeleton of a "Nephilim," or a giant, as it explained.

While everyone else was completely awestruck at these fascinating displays, Gabriel inwardly mused about how Philip could have amassed such objects, and what kind of tricks was he pulling. Gabriel had always considered himself a rational person, firmly believing in sense and reason and scientifically-proven evidence. To him, giants and dragons simply did not exist, but in this museum, he was suddenly faced with tangible proof right in front of his eyes that those creatures did in fact exist at least at one point in time, in a forgotten history, perhaps.

The nearby will-'o-the-wisp shone its unearthly glow from the corner of his eye as if in approval of this revelation. All around him, the people were enjoying the displays greatly. Some teenagers were taking selfies with their smartphones with the skeleton looking down upon them, laughing all the while. A couple on a romantic date was looking at a carved-out cave painting from ancient times, pointing at the human figures painted in black that were carrying spears against a large monster painted in red.

"I used to read about stuff like this as a kid," Gabriel overheard someone saying among the crowd. "I never thought they were real." Gabriel's inner confusion reflected this sentiment. There had to be some trickery to everything in this entire room. Part of him wanted to smash open the glass case containing the will-'o-the-wisp and expose the tiny projector that created the hologram, wherever it was. But upon taking a closer look inside the case itself, he could see that the top and bottom were completely flat and solid. There were no cameras or projectors anywhere inside it.

From the far end of the room, the crowd heard the low, echoing sound of a bell chiming over the room. A silence fell over the crowd, and a voice issued forth from the top of the room.

"Ladies and gentlemen," said the booming, echoing voice. "Welcome, one and all, to the Mystic Theater of Doctor Xoctarius! Please make your way to the main theatre in an orderly fashion. The show is about to begin!"

Gabriel took his place among the crowd, slowly inching his way through a pair of massive doors that opened at the far end of the exhibit hall. The crowd was densely packed and moving through, but past those doors, it opened up into a large amphitheatre. Rows of cushioned chairs were arranged in large arcs around a stage, rising up one row after another.

From among the crowd pouring into the theatre, Gabriel found a familiar face standing over one of the seats in the fifth row from the front. Philip Grafton was in attendance, and the suit he was wearing took Gabriel by surprise. His long black velvet coat was embroidered with golden designs, and his hair was slicked back and tied in a tight ponytail. His beard was neatly trimmed in a goatee.

He smiled brightly as he recognized Gabriel among the crowd. "Mr. Crowell!" he exclaimed happily. "Thank you for accepting my invitation!"

"You're Doctor Xoctarius?" asked Gabriel.

"It's a stage presence, my friend," replied the doctor. "Please take a seat; the show is about to start."

Gabriel walked up three steps and took a seat in the middle of the row. He sighed with relief as he sank into the soft, plush cushioning of the chair. He felt as if he was in a grand old movie theatre, albeit much larger and on a more personal scale.

When the audience was ready, Doctor Xoctarious took the stage to some polite applause from the crowd. He bowed slightly, and stood in the center of the stage. A bright white spotlight shone over him.

"Welcome, my friends, to my Mystic Theater," said the doctor in a magnified voice. "Your curiosities will soon be satisfied, and your aspirations for adventure will soon be quenched. Tonight, we shall venture together into worlds throughout history and imagination, delving deep into the morbid and macabre, and celebrating a safe return, as well. What will follow is a series of visions of my own design that I wish to impart to you all, tales of the deepest despair and the highest triumphs. Behold!" he shouted, waving his right hand above his head.

From out of his gloved hand, a white dove fluttered around the stage and disappeared in a cloud of smoke. Some audience members laughed with delight, but Gabriel could see that it was an illusion; the small white lights lining the stage pulsed in sync with the bird, and its movements were not matched that well to Xoctarius himself. It was a trick, and he could tell.

Xoctarius released another bird from his left hand, and it ascended over the stage, then suddenly it grew larger and burst into flames. From below, Gabriel could feel its intense heat, and the fiery bird evaporated into nothingness.

Xoctarius then turned his gaze to one person in the audience: a very stout man with combed-back brown hair and a thick moustache. Xoctarius pointed at the man and motioned for him to stand up.

"Stand up, please," said the doctor. He did so reluctantly, and his girlfriend next to him squealed with surprise. The spotlight shone over the man as he stood nervously. Beads of sweat poured down his forehead, staining his white collared shirt.

"Hmm, this man is quite a bear, isn't he?" remarked the doctor with a chuckle. The man stifled a smile, and his girlfriend laughed. Then, with a wave of his gloved hand, Xoctarius again pointed to him, and in the man's place was a large brown bear, standing right where he once was less than a split-second ago. From where he sat, Gabriel should have had a clear view of a swap between the man and the actor in the bear costume, but even he missed that. As the bear moved around on all fours, the girlfriend started to panic.

"Bob, is that you?" asked the girl. The bear sniffed at her and licked her face like a dog. She laughed nervously while the audience laughed uproariously.

Xoctarius pointed again, and the bear disappeared in a puff of smoke. Then he pointed one more time, making a motion with his finger and thumb like a gun, and the fat man reappeared from the cloud of smoke. The audience was relieved, and cheered wildly when Bob came back.

"Thank you," said the doctor as the cheering died down. "That is but a small taste of the power I wield in my Theater. Perhaps this will silence any doubts you may have on what may transpire here. I have performed for many, many years, and lately it has been getting difficult to reach an audience. But now that I see we are all ready to accept what happens here, we may begin proper. Before anything else, may I please ask that we all take a moment to silence our cell phones or any other device that may present an interruption to our journey. Whatever may happen here tonight, be assured that no harm will ever come to any of you. My visions may be startling, some even horrifying. Take heart in the fact that at no time will you ever find yourselves in mortal peril.

"And now, I present to you all this question: what is the essence of life itself? What does it mean to live or to die? To be born, or to be reborn? What truths lie in the distant past, and what mysteries lay in wait in an elastic, unshaped future? Mystery is all around us, and in a world as fast-paced as your own, you have forgotten this simple truth. In the midst of coming and going, doing and undoing, there is still the one irrevocable truth that guides all your thoughts, words, actions, and destinies: that the faceless, shapeless future has yet to reveal itself to you. Behold, our first tale for this evening... which I call

'Das Ubermensch.'"

DAS UBERMENSCH

Story
By
Dominic R. Daniels & Doug K. Owen
Written by
Dominic R. Daniels & Doug K. Owen

Los Angeles, California. Downtown, the far future, in autumn. In the shadows of the colossal skyscrapers, two friends sat at an old-time historic 1940's diner on the corner of 1st and Hill Street, which was named The Dip. It was the brick-layered home of L.A.'s famous pastrami and *au jus* roast beef subs. One customer, a clean-shaven, Hawaiian and Filipino man in his mid-twenties, looked at his watch for the fifth time. Their order was very late.

"What's taking so long?" he asked, exasperated. The other person with him, slightly younger and bulkier, slouched lazily in his seat.

"Maybe they're just backed up. Just get over it, Miguel."

The droll of waiting was rudely interrupted as a man in a black ski mask and dark clothes barged into the diner, brandishing a silvery handgun. He waved it around in every direction frantically, yelling until his voice became hoarse.

" Get the fuck down, now!" the gunman roared. Miguel, his friend and the other diners instinctively dropped beneath their tables and covered their heads. Frightened shrieks were instantly silenced. A sexy raven haired waitress with plump breasts in Daisy Duke shorts and ripped denim behind the chrome-plated counter dropped to the ground for cover.

The gunman fired a single round up into the ceiling, the gunshot delivering a deafening and sharp explosion of sound that shook every diner and employee to the core. The round from the gun left a gaping and smoldering hole in the plaster ceiling above. Powdery residue drifted down from the bullet hole.

Then he waved the gun around again at the people in the diner, and stormed to the cashier's desk, pointing the gun at the waitress who lay huddled behind the desk for safety.

"All the money, now, or I kill you!" he demanded tersely. The waitress was wide-eyed, shaking uncontrollably in terror. She very slowly reached up to the cash register and pressed a button. The gunman put a hand into his pocket and drew out a small, flimsy plastic card, and forced it into the waitress's hand.

"Transfer all of it over to that card, now!" he growled, planting the barrel of the gun directly against her temple. She drew short, sharp breaths, trying to slow down her rapidly thudding heart, and took the card from the gunman, swiping it into the card reader. The computer screen on the register came aglow with information about pending transfers. The gunman slammed the butt of his gun against the desk impatiently.

"Faster! Or I'll blow your fucking head off!" the gunman screamed. "Give me the money! Now, you dumb bitch!"

Behind him, Miguel got to his feet in stark contrast to everyone else cowering behind counters and under tables. On the underside of his left forearm, a metallic device was hooked into his bare skin. The device, a cross-shaped apparatus with a blinking red light in the center and four prongs implanted into his flesh, made his muscles twitch and expand. He clenched his fist and locked up his entire arm and clenched his hand into a fist of metal.

He grabbed the gunman's left forearm with the hand that held the weapon, and yanked tightly. Two loud pops issued from the gunman's body, quickly accompanied by an agonized scream. The robber dropped the gun, and it clattered to the floor, then Miguel placed his foot upon it to keep it out of the robber's hands. The robber fell to his knees in pain, clutching his lifeless arm, which dangled uselessly on his side. He could not move his elbow or his fingers; his entire arm was disabled.

Miguel's friend slowly rose from beneath the table and looked on the scene with astonishment.

"How did you do that?" he asked. Miguel simply smiled and pointed to the device on his arm.

"Cybernetics," he responded simply.

At a farm outside of Des Moines, Iowa, a farmer was busy harvesting a field of wheat. The farmer, a man in his senior years, preferred with all insistence to go about his farming by hand as much as possible. The old-fashioned methods were fine for him; therefore, he pulled each piece of the amber grain out of their stalks with his work-worn fingers, and placed them in a bundle. He would carry on with this task for a long time, but it gave him a sense of satisfaction, knowing that it was all done correctly and with his utmost knowledge.

Off to a side, his young farmhand was also occupied with the same work, though at a much faster pace. Metallic devices planted into his arms and chest made him work faster than the old man, and likely even faster than he himself regularly would have otherwise.

"These implants are amazing!" the young farmhand exclaimed to the old man. "It's even better than using a tiller! I'm faster than ever at picking, now!"

"I hate it when you use those things," said the old man. "It's not what nature intended us to be. We should take our time and get it all done right; otherwise, the grains break apart, and they're no good that way."

"But look at what I've collected!" the young farmhand said back, showing off his bundle of perfectly-picked grains. The old man groaned, seeing all the well-kept stalks of wheat in much larger bundles than what he himself spent hours collecting.

"It's not natural…" he muttered under his breath.

"Hey, you wanted me to work for you, and I'm doing a better job than ever," the farmhand replied defensively. "Come on, it's 2063, and we shouldn't have to be picking by hand like it's the Bronze Age! We have these things for a reason!"

The old man said nothing and went back to his job. The young man, however, moved at a dizzying pace through the farmland, working faster and longer than any person within their normal strength possibly could.

Back in Washington, D.C., in the oval office, President Cotter William Marston was meeting with the Secretary of Defense Howard Philips. The president ran his thin, gnarled fingers through his silver wisps of hair while listening to the younger Secretary drone about his report.

An LED screen built into the polished wooden desk flashed various other reports at the same time, splitting his attention several ways. As President, he figured, this was the price to pay for being a man of power and influence in world political affairs: a sensory overload to place even more strain on his already overwhelmed brain.

"Mr. Philips, are they still discussing the clone bill?" asked the President.

"Unfortunately, yes, Mr. President. They're bringing it to the Senate floor for a debate at about 1:00. It's a hot debate. If I may, sir, in all the years that I've known you, I've never once doubted your role in leadership as Commander in Chief. But what is happening with that young Senator Rothman concerns me. He is dangerous, Will. We need to get rid of him," he said outright.

"Simple enough," replied the President. "Anything with his name on it, I'll just put it to a veto. I'm not about to let him have his way and ruin this country."

"But the public will," the Secretary cut in. "The bill already passed last month to release a public sale on cybernetic devices. We're facing a serious problem, William. They're asking for a mandate to legalize clone labour, and they're split on a 50-50 vote. If the clone bill is passed, it'll be total chaos."

"How would that be chaos?" asked the President inquisitively.

"I believe it would be. No doubt you remember history. Does the Civil War ring a bell, sir? Using clones for slavery is not something we should be doing, or even be proud of. I'm deeply ashamed to say that this nation has stooped to its worst low ever. This is very bad."

"Howard, I remember my history well. I also remember that there was a certain precept about all men having been created equal, and that also applies for those created in factories. It's highly immoral what they are trying to do, and I have a hunch that it will only get worse before it gets better.

"Rothman and his constituents forget that they were all made the same way. He's too ambitious. I suspect he's got something up his sleeve. No politician in this damn town plays it straight. You know that as well as I do, and the American people know that too."

The President reclined in the thickly-cushioned chair, passively looking at the LED screen, which came alive with images of clones working in an aluminium mine. He could see their green-tinged faces twisted in scowls as they worked pneumatic picks at the jagged ground beneath them. Inwardly, he wondered about his idea about all men being created equal—if that philosophy in this age was even true to begin with.

"Barbaric," he uttered with contempt. "We are better than this."

"Which means we've got to dig up some dirt on Rothman and get him out of office as soon as possible," Howard interrupted. "The problem is that the people love him, and his views are beyond liberal. He scares me, William."

"Let's leave that to the public, once they see what kind of things have gone into their cybernetics and everything else. Using those green-tinged—things, to do the grunt work for us all… Once they see the inhumanity of how these poor creatures are treated, I believe this insanity will stop."

"I've heard rumours that Rothman is so supportive of the cybernetics movement, that he's volunteered to get himself implanted," Howard pointed out.

"I don't care about that. Let him dabble in his pseudoscience, Howard, if it pleases him. If it winds up killing him, then there's nothing to worry about. Case closed; knock on wood," said the President knocking a tap on his desk for good luck.

"And if it does work, so much for your re-election. He'll ruin the whole country, it may even become worse than that."

The young man standing on the Senate floor received high applause from his peers all around him. Most of the applause, he could tell, was merely for show and not sincere in the least. Most of the other Senators, older men from distant states, deeply resented his views like no other. But the brown-haired and slender Senator Adam Rothman was determined to make his case for the betterment of the people. To date, he was the youngest senator to ever be elected to office in United States history, just shy of 30 years.

"We're all deep into the 21st century, and yet here we are, elected officials chosen to represent the very best that this country has to produce, bickering like it's the 2010 decade all over again! That, gentlemen, simply will no longer do," Rothman declared vigorously. The unblinking eyes of the cameras mounted around the entire Senate floor caught his every nuanced hand motion, every bead of sweat dripping from his brow, and the two metallic bullets lodged into his forehead. The overhead lights shone off of those bolts, reflecting in the eyes of some nearby Senators, who squinted with disdain.

"Senator Rothman," asked another Senator, an older gentleman. "Do you feel that we made a mistake, legalizing the production of cloned labour? We've had protests from the conservative base demanding that we stop immediately."

"Let them protest! Protest over not knowing what's really at stake here!"

"And what do you feel is at stake, Senator?"

"Restoration, gentlemen. That's what's at stake! We've relied on other nations and their resources for far too long! We've been at the mercy of China, India, Japan, and the Middle East for oil, technology, and just about every single product you've ever bought at a discount department store! Now we finally have the technology of our own to get back on our feet and become the self-sufficient nation we've always been meant to be! We don't need them anymore! They need us!"

"And you think that these cybernetic implants and clone slaves are actually going to make that happen?" asked the puzzled Senator.

"Absolutely, Senator. There's no better example of 'Made in America' than cybernetics! We have made people faster, stronger, smarter, and healthier than ever before! We've increased life spans with these devices! Can any other nation claim that they have achieved such scientific advancements as this?"

"Advancements?" repeated the older Senator. "You call slapping on those mechanized devices to the human body *advancements*? It all constitutes an unfair advantage to the common man! You can't just go to a mall and turn yourself into a machine!"

"Why not?" Rothman shot back. "Why can't we allow our citizens to alter themselves? That's what has made this country so great in the first place, the freedom of choice!"

"And what of those clones?" asked the older Senator again. "It's bad enough that such things even exist in this country, but now the questions have been raised to grant them equality under Federal and State law."

"The clones are all grown by the Genome Consortium. Therefore, they are the corporation's property. As such, it's a waste of time to even talk about whether or not they're human."

Another Senator from near the back wall stood up and pointed an accusatory finger down at Rothman.

"You are lying, sir!" the female Senator yelled. "Those clones are every bit as human as we are! Where do you think their genetic material came from?"

"Senator Ingrid," muttered Rothman casually at this accusation. "It's has come down to a matter of simple economics. Those companies require the capital to keep their operations running, and so they created the clones. Every single one of them is stamped with those companies' digital signatures, when they're grown in the labs. They are company property, and they are conditioned into that for their entire lives. That's called good business, and why is this fine country of ours in business? I will tell you why, Senator: TO MAKE MONEY and further prosperity for our nation."

"It's bad enough that you've been campaigning on issues to legalize bigamy ever since your nomination, Rothman," she accused. "The people are divided on such moral issues. But is this really what you'll have us become if you're elected President? Are you going to have us create an entire class of slaves while you let the people turn themselves into machines? What about the riots and protests in Florida and Texas?" she demanded. "Do you want this country to decend into total chaos?"

"Like I said, Senator, they're protesting against the future. And the thing with the future is: it's always coming, whether you like it or not. They'll either accept it one day and get with the times, or they won't. You cannot please everyone in this country. Those who want to progess will progress, and those who do not want to will not," said Rothman confidently, calm and calculated as a true strategist in this debate of views and matters of opinion.

Several news vans and reporters were camped outside the steps of the Capitol building. The congregation of reporters and technicians swelled around the massive, spotless-white structure, waiting in anticipation. The famous Senator Adam Rothman would be due to appear at any moment, the great man of the hour, the Presidential hopeful that promised sweeping transformations down to the very foundations of the United States. The so-called Cyber Champion, as he was labelled in the media, was a force to be reckoned with.

As soon as the man with the two metallic bolts on his head appeared, the reporters swarmed over to him in an instant. A cacophony of questions bombarded him from all sides, and microphones were shoved into his personal space by an army of reporters. To him, it felt like being back on the Senate floor, only this time, his audience was invading his personal space.

"Mr. Senator, is it true that you've invested in Cerberus and Parson Industries after the clone breakthrough?" asked one reporter.

"Mr. Senator, what is your response to the allegations of breaking down traditional values from the Human Focus Group?" asked another, at the same time.

These questions and more followed, to the point that they all merged into one giant hum of questions from a desperate public. Rothman calmly held up a hand to try and quiet them down, and the noise started to subside slightly.

"Yes, to answer questions gentlemen, I have given some support to those companies," Rothman stated. "And yes, I have shown support for some, shall we say, alternative perspectives on modern living. However, the most important issue in this nation is the creation of jobs here at home in America for all her people."

"People?" asked another reporter. "What about those slaves grown in labs?"

"Technically speaking, these are autonomous bio-engineered products, just a step above Class 9 robots. They may look like human beings and even act like them in subtle behaviour, but they actually are fully-artificial organisms, designed expressly, and unable to think for themselves or even reproduce. If you want to talk about civil rights for them, you may as well also ask for civil rights for your toaster ovens."

He was then met with the sounds of laughter from the crowd. He smiled slightly at the sound of his own joke, then he placed his forefinger on one of the bolts sticking out of his head.

"These devices," he started. "These are neural enhancers. Think of it as having a second brain to think with. It's an absolute marvel to be able to think with twice the capacity, and you will soon be able have this power as well! Don't let a good thing go to waste, my friends; opportunity is where you look for it."

The crowd hung on to his every word, excitedly. Across the vast web of cyberspace, viewers online were also entranced by his presence.

"These implants and the clone labour will make this country rich beyond all our wildest dreams; all of it, my friends, is the future of America, which we, as citizens of the States, will change this country into a financial powerhouse of success, a new industrial revolution for the modern times we live in, and you will all have the great privilege to witness such a historic moment as this!" Rothman bellowed mightily.

"These new industries are providing not just much-needed jobs, but they are paving the way for new opportunities for the entire human race! If you want to be stronger and faster, it is now within your grasp without exerting yourself! We have always sought to become exceptional, and now we all finally have the power and the technology to do exactly that! We can leave the most dangerous tasks to cheaply-grown clones and can create jobs with the promise of a better economically prosperous life for all our citizens!"

"And what about the religious and moral organizations who are against cybernetics and clones?" asked a reporter off to a side, trying to get his voice heard over a chorus of cheers and applause.

Rothman simply smiled. "They can't cling to their old ways for much longer. The future is coming. Though I do respect their views and practices, it is not right for our laws to be based entirely upon the ideas of a few for the many to be beholden to. That's why there is the separation of the church and state, and thank God for it."

The reporters were stunned by the verve and cleverness of his carefully-chosen words. As Rothman started stepping down the steps of the Capitol, the reporters cleared a path for him. Rothman walked on with a clear personal space, as if he had his own field around him that no one could enter.

Broadcasts nationwide were being seen on holograph and TV screen, and his words of inspiration reached every person natural-born and lab-grown alike. Some people smiled and cheered for their futurist messiah, while others cried with rage at the ideologue with an agenda to reshape the nation in his own twisted image. Across the country, opinions about Adam Rothman were evenly split; many adored him, while others despised him. Some even wished he was dead.

A black limousine was parked across the concrete lot, to which Rothman casually walked while the reporters and onlookers gave him space. The limo was a classic stretch model; long and black, adorned with thin lights on its side between the tinted windows. Rothman simply smiled and waved at the crowds gathered around him, occasionally pointing at the two implants in his forehead with pride.

"Frankenstein!" came a shout from among the crowds. "Terminator freak!"

Rothman stopped in his tracks and threw a disparaging look in the direction where the shout came from. Among the crowd was a middle-aged man with a thick moustache and an American flag T-shirt.

"Care to repeat that comment, sir?" Rothman growled.

"You heard me!" shouted the protester. "You're nothing but a fucking mutant all stuffed up with wires! And you want us all to be that way; it's not right!"

"Mutant or not, I'll have you know that these implants saved my life two years ago when I was in a car accident!" Rothman shot back with a similar verve back on the Senate floor. "If it wasn't for these implants, I would be in a coma by now!"

"You'd be better off that way!" the protester replied bitterly. His rants were quickly cut off by a counter-protester shoving him on the back of his shoulder. Rothman could see a cybernetic device on his arm, and Rothman flashed him a smile.

"Dumbass, you're talking about devices that can save people's lives! You can't go outlawing things just because you don't like them!"

"Fuck you!" the anti-cyber protester yelled, and began scuffling with the cyber-enhanced counter-protester. The crowds and the reporters cleared a small space for the two protesters to exchange blows. The anti-cyber protester swung his fists wildly at the other man, whose attacks were composed and left the other man clutching a bloody nose. Rothman said nothing at the scene playing out before him, and instead ducked into the limo. From behind the tinted windows, he could see the two protesters still fighting, their shouts muffled by the closed doors and windows.

"Thanks for proving my point," he muttered under his breath, careful not to be too loud. The opposition could have spies or lip-readers everywhere in Washington.

The limo took Rothman through the crowded streets of Washington, D.C., where the skyscrapers cast long shadows over the streets in the late afternoon. Rothman glanced out his windows, looking at the decaying storefronts and homeless people huddled under canopies. He heaved a sigh, seeing all the destitute souls right there in his own city. Inwardly, he felt his strength of resolve start to grow; everything he did on the Senate floor would benefit everyone, especially people like those wrapped up in dirty, fraying parkas huddling by steam vents in the sidewalk to keep warm. Of course, his conservative voter base might accuse him of having *caused* their homelessness due to the laws about clone labour. He may have a secondary cybernetic brain, but even he could not predict the outcome of his legislation.

These thoughts swirled through his head as his limo exited the urban areas and into the residential areas. One particular suburb that the limo crossed into featured houses that were built almost exactly the same, such that even Rothman sometimes had difficulty telling which house was his.

The limo stopped at one of the houses, which was Rothman's own home. The lawn was green and well-trimmed, and every panel of painted wood on the house was spotless, and the surroundings practically advertised domesticated suburbia.

Inside, Rothman collapsed into a cream-coloured plush armchair, pouring himself a glass of liquor from a table next to the chair, and turning on a holograph player. The wall facing him came alive with three-dimensional images of pundits at desks with the Capitol superimposed directly over them.

"That's the problem that faces our nation today!" said the image of a white-haired, portly pundit on the right side of the holographic desk. "With every new law that gets passed by Senators and Congressman like Rothman, we are witnessing the breakdown of every facet of American society! There will come a day when those cybernetic devices that he's so in love with might even be made mandatory for everyone! What message does that send to our children? It would say that your own God-given talents aren't enough, and that you have to go through artificial, false means just to get at the same level as everyone else! Its's a disgrace," he said.

"I disagree, Mr. Bosch," replayed the image of a light-brown haired female pundit sitting opposite him, whose dark red business suit shimmered with a holographic glow. "Nobody's standing outside a climate, forcing people to buy them. In fact, Cerberus and Parson sales are still not very high, even with Rothman's legislation."

"That's exactly what I said on the Senate floor," Rothman thought aloud. His secondary brain alerted him to the footsteps coming up behind him.

Rina Rothman, Adam's Spanish-Indian wife, 28, was a brilliant biologist and medical doctor, and she walked into the room. Her beauty was as graceful as a young doe and tender as a robin; she was slender and her skin was soft and delicate with the color of olive light brown. Her lips were moist and red as a rose, and her eyes were filled with vitality of emerald green, and her nose was short and proportionately pleasing. She had long locks of dirty-brown hair like a sea siren; her breasts were plump and soft, and she was dressed in ladies business dress and high heels, pretty in shades of pink and fuchsia, the chic style of that a socialite would wear on a day out in Beverly Hills.

Rina had a kind and sassy nature, and she was a very nurturing person, always with the best intentions to please her husband, which made him wish to please her equally in turn, and they loved each other.

"So how was your day, dear?" she asked.

"Long, overly eventful, and tiring," Rothman exhaled.

"Your constituents I saw on TV: they're giving you quite a hard battle," said Rina. Adam nodded.

"I just wish they'd understand this the way I do. I am trying to help people have a better life; is that so wrong?"

"They will see in time, dear. It takes time for people to accept new ideas in society, especially on something as controversial as this."

"In time, I suppose. That's alright. How's Marylin?" he asked calmy. Adam had been so busy he had little time to spend with his wife and young daughter. He missed them often, but the demands of being a servant and politician to the United States had to come first. Serving his country and fellow countrymen had to come first as top priority; it was they way of things.

"She asks about you every day. She wants to know when you'll come home and spend time with her." Rina's voice suddenly became tinged with worry. "I really wish you'd take some time off the campaign and spend some more time with us. You hardly ever come home."

"I know, but that's the price I pay," Adam sighed. "I promise, as soon as I'm elected President, we'll take a long break somewhere. Just name the place and we'll go to it."

"Alright," Rina replied. "How about Europe?"

"Europe it is, anywhere in the whole continent." Adam got up from his seat and finished off his glass of whiskey. "Is Marylin here?"

"She's upstairs, and she's not feeling too well," Rina replied.

Adam walked upstairs and turned right in the hallway to enter his daughter's bedroom. Six-year-old Marylin was tucked in bed, surrounded by an array of stuffed animals and life-support machines. She wore a pink nightgown, and her dark brown hair fell in curls over her pillow. As the bulky breathing machine kept whirring next to her bed, she clutched her favorite teddy bear. She smiled through the thin plastic tubes on her nose as Adam entered.

"Hi Daddy," she said with a light voice.

"How's my little angel doing?" asked Adam sweetly.

"I drew a picture for you, Daddy," Marylin said. "I did this today." She pointed to a piece of paper on the wall behind Adam. He turned around and found taped to the wall a drawing of three hastily-coloured figures, each with a name: "Me," "Mommy," and "Daddy." Adam noticed that "Daddy" had two small grey dots on his head.

"Marylin, I promise that things will get better for us soon," Adam reassured her. "What's one thing you want more than anything in the whole world?"

"I want to walk again, Daddy," came the reply from the little girl. Adam nodded.

"I know just the things we can get for you to make that happen."

"Do they hurt?" asked Marylin. "Those cyber-things?"

"No, my dear. They don't hurt. All I need to do is just a few more weeks of work, and you can have them. You'll be able to walk, run, dance, and everything. Would you like that?"

"Yes, Daddy. I would." She propped herself up in bed and held out her arms. Adam stepped in to embrace his daughter.

"I love you, Marylin," Adam whispered in the hug.

"I love you too, Daddy," Marylin whispered back, muffled by Adam's body.

In the master bedroom, Adam Rothman took off his coat and tie, and he rested on the bed. Rina was behind a dressing screen, getting into a lace-laden nightgown. Adam restlessly gripped his head, plagued with worry.

"Why can't they just shut up?" he complained bitterly. "Why can't those people understand all the good I've done? I wish they would see things from a better perspective. This damn business of politics is so frustrating. Sometimes, I wonder why I choose to go into this career. I should have been a lawyer: less headaches to deal with and more money to make."

Rina stepped from behind the dressing screen. Her nightgown partially exposed her breasts, and it curled tantalizingly at the bottom. She went onto the bed next to her husband and placed a long hand on his shoulder.

"You worry too much, Adam," she said. "Let's just have a moment together. Please? we hardly ever do this anymore."

Adam turned around, and they shared a tender kiss, then another which lasted longer. Rina cooed pleasurably with that kiss.

"Make love to me," she said gently, and he smiled in return and obliged.. They made love in the darkness with passion, and he wanted to get away from everything and so did she, just for one hour. The world was theirs, together, and nothing else mattered.

A while later, the campaign office was buzzing with exciting energy. Volunteers, staff members, and reporters were counting down the seconds until the end of Election Day 2064. After months of campaigning on the platform of expansions in cybernetics and clone labour, Adam Rothman was poised to become the nation's newest and most progressive president in recent memory.

Rothman and his family stood on a large stage where several holographic images repeatedly flashed his campaign slogans such as "America: Evolved," "Opportunity Through Power," and "Strength Through Science," along with images of Rothman, as well as a slideshow of people using cybernetic devices to lift boulders or build houses. The savior of America had come.

Then a hush fell over the excited crowd, and the screens went dark. A booming voice could be heard over the speakers lining the auditorium.

"Ladies and gentlemen, the results are now in from all districts! Meet the 56th President of the United States, President Elect Adam P. Rothman! Congratulations, Mr. President! You have won by a landslide!"

The crowds exploded in jubilation. Confetti in red, white, and blue cascaded down upon the heads of the joyous Rothman supporters as they cheered and screamed in elation. Rothman and his family then took the stage, with Marylin in a motorized wheelchair. Rothman waved at the crowd, smiling all the while. The crowd began a fervent chant of "ROTH-MAN! ROTH-MAN! ROTH-MAN!" Rothman waited several moments for it to calm before making his speech.

"Fellow Americans," he spoke with his voice electronically magnified. "We now stand on the threshold of a brave new world, a world where America shall become the unchallenged leader in science and innovation! We shall reclaim our true role as leaders of the free world! Unite with me, in the cause of a better tomorrow, for our generation and for future generations! For your children, and their children, we shall remain united! We shall be victorious!"

The crowd cheered in response.

"Soon, the entire country will feel the might of cybernetic enhancements! Soon, the most menial of tasks will be left to the green-blooded labourers built in our own image! We will overcome weakness, conquer infirmity, and become at last the masters of our own destiny!

"With the cybernetic enhancements from Cerberus and Parson Industries, even my own daughter, Marylin, will finally be able to walk again!"

Marylin stirred in her wheelchair, and she began to feel a twitch in her right leg. A cybernetic enhancer on her kneecap and lower leg. She closed her eyes and tried to focus, and then gradually she moved her own foot out of the chair. With more effort, she bent both her legs, and slipped out of the chair, feeling her own feet touching the floor. Adam and Rina looked on from her side, along with the rest of the congregated crowd and the world via holograph, as she tried to gain her sense of balance with her feet on the ground.

She righted herself, and took a step forward, catching her balance and taking another step, then another. Her steps were slow and careful, and she started to walk faster, breaking out into a trot around the entire stage. The crowd joined Adam and Rina in cheering for the girl who could finally walk again.

As the months passed in his new elected office, the new president had achieved the impossible: Congress and the Senate had fully legalized the public sale and distribution for cybernetic enhancements and clone labour for all fields of labour and industry including agriculture, mining and construction.

The cyborg markets soon emerged for those who were terminally ill and wished to expand their lives by having brain transplants into full cybernetic bodies, becoming the machine, leaving their frail previous humanity behind them.

The country exploded in economic growth with the increase of productions in cybernetic manufacturing, and thousands of factories and plants opened all around the nation, creating jobs and abundance like never before.

America was gaining an edge over her European and Asian counterparts; oil was later abandoned for the production of renewable biodegradable fuels using vegetables and animal waste, and there was also the advancement in eco- friendly technologies and filtration systems used to clean up the atmosphere in many of the nation's smoggiest major metropolitan cities. All of these new innovations came from original cybernetic technologies from the Genome Consortium.

After two years in office, President Rothman had made the United States of America into a powerhouse of capitalism and success, much to the distaste of the heads of state in the United Kingdom, the Middle East, and Russia. They were angry because the USA had enacted strict trade embargoes, which crippled these other nations, and the only countries that still conducted any form of commerce with western society were Japan and China on a limited basis.

But a change was happening in Adam Rothman; it was a change that was noticed even by members of his own family and cabinet who began to feel that his push for technology may have been taken too far. As for the rest of the Senate and Congress, they were beginning to feel everyone had made a drastic mistake in making him

President and many said that those who voted for Rothman have sealed their own fates.

In the Oval Office, Adam Rothman sat at his opulent desk and adjusted the two new cybernetic devices underneath his coat. The silver crosses hooked into his arms were starting yield that familiar and wonderful flow of energy through his body. He could feel himself growing stronger physically, but he felt a need to pace himself, as if by moving normally he could accidentally break something with tremendous force.

The other implants in his body also heightened the effect. He could see things with increased clarity, catching the smallest details of the wooden bust of Abraham Lincoln sitting across from him in the office. He could hear the slightest whisper from behind the insulated walls. All those new technologies were embedded into his body; he was a walking advertisement for human perfection.

More cybernetics had been placed into his body, as well as an entire extra pair of robotic arms jutting from the sides of his torso, which also flexed and moved with his nerve impulses, and he had become addicted to designer surgery. This form of vanity did not help his image with the public or his fellow constituents. The effect made him look like a robotic spider, which may have frightened some of his voters and delighted others.

"I could've been voted Mr. Universe," he quipped to himself, flexing his enhanced muscles. "If only they'd allow things like this in the competition."

Despite his guns and the advances that took place under his watch, there was still some very stiff resistance from certain groups. Rothman turned on a holograph projector in the Oval Office, and an image of a news anchor materialized in front of him.

"The so-called Human Focus Group, labour unions, and other organizations have publicly come out against cybernetics and clone labour," said the reporter's translucent image. "Among their complaints is that cybernetics are against traditional moral values, as well as concerns about the nationwide rise in cybernetic-involved street crime. With homicide rates increased 45% over the national average in the last year, many of these groups are calling for nation-wide bans on all cybernetic devices to end these grizzly killings and the wave of senseless violence."

The holograph changed to show the image of a middle-aged man not too different from the one who spoke out to him outside the Capitol all those years ago. This one was thin, bald, and wore an expression of discontent.

"It's against everything that makes us people!" the interviewed man complained. "I lost my wife to gangbangers with cybernet-ics! My kids are scared, my whole community is scared, and it's all thanks to Rothman! He brought this menace upon all of us just because he believes that people aren't good enough the way they are, the way God made us!"

"And what would you say to everyone watching this broadcast, sir?" asked a voice from off the camera. The man pumped his fists angrily.

"Protest! Repeal everything having to do with cybernetics and get Rothman out of office as soon as possible! Worst president ever!"

Rothman turned off the holograph with a snarl. Again and again, this charade of the anti-cybernetic movement was playing out across the country, and he was being made the sole target of their jabs and insults. Rothman sunk into the plush leather seat and contemplated.

What would it take to get these people out of his way for the betterment of the nation? He knew that the economy had grown at an astronomical rate since he enacted the first of the cybernetic-expansion laws, and he had made America more wealthy and pros-perous for every citizen of the social classes than the country had ever been in than in the last 80 years of the nation's existence, but the people were still not happy. What could he do to just shut them up? There were still those people who not only refused his gift of cy-ber-enhancements, but they were going well out of their way to stop them completely. He knew something had to be done, and quickly.

He pressed a button embedded in the desk, calling his PR representative. "I'd like to address the nation," Rothman said into the intercom.

"My fellow Americans," Rothman said before the camera, broadcasting his holograph nationwide. "There is a cancer in this nation, and it is growing at an alarming rate. It cannot be cut out or easily treated. That cancer is known as ignorance—willful and divisive.

"I'm sure everyone is now well aware of the events unfolding across the nation. In countless towns, we have seen blatant acts of terrorism perpetrated by certain organizations seeking to rid themselves of what has made this nation strong and independent. These violent degenerates declare themselves to be so-called 'freedom fighters against the evils of cybernetics,' and that description could not be farther from the truth."

He paused a moment to recompose his voice. The cybernetic implant in his larynx was beginning to kick in, soothing his vocal cords.

"This movement only seeks to undo all the good and growth that has been achieved over the past two years! If they had their own way, we would lose all our technology, and the economy as we know it would shrink back down to levels not seen in decades! These urban terrorists kill in the name of freedom and liberty. As such, it is the excuse that all terrorist make, and I say that they only kill in the name of their own selfish and outdated ideology, and I will not tolerate it anymore!

"Under emergency executive powers and the regulatory laws passed against acts of treason and sedition, our party will quell these uprisings, and anyone who is caught in acts of malfeasance against government officials or cybernetic facilities— either publicly or privately-owned— will be considered immediate enemies of the state and prosecuted vigorously.

"Rights of trial and habeas corpus shall be temporarily suspended for all agitators. The punishment for the offenders of such heinous crimes commited against any fellow American citzen shall face life imprisonment or death by public execution. Let this be a declaration of judgment to the inviduals and groups who are responsible for these killings: we will make examples of those who dare to defy and betray their countrymen and fellow patriots of the United States of America. Freedom and liberty shall stand her ground forever. We shall prevail!"

The holograph was disseminated throughout the nation on every channel. One place it was seen was a local bar in Boise, Idaho, where most of the patrons were sporting cybernetics on their bodies. One patron slammed his glass of beer against the counter with such force that the glass shattered, sending soaked pieces of glass flying into the air.

"Those bastards are trying to take away our cybers!" the man shouted. "We should hit them before they hit us! Let's kill the bastards!"

The cyber-enhanced patrons rose to their feet and shouted angrily in assent. "It's the American way!" another patron yelled, and the group went out of the bar into the streets. Down the road, several anti-cybernetic protesters were holding signs on a street corner, with slogans such as "Stay Human!" "Say No to Cybers!" "Don't Change what's Already Perfect!" and "Men, Not Machines!" In a fleeting instant, the crowd of angry cybernetic-users made a beeline for the protesters and began attacking them with single-minded ferocity.

The anti-cybers fought back with their bare fists, but the cyber-users tore right through them with more strength than their entire non-enhanced group could muster. For every punch that slowed down a cyber-user, they would respond with a skull-shattering onslaught.

Rothman saw the news footage from the Oval Office of the riots that kept spreading across the country like a wildfire of destruction; disgusted and angered by this act of defiance, he turned off his Holograph and tried to think of a solution to end the chaos.

Out of nowhere, his beloved wife came into the room, her eyes were full of tears, struck with grief at what actions her husband had taken to bring the country to its knees. He had become hard as a dry angry old man; he was cruel, cold, and filled with contempt for his fellow human beings. Bitterness had torn his soul apart.

"What do you want? I am extremely busy; this had better be good," intoned Rothman coldly.

"You are always busy, Adam; you don't even see your wife or daughter anymore," said Rina.

"I have a country to run, dear. Understand the political powers that I have to contend with on a daily basis in the office, and the pressure of leadership and being a man in the most powerful position in the world," rebutted Rothman.

"But what about us? Don't we still matter to you at all?" she asked.

"Of course you do, my dear, and our daughter too, but sacrifices have to be made for the betterment of the people; it's my job," said Rothman reluctantly.

"And, what about that trip to Europe you promised me two years ago," said Rina

"Rina, my dearest wife and friend, our country is about the break out into potential civil war, and all you care about is going to damn Europe. My dear, you have become a selfish, narcissistic, and vain creature; you disappoint me, " said Rothman.

"Oh, you're calling me a narcissist and vain? What about all those things on your body, you look like a walking can opener!" she said, raising her voice.

"Don't you talk back to me, my dear. Without me, you would have never reached the societal status you were given to be the First Lady of the White House. No, you would be slaving away in a government lab testing rats with serums, so don't you ever again speak to me that way," said Rothman raising his voice but keeping his composure.

"You are not being fair, Adam," protested Rina.

"Am I? My dear, it takes mutal cooperation, for a marriage to work out, and you're choosing the make things very hard for the both of us. You should know that more than anyone else. Understand that being a politician is my business! I am sorry if you don't like it," said Rothman, angry.

"Is there a part of you that is still the man I once loved? You have changed so much over the last two years, not just with this body, but your personality has too. You're starting to frighten me, and you're frightening our daughter too," said Rina.

"This is part of me now; it's who I am, and if you wish to remain my wife, you will need to learn to accept me for who and what I am. If you do not, I will consider to get a divorce," replied Adam.

"You have become so cold Adam. Why?" she said shocked.

"These devices, these arms: it's who I have become, and nobody can ever take that away from me."

"But that's another problem right there!" Rina shot back. "Look all around you, at what those cybernetics have done to people! It's caused way more harm than it ever could've been worth! Please, just let go of those things and come back to us!"

"I have a job to do, so unless you would like to discuss this another time, please leave me alone," said Rothman.

"There is not going to be another time Adam," said Rina, sealing her fears that her husband was lost.

"What are you saying?" said Rothman taken by surprise.

"I'm leaving with Marylin today. I just wanted to give you one last chance to make things right," said Rina

"Take the damn brat then, you ungrateful wife. I saved our daughter's life, and you don't even care about that," said Rothman.

"That is not true. I do care, but I also care about a having husband who will be there for his wife and child. I guess its just being a concerned mother. I'm sorry," said Rina sadly.

And with that she left with her daughter with a luggage bag on the next flight out to see her family in Madrid, Spain.

"Damn bitch! You can't trust any woman anymore," said Rothman after she left the White House. "Unfaithful cunt; I thought she said for better or for worse. Using, self serving, selfish, whore," he complained in an angry tirade he sulked to himself quietly.

Then he calmed and thought deeply with regret. "Maybe though, I do deserve this. I tried to make her happy and my country happy. How was I supposed to know it would all come down to this? God help me. God help me," said Rothman feeling some remorse in his heart as he buried his face in his main hands, but his anger plucked any sympathy out, and he rose from his seat, embittered and full of disgust seeing his fellow human beings. He just did not care anymore.

Rothman was seething when he was brought before a special session of Congress. All those Senators that he once sat shoulder to shoulder with, now we're looking down on him with the utmost contempt. Outside, the sounds of gunfire could be heard echoing.

"President Adam Rothman," spoke the Speaker of the House, an older man with a mane of silver hair. "These impeachment proceedings will now begin against you for dereliction of duty to the Constitution of the United States."

"Spare me your bureaucratic babble, Senator, and get to the point," Rothman growled.

"Fine, then," said the Speaker. "The charges against you are as follows—"

He was interrupted by the sound of hurried footsteps down the vacant marble floor. One of the Senators rose from his seat and rushed towards the President in the center of the room. From out of his jacket pocket, he drew out a snub-nosed pistol and pointed it squarely at the President's head.

Before he could fire, Rothman leaped several feet in the air out of the bullet's trajectory and landed directly behind him. With his two organic arms, he took hold of his assailant to restrain him, and with one of his spindly mechanical arms, he grabbed the Senator's gun and threw it off to a side.

The attacking Senator struggled fervently against Rothman's grasp, trying to squirm his way out of his powerful grip. Then, in one move, Rothman balled up his cyber-enhanced fist and slammed it into the Senator's skull, leaving a deep crater where his head once was. He released the lifeless body, which slumped to the floor, leaking blood and brain matter onto the marble floor. Rothman then looked around all the frightened faces staring at the scene that unfolded.

"Anyone else want to try to kill me?" he asked sarcastically and was met with frightened silence. "Security!"

The doors in the back of the Senate hall flew open, and scores of armed guards poured into the room. Every one of them was armed with heavy assault rifles, trained on the insubordinate Senators.

"Open fire!" Rothman commanded, and with disciplined accuracy, they made short work of every Senator and House Speaker in the room. Their shouts were drowned out by the sounds of gunfire until only Rothman and his private army were left alive.

He stood before one of the still-active holograph cameras and addressed the nation.

"What has just been seen are the opening throes of a new order in this country!" Rothman exclaimed. "From this day on, I, Adam Rothman, declare myself as acting High Chancellor of North America! These insurrections will be stopped by all means necessary! All conspirators shall be put down as if they were dogs. Any who are not loyal to the state shall be immediately executed!"

On his orders, civil war broke out in every city and state that very day. The entire population was spilt between cyber-users who supported High Chancellor Rothman and the staunch anti-cybers.

The war lasted at three years, and several cities were occupied by either side, then retaken or outright destroyed. The anti-cybers fought with heavy-grade weapons and assault vehicles, while their enhanced opposition only needed their own devices to fire concentrated energy bursts –though at great personal risk— to decimate the anti-cyber forces.

In the end, the country was left in ruins. The Chancellorship of Adam Rothman led to disaster until his eventual death in an anti-cyber assault when he wasshot in the head. The cyber-users, in retaliation, accelerated the force of their own attacks until nothing was left of the country but burning cities and fiery rubble. America was no more. Destroyed and undone, the great Empire of Democracy that stood once proudly for close to three hundred years in its history was no more.

Then the invaders came from overseas. Warships from Europe, Asia, and the Middle East anchored at the coasts of what once was the United States, and their soldiers poured out into the ruins, looking for any spoils that remained.

The scenes of chaos and desolation disappeared, replaced with Mystic Theater. Some audience members were taken aback, terrified by what they had seen, and they prodded Doctor Xoctarious with questions. Some people were sceptical, taking the whole story as cheap entertainment, wondering how Xoctarious was conjuring all the images. Surely it was nothing like any movie screening that they've ever seen.

"What you have just seen," announced the doctor, " was just one vision of a possible future, in which one man's beliefs ran rampant over an entire nation which he twisted and reshaped into his own image, fancying himself a god among mortal men. Guard yourselves, my friends, for those possible Rothmans may yet reveal themselves to assume command over everything you have ever come to believe in."

The doctor continued to speak as the visions continued. "Now I bring to you all an important question. What causes? the absence of faith in the Divine? It is the fear and doubt of unbelief. It is what drives men to question all things.

"Does God exist? Why is the world in the trouble that it is in? If there is a God, why won't He do something to fix it? Why is there so much pain and misery if there is supposed to be a loving God? These questions are normal to those who are suffering and longing for peace.

"We all seek answers. Some of us turn to reason and logic to ease our worries; others turn to ignorance and arrogance to avoid the higher truth. But there are some answers that are never meant to be known, and there are some things beyond the veil of uncertainty that, if glimpsed, can irretrievably ruin an entire life. Such actions bring a terrible darkness; when a man faces not his own inner demons and fears, but when he faces the power of evil itself, incarnate, in living flesh and blood," he said. "Behold this story which I call 'Shadow People.'"

SHADOW PEOPLE

Story by Dominic R. Daniels
Written by
Dominic R. Daniels & Doug K. Owen

1

The walls of the Mystic Theater disappeared, replaced with crumbling plaster walls to form a tiny apartment room lit by a flickering light bulb hanging by a slim, dust-laden wire in the ceiling. The bulb's light continually sputtered, going from light to dark in seconds, and the smell of damp condensation from the moist mold was on this man's cracked plaster walls, chipped with showing signs of loose red bricks on the walls.

The walls themselves were fully covered in hand-painted murals containing the morbid, the twisted, and the deranged; they were images of demonic fallen angels with large, imposing, black-feathered wings with grotesque heads of filthy black birds, horned goats, and shadow specter-like creatures.

The murals were monstrous abominations of people being slaughtered and torn apart in different methods of torture : being broken on the rake, impaled on a giant dead tree with spikes that resembled thorns on a rose bush as the victims' blood drained and poured down the dry branches of the tree and flowed down on the ground into a silver bejeweled chalice for a sacrificial offering to the profane.

Inverted crosses were on the walls, burning in flames with the writings of blasphemy, saying: God is Dead! There were images of people who had committed suicide by other techniques, like paintings of people stabbing each other with long blades, a picture of an older man blowing his brains out of his skull with a pistol as he held it against his temple already pulling the trigger with a burning shot erupting fire, splattering fragments of bone, blood, and brain all over the place. It was a hideous and a sick sight to see and take in.

But these pictures of the macabre were not all the sights to see on these walls, on other parts of these worn walls was visions painted of the heavens, of holy saints and Arch Angels such as the angels known as Raziel, Michael, Ariel, and Metatron. They were undefiled images and were worshipping a luminescent light above them with a giant hand descending down from the clearing clouds and a white dove coming down on the beings below who worshipped it.

In other corners of the candlelight room were oil painted canvases which stood on multiple wooden easels with pictures of Catholic saints such as Saint Francis of Assisi and Saint Padre Pio, bearing the marks of the Stigmata with the bloody wounds of nail marks that pushed into their hands bleeding and raw from agony, suffering for the glory of the eternal Holy of Holies.

A young lean muscular man with long blond hair and a handsome face blue eyes was wearing a white tank top undershirt and black leather pants, and he was bare foot and sat on a tall wooden stool while painting vigorously his visions of the ever-after on canvas.

The images burned in the his mind from the nightmares he suffered night after night, and he could not sleep nor eat, and his diet was willpower along with the byproduct of drinking large cups of caffeinated black coffee and Jack Daniels whiskey.

He was chain smoking on leftover butts and nubs of cigarettes, taking in whatever drag he could get off one until the last bit of tobacco burned the end, which he extinguished into a obsidian ashtray on a small table next to him where his palette of multicolored paints were scattered along with paint cleaner in a dirty water filled mason jar full with used paint brushes.

His nerves were shot, and he was tired from the lack of sleep, but something drove him to continue paint up to seventeen hours at a time. He had not slept for two straight weeks, like a meth addict. The only other signs of a living arrangement in this loft were a small miniature bar refrigerator that he kept stocked with hard liquor and canned food, along with a dirty mattress he slept on the floor with no bed covering and an old feather-stuffed pillow with assorted hand stitched patches that covered the holes. It was 4:00 in the morning, and he stopped and rested; it had been a long night's work.

Twenty-eight-year-old Darren White cursed his rotten fortune as he feverishly kept painting on the canvas, his sleep-deprived hands quivering uncontrollably even after he set down his paintbrush and picked up a cigarette from a small carton on a cinder block that doubled as a table for him.

"This is my life," he muttered bitterly to the morbid paintings on the walls that were his only companions. "I never did anything to deserve this." He lit up the cigarette with a small lighter and tried to inhale a deep draft of the smoke, but as his entire body kept trembling violently, and the cigarette kept falling loose from his lips. Frustrated, he tried to steady it with his other hand, and kept puffing faster as he laboured draws from the cigarette.

The smoke that filled his lungs started to calm him down slightly, but his mind was still harried and unfocused. His vision started to go dark and blurry, and his limbs dangled as if they were weighted down, unable to move. He stumbled two steps from his stool in this deprived, caffeine- and tobacco-fuelled stupor, and he finally doubled over and collapsed on the dusty wooden plank floor. He laid in a bent, awkward position on the floor, still trembling and convulsing even as he lost control of his body. Then all went black and the darkness came over him.

Then, the nightmares returned in all their livid, visceral grandeur. Darren found himself chasing after a demon in the form of a young man with a deep red complexion, a muscular form, and leathery black wings. Its eyes burned a bright red, as if two candles were lodged into its skull. The demon, with its mouthful of long and pointed fangs, laughed scornfully in a high-pitched voice that rang harshly in Darren's ears. The demon laughed at Darren as it flew overhead, holding in its clawed hand what Darren knew was a pouch filled with money that Darren so desperately needed.

He did not know where it came from, only that the pouch contained money and he was desperate to have it, so he ran in pursuit of the winged menace. Still, he kept running after the demon, through a desolate marshland with a sickly yellow and brown fog canopy all around him. The demon kept flapping its wings through the fog, trying to outrun his opponent, but Darren struggled against the waist-deep pits of thick, viscous mud that held him back from his prize. More and more he kept struggling to lift his legs and pull himself forward towards the nameless, malicious beast that stole his money. Darren ground his teeth and growled some choice swear words as the mud started to consume him from the waist up.

"You damn bastard, come on and fight! I'll kill you!" raved Darren fearlessly. Demon or not, he did care. He wanted to nail this thing and get that pouch.

The flying demon turned around and realized that Darren was stuck, and it relished the opportunity to dive down from the sky and swoop over him, tantalizing him with the money pouch.

"This money will never be yours!" the demon taunted him, laughing as he held the pouch over Darren's head. Darren waved his arms around frantically trying to reach for it, but the demon kept yanking the pouch just out of his reach. From out of the polluted fog and muck, the shapes of other creatures came into view, every bit as hostile and grotesque as Darren's tormentor.

Deformed, disgusting entities emerged from the fog, encircling Darren as he remained stuck in the thick mud. Many of the monsters had humanoid forms, but the similarities to a human form stopped there, as they sported black and feathery wings, long, sharpened horns jutting from their foreheads, and pitch-black, taut skin that made them look like corporeal shadows.

Other creatures in the unholy menagerie looked like crosses between wolves, eagles, and horses. Each of those cross-species amalgams sported bloated, diseased bodies with raw, dripping skin, and all of their beady, bulbous eyes were pointed squarely at the young man stuck in the mud. They erupted into a chorus of scornful, sadistic laughter at the defiant young man before them. In response, Darren balled up his fists and gritted his teeth.

"Why don't you just fuck off and get a job?" he derided the creatures all around him.

"Because you're just too fun to fuck with. Besides, you're the bum; not us!" replied one particular demon with a long, giraffe-like neck, poking its thin, mucus-slick skull in Darren's face, looking at him with glowing eyes like embers.

The creature's laugh joined those of the others around it, overwhelming Darren's stoic stance against them. The host of demons gathered close around him to jab at him with clawed, gnarled fingers from all directions, puncturing his flesh from every angle. He tried to wave his hands around him to defend himself, but two slimy tentacles wrapped around his wrists and held him in place, leaving him defenceless against their brutal onslaught. Some of the creatures grinned deviously and laughed with bloodthirsty glee as they sank their long claws into Darren's chest. Darren screamed in the rawest agony with every stab and poke from the creatures all around him. There was no escape for him, no respite, and no mercy from the monsters all around him. He was destroyed.

Darren awoke with a sudden gasp, and then fell into convulsions while still splayed out on the floor of his apartment. His head felt it had shrunk several sizes with his brain about to explode right out of his skull. His limbs felt like lead, lacking any strength to move. Every time he even slightly moved his head around, the pain in his head multiplied sevenfold, and he shut his eyes and growled with the pain. Both of his nostrils began to drip with blood, and he could taste the salty sensation of blood in his mouth as well. It filled his mouth until he spat it out all over the floor and snorted it out of his nose.

Those nightmares were starting to affect more than just his mind. For years, he had to deal with those scenes of torment and death that erupted in his imagination, and it caused him plenty of psychological damage as it was. Now these visions left him with unbearable headaches, cramps in all his limbs, and frequent nose-bleeds. He figured maybe he should get himself checked by a physician, but then he realized that took the money which he didn't have.

The window in the back of the room spilled rays of sunlight over his pale body, so much that he tightly shut his eyes to save them from the brightness A sudden pounding outside his door amplified his already throbbing headache. He growled angrily at the unrelenting slams against his door.

"White! Your rent's due today!" came a shrill voice outside his door. "Get your ass out here NOW! You hear me, White?"

Darren grumbled and mustered up enough strength to pull himself onto his feet. He wobbled on his feet, unbalanced, and tried to steady himself by gripping the stool in the room, then going from there to the art-covered walls. His legs throbbed with pain with every second upright.

"This ain't a damn charity case, White!" roared the voice outside. "Get me my money, or I'm kicking you out!"

Darren stumbled to the door and slumped against it. "I'll get you your money soon," he protested. "I mean it this time, Mr. Pratt."

"Five days!" replied the gruff voice of Mr. Pratt behind the door. "Five days, or you're out! And you're damn lucky to get that much time! No more extensions!"

"Fine," Darren conceded, and he could hear some heavy footsteps going by his door. His landlord had left, and once again, he only had his macabre handiwork for company. Darren heaved a loaded sigh and collapsed onto his stained mattress against the left wall of the room, which was only slightly more comfortable than the hard wooden floor that was his bedding last night. A loose metal spring was poking out of the frayed cotton batting of the mattress, jamming into Darren's back. That sensation reminded him bitterly of his nightmare about being torn apart by the monstrous army. Everything in the entire room was a testament to the lowly, burdensome life that he had.

"I hate this…" he whispered. "I hate this. I hate this. I hate this."

Again and again he repeated this phrase, each time with more raw emotion, until he found himself screaming.

"I HATE THIS!"

He pounded his fists against one of his paintings of a stigmata-afflicted saint until the canvases burst, leaving a fist-sized hole right where St. Francis's face used to be. In a frenzied rage he began ripping into some other pieces of artwork that were unfortunate enough to be in the vicinity. Darren punched the images of saints and angels, and tore right into the paintings of demons and monsters, ripping into them with every bit of ferocity as the creatures in his nightmares had previously done to him.

Another painting was destroyed, then he tore off the wall, and his framed Bachelor of Fine Arts diploma he angrily slammed to the floor, shattering its glass casing and leaving jagged glass shards everywhere.

Darren fell to his knees, trying to breathe the raging fire out of his body, cursing everything in his life. He hated everything about his life; he hated his tiny shithole apartment, he hated being broke all the time, he hated the fact that very few buyers anywhere wanted to take any of his pieces that he worked himself senseless to create, he hated his strict Catholic parents' upbringing, hated those bleak and horrific nightmares and visions, hated being alone aside from the monsters in his mind and the unrelenting Mr. Pratt, and above all, he hated having absolutely no means to support himself.

"How the hell am I going to come up with that money?" he said as he started to weep. "Oh, fuck me! I want to DIE! I WANNA DIE!! Nobody gives a shit about me anyway! FUCK EVERYONE!"

he moped as he cried bitterly, falling to the floor immobilized by his own despondent grief, and he laid helpless and numb to his life like a dead rabbit twitching, his inner turmoil brewing within his empty soul.

He crawled on the ground over to his mattress and pulled out a derringer pistol from underneath his beat up pillow, the gun already loaded with six shots in it.

Playing with the weapon in his hands, his eyes began to flutter, tension rising in his veins as he boiled with hate, only hate. He jabbed the gun into his forehead, wanting to blow his head off. In a second it would be over, a quick merciful death. This was more merciful than living; no living on a day-to-day basis in squalor was true Hell.

Debating whether to do the unthinkable, he trembled with the gun in his palm, then he set the gun down on the floor and just stared at it. He just kept sitting there, staring at that pistol for over an hour, and he felt that time ceased to exist.

He then got an idea, and putting the gun in a small suitcase with two of his paintings, he went down to the local pawn shop on the corner that was three blocks from his loft down the street. He went there often to sell his paintings. The owner was named Billy Roderick, a middle-aged two-bit low-life and loan shark who knew Darren as an acquaintance, and he gave him business once in a while out of sheer pity.

It was about eleven in the morning, and Billy had just opened his shop about an hour before, and Darren saw the sliding gate cover opened and the door unlocked for business, so he went in and met with Billy at the counter.

"Hi Darren, how you are doing?" asked Billy calmly. "Been a while since you came in last time." Darren placed his suitcase on the glass counter and opened it up, revealing the wares inside.

"What have you got for me this time?" Billy said to Darren as he rifled around the suitcase.

"Not much, but it's something you might be interested in," replied Darren, showing off the small Derringer to Billy. He took it with curiosity and squinted, noting all the fine details on the gun.

"How long have you had this gun?" asked the shopkeeper.

"About a year. It's never been fired before, though. It's brand new."

"What did you pay for it?"

"About $250 I think; I don't remember."

Billy set the gun on the counter. "I'll give you $150 bucks for it. What else do you got?"

Darren showed him two of his newer paintings. Billy marveled as he saw a painting of an armoured saint on horseback, plunging a spear into the belly of a ghastly European dragon with black scales and horns on its serpentine body and blasts of orange fire that spewed out of its horrid mouth that were full of little sharp teeth and fangs.

"That one's St. George," Darren explained.

"Nice," remarked Billy. "This one's good. $200 sound alright?"

"Fine with me," Darren agreed. "Here's another one I did recently."

Billy took in his hands another canvas painting; this one was of an old man with a grey beard and deep red markings on his hands and feet.

"Very detailed," Billy noted.

"That one's Saint Padre Pio," Darren clarified to him. "Those marks there are called stigmata. It's kinda hard to explain—"

"I'll take your word for it," Billy cut him off quickly. "This one looks like it could fetch a hundred."

"You've made my day," Darren said, taking the cash gladly.

"Darren, you've got some talent here," said Billy. "Ever considered selling some of this stuff to the church?"

"I've done that. Problem is, the market's oversaturated."

"There's a market for religious art?" asked Billy incredulously.

"Sure there is, and on top of that, the Los Angeles Archdiocese is very selective."

"You know, I've seen some of your other stuff, that more twisted shit that you do," Billy said. "I don't know, maybe some kind of heavy metal band would want an album cover, or one of those underground comics or something. Gotta be someone out there who'd want stuff like this."

"I sell to the record labels once in a while, but not that much and not that often. The competition is a bitch. If I don't get into a gallery soon, I'm gonna be left on the street."

"Let's hope it doesn't come to that," said Billy.

Darren pocketed the cash on the counter and shook hands with the shopkeeper. "Thanks, Billy."

"Anytime, kid. You ever need anything, you just let me know."

The area of Downtown Los Angeles was swept with litter and dust. Darren walked past graffiti-covered storefronts and past filthy panhandlers begging for spare change, and he walked over to one of the few remaining pay phones in the area. Darren cancelled his cell phone contract long ago; it cost him too much money. After inserting a few quarters, he dialed in the number of the only people with whom he could still hold a conversation.

"Hello?"

"Dad? It's Darren. Just wanted to see how you're doing."

"Been decent," came his father's reply. "Your mother and I hadn't heard from you in a while. How have you been?"

"Not so hot, really," replied Darren. "Only just getting by here and there. Sales have been slow lately."

"Still painting, I see?"

"It makes me happy, Dad. Nothing else does."

"I still don't get it. You're a brilliant kid, and you just had two months left on your Criminal Law degree, then you just pass it all up just so you could paint pictures. Is that really what you want to do with the rest of your life, being a starving artist? Broke?"

"Dad, you never understood me," Darren stammered slightly. "You never had to live with that—thing, that I have."

"Don't start with that crap again," his father warned him. "You know that's all in your head. Always was."

"Yeah, all the shrinks you guys took me to kept saying that. I went to the counselling, I took the meds, and none of it worked."

"Wasn't our fault. We did everything we could for you."

"Do you think I could come back home for just a few months?"

"Darren, we've supported you for 22 years already. You had every opportunity to come work at my firm, but you turned it down. You're on your own."

Darren pulled his head away from the receiver and sucked in a breath, trying not to unleash his rage at his father, so instead he kept the conversation going.

"How's Mom?"

"She worries about you a lot. I do too."

"But you still wouldn't let me come home, would you?"

"Not unless you're willing to drop this whole painting thing and start becoming a lawyer. Think about it."

Darren was about to respond, but an automated voice cut him off promptly.

"Please deposit 50 cents to continue your call."

Darren rifled through his pockets, not finding any remaining loose change, so he hung up the phone and went on his way, feeling bitter about the conversation. Even his own parents were against him. He knew that his parents never believed in him or in his work, and they never knew the release that it gave him from his tormented visions.

Every morbid image that he painted was his own way of purging his emotional demons, exorcizing them onto a canvas out of his head. Without that release, he figured he would be driven out of his mind by the constant attacks that came to him in dreams and visions and put into a mental hospital as a basket case.

His helicopter, domineering parents, during his youth, took him to various psychiatric specialists to pin down a cause for these nightmares, only giving him a myriad of drugs and counselling sessions, all of which did nothing for him. He tried telling himself that he was not crazy, but he was no closer to any source of his torment aside from living in poverty and rejection.

He went home feeling down, and he paid his rent as he promised to Mr. Pratt, then he went inside his loft and sat down to drink. Two days passed, and he was in a stupor of intense depression, when had a dream of a tall man, dressed in a white business suit telling Darren as a little boy of ten years old, crying for help. "GROW UP!" said the man in the white suit, and then Darren woke up. It was a wake- up call to take charge of his adult life; after all, no one else was going to do that for him.

Meanwhile, to keep things from dragging, Darren decided that if he was going to change his circumstances in his pathetic life that he alone had to be responsible for his outcomes. He chose to man up and stopped putting the blame on others, and this gave him inner courage and great tenacity with an unyielding stubbornness to win, and he would work any side job he could in order to prove his family wrong and to also succeed in becoming a world famous painter.

In his ideology, an artist no matter of what practicing medium had to stay true to his or her vision and dreams, for if a creative human being decided to let others tell that individual what he or she could or could not accomplish in their own life, what good was having personal goals and dreams? They would be swept away by the winds of doubt and fear.

"To Hell with them all," he said to himself in his thoughts. "I'll prove them wrong! I'll prove them all wrong! And nobody will stop me!" he made this sacred oath to himself in his heart, and he would not stop until he conquered not only his own inner demons but to gain his family and society's approval. Revenge through massive success was a dish sweeter served than all the finest desserts and brandy in the world.

Revenge and justice would be his and his alone. This was a recurring problem he had faced in his earlier years as a child while in school; despite having excellent grades and being very bright in his classes, he was often mocked by his peers, bullied and often beaten up and thrown in garbage cans by large Andre the Giant size school bullies.

His crime to deserve this was nothing; in his young life, he was mostly an outcast. He kept to himself and read poetry books and drew pictures of animals, mainly tropical birds, mostly in his spare time. Hardly saying a whisper to anyone among his classmates, the teasing continued, and he would not respond to the severe psychological abuse he faced on a daily basis because he did not know how.

The other children saw him as mentally challenged, but this was not true. He would just go emotionally cold, and he would psychologically lock himself up in his own mind and thoughts, he could not handle the abuse so he ignored his peers on purpose, but he started to have the visions even before his elementary school years. He never said a word about it to anyone becausehe just didn't know how. The dreams of fallen angels and pious winged agents of Christ continued to grow stronger with each passing new year, and he also began to experience his nightmares, visions of the past millenniums, and he saw many famous events that had happened far back in the ancient world, which included the crucifixion of Jesus of Nazareth, the green crown of brittle sharp thorns that pierced the Lord's brow with cuts, blood, water, and sweat digging into his flesh.

The pain was beyond excruciating for this man as the Roman soldiers mocked him. Darren could see the Lord being whipped by spiked ropes, His body cut to bits of hanging pieces of flesh and blood flowing out of his veins like a river of pain. Darren flashed forward to see when they took the iron rusted nails and hammered them into palms of flesh of the Son God, and Darren, though a not religious man, felt utter terror and sorrow, and he not could understand why, but he had tears running down his face and he wept.

Then he was transported like being shot through a portal of fire to the infamous burning of Rome that was caused by the evil Emperor Nero.

He saw the accension of the Savior himself floating up into Paradise with the Twelve Apostles who saw the miracle happen before their very eyes, and it was just as if Darren himself was transported back in time, 3,000 years ago, observing these strange events with the disciples side by side.

Among these holy servants of God who saw these historic moments happen many millennia ago. This phenomenon he began to experience was as early as the age of just three years old. When he was but a little boy, he tried to explain to his mother and father the horrors and monsters he saw either awake or asleep before his eyes during the day, all the day and all the night. The visions came about every two hours, and it was like some kind of mysterious divine force was trying to reach him, and yet he felt within his very soul that it was also protecting him from unknown harm at the same time.

These strange questions of what this power he had acquiredrang like a bell in his mind. As he got older, he tried to wake up to realize that he was different, and for the most part he was meant to be different. Normalcy was a foreign word to him that had little to no meaning in the real sense. Perhaps it was some awful hand of fate that guided him and not simply delusion, which was what his family had come to believe.

During the coming days, he got out of his little turtle shell of an apartment loft and went down to the local public library to apply for jobs on the internet; he applied for anything and everything he could get his desperate hands on: Clerical Work, Janitorial Positions, Fast Food Preparation Jobs, Waiter Jobs, Bussing Dirty

Dishes, Security Guard gigs— he even attempted applying for those shady jobs on Craigslist to donate his sperm for few quick bucks, but to his surprise all the employers responded in the same exact answer: "Over Qualified and a low sperm count," they said.

But that didn't stop him from pushing forward. Persistence and stubbornness was the key. He dumbed down his resume and lied during interviews to get any job he could, but the answer was still the same.

Even though he had seven years of solid general work experience under his belt, and an additional background in professional commercial illustration for sleazy rock-and-roll night clubs and music production companies, he started taking temp jobs in mail rooms at a few low-paying television agencies to grind out a living.

He worked long overtime shifts over a period of eight months and was able to make a fair living, but unfortunately, during the coming winter month of December, the job ended abruptly and without any notice given, despite the coming Christmas holiday. This was horrible timing.

Most of the staff was let go due to budget concerns, and he felt like dog shit on the day he handed in his pink slip, despite all his hard work and the respectful attitude he maintained at all times to his employer and coworkers.

Unfortunately, the job only paid him as an independent contractor and that meant no unemployment benefits, and with the monies already gone to pay the current month's rent, he had just enough to cover for basic utilities and having some decent food in his home.

To keep himself busy from getting angry, he began to paint again and began to expand his work based on new visions and nightmares he was experiencing, and this time the dreams had a more fantasy-world tinge and was less religious, so he went down to the farmers' markets and the horror film conventions to sell his work.

He was able to make enough to money to last him another month, but after paying all the months expenses to get by, he had only $100.00 in his savings account, and it was not enough to make ends meet.

His anger and depression came back, and he began to fantasize, morbidly curious, about killing people to get back at the society and the world that cheated him out the basic human right to survive and live with some human decency. He fantasized about killing everyone. He wanted to chop them up into little pieces and choke the life out of them.

He visualized these dark thoughts, not for pleasure, but just because he wanted others to feel the same pain and suffering that he felt. He wanted others to learn the meaning of society's cruelty, and maybe then this wretched world could change, but he knew in his heart that if he began to act such thoughts out in reality, he would have no career or future. If he did harm anyone, he would not get away with it, and he would be rotting on death row or be taking a dick up his ass and then be killed by fellow inmates in San Quentin.

So he decided to put these hellish desires to good use by writing crime stories of his own fictionalized villains as serial killers, and he also took an interest in crime-related news article, stories of traditional Satanism in various murder cases and instances of ritualistic human sacrifice, and he also became curious about sorcery and of the tales of witches.

These were not the peaceful white witches who were healers in the traditions of Wicca, but the dark side of magic, of the Left Hand Path systems of demonology and death cults. He began especially to read pulp magazines and weird tales, such as fiction from the demented short stories of H.P. Lovecraft Edgar Allen Poe.

He then started submitting his finished fiction works to various book contests on the internet and in horror magazines, many of which he received recommendations and award nominations for his work, which this made him very happy and the anger left him for a while. Darren began to feel some level of accomplishment, and he was very thankful that he did not make a hasty decision to ruin his future.

He decided he would become a crime-fiction writer and continue to paint his heinous art work on the side. He began to submit his work to different literary agents and publishing houses, and yet while they found great promise with this talented young man, it was hard to take on new writers who were not already commercially well-known.

The book industry had suffered and also changed with many publishing houses closing down in competition to the rise of power in the self publishing industry. The power was no longer in the hands of corporate publishing companies put in the hands of the individual writer and the readers.

But he kept on hoping and kept on writing, including sending out those query letters. This made him very happy, and finally his nightmares and visions were actually helping his creativity, not inhibiting him. But it was still a very hard time.

For just a few days, he landed a day laborer job selling cigarettes off work trucks to construction crews, but that job ended quickly and there was no more work available. He later managed to get an agent for his books, but it fizzled out after a few months, while selling some more paintings to make an income, but the answer from the publishing houses was still the horrible same: "NO! NO! NO! And NO!" he just couldn't get a solid break.

After that, all forms of employment came to a dead halt. The economy had grown worse, and more and more Americans were losing their jobs. For the first time in his life, he began to lose all hope and began to pray often to the God whom he'd rejected in his youth to help him. The rejection was projected at his former faith because of the hardship he had faced for so many years, not knowing how or why it had happened to him.

But now, he did not care. He needed help and he needed it badly, so he prayed and prayed relentlessly for an answer, for some ray of hope for a better future because even to survive was better than to rot in misery or face eviction.

But none came, which made him hate the God of his childhood even more, and then tragedy struck him like lightning hitting a conductor rod during a storm.

At around 3PM on Monday, January the 12th 2015, it would be a day that would forever change not only his life but his entire perspective on life for years to come. It was on a cold winter day, a bitter windy day, so cold that frost appeared on the glass panes of his windows. His heater had broken during the night with his breath becoming like mist, and as he huddled in his black leather jacket, the thick lining was the only comfort he had to keep him warm other than a small bottle of port bar wine and the many lit candles he had that give off little heat.

Darren went downstairs in the main entry way of the building to check his mail at his little mail box slot# 765, and taking his small brass key out and inserting it into the lock, he slowly turned the key as the mechanism inside the mail box unlocked and the door opened. Peeking inside the mail box, he noticed a small telegram letter, and the envelope was dark tan in color and the material that was made of recycled paper that smelled of former super market paper bags, a musty odor and somewhat unpleasant. He pulled out of the metal slot, closed it, and locked it. As he walked back to the old cage elevator lift and pushed the button, and while waiting for it to come down, he carefully tore open to letter and read its message. It was a message that shattered his heart like fragments of glass. It stated:

The Montez Telegram Corporation:
January 12th, 2015
12:00 PM
Los Angeles, CA
Dear Mr. White,
We regret to inform you with our deepest sympathies for your loss at this time. Your father, Marshall J. White, has passed away; he was killed in a car accident this morning while he drove to his office. Funeral services will be held on Thursday January 15th, 2015, at Saint Monica's Catholic Church in Santa Monica, CA. Time of service is 4:00 PM in the afternoon. Mrs. White had contacted us to send this notice to you rush delivery, A.S.A.P. Once again, we send our sincere condolences to you and your family.
Respectfully,
Elisa C. Whitmore
Sr. Dispatch Agent

His whole life just fell to pieces as if someone dropped a priceless Ming vase, shattering it in a million parts. He could not even speak or think, and anger rose in his mind. The throbbing and jarring pain he felt as he heard outside the lobby door as construction workers who were drilling into the sidewalk concrete with a jackhammer.

Blood dripped out of his nose and his ears, and the sound was so physically painful, it was like someone stuck an ice pick right into his brain and twisted it, intensifying his own torture. The visions had somehow increased his senses of hearing and sight as light that shone through the glass entrance door hurt his eyes; the stinging light was as if someone had put rubbing alcohol on his eyelids. It hurt like a bitch.

Then the pain ceased, and he let out a delayed wail as he began to cry uncontrollably, the tears rained down his face like a waterfall as he tasted the bitter sweet salt of them as they touched his lips. His father was dead.

A few days later he attended his father's wake, and the service was over as he sat at in the funeral home looking at his dad's coffin. The lid had to be closed because the body had been too mangled to be seen in the open. The place was empty; everyone who attended the service had gone home, and only his mother and he remained in the room. She stepped outside to have a cigarette to calm her nerves; it had been a tumultuous day.

That night, when Darren came home, he just sat up all night, staring at the flickering light bulb on his ceiling; strangely enough, he had no visions this time. They had stopped completely. He did not speak, he did not sleep; he just sat there and looked at the walls, seeing his hellish world around him.

He would not be able to win his father's approval; the prize was lost. He began to drink heavily after that night, without eating or sleeping very much and went back to writing his books and sketch drawings for his new paintings. It was the only thing that helped him deal with his loss.

His mother's personality changed as well; after the death of her husband, the grief she felt had cause for her to lose her own sanity, and one day, Darren learned from a family friend who wrote to him that his mother was taken by the state to live in a sanitarium. This broke him even more, a millstone tied around his neck, which added additional sorrow to his already fucked up life. This had happened by some strange synchronicity; everything was at least somewhat fine, and now bad things were happening to him from every corner and this strange string of misfortunate events did not seem to want to stop.

Then came the day that he hated most each month: the day the rent was due. That intolerable day. This time, he had no money to pay and he owned very little left to pawn to get that weasel Pratt off his back. Darren had already sold off most of his work to Billy at the shop to take out a loan.

Now, Pratt would show no mercy. Darren was mentally and undeniably fucked in every way possible. Two days later, he was served with an eviction notice in writing by the county, and while Darren could contest it in court to have two additional months to let him stay in his place, he knew that Pratt would make his life a living hell every moment of everyhour just to get him out of his building.

He packed up his last possessions in a small suitcase: the remainders of his clothes, a small steel pocketwatch, a Swiss army knife that he kept for protection, and a small tin flask that he got for a gift on his 26th birthday two years ago. This suitcase was his whole life that he would be living with while in transiency. He held that case in his hands at turned to look one last time at the empty room that he lived in and once called home. All that remained was his memories; even the walls had been repainted bare naked white, a day before by that crusted gezzer Pratt, who was eager to vomit Darren out of his sight forever.

Defeated and humiliated in shame, Darren walked out the door, and a chapter in his life closed as he heard that creaky old door slam shut.

2

Over the next 7 months, Darren stayed at various rescue missions and homeless shelters in the confines of the city; he worked in vain at hustling to try to get a job to get back on his feet, even to work even in a menial position, but no work came in. Destitute and friendless, he managed to scrap food together by stealing from bread trucks in the early hours of the morning on the streets near the supermarket in-take centers which took orders in shipping and receiving after midnight.

He squatted in abandoned rat-filled tenements that had been condemned for years, hoping for what it was worth that just maybe he would have some misfortune, although fortunate for him, if the whole building would collapse on him from an earthquake and bury him, letting him die in peace, but none came.

He wanted to commit suicide, but he didn't have the balls to go through with it. During the days, he begged for change on the street and ate out of garbage cans when stealing was not an option. He bathed at the shelters to keep clean and to avoid catching skin diseases, and then one day he said to himself in his frustration and anger: "I have had enough of this shit! I swear to all of Heaven and Hell, if there is such a place. Curse the damn day my parents banged and had me! God, I hate you! You unfair asshole in the sky! What did I ever do to you? I'll make it even if I have to give blow jobs and take it in the ass on the street! I'll rob and kill people! Fuck you all! FUCK YOU ALL!" he screamed at the world as he wept without a bit of pity left in his heart for anyone else or himself.

He loved nothing and no one else anymore. The only thing he could love was enacting retribution on anyone who crossed his path. He was forsaken and he knew it; his parents were taken from him, his dreams were taken, his very human dignity was taken from him. He was lifeless, like a walking, soulless corpse.

And then the visions returned, more terrifying than ever before, but this time there were no beings of light in his sight, only malignant spirits of shadows and darkness whom he saw awake and his dreams, night after cold-blooded night. He started to wonder really if he was what others had been calling him his entire life, a psychopath and secretly a warped man who had the qualifications to become a serial killer in his heart.

He actually never killed anyone before in his waking life, but only in nightmares and dreams of despair that he suffered from so greatly. But Darren knew in his heart that he was not insane at all, and the visions were too real to be a delusion.

There was even one time when recalling his childhood years, he saw a man in a white gown before him for a split second in the corner of his left eye while he crossed the street, and a speeding pick-up truck driven by a drunk driver almost hit him, but miraculously, he was pulled out of the way by unknown hands that he felt jerk him to the sidewalk, and when turned around to see who it was that saved him, nobody was there.

He was safe and alive, but he thought that maybe it was all just in his mind. He never really believed much in the afterlife or in angels, for that matter, but maybe, just maybe there had been a reason for this so-called curse he possessed for so long.

But his constant anger clouded his judgment, and the only concern he had was to get out of his problem; he vowed from that moment on, he would do whatever it took to get ahead in life, even if he had to lose every shred of his humanity and morality to achieve the success he craved so badly.

All he ever really wanted in life was to be loved and to find acceptance, even if it had been from just by one person only, someone to share a tender moment of compassion and warmth with; that would have meant the whole world to him. But no one cared. He wanted to have a friend and was filled with sorrow each day.

The loneliness and empty life he led was enough to drive the sanest man to madness. Even if Darren could find a stray dog for a pet to ease his emotional loss, that would have given him some level of affection, and he could have appreciated that. He could relate to the suffering of that poor animal who also did not have a home, and he could have given it love in return that it needed, much more easily than giving compassion to selfish human beings in this cruel, miserable world which treated him and many others like him; they were nothing more than garbage, just because they were homeless. Sad that he was treated that way.

What crime did he commit to endure so much suffering? What evil had he committed? He began to take notice of the kind of harsh treatment among the street people that was inflicted upon them by the regular citizens who appeared to have meaning in their own lives. Darren watched as he saw these types of people who abused other homeless souls like him. They spat on him, cursed him, calling him a loser and a bum. "Why can't you get a job?" they said, mocking him, not even understanding his situation or others, or how they got into the situation that they were in.

Darren tried to understand the nature and discrimination of his plight as he would talk once in a while to other members of the homeless community. A few new faces here and there were who became familiar acquaintances with. Many of the other homeless folks he would sometimes congregate with and talk to were young people just like him, and many had lost their jobs, or came from broken and abusive homes that they were desperate to escape, and they wanted to find the freedom and acceptance that they wept for, just like he did.

He felt sorry for his fellow brothers and sisters of the streets, and he was like them, and they were like him. Abused, unloved, and unwanted by a world of conceited assholes that did not care. Treated like shit for no reason at all.

Darren began to see things differently; the world was evil and a cold place to exist in. Where was the dignity and compassion from his fellow man who should do the loving moral deed to help others, as in the past when he always tried to help out others in need? He never asked for anything in return, not even a thank you. Doing a kind deed was enough reward for him.

Did people even have a sense of honor and humility in them? The answer to him seemed to be no. It angered him that no one would even lift a finger to help him or the other street kids like him, kids who just wanted to find a job and have a place to live. An honest job, with honest pay and decent hours to make a simple living: was that so much to ask for?

Darren did not understand why. What did he do wrong to deserve such a mean existence? Did he kill someone in a past life, if he had one? Did he break the heart of girl in his past and never make restitution for it? Even if he did, he always tried to makes things right with the people he had hurt. But that was long ago.

His heart was crushed with grief. What force was it that drove him to suffer this way, and why was his life so hard? He thought about these things and often compared his situation with other people he met who were in similar scenarios. Decent people like him were also stepped on by society, for no reason at all.

He just did not understand, and of course the question that stuck in his head constantly was this simple little irritating whisper: *WHY?* He used to be innocent, kind, and understanding in his personality a few years before, but his heart became hardened with bitterness. The innocence was lost, and only instinct and a will to survive remained: the most debased primordial urges of a human being consumed with a limitless hunger inside which needed to be fed, a deep hunger.

Over the next week, Darren made a contact at a popular bar named Vicenza's in Beverly Hills, a place that he would sometimes frequent to make connections in the art world, despite being home-less. With a bit of ingenuity, he managed to clean up his appear-ance and shave to look presentable, and he took his only clothes left down to a local Laundromat and pressed his shirts and pants and shined his shoes to go network and make connections in public.

Scrounging up some cash from selling off his drinking flask and his pocket watch, he managed to purchase a second-hand black cotton business suit with a collared shirt and black tie from a vintage thrift store near his squat, and he also printed up some business cards for pennies on the dollar, advertising his services as a male escort.

Though not very sociable in his former private life, he learned to fake it until he made it, pretending to be a man of class and of substance, not with material things, but with wit and charm.

He also learned how to influence others while studying self help books at the public library and the black hat techniques and strate-gies from Pick Up Artist manuals and How-To sex books to seduce any woman he could, as well as men.

Sex was an activity not unfamiliar to him. He was born with large endowments and was a good lover with the past girlfriends he had relationships with back in college; he often worked out at the local community center which had a free gym for anyone to use at their leisure. He did this to keep fit and so he increased his muscle tone, and he also used the swimming pool at the facility to keep a lean physique; he had to because of the diet he was living on at the time, which consisted of store shelf Ramen and canned dog food that was anything but healthy.

He thought about applying as an actor in the adult film in-dustry, but the idea of having his face plastered on the plastic box porno covers of Blu-Ray and DVD discs in every novelty sex shop soured that idea, so escorting was better for him, and so that is how he turned out in his new lifestyle so to speak, leaving the idea of killing people out of it, which was a stupid idea he did not choose to embrace.

He began to pick up clients of all kinds: businessmen who wanted a different type of sexual experience, attractive and rich house wives who were bored out of their minds in their weak marriages, college girls who wanted to screw for the sake of it by being enthralled with a hunk that was gifted with a big cock, even couples both gay and straight who wanted to have sessions together at private sex parties.

It did not matter to Darren, though; if they had the cash, he would give up the goods, and he would please his clients better than the ladies who worked in professional Nevada whorehouses.

He was just good at what he did, and he what he was good at was fucking. He actually started to like having sex with multiple partners. It became to him the supreme thrill, a sport in reality and, oh boy, how the money started to roll in.

He was making an average of $7,000 dollars a month, and that financial cushion was able to provide him with a nice comfortable lifestyle and a fairly upper class apartment in West Hollywood. But that was small pickings for him, and he wanted more.

Wanting more money and more power, he started dealing cocaine on the side with the contacts he made at the racetrack who were involved with crooked gangsters and shady film producers in the movie industry. Crime was paying and paying well, and more cash flowed to him like striking gold in a vein of solid rock. His investment in debauchery was paying off, and the school of hard knocks became his true education about life; however, he still felt lonely at times and did not have a woman in his life to love him.

He started to long for a companion, but then again, who in their right mind, least of all a respectful person, would date – much less marry – a career male gigolo drug dealer.

In his spare time, Darren continued to write books. He had about 15 completed novels under his belt, so he decided to switch off genres in crime-fiction and make a move towards the horror and fantasy book market. His nightmares lessened and the visions lessened as well.

They were still morbid and sick, but he kept the ideas for new stories and characters and used them in his books. He also began to paint again in his spare time, but he decided to paint things of beauty in contrast to cheer up his spirits when he could, and his artistic skills increased to becoming an adept in his side trade.

Maybe now with a little luck, he could become a successful writer and painter for an occupation, and he enjoyed that much more than escorting. He knew a career like that would eventually in time run its course.

3

In November of the following year, he received an invitation for his sexual services at a private function at the home of one of Los Angeles's most prominent women in the finance world. This included a non-disclosed contract signed and dated by him to be completely confidentially about this engagement. He would not be allowed to talk about it to anyone. His client was strict on such details.

Her name was Veronica Mathers, a respected socialite and a very attractive woman in her early 30s who worked as a successful entrepreneur with multiple businesses, being a multimillionaire included. This private venue she would be throwing the party in was a fancy home which she owned, and which was one of many out in the Hollywood Hills.

It was a cool and calm Saturday evening, and Darren was actually excited to attend this party. Work was a pleasure to him and he longed to make some new friends.

Most nights, when he was not servicing clients, he kept his personal life in total confinement. He may have acquired a new way of life, but the old Darren still lived more in loneliness than ever, strange as that may seem: a gigolo who was also a recluse and a shut-in.

Ever since his father's death, it was hard for him to get close to anyone, though he faithfully went to visit his mother often at the mental hospital where she was staying, but her health had begun to drastically deteriorate and her mental cognisance was slipping fast away. She could barely recognize who her son was, having to ask him his name two or three times to recollect a memory of some kind.

The poor woman would be dead in a few months, and doctors said it was a combined condition of heart and lung disease from all the years Michelle had smoked, which dug her an early grave, but this was understandable and Darren was able to accept it. It made him give up cigarettes for good, and he completely stopped drinking for the betterment of his own health for a time; cold turkey worked effectively well.

That night, the party was to begin late around 10PM, so Darren prepared himself around 8:30 with his beautification routine to look his best. He started out using a delicate face cleaner to absorb any oils in his pores, then an expensive protein enriched hair shampoo in the shower, and after that, he got out a citrus balm cream which he applied as face mask and left on for ten minutes to smooth his skin.

Then he finished with cleansing himself and drying off with soft almond colored towel, and he dressed to the nines in a slick Italian Valentino suit and applied to his face lightly an expensive cologne, a rare edition of Clive Christian C vintage, established 1872, a luxurious scent meant for Chippendale gods of glamour.

Around 9:15, he was out the door, looking like a movie star and feeling very good in a manner of spirits. he had heard good things about this client from other gentleman callers in his trade, and other than the obvious, normally Ms. Mathers paid very well, and a business contact like her could also mean other open avenues of opportunity.

The taxi swung by three minutes later, checkered cab special, and he hopped in and reclined in the cushy back seat of the car. Darren prepared himself mentally for his work to meet his hostess for the night's festivities.

"Where to?" asked the cabbie, a young Persian man with short black hair and light goatee on his face.

"2450 Solar Drive, Hollywood Hills," said Darren.

"Right away," said the cabbie as they drove off out their destination.

As the minutes passed, Darren looked through his side window glass, looking at the bright lights from neon lit signs of the city, their reflection bouncing on the glass like in a mirror, and he turned his attention to road in front of him and checked his watch; he did not want to be late.

"You know that address you want to go to? That house I mean has quite a history here in LA," said the cabbie.

"How so?" asked Darren, puzzled.

"That mansion has had a quite a share of guests over the last few years, and I heard it was just purchased about a month ago," said the cabbie.

"What so odd about that? Lots of people buy real estate all the time," said Darren, unconvinced.

"Not this place. The place we are headed to was rumored to be built on Indian burial ground, and from what I've read in the news, it's had its mix of drug addicts, to gang bangers, to weekend Satanists doing devil worship rituals in there; they say that the compound is haunted if not cursed, and many people have died in that house. I even heard one story that a man was murdered there in the billiards room," said the cabbie

"Probably just a tabloid story and even if it wasn't, you have no idea what demons really are," said Darren.

"What do you mean?" asked the cabbie.

"Trust me, you don't want to know," said Darren.

"Whatever you say. I don't mind, as long as my meter is running," said the cabbie in reply.

Half an hour later, the cab arrived up the cold paved hill on Solar Drive, and the street was lit only by the lights that were turned on from inside the mansion; under the pitch black sky, the stars shined like diamonds, and Darren could see them from at this height in the mountains that displayed an overview of Los Angeles and the Hollywood sign on the other side of the hillside.

"Here it is. Welcome to the Hollywood House from Hell, " teased the cabbie.

"Spare me the jokes, man. How much do I owe you?" asked Darren annoyed.

"$55.00," said the cabbie.

Darren pulled out his leather wallet from his inner coat pocket and handed the driver $65.

"There you go, plus the tip," said Darren.

"Thanks. Enjoy your night, " said the cabbie.

"Hey, what's your name?" asked Darren feeling a little sorry for being rude to the driver.

"Arman. What's yours?" said the cabbie.

"Darren," replied Darren with a half smile on his face. "Thanks for the warning, Arman. Have a good night," said Darren.

"Anytime. See you around," said Arman, smiling, and with that, Darren got out and shut the back passenger door behind him. He walked toward the main front door of the mansion as the taxi sped off in the darkness.

Knocking on the front door, he rang the bell to let the partiers inside know of his presence. The door was opened by a ravishing enchantress, a fiery red haired angel of a woman, dressed in a peacock feathered dress and wearing a jeweled diamond necklace around her neck and hanging ruby earrings from the short lobes of her pierced ears.

She was so enticing; her eyes glowed a vibrant green like that of pure jade, her lips were red as blush lip gloss, and her nose was short and perfectly proportioned; she had creamy soft skin full of vitality and grace. She had naturally long fingernails that were painted dark aqua to match the colors of her dress, on her right ring finger she wore a rare black pearl ring.

"Good evening, Miss. I'm Mr. White. Darren White," said Darren poised extending his hand as she extended hers with warm handshake.

" My name is Veronica: Veronica Mathers," she said, smiling lusciously.

"Charmed. Thank you, my dear, for inviting me," said Darren politely kissing her hand like a gentleman.

"You have manners. I am glad you have respect for our elite kind," said Veronica.

"Of course," he said.

"Excuse me, please come in. My other guests, I'm sure, will be delighted to meet you," said Veronica.

"This is quite a mansion you have here, Ms. Mathers," said Darren admiring the sixteen-century antiques that layered this large home, including an arrangement of French furniture which included a large comfy sati couch, leather trim chairs in the study, and a grandfather clock that was made in 1899.

They walked into the main parlor living room that had separate leather sitting chairs and a large sofa with a brass counter top bar on the side stocked with bottles of expensive champagne, Don Perignon and Louis the 13th cognacs, including a vast collection of aged wines that even the pickiest connoisseur could savor.

"Call me Veronica; you don't have to be so formal here. Tonight is just for us all to have some fun," she said seductively wrapping him around her fingers, as she kissed him on the lips freely, no modesty needed; it was a very enjoyable way to start the night.

"Hungry for action so quickly," said Darren, impressed by her skills. Her lips tasted sweet like sugar coated strawberries.

"Not yet," she teased. "Later. right now let's have a drink, shall we? My friends you will like," she said.

"Certainly," said Darren politely as Veronica ushered him to meet her other young guests, who all were vainly attractive in their late 20's to early 30's.

"Darren, I would like you to meet Mr. James Barnesworth, Vice President of TechWare Enterprises," said Veronica.

"A pleasure to meet you," said James, extending a warm handshake.

"The same to you," said Darren

"So, what it's like to be an executive for a computer firm? " asked Darren curiously.

"It's an enjoyable business to be in; we mostly design new type of micro processors in competition with IBM and Apple Macintosh. But our specialty and my personal choice is programming and development in video games for next generation console systems; it's a good trade," said James.

"That's great. You have a very fun job; that's pretty cool," said Darren, intrigued.

"We try to keep it that way," said James. "So what do you do?" continued James.

"I provide dating services to lonely ladies," said Darren, half joking.

"A player; very nice, very nice," said James

"It's interesting work, but actually my true passion is writing novels and painting," said Darren.

"Are you published?" asked James.

"I would like to be; I am trying to get a new agent at this time," said Darren.

"What type of books do you write?" asked James

"Horror, fantasy, crime and mystery mostly; I have 15 finished to date," said Darren.

"That's good. Everyone likes a scary story. You should be famous," said James

"The dream lives on," joked Darren with a certain dryness.

"What about your paintings?" asked James.

"They are intesteresting. My style is a cross between the sacred and profane, you could say. It's very dark art, but I have a talent with morbid subjects, so I paint them," said Darren, poised.

"I would like to see some of that sometime, if you don't mind," said James.

"Are you a collector?" asked Darren curiously.

"Yes, actually I am. I have a passion for exotic paintings of all kinds, including rare sculptures; there is a good market for it with certain museums. I also am friends with some of the biggest gallery owners in Los Angeles as well as in New York," said James.

"I would be more than pleased to show some to you. That makes me very happy; thank you so much," said Darren gratefully.

"Excellent," said James, handing Darren his business card, and Darren handed him his.

"Will you come and see me?" asked James

"Oh yes, I will be more than happy to," said Darren.

"Fabulous. Come see me next month, right before Christmas, and I'll see what I can do for you, though it may take time to get you into a gallery— if you're work is as good as you say it is," said James.

"It is; trust me. Thank you very much, James; you're extremely generous," said Darren, amazed by such a random act of kindness from a complete stranger who he'd just barely met.

"Don't worry about it. The world needs good culture," said James, smirking.

"Oh, forgive me. Here are our other friends," said James to Darren.

"This is Monica Stevens and Bartolommeo Peters, head executives to the Sanderson Banking Corporation; Monica, Bartolommeo: this is Darren— I am sorry; I did not catch your last name," said James to Darren.

"White, Darren White," said Darren nervously.

"Nice to meet you, Mr. White," said Bartolommeo

"How do you do," said Darren in return.

"Hi," said Monica.

"So how did you come to meet Veronica?" asked Monica.

"I heard about her from a mutual acquaintance of mine by the name of Jay Thompson, " said Darren.

"Oh, that is right; Jay comes to our monthly events now and then," said Monica.

"You mean these special gatherings are held often?" said Darren.

"As often as we like. This small group is sort of little social club of ours; it has its function in making business contacts and satisfying, shall we say, other appetites," said Monica.

"So I've heard," said Darren.

"Then you understand the discretion of you being here this evening; normally, we do not invite outsiders to these meetings," said Bartolommeo.

"Yes, I understand," said Darren.

"That is good," said Bartolommeo firmly.

"Is there anyone else attending tonight?" continued Darren.

"No, it's just us, but there is some other guests here, there in the other room enjoying a few cigars and drinks," said Bartolommeo.

"Ladies and gentlemen, if I may have your attention, please," said Veronica ringing a little bell she had on the bar top.

The other guests, consisting of three men and five ladies dressed in black tie, heard the summons and came into the room immediately, as if waiting to be commanded by the mistress of ceremonies.

"I would like to propose a toast, to our recent success in our takeover of Jamestown Industries; as of this momement, our think tank collective is now the proud owner of 99 % of our previous competitor's stock, and we are making a killing," said Veronica smiling spitefully.

The other guests clapped their hands in jubilation and raising their glasses, sipping a superb $15,000 1999 chardonnay.

"Thank you; now then, let's have a change of focus; it's time to indulge in tonight's affairs, turn up the music, and let the good times roll," she said charismatically.

One of her other guests turn up the volume on the jukebox in the room, with a selection of smooth jazz that help turn up the heat for passion play.

They began to slow dance with each other, guests with other guests, men and women, and men with men: slow romantic play, gentle yet very robust.

"Darren, come here, "ordered Veronica softly.

Darren obeyed as he set down his drink and took Veronica in his arms and danced with her. He was surprised by her transparency, even surprised how almost instantly she was smitten by him, and he became smitten with her, as they danced in the dimmed down room with lights fading to provide a touch of elegance.

As the night proceeded, the raw energy flowed, filled with wanton nudity, sexual games of passion, and hot and heavy ecstasy. Darren pleasured everyone one of them, including Veronica, in voracious foreplay and action, the women screaming with passion until they reached climax, the men kissing their large breasts and ejaculating on the ladies' bodies, driving the ravenous women to beg for more and more. There were ven orgies, as this had their limits of respect, for these women were not pieces of meat to be consumed without regard, but they were to be given devotion of equal voice and desire to be fulfilled.

By three in the morning, the party was over, the guest had already cleaned themselves up and tidied up the room; it was late and Veronica was exhausted from all the sexual playing, too tired to show her guest the door.

Darren took over and thanked them for coming and for inviting him, and they all were well pleased with his services and each paid him a large check. In combination, he made $20,000 that night, just one night worth of work.

After they left for the remainder of the wee hours in the early morning, Darren saw Veronica sprawled out on her couch still partially naked and covered with a white bath robe after bathing a half hour earlier, and he lifted her up in his arms as she slept and carried her off to a bedroom he saw nearby in the next room, tucking her in like a gentleman as she slept soundly. He left his card on her nightstand and went down stairs to sleep on the couch, and he was too tired to call a cab and assumed that Veronica would not mind. In truth, if he had asked she wouldn't have minded, so he found a clean couch in the study and rested as he was dressed in his clothes, after hours of pounding multiple orifices away, and he decided to break his pledge to himself and have a small nightcap by pouring himself a glass of brandy, sipping it slowly.

Then he fell asleep soundly. This time he did not dream at all; it was a peaceful sleep, something he had not had for years.

At around 9'o clock in the morning, on a sunny fine day, he awoke and decided to do something nice for his host by preparing her breakfast in the kitchen. Darren was very good as a cook, and he enjoyed cooking in his spare time at home; He prepared a lovely plate of fresh gourmet hot cakes loaded with black berries and freshly made whipped cream with a saucer of sweet butter cream and pure maple syrup on the side. He also prepared some organic turkey bacon in an iron skillet with two fluffy white eggs, sunny side up and a cup of fresh black coffee, French roast. As he set the plate of food and the coffee on a carrying tray and brought it to Veronica's room, as she just was barely waking up.

"Good morning, Veronica," he said

"Good morning. Oh, how thoughtful of you, Darren. You're so kind to do this for me. I thought you went home with the others last night; I was so tired, and I apologize for passing out," she said.

"Nonsense. Here have some breakfast; it will give you some strength," said Darren as he poured her coffee for her from a metal coffee pot.

"You made this for just little old me?" she asked.

"It's just my way of saying thank you for the business and for a wonderful time last night, if you'll excuse the expression; you are a good lay in bed. I think we both came five times in a row," said Darren

She chuckled.

"Your guests paid me very well. It's a pleasure doing business with you, and I hope I can be of assistance for you again in the near future," said Darren.

"Of course; you will be. Go to my dresser and you will see a check that is already signed and dated for you sitting on top of it. I wrote it out in advance last night, but I was too exhausted to give it to you at the end," she said.

"That's alright, I understand," he said as he went to main dresser which had a makeup mirror and picked up the check on it. The amount was for an additional $5,000 dollars.

"Thank you very much, Veronica," said Darren gratefully.

She began to dine and taste his food.

"This is delicious; you cooked this?" she asked.

"Yes I did; my Italian grandmother taught me to cook when I was younger," he said.

"You know, I could use a personal assistant here at home; my work schedule is very busy," she insinuated.

"You mean a butler?" he asked.

"Something like that. Personally, I'm too tired to cook and clean when I come home. Besides, you know how to take care of me already sexually. I would not mine the company at all," she said.

"You live alone," he asked.

"Yes, and it gets very lonely here at times. For a girl like me, I get sad sometimes. I like you," she said, soft-spoken.

"So this arrangement then is a mix of business and pleasure; is that what you want from me?" he asked openly.

"Plainly speaking, yes. If you would take the offer, I'll pay you a good salary. The arrangement would be that you would work exclusively for me and no one else, and what I ask you to do, you will obey me as my personal servant and continue to please me and my guests at parties like the one you experienced last night," she said.

"What about money?" he asked. To Darren, business was still business.

"Well, that's easy. How much would you like to make each month, including with your additional skills?" she asked.

"Butler and in-house lover, hmm; let me see. How's about $180,000 a year flat? No additional charges for extra services provided. I'll even work for you on holidays. 7 days a week, whatever you would like?" he said.

"That's fine; done. It will be more appealing than your current status of employment and more steady too. Wonderful, and of course you will have to give notice to your current place of residence about your move. I will make the arrangement for you to transfer here in about a week. Does that sound reasonable," she asked.

"Of course it does, and thank you for your patronage. I appreciate it," he said as they shook hands sealing the deal on this new business relationship.

Darren had just moved up in status. This was good for him and for his employer; the short time Veronica had spent with him in session had not only appeased her lust for sex but a lust really for true companionship. Money could not buy love, but it could buy pleasure, and he was the perfect lover. Out all the men she had over the last few years, he was the best in his performance she had ever had, and so a new life for Darren White was about to begin: a life of power and success, and his hunger was being satisfied and so would be hers. It would be a partnership of no limits.

4

Over the next few months, Darren worked his magic on Veronica, and she equally worked hers on him: pleasing each other and he her guests often at her monthly sex parties and in daily life as a personal butler and house chef.

Their relationship grew into something much more than just professional; even with passions came limits, but to both of them, they had begun to truly fall in love, madly in love.

Through Veronica's connection to Mr. Barnesworth, she was able to get Darren signed to various prestigious art galleries in Los Angeles, New York, and even a few medium-sized ones in Chicago, and Darren was painting like a madman every day and selling more works of art faster than he could paint them.

He also was finally signed to a boutique book publisher which gave him decent distribution to major corporate and independent book stores across the country, along with a handsome advance for all his works. He was doing book signings at least twice a month and interviews for many celebrity magazines such <u>Life</u>, <u>Time</u>, <u>People</u>, <u>Rolling Stone</u> and art house web 'zines; he had become what his family had never believed in: a super star author and artist.

He had proven them wrong, and it made him happy to know that for once in his life, he was given the respect, recognition, and the basic humanity that he had craved so desperately for close to 30 years; his days as an outcast were far behind him.

In that time, he formed close friendships with Veronica's guests at their parties, not just for sexual activity but also in daily life, and he would do anything for them for them as his friends, and they were just as loyal to him. He was happy, but it even made him happier to please others selflessly, especially Veronica; she was his goddess, his queen, his raison d'etre. He loved her so much and she loved him.

Darren was soon becoming a very wealthy man, and to show his appreciation for his success, he began to give back to society by donating large sums of cash to the many charities in Los Angeles for the homeless and needy in his spare time, and he even founded a special non-profit organization called The Hope for the Homeless Foundation, which would empower thousands of homeless people in Los Angeles, especially those stuck in the tents on Skid Row, to provide them with proper public housing, medical services that they were unable to receive before, free collegial education courses to help them better their own futures, and paying employment to give them jobs and hope for a better future.

That was something the government cared less about. He knew what living on the streets was like, and he vowed to help everyone as much as he could. He was filled with much compassion for others, and he hated to see anyone suffer in pain, and the desire he once had to destroy life was long departed from him.

Now he would use his money and power to save others who could not save themselves, and he did this, not to receive recognition, but because he generally felt sorry for others and felt an inner duty to love his fellow man and woman in society, regardless if others did not.

To him, it was an honor. He wanted to avenge others, to give them justice, just as he had desired vengeance for his previous condition. He chose to not flaunt his success like many young pretentious celebrities, but to be a kind and gracious man, even one as immoral as he was in his private life. Although sometimes he was moody, moving between irritable and kind, the public began to see him as a sort of Robin Hood type of folk hero, and he became very respected by many for his humanitarian efforts. He would never return to that old way of life ever again; the future was shining bright.

But Darren White, the former struggling street artist turned mega star, was not exempt from the tragedies of life just as any regular human being. A year later, his mother died and this grieved him much; he felt so stoic, at times that the nightmares came back, and he began to wake up in the middle of the night screaming in convulsions of terror with sweat soaking his bed sheets.

Veronica tried to ask him what was wrong, but he could not bear to tell his horrible secret, and surely she would think him mad and abandon him, so he lied about it and told her that it was just nerves from the pressure of work.

The visions during this whole time for some strange reason stopped altogether, and and it was only dreams of the damned he saw; he saw this time dreams of demons being worshipped by people in black robes who wore bone masks of animal skulls on their heads, and these hideous figures would have sex with these people and drink their blood in these esoteric rites.

These creatures were human-looking in appearance but their eyes glowed inhuman with a raw urgency of abomination, and the dreams always took place in a strange forest temple then he normally would awake, nothing more. Maybe this was a warning, a foreboding sense of some kind of premonition, but Darren thought it was just all in his head, ignoring it like a fool. Something was definitely wrong and he knew it, but he did not have the will to face it, whatever it was, and he buried this sense of dread deep in the recesses of his depraved fragile mind.

However, he cheered up whenever Veronica was around. It was at this time that he purchased an engagement ring to give to his love; he had hope that she would say yes in agreement to marry him, though he was afraid that she would not enjoy to be tied down in a monogamous relationship to have an open sexual life. To his surprise, she said yes, and they planned their wedding, but the arrangement would not be a traditional type of marriage.

It would be an open marriage, but Darren did not mind; they both were corrupted already. Yet he loved her anyway and over all, she was loyal to him; that is all that mattered, and he was loyal to her; the fact was that he loved her for who she was despite of her chosen lifestyle made their love only more intense for each other and their lovemaking more pleasurable. It brought them close to appreciate their relationship and have gratitude to each other about it.

In the master bedroom, it was a very unique room, accessible with treasures from the most wondrous places around Europe and the Far East – almost every article of their furniture came from Italy and Spain imported and hand made by a master wood carver, and the bed frame was intricately designed by the best metal crafters in Rome of molded gold, brass, and copper all in one, and the mattress was made of space foam, soft to the touch and alone was so plush and comfortable that one could get easily lost in it and want to sleep in it forever to dream sweet dreams, and the tall crystal lamps with their beads on the sides of Veronica and Darren's night stands came from France, and the stands themselves were carved and polished mahogany wood from Germany, and on the ceiling above their bed was a small crystal chandelier hand made in Russia, and a large looking glass mirror to the side of the room made of pure gold and silver imported from China, 14th century to be exact;, it once belonged to the famous Emperor Zhu Di, a rare and valuable find indeed.

One night while in bed together, Veronica wanted to ask her fiancé something as they sat up in bed naked, covered by their soft silk sheets. Though at times she was quite a confident woman and very dominant, other times she was insecure and childlike.

"Do you think I am a freak?" she asked, unsure of herself.

"Now, why would you say that, Veronica? I love you with all my heart."

"It just— well, I don't know. It just feels strange?" she said

"What does?" he asked.

"Two lonely people fall in love, two outcasts like us. And well foolish. I guess I'm just wondering about things? You know, life, us, the future," she said.

"I think that you worry too much. And by the way, how are you an outcast?" said Darren.

"I am not like other people. I am just a saucy bipolar girl with a taste for the finer things of life," she said.

"And what is wrong with that? There is nothing wrong with having a little money on the side. Even if you are different, the most brilliant minds in this world are often called crazy, and the difference is they choose to have success, and the ones who want it, babe, go for it. They don't give a shit about other people's views. It's not their business anyway. You deserve to be happy, and I love you."

" You sure about that? A adventurous type of girl like me? Businesswoman by day, nymphomaniac by night; do you still love me?" she joked softly.

"Yes, and a lovely nymph you are. That is why I love you. You're not an outcast; you are a very passionate person. You choose to live life on your own terms like I do. Is there something wrong with that?" he said surprised

"I don't know. I just feel I don't belong sometimes. Do you ever feel that way?" she said.

"I know it very well. But I don't care. The only thing that matters to me is you," he said, smiling at her.

"Your loyalty is commendable," she said.

"Why wouldn't I be? You gave me compassion when no else would. Because of you, I was given a home to share with someone I cared about. The fact is that you're the only person that I actually do care about. Do you even realize what that means to me?" he said.

"I do; I know what you told of your past, and life was hard for you," she said.

"But you have not told me about yours?" he asked.

"There is not much to tell; I was different than most people growing up. I did not grow up in what you would call a normal family," said Veronica.

"What did your dad... you know?" he asked.

"No, it was not anything like that, but it was a different type of life," she said.

"How?" he said

"Do you promise you won't judge me? What I am about to tell you is very, very personal," she said, not sure she should.

"What's wrong?" he asked.

"It has to do with my religious beliefs, what my parents raised me to believe in and practice?" she said.

"What are you a radical Muslim or something?" he asked.

"No, not that extreme, but shocking enough; it would be shocking for most people in traditional society," she said.

"So what do you believe in?" he asked.

"I believe in many things, many worlds, spirits, and beings of all types," she replied.

"Do you believe in God? Not that I do, I'm sort of an atheist when it comes to things like that," he said.

"My parents brought me up as a pagan," she said.

"You're kidding, right?" he said.

"You promised me, remember?" she said.

"I'm sorry; so what are you?" he asked

"I am a practicing grey witch; my parents and grandparents were magicians and shamans also. They were more of medicine men and woman, healers really. Also herbalists to help heal the sick, but they practiced white magic too to help others. We come from a long line of healers, and as a descendant of the old covens in Italy and Ireland, I am a half breed of both cultures, "she said.

"Are you Wiccan?" he asked.

"Not exactly, more of a polytheist and spiritualist; I pray to many different types of god forms and spirits," she said. "The spiritual traditions I follow are mix of the Hellenistic, The Goddess

Diana, Kabalistic, Egyptian, Hindu, and a little bit of angels and the Hebrew god from the Judeo Christian Tradition; combined, it's a syncretistic faith," she said.

"Interesting," he said.

"I am surprised you are not offended," she said.

"Why should I be? I love you, and what you believe in is your own business. Who am I to tell you what your faith should be?" said Darren.

"You're sweet," she said, kissing him on the lips.

"Thanks," He said.

"I'm just curious; have you ever played with that black magic stuff," he asked.

"Once, out of sheer curiosity, and it did not turn out well," she said.

"So how did you become an atheist?" she said.

"I never was into the whole God thing to begin with. But I will tell you, for a person like me who does not believe in such things, I have had my fair share of weird occurrences that have happened to me," he said.

"Like what?" she said, rubbing his bare muscle-bound chest softly.

"Do you promise that if I tell you, that you won't think I'm crazy?" he asked her seriously.

"Darren, you can trust me," she said.

"I saw things. Things that people normally do not see. I saw what people call demons, angels, mystical shit; I don't know. My family thought I was insane, and I mostly came a secular background, even though we went to church often," he said still in disbelief, and yet he somewhat believed after all these years.

"Then you are very mistaken. Don't you realize how gifted you are?" she said, surprised.

"What do you mean?" he said.

"Darren, you have been given great power, a large spiritual gift. You're a natural born prophet, perhaps of a reincarnation of a great god or mystical healer, maybe even a Holy Saint or Ascended Master. I have heard that the Higher Powers have used people like that to do great good in the world, to help others fulfil their divine mission on earth and to heal many people who are dying of illnesses to give them faith and hope," she said

"You call having visions and nightmares almost 24 hours a day, a gift? It's a curse," he said.

"So that is why you were having all the nightmares," she said. "Why did you lie to me?" she asked, disappointed.

"Because I thought if I told you, you would leave me," he said.

"That is ridiculous; I love you, and I would never do that," she said.

"I believe that now. It's just I have been having a strange feeling lately like something really bad is going to happen, and I don't know what it is. Part of me does not want to know," he said.

"Have you tried contacting your guides to help you?" she asked.

"Guides?" he asked.

"Spirit guides; they are the spirits of your loved ones who act as a guardian protector for their living relatives," she said.

"I don't believe in that stuff, but I would do anything do to get rid of the visions, though: anything. I just want to have a normal life and to be with you always," he said.

"You are very kind," she said.

"No, I'm not kind, not really. I do care about others but…"

"But what?" she said inquisitively.

"I'm a stubborn asshole, okay? But I do believe in the decency of helping others. It's called being human," he said.

"*Teach him; he is chosen,*" a voice said in the room with them.

"What the hell was that?" said Darren startled as he jumped out of bed.

"That is my familiar. He normally comes to see me in my dreams, so this is a first time I have heard his voice in the real world," said Veronica, taking it like it was nothing.

"Bullshit! Bullshit! This is not real," he said.

"I am real, human!" said the voice.

"What the fuck!" said Darren shocked.

"You don't believe?" said the voice.

"All right. Cut the jokes; whoever is in here, show yourself, or I am calling the police," he said.

The invisible voice just laughed.

"Hahahaha! A young man. Such a fool," it said.

"What are you? A demon? An angel?" said Darren.

"None of the above," said the voice.

"Then what are you?" said Darren.

"A familiar. I am a dragon spirit. My name is Zagan," said the dragon spirit.

"Then, let me see you," barked Darren agitated.

"No, you will not see me unless I allow it," said Zagan

"Okay, I am not crazy, and I just heard that?" said Darren.

"No Darren; you never were crazy. You have had a great gift your entire life, and you have vast powers to help others," said Zagan. "Powers that you do not realize you possess; listen to Veronica, and she can teach you the control this power if you choose. The gods have chosen you, even the god of your parents' faith wants you to use your gifts for good, but only you can decide to take that path; free will is in your hands," said Zagan.

"I don't care about having strange powers! I only want to have a peaceful life with my wife-to-be. If you are a spirit and what you say you are, then take this damn curse away from me," said Darren.

"Are you sure that is all you want me to do for you?" asked Zagan

Darren hesitated and thought for a brief moment.

"No, that's not all. My mother and father are dead. Tell me if they are they in this so called heaven, if there is such a place? I have to know!" said Darren obsessed, craving the truth.

"I will not tell you that, for I do not know. There are many realms of existence that a human soul travels to after physical death. But you can learn of such secrets if you become trained in the magical arts. Will that satisfy your curiosity if you do?" said Zagan.

"I would like to be at peace. If this damn curse will be removed, then I will do it," said Darren.

"Veronica, do you agree to bring him into the light?" asked the dragon spirit.

"Yes, I will train him; it is my duty to teach others the sacred mysteries to have ascend in the Universe," she said.

"I don't care about any sacred mysteries or higher purpose. Just free me from this shit, and I'll do whatever you want," he said angrily.

"A waste of such potential, but that will change in time, " said the familiar spirit, then it departed, and it was only Darren and his lover with him in the room.

Darren just took it in his stride.

"Oh, forget this; I must be out of my damn mind. Good night, babe, " he said.

"You're not," she said.

"Let's just talk about it in the morning," he said, as he closed his eyes and so did she as they went to sleep.

The next morning, Darren and Veronica sat down at the breakfast table still in their bathrobes. Veronica explained to Darren some of the finer points of her Kabbalistic dealings, including different rituals and observances intended to conjure up spirits to seek advice or to do her bidding.

Darren listened intently, but with some hesitation; most of the concepts she explained to him made very little sense to him. What were those "sigils" that she mentioned, or "revibrations" or anything of that sort? How does one summon spirits, and how do they give people piles of gold or mind-blowing sex? Still, if Veronica believed so heavily in this stuff, who was he to judge? Besides, after last night's encounter with the invisible dragon spirit, he was willing to take a leap of faith, especially if it meant finally being rid of his dreams and visions. Still, why would Veronica consider those horrific scenarios that kept repeating in his addled mind a "gift?"

"... So that's how a resting ritual is performed," explained Veronica over breakfast. "I use that almost all the time myself. It's quick, easy, and you don't have to spend anything on easy-listening music or whatever."

"So, how do you start with all this?" asked Darren, puzzled by everything that he was still trying to absorb. Veronica could tell he was confused, and spoke plainly to him.

"If you want to learn about these powers and magical systems, there's only so much I can teach you. You can join my coven. It's based on the traditions of The Golden Dawn's magical system, we call our group the Order of the Black Moon."

"Okay, so it's Black Magick then, right?" asked Darren. He recalled having read about black magick before when researching for his novels.

"Not exactly. There are shades of grey in everything, you know," Veronica corrected him. "Magick is an experimental science and an art, in causing change with our mental and spiritual willpower. But our knowledge only goes so far, but if you stick it out you could become what we call an 'Ipsissimus,' a higher master of the arts."

"What about those dreams I keep having?" Darren stammered. "I never asked for those, and you keep calling it a gift? I never wanted it!"

"Darren, please," Veronica tried to console him. "I think it may be your destiny to undergo training. You've been given these visions for a very good reason, and if you don't learn to channel them and harness your own energy, you'll be out of balance until the day you die."

Darren paused for a moment, swirling his cup of coffee. The black liquid sloshed around in the white china cup, and he heaved a sigh.

"Alright, I'll give it a shot."

"It's not something you 'give a shot,' Darren," Veronica added. "It's something that changes your life forever."

A full moon shone over the graveyard at midnight. The green grassy field was littered with short, squat headstones and tall obelisks to denote the long-deceased people buried beneath. A thin blanket of fog enveloped the field, making the tombstones look as if they were partially dissolving into the mist, anchored in the ground despite the simple truth that they were much anchored. In the distance, in a clearing surrounded by tall, stone-built crypts, a bright orange glow illuminated the nearby headstones.

A roaring fire was built in the centre of the clearing, filled with masses of wood and kindling. Over the hissing, popping sounds of the burning wood, a congregation of black-robed men and women sounded chimes and bells in celebration. These people chanted in different languages, their primal sounds echoing through the night. Darren did not understand anything they were chanting, but Veronica, standing next to him, explained that those chants were Gaelic and Latin, powerful languages in Magick. They were invoking the names of spirits and long-forgotten gods.

Darren stood in the centre of an intricately-drawn circle in the dirt, which was adorned at odd ends with symbols and various letters. Right where his feet were was a five-pointed star. Veronica told him sternly not to move from the centre of the circle. His neck and shoulders were weighed down with a heavy chain, which held a silver amulet over his chest. The amulet was in the shape of a large five-pointed star, similar to the one drawn on the ground at his feet. The metal felt cold and heavy on his neck, even with the thick black fabric robe he wore beneath it.

Around him, the chanting was reaching a fever pitch, with words and evocations that Darren still could not decipher. What he did recognize, though, were the faces of the people around him. He recognized James Barnesworth, Monica Stevens, and Bartolomeo Peters, all of whom were frequent guests at Veronica's parties. Darren never would have suspected that they too were practitioners of Veronica's religion (if he could call it that).

"Brothers! Sisters!" Veronica called out in a suddenly booming voice. The chanting abruptly stopped, as did the chimes and bells. The air became deathly still, and all eyes were fixed on Veronica and Darren. Darren tried to steady his breath, knowing that he was facing a different side to the people he once knew and had sex with. All of a sudden, he felt like a child who stumbled into a lion's den.

"Darren White has the gift of prophecy!" Veronica announced. "He is to become initiated into our sacred Order of the Black Moon! Let him be embraced tonight as our newest neophyte!"

The crowd responded with a loud cheer, as well as some more chants and phrases in their obscure languages. Veronica turned to Darren and stared down at him with a piercing, icy stare from her suddenly illuminated green eyes.

"Darren, do you so swear by all that is, seen and unseen to uphold the tenets of the Black Moon, to hold all knowledge in confidence and to defend the secrecy of the Order and its members, for all the days of your mortal life?"

Darren paused, speechless. He was afraid from all the peering eyes watching over him, illuminated by the roaring fire. The stone crypts now seemed taller than usual, like giant entities looking down at the insignificant human that he was, like a little butterfly trapped in a killing jar.

Veronica winked, and whispered from a corner of her lips *"Say yes."*

Darren caught the hint, and nodded. "Yes!" he asserted.

"Then let us begin the ritual of consecration!" Veronica announced. Turning to Darren, her voice dropped back down to a terse whisper. "Stay in the circle, close your eyes, and don't move a muscle. If you move, everything will go wrong. Don't move and keep the amulet on you. Got it?"

Darren nodded. Around him, the entire congregation took place in different parts of the circle, stepping delicately over the mystical symbols and letters drawn in the dirt. Darren kept his eyes firmly shut, wondering inwardly what was about to happen. He knew that Veronica would let no harm come to him, but his mind conjured up different ideas of something painful, humiliating, or at the very least disgusting, for him to endure. Still, it couldn't have been any worse than what he endured on the streets.

"Sentio. Sentio," the worshippers chanted slowly and methodically around Darren. *"Tenebrae operient velamento diei. Lux lucis, et dissipabitur arcus noctis. Isis, Thoth, Osiris. Egredere. Freya, Aradia. Egredere. Dianam: Egredere. Sentio. Sentio. Sentio. Hoc efficiunt servum novum."*

The congregation kept their hands outstretched before them, pointed directly at Darren in the centre of the circle. Slowly, Darren could feel something start to stir inside his body. He kept himself rigid by Veronica's instructions, but the sensation welling up inside him was becoming too great to ignore, like a sudden stomachache. But this was no more discomfort that started to manifest in his body; even he could tell that those people were doing something to him with those Latin chants. Still, he kept himself solid and unmoving.

Around him, unseen by his shut eyes, the congregation began channeling energy into his body. Beams of unearthly green light shone from their palms and were directed like flashlights into Darren. They each remained as rigid as Darren himself, still chanting the rhythmic, mystical incantations. The fire in the centre of the room continued to burn brightly, but the emerald-green glows from the congregation proved brighter than even the fire.

Again, they chanted, channeling their energy into their neophyte in the centre of the circle. Darren willed himself not to move, not to think about anything at all. But everything in his mind was screaming for relief from the strange sensations in his body. He could feel something moving around in his chest and arms, as if a colony of ants had crawled beneath his skin and were taking over his whole body, organs and all. Every bone, every muscle, every piece of his body was taken by these foreign, bizarre feelings, and it was rapidly becoming unbearable. He let out a slight gasp of pain, but he heard a shrill voice from among the slow, steady chants: *"Don't open your eyes!"*

Veronica's rule about not moving was being ignored. Darren tried to move his left arm, as if to shake away some of the unseen spirits squirming beneath his flesh. Around him, the congregation kept their stances and more energy flowed into him. Above the congregation's heads, ghostly faces began to appear, constantly morphing shapes and expressions. These vaporous, amorphous, and glowing green entities looked down at their new neophyte, eager to use him as a vessel in the earthly plane of existence. Darren broke into spasms and released an agonized wail that drowned out the sounds of Latin chanting.

"No more!" he begged vehemently. "What are you doing to me?!"

"Enough!" Veronica shouted. The congregation stopped chanting, and lowered their hands. The energy flows halted, and the ghostly faces vanished. The green glow was gone, and the only light by which they could see was the now dying bonfire in the centre of the clearing. Darren fell to the ground, sprawled over the five-pointed star drawn in the ground. His body broke into uncontrollable spasms and he was retching violently. Veronica quickly moved to his side and crouched down near him.

"Are you alright?" she asked. "The initiation can be like that for some people. You'll feel better soon."

Five days had passed, and Darren still was not better. Those outlandish feelings of insects burrowing through his body still happened (though with less frequency and less intensity as that fateful night). Most mornings were spent vomiting in a toilet and trying desperately to clear away the ghostly images that clouded his vision. He could see floating, formless orbs of sparkling white hovering above himself and Veronica. Sometimes they would move in his way such that it would be the only thing he could see. Veronica herself could not see any of what Darren saw, and she tried to console him as much as she could.

"That's a form of astral projection," she explained. "You're separating your earthly body from your spiritual one, and you're starting to see into different planes of reality. Usually this sort of thing takes years just to be able to see what you're seeing. You just need to control it is all."

Darren seethed with anger. "Why the hell didn't you tell me this was going to happen?!" he demanded.

"It's always different for everyone, I told you," she replied simply. "We should start your training now."

Veronica took Darren by the hand and led him through her opulent mansion to a room in a corner on the ground floor, a place that Darren had never seen before in the year that he lived there. The walls in this room were painted jet-black, and the windows had black curtains over them, so that the only light that was in the room was pouring out of the open door which they entered. Veronica lit some candles lining the room with a small lighter, revealing to Darren a shrine room. The candles were held in small sconces on the walls, giving Darren the impression of a medieval dungeon. A wooden altar stood in the centre of the room, about three feet tall, and adorned with stacks of cards, scraps of paper, and several small quartz crystals. She took the crystals and placed them each in the four corners of the room, then invited Darren to come to the altar.

"Let's try to get a harness on your astral travels," said Veronica. "Place your hands on the altar."

Darren did so without hesitation.

"Now, repeat after me: I am master of my element. I assert control over my spirit and command it to return to me."

Darren repeated the words over and over, but his vision was still filled with the strange shapes. He could even catch glimpses of hooded, humanoid figures on the very edge of his vision. These shapes looked back at him with two glowing red eyes. Darren started to panic, but Veronica held his hands firmly.

"Concentrate, Darren," Veronica coached him. "Focus your energy and put some *oomph* into it."

Darren repeated the phrase with more force, and gradually his vision began to clear up. The glowing orbs and dark figures began to fade away in his sight. He sighed with relief when all he saw before him was Veronica.

"Better?" she asked.

"Better," he replied.

"Good. Just be careful with things like that. Astral projection can go really wrong really fast. If you don't assert control, you could wind up losing your spirit in the ether, and I don't think I need to tell you how bad that is."

Darren nodded.

"Okay, now that everyone has their spirits in the right place, let's try some Tarot card reading. This is very basic stuff, and it's kinda fun, too."

The next few hours were spent at the shrine doing Tarot readings with each other. Darren learned the exact placement of the cards on the altar, and what each of the images meant. Ones such as "The Fool" and "The Lovers" were simple enough for him, but others were more abstract, such as "Death," "Judgment" and "The Tower." Veronica explained that each of them had a purpose, and that they take a certain degree of focus to interpret them in the right ways for the right people.

Later, Veronica opened a door in the back of the room, showing to Darren her library. The black walls were overtaken by shelves of old leather-bound books with titles emblazoned in gold on their spines. Darren squinted in the light from the candles in this room, struggling to read some of the titles, such as the <u>Berateth Kalek,</u> the <u>Necrosectorum,</u> and the <u>Yat Utanyat.</u>

"This is where I learned everything that I know," said Veronica, looking over all her books. "There is knowledge of this world and every other world and everything in between all to be found here. Things that even you, with your wild imagination, could barely even believe. Give it some time and practice, and all this could be yours, and you could command wealth and power like no other."

"Wealth and power?" Darren asked, curiously.

"Wealth and power, and then some," Veronica added. "You could raise up spirits, gain hidden insight, maybe even control the forces of nature. How does that sound?"

Darren grinned. It sounded too good to be true.

A year had passed since Darren's tutelage started. Veronica and several other members of the Coven of the Black Moon were highly impressed with his progress. In the course of mere months, he had come to master some of the most difficult areas of magic. He could, at will, project his consciousness out of his own body, peering through walls and even over great distances to find anything he wanted. This was a trick he used oftentimes on Veronica, when she had hidden away a birthday present for Darren, and he used his power to covertly peek into her closet to find an engraved metal drinking flask for him.

He could also accurately predict the outcomes of Veronica's business events with the Tarot, right down to the exact sum of money she would earn. He could also absorb spiritual energies using various incantations; summoning spirits from distant realms and assimilating them into his own body, gaining their strength and knowledge.

Over time, he even learned spells that would let him float up to a foot in midair, and move objects with nothing but sheer willpower. He could make a book fall down from a shelf in the library from fifteen feet away, then cradle it in midair and pull it to his outstretched hand. Even Darren himself was impressed with his rapid transformation; the coveted grade rank of Ipsissimus was very soon to be his.

However, his nightmares were getting more persistent. He started dreaming about hooded figures out in a forest clearing, performing Magickal acts beyond even his understanding. He could hear them chanting in languages far older than Latin or Gaelic, invoking spirits called "Anroth," "Khorn," and "Ymut." With the tall trees standing in the shadow and a large, roaring fire lighting up the small clearing, these hooded people chanted and rang bells that reverberated more than a normal bell ever would.

From out of the fire stepped three figures, two men and one woman. The flames licked around the naked figures, but it did no harm to their bare flesh. Darren was stunned at the perfection of their figures, the definition of the men's muscles and the perfect

roundness of the woman's breasts. Each of their faces were perfectly proportioned; sharp and powerful-looking for the men and
softly serene for the woman. All three figures had eyes that glowed
a bright red, as if some of the roaring fire was inside of them. The
three beings began to dance among the hooded revellers, flailing
about wildly and passionately.

They pulled off some of their cloaks, revealing bare flesh beneath, and proceeded to fornicate with the members. The revellers
partaking in the sex acts gasped with every thrust they delivered (or
were delivered to them by the demons), faster and wilder with each
moment. Every reveller penetrated the demons' orifices or chose
to get penetrated by them. One demon scratched its long, clawlike
fingernails into a revel's bare back while it thrust away at her from
behind. The reveller getting the demonic sex screamed in pain,
then moaned in pleasure.

A conclave was called that night, where Darren as a newly-mint-
ed Ipsissimus of the Golden Dawn led Veronica and the rest of the
Coven in special Latin and Gaelic chanting. Darren kept his hood
over his head, and his hands outstretched above his head, his voice
reverberating with some unearthly power.

After the chanting, one of the Coven members pulled Veronica
off to a side and spoke with her in private in the shadow of the
tall crypts. Darren saw her conferring but he did not mind, and
instead he showed off his ability to levitate to some of his subordinates. With a consonant-heavy incantation, he felt his body become
weightless, and ascend over the dusty ground. The congregation
was taken aback and applauded with delight as Darren floated up
to six feet in the air, high enough that some of the shorter Coven
members had to jump to be able to touch his floating feet. Darren
smiled and brought himself back down to earth.

"Darren?" said Veronica from across the clearing. "I want a word
with you, now."

Darren walked over to the crypt's side, into the pitch-black shadow with his lover at his side.

"What's on your mind?" he asked.

"It's unbelievable, even for me," she said quietly. "You've only been in the Order for a year, and you're already doing things that most people spend their whole lives just trying to understand and study. The flying, the predictions, the astral travel, you never should've been able to do all those in so short a time!"

"What's wrong with that?" asked Darren defensively. "I thought that's what you wanted for me in the first place."

"Well, it is, sort of," Veronica stammered, lost for words. "I just didn't expect it so soon is all. And some of the others in the Coven, they're starting to suspect something."

"Like what?" asked Darren.

"Well, there are some things in magic that even we wouldn't do, the darkest of the dark arts. As soon as you start trying those spells, you're not in control anymore."

"What about all that 'I am in control of my element' shit you told me?"

"That's different, Darren. This is more powerful than anything we do here. It's too powerful for anyone to control, and it always brings negative things to anyone who does it."

"You think I'm not up to it, is that it?" Darren accused her.

"Babe, listen to me!" Veronica begged. "I don't want to see you get hurt."

She trembled slightly, and Darren placed his hands over her shoulders for an embrace.

"I'll be careful," he whispered to her.

"Please, don't do any of those evocations," she replied softly. "Believe me, that door only opens one way, and nobody can get out of it."

Six years passed, and their relationship blossomed. Nearly every night, Darren and Veronica partook in carnal pleasures with each other, making each other reach dizzyingly high climaxes and rich orgasms. Their love grew more and more with each passing day. Veronica's business grew exponentially, and Darren's work as a writer, painter and secret Ipsissimus was ever enjoyable to him. His old life felt like a half-remembered dream, where he was sloshing paint on canvases to recreate his horrific nightmares for just a few hundred dollars in a tiny shithole apartment with an overbearing, unforgiving landlord and parents who barely even remembered his existence.

All of that was different in his life now; he had a wife to call his own, his art and novels made him millions of dollars, and of course there was always the Magick to aid him. The spiritual energies that coursed in his body gave him insight and intuition like nothing else, such that he could avoid getting hit by a drunk driver while walking down a street in an instant. On-lookers around him were amazed at how skillful he was when he suddenly stopped dead in his tracks on the sidewalk, as if he somehow knew that the soused driver of the old green Volkswagon Beetle was going to crash at that exact moment and exact time.

One night, Veronica slept alone in the plush bed that she usually shared with Darren. He was out in the shrine doing some more studies, and he assured her that he was going to stay within his limits. He had already read and reread every single book that Veronica owned, but she inwardly feared that maybe he would stumble upon that other vault of knowledge that she kept, and she felt guilty about having it.

Behind a wall in the library was a secondary room with only just a handful of books to be found. But those books were special; they contained the darkest secrets of Magick, the very things that she warned Darren against using. She only kept them for reference, antiquarian value, and to understand her own limits as a magical praticioner. If Darren ever got his hands on those, learning Solomonic Magick, Left Hand Path Magick or even the higher echelons of Demonic Magick...

She awoke with a sudden sense of urgency. She could feel with every fiber of her being that something was dangerously wrong. She could feel a dark energy, unseen but very real, seeping its way through the house like a flood. Her pulse quickened, and sweat dripped down her brow. In her cream-coloured nightgown, she got up from bed and looked around the darkened house. Turning on a light, she gasped in terror as hundreds of bright, sparkling orbs of energy floated before her eyes. She could also see black silhouettes of spindly, sharp-toothed demons rampaging through her bedroom and every other room.

By instinct, she knew what to do. She closed her eyes, made several hand gestures, and spoke clearly and with full force: "Spirits from realms beyond, in the names of the Holiest of All Holies, Michael, Raphael, Uriel, Ariel, and Metatron, dispel these evil spirits at once!"

Her prayer was in vain, as the spirits laughed scornfully at her and proceeded to rummage through her house, knocking over furniture and tossing clothes all around. Then in an instant, they all went invisible. Veronica looked around wide-eyed, and sighed with some relief. Praying to the higher power that she was aware of certainly had its advantages.

Then she felt something crawling on her back, something unseen and malicious. She gasped, and quickly flailed her arms to get it off. She felt something jabbing and poking at her limbs, like some invisible insect. Quickly she tried to brush away what unknown force was attacking her, then she felt herself getting lifted a foot up into the air with some invisible bonds. She was thrown against a mirror on the wall, cracking it with the force of her body, and slammed against the far wall. Small cuts started to form on her arms where the poking and scratching sensations were, until large claw marks formed on her upper chest, torn through her nightgown as if by an invisible taloned creature. Blood dripped from her open wounds as she was suspended in midair, then she was thrown against the walls and floor like a rag doll.

Sprawled on the floor, she was sliced up, bruised and bloody. The carpeted floor was stained a deep red where she lay, and it was spreading fast over the floor. Veronica slowly got up, trying to regain her strength, and bolted downstairs into the shrine and then the library, looking in horror to find the gaping hole in the wall where a bookshelf was, and the light coming from beyond the wall. Her worst fears were confirmed, and she ran into the hidden room.

Inside was a small table and only a few leather-bound, dusty books, one of which was open. In a corner of the room, Darren, in his black robe was having sex with a naked woman that appeared to have long, curved horns jutting from its forehead, and glowing red eyes. Veronica was stunned, and pulled Darren off of his succubus lover, throwing him to the floor hard.

"Darren!" Veronica exclaimed. "You are cheating, lying bastard!"

"What else do you want to call me?" asked Darren, getting to his feet to tower over Veronica. "How about 'Magus,' or 'Living God.' I got the power, and there's nothing I can't accomplish. You should try it; it's better than sex mixed with blood,'" he said, drunk on the dark energy that coursed through his viens. He was no longer the Darren she once knew. His true soul was gone. Only the demons now lived in his body and mind.

"I told you to stay away from the Goetia!" Veronica shouted, pointing at the open Grimoire on the table. "Now look what you've done! Look at me!" She pointed to the ragged wounds on her body, still streaming with blood.

"Not a problem. I can heal that."

Darren pointed to her and muttered a choice incantation, and Veronica's wounds started to close miraculously. He then looked to the naked succubus and waved it away.

"Be dispelled!" he ordered, and the creature evaporated into nothingness. Veronica slammed her fist into the side of Darren's face.

"You bastard! You fucking bastard!" Veronica shouted. Darren said nothing, instead grabbing Veronica's wrist to stop him from getting punched again, and smashed his own fist into her stomach. She doubled over in agony and fell to the floor, with Darren leering above her. Several demonic spirits materialized around him, looking hungrily and lustfully over her.

"Take her," he commanded the spirits. "She's yours now."

The demonic spirits descended upon her, and she flailed and rolled around wildly, trying to bat them away. The demons assaulted her viciously like ravenous birds, pecking and slashing at her. Above her, Darren forced her into place and proceeded to rape her, harder than he ever penetrated her before. She shrieked and clawed at him with her nails, but despite spilling much of his blood, he still kept at it upon her.

In desperation, she made one last effort to save herself, something she swore she would never do. The door opened one way, she remembered herself saying.

"Hes in makal tehah'rakan!"

Behind Darren, a sudden burst of flame erupted, spreading over an entire wall of the secret room. Darren looked up from raping his wife and gasped in horror at what he saw emerging from the flames. A man walked out of the fire, seven feet tall with fine blond hair and leathery black wings jutting from his back. His face morphed from being human in appearance to becoming flat and reptilian, with glowing scarlet eyes.

"Take him, Lucifer!" Veronica shouted. "TAKE HIM!"

"No!" Darren shot back. "*I* am the Magus! I am a god! I control YOU! Obey me, you evil spirit!"

"Fool," said the Devil. *"You control nothing."*

Without another word, he pulled Darren's throat with his clawed hand. Darren gasped in the Devil's grip and struggled vainly. With that one clawed hand, the Devil squeezed his throat until blood oozed from between his long, thin fingers. Darren's eyes went lifeless, and his skull rolled off of what little was left of his neck. The Devil caught Darren's severed head in his other hand neatly.

Down on the floor, Veronica tried to collect herself, and sighed with relief. The spirits that assailed her had dissipated, fearful for their master.

"What took you so long?" she muttered.

"Still playing games with mortals, are we?" asked the Devil.

"He became an asshole."

"You serve me well with these new souls to collect."

"It would've been sooner, but things got out of hand."

The woman, the Devil, and the hidden room all vanished. The last thing the audience saw the Devil was him staring directly at them, as if this was more than just an illusion, but something real and affecting them in every personal way.

The audience was horrified. Some fainted, some even screamed chills of blood-curdling terror. But the doctor turned on the lights and the vision was over, as light conquers darkness. In closing this story he spoke: "As tempting as knowledge is, there are certain things best left unknown; such was the case of this unfortunate young man. You see, God was there waiting for him to come home to repent, but Darren just never did. I know this from experience."

As soon as everyone found their seats after a brief intermission, the doctor took the stage. The overhead spotlights shone brightly upon him, such that he squinted slightly to be able to see his audience through the light. He waved a gloved hand, and from out of his fingertips came a flurry of red rose petals, which fluttered in the air as they fell to the stage floor. Then, with outstretched arms, he curled up his fingers, and a hush fell over the crowd.

His hands started to glow a bright red with some mysterious energy. Above him, the stage lights started to dim out, making the only real source of light the doctor's glowing fists. The doctor then released his grip, and from his open palms issued a great burst of energy like an electrified cloud, which illuminated the theatre in bright crimson.

The crowd collectively gasped as the vaporous cloud shifted shape right above the doctor's head. It shimmered with red light and turned from a formless cloud into a gigantic bird of pulsing energy. Its wings were wide and adorned with sharp prongs where its feathers would be.

A crest of cloudy vapor stood on the top of its head, and as it looked around with glowing red eyes, it issued from its beak a booming call.

The bird outstretched its mighty wings and flew in circles around the theatre, close enough to the heads of onlookers that some even tried to stand up with outstretched hands, hoping to touch it as it flew by. The energy-filled bird raced overhead around above the audience, leaving a glowing trail of light in its wake, making ribbons of light where it flew.

It called out a loud, screeching "CAWWW!" sound with each revolution around the theatre. The doctor, still upon the stage in the centre, moved his hands around over his head to control the motion of the bird, like a conductor in a symphony. He smiled with delight as he made the energetic bird fly high enough to almost touch the ceiling of the theatre, then reverse course and swoop down directly over an unsuspecting audience member.

The middle-aged man who was sitting directly in the bird's warpath looked up slowly and then yelped with alarm and covered his head as the bird descended quickly over him. Then at the last possible second, when the bird could have been mere inches away from the man's bald head, it changed course and veered upward and away. The man slowly uncovered his head, realizing what just happened, and sighed with relief.

From the middle row where he sat, Gabriel sat entranced by the spectacle unfolding before him. If this was an illusion, it was far more advanced than anything he could possibly comprehend, especially if it was moving this close to people. *What could be his secret?* He wondered inwardly. *How is he doing all this?*

The cloud-and-energy bird made one last turn around the theatre, and then it swooped over the centre of the stage. It began to shrink in size, small enough that it could perch neatly on the outstretched left arm of Doctor Xoctarious. The doctor smiled and nodded with the bird perched on his forearm, and the crowd began cheering wildly for the astounding spectacle that was just presented. Even Gabriel stood up with the rest of the crowd, clapping his hands quickly and loudly. Some people even whistled with delight and satisfaction. The doctor then raised his left arm, scattering the vaporous bird into a fading puff of smoke and took a bow. The applause reached a fever pitch, and when the doctor finished bowing, he raised a gloved hand to try and silence the jubilant crowd.

"There's still more to come, my friends!" he bellowed jovially, trying to get his voice raised above the sounds of clapping and cheering. "I've more delights to share with you in my Mystic Theater!"

The sounds of the crowd began to die down in anticipation of his next move.

"It is part of the human experience to seek out thrills in all their forms, is it not? What kind of person would not dare leave for even just a moment the never-ending drudges of the world? Life, with all its complications and demands, is always meant to be enjoyed. Trickery can be wonderful! Cast aside your beliefs in what is real and accept for a moment the illusion of the fantastic! Leave behind your cares and burdens for just a moment and allow your spirit to drink deeply from the wellspring of imagination and wonder!"

Some scattered applause from the audience accompanied these words.

"Well, I admit I can be somewhat poetic if I need to," said the doctor. "However, the escape into fantasy must be temporary, for if one is led too far astray, it can be very difficult to find one's way back. Now, I invite you, dear friends, to join me into the medieval realm, where knights and lords wage endless conquest, where the clashing swords and war cries sound over the battlements! For in this year of 1336, this is where we shall come face to face with 'The Enchantress.'"

THE ENCHANTRESS

Story by Doug K. Owen
Written by Doug K. Owen

The lights overhead darkened out, and the audience fell silent in anticipation. Gabriel could feel his pulse quicken with every moment in the blacked-out theatre. Instantly, the lights came back on, and where the theatre once was, there was instead a completely different place entirely, as if in an instant, the entire building was replaced or the audience was transported to some distant land.

The walls that were once spotless white were grey, uneven stones. The carpeted floor was now a field of brown and prickly grass. The ceiling and the overhead lights were gone, replaced with an ethereal blue sky and a punishingly hot sun.

Where the doctor once stood, there were two armoured knights engaged in a vicious bout of sword-to-sword combat. The sun gleamed off their shiny metallic breastplates and cylinder-shaped hems, as well as off of the long broadswords they swung at each other with two gloved hands on each hilt. One knight had red trim on its suit beneath the armour, and one had blue and green trim— signs of their respective factions. The audience sat captivated at the scene, watching the two combatants expertly slash and parry at one another. The swords rang with a metallic clang on each impact, accompanied with an occasional electrical spark at the point of impact. The two unrelenting warriors fought with disciplined, powerful moves against each other, willing themselves to break their assailant's defence and score that killer blow to win the battle.

The knight in the red trim, in a sweeping motion, swung his sword upwards against his enemy, knocking his enemy's sword completely out of his hand. The airborne sword flew upwards, spinning fast, and it landed point-down into the ground near an audience member in the space that once was a walkway between theatre rows.

"Enough!" cried a voice from across the battlefield. "This battle is won!"

The two knights stood at attention to the nobleman seated beneath a canopy of blue and green fabric on the far end of the field, against the stone wall. Flanked by two guards as similarly armoured as the defeated knight, the old nobleman with the white beard and a golden band around his head rose from his ornately-carved wooden seat. His face was lined with age, but his smile was amiable and bright. He wore a flowing robe of dark blue velvet, far more expensive and regal than the rest of the people watching around the battlefield. Many of the other spectators wore suits of muted colours, and some were clad in little more than roughly-hewn burlap. Nevertheless, both the nobility and the peasantry thoroughly enjoyed the exhibition fight.

"Well-fought, you two!" the nobleman proclaimed to the two knights standing still. "It seems that the prowess of Lochaven's battlers is unmatched even to our best! To that, well done, fighters from Lochaven!"

The knight with the red trim bowed slightly to the nobleman. "I save my best talents for the battlefield, for when I face Ravenwall."

"And Ravenwall is right to fear you," the nobleman assented. "Let us now welcome our other guests to bring their own brand of diversions for my court!"

The two knights exited the field, and in their place came a crew of men and women in brightly-coloured costumes. A blonde-haired woman in a flowing emerald-green dress, accompanied a young man with close-cropped brown hair and wearing a leather jerkin emblazoned with symbols in red and blue. The symbols were mostly geometric shapes, crosses and stars. The woman's features were very slender and fine, with emerald-green eyes and a wide smile.

The entertainers bowed deeply before the nobleman. "Our thanks to you for hosting us, Edmund, Eighth Earl of Arunford," said the man in the patterned suit. "With our Lord's permission, we intend to demonstrate feats of illusion and wonderment to befuddle the senses and raise spirits high!"

The nobleman nodded, and held out a hand gesturing them to proceed. The woman turned to the suited man, and embraced him slightly.

"I'm ready, Cadfael," whispered the woman. "Everything's in place."

"Work your magic, Philly," Cadfael replied quietly, so as not to be heard by the Earl. Cadfael stepped back to work with some of the other performers, while Philly entered the centre of the field. She bowed to the Earl, and her assistant in a green form-fitting suit provided a wooden box filled with various potions and mirrors. She took in her hand a glass flask filled with a clear liquid, and a small mirror.

"Behold, most noble Lord, the wonders of Philena!"

She poured a large volume of a clear liquid onto the mirror, and instantly it ignited with flames of bright red and violet. Sparks popped and flew from the small inferno she held in her hand. The nobleman and all members of his court looked on with disbelief and wonder as she began to dance with the fiery mirror in her hands. She spun her whole body around while keeping the blazing mirror held level the entire time, as if it was held in place by invisible hands while she twirled and kicked. Rarely did the mirror move at all in the course of her dancing. The Earl was astounded, but at the same time terrified; what if her dress would catch one of the sparks from the fire? Still, the fact that no such thing happened put his mind at ease.

In one sweeping move, Philena leaped into the air in a somersault move with the fiery mirror leaving her hands. The crowd gasped as she stuck the landing on the brown grass, and caught the mirror with the fire still burning on its top side. Then she took in a deep breath, and blew a long draft of air into the fire, making it expand into a great burning cloud of violet. As quickly as it ignited, the fire petered out and died, and Philly placed the mirror on top of the wooden crate with her supplies. The nobleman and his court applauded enthusiastically for the act they had just witnessed.

Philly smiled wide, savouring the accolades from the people all around her. Everyone from the shabby-dressed peasantry to the gaudy Earl were thoroughly captivated by her performance and showered her with appreciation for what looked like a dangerous and foolhardy act, gracefully performed. Philly had always loved performing, and working as part of Cadfael's troupe was the fulfilment of her every dream. She could charm everyone with everything from simple tricks to elaborate stunts such as the one she had just performed.

The Earl rose to his feet, clapping voraciously. "Well done!" he exclaimed. "Well done, Philena!"

In a separate part of the castle, two sentries were standing guard on either side of a heavy wooden door, which was locked with a thick iron padlock. The guards could hear the sounds of cheering and music outside, and inwardly they yearned to be outside taking part in the revelry instead of being relegated to sentry detail outside the Earl's strong room. The guards leaned lazily on their tall halberds and struggled to keep their eyes open. The polished metal helms and breastplates were starting to grow heavy on their weary bodies.

From down the hall, three men approached the door to the strong room. The guards snapped to attention and crossed their halberds in front of the door, barring them access. The three men were Cadfael and two of his performance cohorts in lively, bright costumes of gold and purple, with their faces painted in similar colours. Small bells adorning their costumes jangled with every step they took.

"Afternoon, gents," said Cadfael. "His Lordship wouldn't want the two of you to sit upstairs bored senseless, so he asked us to give you a small taste of the festival."

Cadfael nodded to his cohorts, who proceeded to do some small acrobatic tricks before the guards. They did cartwheels and handstands in the hall for starters. Cadfael stood aside, and the two tricksters joined hands together and somersaulted on the floor with one over the other, making several turns on the floor like a giant wheel. The guards eased their stances slightly and smiled, amused by the tricksters' antics as they got back to their feet to take a small bow.

Then in a sudden move, both of the tricksters grabbed a ball from their costumes and in unison, threw them on the ground, producing massive bursts of smoke. The guards doubled over, coughing and choking on the thick white smoke from the bombs. From a distance, Cadfael looked on with a grin.

"Grab their keys!" he commanded. The tricksters both searched the guards while they were afflicted by the smoke. The performers both were keen to hold their breaths and squint so as not to be affected as the guards were. One of the tricksters found a key off one of the guards, and nodded to Cadfael.

"Let's see what he's got in there!" said Cadfael.

The tricksters opened the heavy door, and the contents of the strong room lifted Cadfael's spirits greatly. Stacks of burlap sacks and wooden kegs filled the room. One of the tricksters opened a bag to find masses of gold coins inside. He silently nodded to Cadfael with a big smile, which Cadfael returned.

"Get as much as you two can," ordered Cadfael. "And be quick about it."

The guards were still incapacitated when the two jesters had finished removing several large sacks of gold from the vault. They had reddened faces and stinging tears in their eyes. One of the jesters stuck his tongue out at a guard as he casually walked out of the strong room.

Outside, the Earl was still engrossed with single mindedness at the further acts performed in the field. Performers in the form-fitting costumes were juggling small daggers with ribbons tied to their hilts. Ladies in scandalously minimal outfits wielded flaming torches, with one of them blowing a massive fireball from her ruby lips. In the centre, Philly was dancing on two thin strands of rope suspended six feet above the field. She moved gracefully and artistically across each tautly-stretched strand, spinning and kicking with poise and verve. All the while, never did she slip or lose her balance, much to the relief of the sometimes worrisome Earl. At the end of her act, she vaulted off the ropes, spinning in midair, and landed neatly on her feet.

The applause from the Earl's court was loud, and his smile was infectious; even the stalwart guards around his seat were grinning across their faces. All the other spectators in his court were equally as astounded, and the roar of applause was deafening. Over the clapping and cheering, it was difficult for anyone to hear an errant voice with an accusatory tone.

"Witch!" cried a voice from among the throng. "Witch!"

From out of the cheering crowds came a middle-aged man in a black robe, pointing an accusing finger directly at Philly. She stood in the centre of the field, unsure of what was going on with the mood suddenly being broken.

"She's a witch!" the man shouted. "Those tricks were of the devil!"

The Earl tried to calm him down with a gentle gesture. "Nonsense, man! Such grace and skill could never have come from the devil!"

"Thank you for vouching for me, my Lord," replied Philly with a bow. She exited the field, along with the rest of her troupe. Coming out from a nearby tower was Cadfael and two other performers, each one hefting large burlap bags.

"Move quickly," Cadfael hissed with clenched teeth. "They're on to us."

Philly broke into a fast walk with the rest of the troupe as they loaded up their brightly-painted blue carriage and headed for the main gate. The gold and all the other supplies were loaded and kept out of sight. They bowed several times to the Earl and his court on their way out, then broke into a fast trot with their sacs? out the main gate. Once they were clear of the gate, the troupe dashed for a nearby thicket of trees on the horizon, thousands of feet away from the castle. Behind her, Philly could almost hear some harried screams in the castle.

Philly rested on a large, flat boulder in a forest once the carriage stopped to let everyone out. They were a very fair distance away from Arunford Castle, and it would be a while before anyone from the Earl's court could track them down. Cadfael emerged from the carriage with one of the pilfered sacks, and brought it to Philly. She opened it up to reveal masses of glittering golden coins. Plunging her hand into the coins, she could feel their cool, smooth texture against her skin, and she smiled with delight.

"This might be our best haul yet," said Cadfael, sitting next to her. "Those Arunford fools didn't even know what hit 'em."

"Sure beats working as a courtesan for those spoiled old goats," Philly added. "Have you seen the women with the Earl?"

"I didn't get that good a look. How were they?"

"Hideous!" Philly said forcefully. "Maybe the Earl has a way of pulling all the beauty out of women and leaving them looking like that! And to think they called me a witch!"

Cadfael hugged her lightly. "You're not a witch, but you sure can cast a spell."

Philly kissed Cadfael on the cheek with a devious grin and a giggle. "Wouldn't it have been a crime to keep me locked up years ago?"

Cadfael nodded, remembering that distant time when Philly was arrested for picking a noble's pocket and was left to rot in a dank prison cell. One night, while Philly lay slouched against the cold, uneven stones that made up her cell wall, she heard a slight picking sound coming from the heavy wooden door holding her inside the cell. The picking became louder, and then it swung open. She cowered back in fright, thinking it might have been a guard sent to harass her. Instead, it was a younger Cadfael, who looked around and scowled.

"Ugh, this isn't the strong room!" he muttered, and then he saw young, trembling Philena on the stone floor. He crouched down next to her and placed a reassuring hand on her shoulder.

"Did they lock you up in here?" he asked, and she nodded meekly.

"Let's get you out. This is no place for a lady like you."

Years have passed since then, and Cadfael took on the role of a surrogate father to Philly, though she saw him as more of a surrogate brother if anything. Cadfael taught her some tricks to perform with the troupe, but Philly added her own unique brand of flair into the performances.

Where Cadfael taught her to walk across a tautly-placed rope, she danced on it. Where Cadfael taught her a sleight of hand trick, she made it her own, adding her special style into every movement and trick. Cadfael knew there had to be something by which even she could be challenged, so he rifled through the pages of the ancient book *Secretum Philosophorum* to find some kind of trick that would challenge her. That attempt was to no avail, as Philly continued to astound him with an almost natural talent in graceful, fluid and amazing motions with her body. Every dance, every flowing motion with a coloured scarf... There was nothing that Cadfael could possibly see that would be errant or overdone.

Philly remembered the whole event just as well, along with everything that brought her thus far with Cadfael and the troupe. Since then, she had grown increasingly fond of Cadfael, savouring every moment spent with him. The other troupe members were like family to her. She stretched out on the boulder and lay down to relax with Cadfael at her side. She looked around and saw the acrobat twins in their gold and indigo costumes: the juggler with a glass orb in his hands, and the towering, long-haired, painted-faced Piangi with his two jester students.

Earlier, they were the ones who helped Cadfael raid the Earl's vault. Piangi spoke to them in a low volume, but Philly could see him, gesturing his hands about wildly to get his points across to his students. Piangi turned to Philly and gave a small whistle, which Philly ignored. He whistled again, and then gave a special whistle with a tune that went from low to high. Realizing Philly's disinterest in him, he whistled from high to low.

"Where's our next performance?" asked Philly. Cadfael withdrew from his pocket a small map on yellowed parchment and traced his finger across some of the hastily-drawn forests and towns.

"Well, we've already gone to Arunford's, that's right here. If we keep moving east, we'll find Ravenwall."

"I've heard of those people," muttered Philly. "I don't think they even know how to laugh."

"I've heard that too," Cadfael replied. "I guess they sold their sense of humour for coin, but it'll be ours soon enough. Are you ready for another show?"

"Always ready, my dear," Philly giggled.

"Great, let's get to it." He stood up from the boulder and cupped his hands together to amplify his voice. "Everyone, let's get into the wagon and head east! Ravenwall awaits!"

As everyone else piled into the carriage, Piangi gave a series of whistles to Cadfael, gesturing with his hands in some cryptic way.

"Not right now, Piangi," Cadfael muttered. "Come on, we're heading out. And for God's sakes, please speak English."

As Cadfael walked to the carriage, Piangi stood with his arms crossed, clearly offended.

"Oi, it's called stage acting,' ya bahstad!"

Revenues grand hall was built with smooth grey stones and the long wooden tables were laid out in a wide C-shape, so that it afforded a large space in the centre of the room while the Duke and his court could sit comfortably. Philly looked around the room with a sense of awe, noticing the artwork on the walls. Ornate tapestries of royal singles such as lions, dragons and crossed swords were emblazoned on the long fabric drapes in green, blue and white. Imposing portraits of long-deceased royals in full regalia stared down over the grand hall with frozen, unflinching stares.

All the while, several people making up Ravenwall's court, dressed in finery, gave similar stories to Philly and her crew with a sense of anticipation. In the centre of the largest table sat the Duke of Ravenwall. He wore a suit of black and red trim, and his black hair was well-groomed His beard and moustache were short and trimmed to points. Sitting next to him was a gaunt, armoured man who kept one muscled hand on the hilt of his sword, His hair was shorter and lighter than the Duke's hair, and surveyed the scene with steel-grey eyes. Philly shuddered slightly; this was going to be a very difficult audience to appease.

She nodded to Cadfael behind her, who returned the nod to her. The acrobats, the juggler and Piangi were also on hand, getting ready to perform. She turned to the duke and bowed slightly.

"Most honoured Duke of Ravenwall, we present for your enjoyment a series of talents!"

The duke nodded without a word, signalling them to begin.

Elsewhere in the castle, Cadfael led the two tricksters down the furnished castle halls to find their strong room. Cadfael knew it had to be a door with the most guards standing by it, as was the tradition that he noticed on his many heists. Rounding a corner, one of his cohorts almost bumped into a large wooden cabinet. The bell on his left foot jangled loudly, and he muffled a choice curse word under his breath.

"Keep it down, you fools!" Cadfael hissed at them through gritted teeth. Ahead of them, down the wide hall was a very conveniently placed door, flanked by four armoured guards. Cadfael knew that the Ravenwall court was known for having a less-than-great sense of humour, but to appease four of them would be very difficult.

But as soon as Cadfael led his jesters over toward the door, the guards slumped to the floor in total unison. Cadfael stopped in surprise, and took a slow step towards them to find out what was going on. The jesters had not thrown their gas-filled bells on them, and he could not smell anything that would have caused the guards to fall like that. A faint rustling came from the rafters overhead, and one jester tugged on Cadfael's tunic, frantically pointing overhead. What Cadfael saw, slinking into the shadows, was the figure of a man with a small crossbow in his hand.

"An assassin?"

The Duke of Ravenwall was stifling a grin when Philly did her flaming mirror dance, seemingly more concerned with the residue falling off the mirror and onto the freshly-swept floor than with the dance itself. Philly knew that she was not getting through to this non-cheering court, so she redoubled her efforts. She added more of the clear potion from the bottle to make the flames leap even higher off the smouldering mirror, and resumed her dance. Philly always knew to keep the mirror well balanced when dancing, and she focused with single mind on making her movements as graceful and smooth as her body could allow them to be. She performed a clean pirouette and kick, and caught the mirror with her foot. Then she kicked the mirror overhead and caught it fire-side-up in her hand. She was breathing hard and sweating profusely after the trick was done, looking around at the Ravenwall court. There was barely even as much as a clap or a cheer from anyone.

Not even the silly whistling and squeaking of Piangi near one of the court ladies was enough to garner a positive response from anyone. When Piangi leaned over the wooden table in front of a court lady with long brown hair and fine features, he made his high-to-low whistling sounds from her. The lady winced in disgust, and Piangi withdrew, stifling a frown.

From the back of the main hall, Philly heard panicked voice that she instantly recognized as the voice of Cadfael.

"PHILLY, GET DOWN!"

Philly hesitated, then she heard something whiz by her head. A small arrow had lodged itself into the spotless wooden table that the Duke was seated before. She ducked down as another arrow flew by, then another. Two members of the court were shot, and they doubled over in their chairs dead. It was not long before Philly found herself crawling beneath a storm of arrows coming from the rafters. Shouts of panic came from all sides of the hall, from the court and from the troupe. Philly caught faint glimpses of several men in black suits firing crossbows from above, sending arrows indiscriminately into the air, sinking into targets of both wood and flesh. An arrow fell right near Philly's head, bouncing off the stones. She ducked down and remained still, hoping that the assassins would assume she was dead.

The assault was over in what seemed to Philly like an eternity. When the last bus of an airborne arrow stopped, she waited a little while longer to poke her head up from the ground to look around. When she did, she instantly regretted the decision. All around her were dead bodies of nobles and performers. She gasped in horror to see the acrobat twins riddled with arrows and blood pooling up around them. Off to a side, even Piangi was struck by the onslaught of arrows, his painted face now streaked with blood and his features frozen in a look of horror. Other nobles were similarly killed, the fine velvet and silk wardrobes on the bodies all shredded and bloodied.

The table in the centre started to move slightly, and the Duke of Ravenwall got up from his hiding place to survey the damage. He gasped wide-eyed in horror as he saw the devastation. Next to him was the armoured man, who unsheathed his sword and stood close to the Duke, ready to defend him from whatever was yet to come.

"What…? How did they…?!" the Duke growled, and then he let loose a loud scream of rage that echoed off the stone walls through the entire hall. He pounded a meaty fist hard against the splintered table.

"Damn to Hell those Lochaven jackals!" he stammered. "Damn them all!"

"My lord, are you hurt?" asked the armoured man with the sword.

"I'm fine, Hiram!" the Duke growled. "My guests… my court… Lochaven will pay for this! Rally the Knights and prepare them for battle!"

As the Duke kept ranting, several survivors of the royal court got up from hiding and cowered in terror. Many of them rushed for the doors of the great hall in a panic. Philly found herself caught up with the terrified crowd and moved along with them towards the door. She caught a glimpse of Cadfael hiding in a shadow in the corner of the room nearest the door, hidden by a large wooden cabinet. She reached out her hand for Cadfael to take, and pulled him through the crowd, out of the room. While the rest of the surviving guests collectively ran down the halls out of the castle, Cadfael held Philly in an offshoot of the hall near the door. He was unhurt, much to Philly's relief, but the images of her family and friends lying dead were seared into her mind. Seeing Cadfael, however, was reassuring.

"Are you alright?" asked Cadfael, holding Philly close. Philly nodded, trying to hold back pained sobs.

"Shh," Cadfael whispered. "It'll be okay. We're still safe."

"Those performers!" Ravenwall hollered from the hall. "They must've known all along about this! Find them!"

Philly and Cadfael heard him, and looked around for someplace to hide. Nearby, they could hear the sounds of hurried footsteps coming towards them. Cadfael's eyes darted around, and then he turned to the rest of the hall where they stood.

"That way!" he hissed, and took Philly by the hand, sprinting down the deserted hallway. Together they dashed down the stone steps into the lower parts of the castle. Cadfael ran for the nearest door and darted inside with Philly, slamming it shut and looking around. They found themselves in a torch-lit wine cellar, where a row of five massive wooden barrels was set up resting on their sides against a wall. The bright light from the torches in iron sconces left plenty of shadows between the large kegs, which was where Cadfael took Philly to hide.

The shadows offered scant protection, but nobody else was in the room, and the heavy wooden door was shut. Cadfael and Philly sat together in the shadows with their backs to the woods kegs, trying to catch their breath and reflect on what happened. The space between the dusty, splintery wooden kegs was very small for two people, which made the hiding spot uncomfortable for Philly. Despite the fact that Cadfael was with her, Philly could not help but to start weeping.

"Philly, don't!" whispered Cadfael sharply. "They'll find us!"

"They're dead!" Philly whined. "Everyone, the whole group! They're gone!"

"It'll be alright," Cadfael reassured her. "We'll get out of here and we'll find a way to carry on together. At least we'll be safe."

"Cadfael, do you think there's going to be a war?"

"If there is," Cadfael mused. "Then it'll put entertainers out of business."

"We need to stop them!" Philly remarked. Cadfael shook his head and held on to Philly's shoulders.

"You saw what happened in there, Philly. There's no sense in swaying anyone from going to war."

"Cadfael, please!" Philly begged, struggling against his grasp. "There's no way we'll recover from this unless we stop them!"

"How do you suppose we do that?" asked Cadfael. "How are we going to stop that Duke from going to war? And what about those assassins from Lochaven? How do we stop them?"

Philly paused, then her eyes lit up as an idea began to take shape in her mind.

Deep within the castle, the Duke retreated with Hiram to the keep, the last refuge for a noble under attack. The tower stood tall over the entire castle, offering a panoramic view of the land all around. The stone walls were built much thicker than the rest of the castle, and it was heavily fortified with a contingent of guards armed with swords and halberds. The Duke of Ravenwall knew that he would be safe there, away from the prying eyes of Lochaven's assassins. His Deputy General Hiram accompanied him along the way, constantly vigilant for any assassins that may still be lurking in the castle.

As soon as the Duke and the Deputy General entered the keep, the thick wood and iron doors shut behind them. Inside, Ravenwall's entire force of knights was gathered, all of them fully armoured and prepared to fight for their Duke. Their helms, Pauldrons, gauntlets, greaves and breastplates were spotless and shone brightly with the light from the overhead wrought-iron chandelier and several torches lining the room. In the centre of the stone chamber, atop a round stone pedestal, was a map of the region written on parchment. The Duke and Hiram walked to the pedestal and addressed the knights.

"Knights of the Order of Ravenwall," the Duke started with a loud, authoritative voice. "You have been summoned to serve your Duke upon the field of honour! Lochaven has dared to send his assassins after myself and my court, but he will gain no victory for me! Those insufferable knaves shall fall by Ravenwall steel, and be sent back to the yawning pits of Hell from whence they came!"

Some of the knights roared with approval and raised their swords on high, filled with the same sense of purpose and rage that drove their Duke. Amid the speech, not one of the assembled knights noticed two other armoured warriors silently and clumsily entering the room. These two particular knights moved with an awkward stride and tried to file in line at the very back of the congregation.

"Lochaven's lair lies to the south," the Duke continued. "We will march along the southern passes that run along the valley, and reach Lochaven in two days. From there, we will mount a full assault on their lair and pound them into submission!"

Several more cheers came from the ranks. One night, however, moved closer to the pedestal from among his comrades, and cleared his throat.

"My lord," said the knight, his voice muffled by the lowered visor of his helm. The duke and Hiram turned to him, each with a sour look on their faces for having interrupted the mood.

"What brazen knight is this, who intrudes so boldly before his Duke?" demanded Hiram.

"With my Duke's permission," stated the knight. "I believe I have spotted the Lochaven forces' route move northward, towards the hills."

"Northward?" asked the Duke incredulously. "Did I not already say that their lair lies to the south? Were you not paying attention?"

"I have heard my Lord speaking… my Lord," replied the knight meekly. "And full well do I know that their lair lies to the south. But I know what I have seen. It is possible that Lochaven has an encampment on the north. They might expect us to move against their southern lair and assault the castle while it is defenceless."

The duke scratched his beard in wonder, and Hiram shrugged. "He's got a point there," said Hiram. "Those Lochaven dogs could be lurking somewhere we would not expect."

"Are you certain you've seen the assassins move to the north?" asked the Duke.

"Upon my honour, my lord," responded the knight promptly.

"Then north is where we shall go. It's possible the caves in the north may be their refuge."

The duke traced a finger around some hills drawn on the map. The hills were inked in grey, with a ghostly face painted directly over them.

"Death to Lochaven!" Hiram shouted, raising his sword aloft. "Death to all who dare stand against us!"

The rest of the knights roared in assent, howling with fury and adding their own war cries to a growing, powerful cacophony. Amid the cheers and armour-pounding, nobody noticed the two awkward knights slip out of the castle's keep and out into the castle grounds. Unseen, they ducked behind a shabby wooden stable and quickly took off their helmets, revealing Philly and Cadfael struggling to catch their breath.

"Do they actually fight with all this metal all over them?" asked Philly rhetorically. "I could hardly even walk in all this armour!"

"Looks like they took the bait," Cadfael remarked. "Now let's see if the others are willing to play along as well."

Night had passed over the Lochaven encampment several miles south of Ravenwall Castle. The Duke of Lochaven was a large, muscular man with a mane of blond hair tied back behind his head. His blue eyes were pointed down and his mouth was curled in what looked like a permanent snarl. His robes of black and red velvet dragged slightly on the dusty ground and his black leather boots had some small mud stains on them.

Around him, a contingent of knights and assassins was huddled around a campfire to stay warm. Most of the knights were out of armour, and some were polishing their armour, sharpening their swords with small grindstones, or trying to warm themselves by the fire.

The Duke of Lochaven, however, stood farthest from the fire, surrounded by four armoured knights. He took off his robe and let it fall to the ground, stepping over it. The rest of his wardrobe was a simple black shirt, vest and pants. He hefted a sword from a nearby knight, and stared down the four knights around him.

In an instant, he attacked the knights, slashing at them with his blade. The knights had little time to react and tried desperately to parry his attacks. The Duke was relentless and calculating in his every swipe, slash and twirl of his sword, aiming precisely for those small, unprotected areas on the knights' bodies where their armour was of no use. Their abdomens, shoulders and underarms were all targets for him, which he exploited ruthlessly. The swords clashed and clanged loudly, their sounds echoing through the night. One knight was felled as the Duke's blade carved into his neck, staining his breastplate with a crimson glow. Another knight had his sword parried effortlessly, throwing the knight off-balance, and met his end as the Duke stabbed him in the back. A third knight was downed with the Duke pirouetting around him and slicing through his unprotected back.

By the end of the battle, only one knight as left standing before the Duke of Lochaven, wounded but still alive. The knight gripped his bleeding shoulder and knelt down before the Duke, who pointed his sword directly at the knight's forehead.

"Do you dare challenge my authority again, sir knight?" asked the Duke coolly.

"Never again, my lord, and I beg my lord's forgiveness."

The Duke withdrew his sword, and nodded to some attendants nearby. Dressed in simple fabrics, the attendants helped the wounded knight to his feet and took him away to rest and recuperate.

"Let that be a lesson to you, sir knight!" shouted the Duke as the knight was being escorted away. "Where's Tybalt?"

"Here, my lord," said a man who entered the field. He was bald and had a wisp of a beard on his chin, clad in full red and black armour aside from his helm. "At your command, my Duke."

"Have the assassins returned from Ravenwall yet?"

"They have, and I present their report."

"Let's have it then!" shouted the Duke harshly.

Tybalt drew in a breath, and wiped a bead of sweat off his bald head. "My lord, they report that most of Ravenwall's court has been killed, as well as several of his guardsmen."

"And Ravenwall himself?"

"There is no way to know if he survived."

Lochaven tightened his grip on the hilt of his sword, and raised it to strike.

"Does he live?!" Lochaven growled. Tybalt winced back a step, trembling in fear. Lochaven lurched forward, still brandishing the bloodstained blade.

"I asked you a question, damn you! Does Ravenwall still live?!"

"He does, my lord!" called a voice behind the duke, who spun around quickly to face the speaker. One of the assassins sent to Ravenwall stood before him, still masked and clad entirely in black, such that it would have been easy to miss seeing him in the night. Were it not for the light of the fire reflecting off his eyes, he would have been completely invisible.

The duke was fuming, and pointed the sword at the assassin. "You and your brigade have failed me for the last time!" Lochaven roared.

"My lord, there is still time to write him. Revenue is—"

The assassin was quickly silenced with a blow to the stomach from the butt of Lochaven's sword. The masked assassin doubled over in agony, clutching his struck chest as Lochaven stood over him.

"I've already settled one trial by combat tonight," muttered the duke as he raised his sword. "I suppose it's time for a regular execution."

"My lord, Ravenwall is coming with his entire force!"

Lochaven paused and looked down on the wounded assassin with disbelief. To his side came Tybalt, who crouched down to get a better look at the assassin.

"How long until they arrive here?" Tybalt whispered.

"Two days at most," replied the assassin, still clearly in pain. "They plan on flanking us from the south, in the mountains! They'll ride over us all!"

"The mountains?" Tybalt echoed him. "Why would they do that?"

"Because we would least expect it, and they would be unassailable at the top of the mountains if they needed to retreat. I heard all this from Ravenwall him! I swear it!"

Tybalt turned to the Duke of Lochaven with a slight nod. After a tense pause, the duke withdrew his sword and turned away from the downed assassin.

"Knights, mount up!" shouted the duke to his army. "We ride for the mountain pass to ambush Ravenwall!"

The fire was put out, and the knights gathered all their belongings. The lone assassin slipped away from the hustling army and their loud, domineering duke, into a darkened grove of trees several feet off in the distance.

The assassin removed his mask, exposing the face of Cadfael. He was still frowning as he still felt the pain in his stomach from Lochaven's strike.

"Took some doing, but I think Lochaven took the bait," grumbled Cadfael to Philly, who was resting on a tree branch several feet over the ground. Philly dangled her feet over Cadfael's head and giggled slightly. Cadfael looked up and tried to playfully swipe at her feet, but Philly pulled herself up onto the branch out of his reach.

"Amazing how easy it was to get that assassin's outfit," Philly observed, looking to the north. "Lochaven's castle isn't far from here. We'll take their strong room while everyone's out in the mountains looking for Ravenwall."

"Anything to rebuild the troupe," Cadfael added. "Not to mention to punish them for having started this whole mess in the first place."

"Speaking of which," Philly remarked. "Let's also rob Ravenwall while he's gone too, for blaming us for the attack."

"Sounds fair," said Cadfael. Philly, then stood on the branch upright, and leaped off of the branch onto the ground, landing perfectly on her feet. Cadfael smiled; truly this woman was a marvel, and he wondered how he ever had the good fortune to have found her. He could not help but to embrace her in his arms and kiss her directly on the lips. Philly returned the kiss, and they both held each other closely, rubbing their hands all over one another. Philly moved her hands beneath Cadfael's black assassin costume shirt, and started to peel it off of his body. Cadfael did not struggle as Philly took it off of him and let it fall to the grassy ground. As such, Cadfael removed Philly's green blouse and let it drop onto a nearby tree root. Philly shivered in the cold, her bare flesh riddled with goosebumps, and pressed herself against Cadfael's lean chest.

They fell to the ground together and made love in the darkness, unseen by human eyes. Cadfael lay down on the ground with Philly on top of him, and he clasped his hands over her bouncing breasts.

Philly gasped and hummed pleasurably with every motion that she and Cadfael made against each other. Beads of sweat dripped from their bodies from the vigorous, intense action.

The two armies were easily tricked and kept away from each other, thus averting any chance of war. Philly and Cadfael had gone from losing everything to gaining the promise of a new and brighter future than any of them could imagine.

Together, and passionately in love with one another, they would rebuild their travelling troupe with the gold stolen from both factions. Together, they would entertain royals in more imaginative, creative ways than ever before, such that even Philly's fire dance would look tame by comparison. They would never tire of each other, never get bored with the same routines, and never abandon their dreams of performing, entertaining and inspiring wonders in the hearts of anyone so fortunate as to witness their spectacular feats.

They stayed together in each others' arms until dawn, when the first few rays of the sun were starting to pierce the veil of night. Cadfael let out a long, deep yawn and stretched out his limbs, still lay down on the ground with Philly resting on top of his body. He smiled and closed his eyes, caressing Philly's shoulders and back. Philly rested on Cadfael's chest, her head moving up and down with every breath he took. Cadfael rested in perfect serenity; he never wanted this moment to end.

This was perfect: the clouds catching colours of orange and yellow with the rising sun, the chirping of crickets, the soft, green grass on his back, and his dearest love wrestling with him. Cadfael cherished this moment for all it was worth. Sooner or later it would be over, but this moment would live on in his heart forever. Soon they would be raiding the treasuries of two clueless factions and be riding away into the distance with more gold than they had ever amassed before.

But something began to take shape in Cadfael's mind: a thought that corroded the blissful serenity with a growing sense of foreboding. Something was dangerously wrong, and it had to be dealt with swiftly and decisively, or both he and Philena would be certain to suffer for it.

"I think we'd better find Lochaven."

"What do you mean?" asked Philly, stirring from her sleep.

"If Lochaven gets up there in the mountain pass, I don't know if they'll ever come back down. You know how it can be up there. Those passes are narrow and steep. Nobody in his right mind would rush an army up there."

"So what?" Philly remarked. "They'll die up there and we get their gold. I thought the idea was to make sure they never start a war, remember?" She got up from off of Cadfael's chest and reached for her blouse to cover up. Cadfael stirred, and pulled himself upright.

"You're right, but when have we ever had to kill anyone before?" asked Cadfael. "If this is to be a new start for all of us, let's not stain it with anyone's blood. Otherwise, we're no better off than Lochaven, right?"

Philly sighed as she got dressed. She did not like the idea of having to come to Lochaven's aid, but she could at least understand Cadfael's concern. With all the tricks they have played on unsuspecting nobles in the past, never have they employed any lethal tactics against anyone. Of course, a guard would be unconscious for a few minutes and the nobles would be left fuming when they were robbed, but never has anyone died as a result of their trickery.

A single trail weaved through the tall, jagged mountains, slick with a thick cover of ice. Philly and Cadfael lost their footing several times while navigating the treacherous path, and had to lean on each other to stay upright. Frigid winds bit mercilessly at them both, despite Cadfael's assassin mask over his face. The towering crags stood over them like scornful giants. Small, bare stalks of plants poked out from among the jagged rocks lining the path, bending in the wind. Beneath the translucent ice sheet, Cadfael could see some footprints in the dirt road.

"They couldn't have gone far," Cadfael noted, and picked up the pace. The path snaked around the side of a mountain, where to the right was a steep, yawning chasm several hundred feet down over sharp-looking rocks. Philly and Cadfael stayed close to the cliff wall to the left, avoiding that chasm as much as they could. Philly shivered in the cold and in fear, but she kept going with Cadfael through the mountain pass.

They came to a more stable area of the mountains, where the path dipped down slightly into a small valley surrounded by boulders and bare, gnarled trees. The chasms were behind them, so the two stopped in the centre of the valley to catch their breath.

A single arrow whizzed through the wind and landed on the ground right by Cadfael's feet. They recoiled in alarm, and beheld several figures poking their heads out from among the boulders and trees. Assassins and knights from Lochaven's regiment stared down at them from all sides, blocking every way out of the valley.

"Come now, assassin," said Tybalt, emerging from the group. "I trained you better than that. Casually walking in plain sight with a woman on your arm, and here of all places?"

"Sir, I…" Cadfael started, but Tybalt silenced him quickly with a sword pointed to his throat. All around, the knights and assassins were gathered with their weapons at the ready. Swords, spears, and arrows were trained directly on Philly and Cadfael. From among the crowd, the Duke of Lochaven saw them as well. His hair was untied and blowing in the breeze.

"Who are you, really?" demanded Tybalt with a low, ominous voice. "We've been marching up these mountains all night, and we haven't seen any sign of Ravenwall."

Cadfael sighed, and removed his mask and flipped his hood down. Philly held on to Cadfael's left arm tightly.

"Your assassins killed my friends at Ravenwall's court," Cadfael said to Tybalt with a hint of rage behind his voice. "We were the entertainers."

Tybalt kept his sword pointed at him. "And you thought you'd get the best of us by sending us up here, thinking that we'd all perish?"

"We came back here to save you!" Philly cut in. "We could've left you here to die, after what you've done to us and our family! But we came back!"

Tybalt readied his sword to strike, but Cadfael stood defiant and steely-eyed. Philly clung to Cadfael's arm and shut here eyes, bracing for the inevitable attack. She figured this would be the end of everything, and that the love of her life was going to die in a matter of moments.

"Hold it, Tybalt!" ordered Lochaven from across the frozen valley. Out of his comforting robe, he stepped down into the valley and took the sword from Tybalt's hand. Tybalt withdrew back into the crowd, and Lochaven turned to Cadfael with an expression every bit as spiteful as Tybalt gave him earlier. Still, Cadfael stood his ground without even a wince.

"By our laws, an act of malfeasance against the Duke or his Order calls for a trial by combat to the death," Lochaven explained in a low, menacing voice. "As the offender, you are obligated upon your honour to accept this challenge."

"I accept," Cadfael responded simply. "Philena, stand aside."

"I'm not going anywhere!" Philly protested.

"I'll be fine, beloved. Trust me."

Reluctantly, Philly released her grip on Cadfael's forearm, and walked to Tybalt on the edge of the valley, near one very large boulder. Without Cadfael's bodily warmth, the freezing wind assailed her more than ever. Tybalt placed a gloved hand on Philly's shoulder to keep her in place. His grip was tight and painful on her shoulder, making Philly wince.

A sword was given to Cadfael by one nearby knight, the same one-handed model as that which Lochaven wielded. The blade was thin and sharp, and the metal crossguard led down into a hilt wrapped in leather bands. Cadfael hefted the sword and tightened his grip on it, staring down Lochaven with a steely, determined look. He took a strong stance, slightly wobbling on the ice that covered the ground. This was not going to be easy, he thought.

With everyone watching, the trial by combat began. Lochaven attacked first with an overhead, downward slash, but Cadfael parried it out of the way. Lochaven kept on the offensive with several more slashes in horizontal and diagonal directions, and still Cadfael blocked them.

Philly watched on in terror, forced to witness what could very well be the death of her lover. The two combatants kept slipping on the slick ground, making it impossible for anyone to keep their balance, let alone remain focused on the combat. The blades rang harshly with each clash, echoing in the wind.

Lochaven pulled his sword back, and thrust forward, expecting to impale his opponent. But in one masterful move, Cadfael slid on the ice off to the left side, so that Lochaven's sword only pierced the air in front of him. The duke slipped and fell forward on the ice, by the sword clattering to the ground out of his hand. Cadfael slid around and stood directly above the downed duke, pointing his sword down on his neck. Around him, Tybalt and the guards readied their weapons, but Cadfael kept the Duke in submission. He looked around at everyone, and at Lochaven, silently daring anyone to make a move that would result in spilling blood. Philly sighed and smiled with relief; Cadfael's artistry was in full effect, and it saved his life.

"I've done your pathetic trial by combat, Lochaven," Cadfael growled. "I think it's safe to say that I passed."

Lochaven shut his eyes and willingly nodded, as if the very act of submitting was highly foreign and revolting to him. Cadfael withdrew his sword and pulled theduke to his feet.

"If you want Ravenwall so badly, we sent them to the northern caves, where they'd never find any of you."

"The northern caves?" Lochaven repeated in disbelief. Cadfael silently nodded. All around them, the knights collectively gasped in horror and muttered among themselves. Cadfael looked around, wondering what was going on.

Tybalt walked over and grabbed Cadfael by the forearm, making him drop his sword. "You insufferable charlatan!" he bellowed. "Do you have any idea what you've done by sending them there?"

"What's going on?" asked Cadfael.

"To the north is the Banshees' Cave, you dog! Haven't you heard anything about that?"

The Lochaven regiment marched down a slowly inclining mountain pass to the north, keeping Philly and Cadfael as hostages. They were both bound with ropes on their wrists and pulled forward by several knights, others of which had spears trained on them. Cadfael moaned with every step they took out of the mountains and down into the valleys below.

He remembered Tybalt's long lecture about the Banshees' Cave, how past generations claimed it was a cursed place filled with damned spirits that remained imprisoned for all of eternity. Anyone brave or foolish enough to venture into the caves would disturb their imprisonment and release them into the world. They were said to be vicious, bloodthirsty ghosts that would attack at random and without mercy.

Cadfael never believed in those superstitions, but it was enough for the Lochaven force to move quickly northward to call a truce to rescue their own mortal enemies of Ravenwall. Cadfael never even knew why Ravenwall and Lochaven were at odds against each other in the first place, but those were matters of nobility that he largely ignored. All that mattered was that Lochaven was terrified of what would happen if anyone, even Ravenwall, disrupted the slumber of those supposed spirits.

The ride north took them through green, rolling hills and through thick forests. It was noon before they reached a hilly, grass-covered terrain with several boulders poking out of the green blanket at odd ends. Ahead of them was a hill with a massive opening cut into the very hill itself like a gaping, dark wound.

"The Banshees' Cave," Tybalt observed. Then he turned to the captives Philly and Cadfael. "No matter what happens here today, whether we make it out or not, you both are going to hang for this."

Philly trembled in fear, but Cadfael maintained his stoic composure. After having defeated Lochaven in combat, nothing that their army could threaten him with would ever scare him.

The inside of the cave was gigantic, far bigger than anyone would have guessed from outside where it looked like a simple hill. The knights lit some torches with flint sparks from the stones onto some tree branches. These makeshift torches lit the way for them to proceed, through a deep, earthy tunnel far beneath the hills. The rock walls had a jagged, uneven texture not unlike the mountains, and the stone floor was slightly wet with dripping water from above. Some drips fell onto the tops of Philly's head, and she shook them out of her blonde hair.

Philly kept her gaze pointed down at the ground as they proceeded, not caring to look at her captors around her. With every step, she noticed something strange: the smooth, moist ground was beginning to glow an unearthly tint of bright green. At first it was barely noticeable in the firelight from their torches, but it gradually began to get brighter and brighter until the glowing ground was so bright that it easily outshone the torches. The rest of the army noticed it as well once it was bright enough, and they began to feel uneasy. Tybalt and Lochaven kept them all moving.

Ahead of the group was a massive chamber, where the ceiling was hidden in shadow, but the ground was a vast oval of the unknown green glow. It shone off the walls, casting harsh shadows all around them.

"Look!" cried out one night, pointing up with his spear. Every gaze turned upward to behold, several figures floating above them. At first it was difficult to distinguish them, but one figure struggled against whatever force held him aloft, as if he was swimming in an invisible current of water. When he was low enough to the ground, the green glow illuminated him in greater detail.

Philly looked up and saw the form of the Duke of Ravenwall, clad in armour and struggling to stay low to the ground. He was constantly being pulled up away from the glowing floor as if by invisible strings, but he battled fiercely to reach the ground. Philly and the others could see that something was on his face. Closer inspection revealed that the Duke of Ravenwall placed some dried mud directly over his mouth, so that every sound he made was muffled. His eyes were bulging in terror at seeing Lochaven in the cave with him.

"Ravenwall?" asked Lochaven softly. Revenue shook his head hastily and tried to struggle even more against his invisible bonds. Panicked muffled sounds came from beneath the mud on his face.

"Answer me, man!" Lochaven demanded. "What is going on?"

As soon as he finished speaking, the ground's glow became brighter, so bright that Philly and Cadfael covered their eyes while everyone else was blinded. The cavern shook violently, and the sound of a loud, shrill wail emanated from beneath them. In the centre of the room, several feet away from Lochaven, a vaporous cloud burst up from the ground. Amorphous arms and a head formed in the cloud, like the form of a human, but with a shifting, translucent, and glowing figure. Its face was contorted in a shriek of panic and hatred, and its cry echoed brutally against the walls. Everyone tried to cover their ears, though Ravenwall and his army were still bound by the invisible forces. Some of Ravenwall's soldiers dripped blood from their ears, which spattered to the ground.

More formless shapes emanated from the ground, each one taking on another ghostly humanoid shape, and each one screaming the same ear-splitting yell. The phantoms spiraled all around the cavern, wailing all the while. Then they turned their gaze on the armies gathered in their cave. The soldiers readied their weapons, looking all around in fear.

Then the ghosts descended upon them like birds of prey, pulling the Lochaven regiment off the ground and yanking their limbs right off their bodies. Cadfael and Philly found themselves in the middle of a bloody rain with flailing arms and legs, with an occasional head as well. The soldiers screamed in terror as their spectral executioners made short work of them. Soldiers from both Lochaven and Ravenwall alike were not spared from their wrath. Armour and helmets were no match for their wrathful grips.

In the centre of the room, surrounded by the flying banshees was a much larger ghost, which had a face with a large wailing mouth and eyes turned down in abject despair. It looked on, still wailing, as the smaller ghosts continued their onslaught against the soldiers caught in its trap. Philly looked up at it, wondering if perhaps that was a leader of some sort of the ghost (or even if ghosts answered to a leader of any kind). With her captors torn apart right over her head and nobody to hold her rope, Philly marched away from Cadfael toward the largest of the ghosts.

"Philly! What are you doing?!" Cadfael protested, but Philly walked on.

"I'm ending this!" Philly stammered. "Nobody else is going to die because of me!"

Cadfael tried to pull her back with her rope, but Philly pulled her own arms back and jerked the rope in her own hands out of Cadfael's reach. A ghost soared right next to him, and Cadfael froze in fear. All he could see was the silhouette of Philly standing before the lead ghost, the green light from the floor pulsing brightly, blurring his vision. Cadfael shut his eyes, forsaking his own safety.

"Philly!"

It was over in what seemed like an eternity. When Cadfael opened his eyes, the glow was gone, and the cavern was in complete darkness. The cacophonous screams were passed, and not a single ghost was seen or felt. Cadfael looked around, not finding anything or anyone. In silence, he looked for the cave's exit, and upon finding it, he sprinted out of the chamber and out of the entire cave. His outfit was soaked in blood, and he collapsed on the ground retching in disgust.

Ahead of him was a small group of survivors from the attack, hailing from both sides. The two Dukes of Ravenwall and Lochaven and some of their knights were still alive, though they too were similarly bloodied. The mud from Ravenwall's mouth was cleared away, replaced with a gaping mouth and a paralysed look of disbelief.

"It was that young woman," Ravenwall remarked. "I saw her stand before the banshee and plead with it. She mentioned that she felt guilty for everything that transpired, and offered up her own life in exchange."

"She couldn't have!" Cadfael sharply exclaimed, still on the grassy ground. Blood dripped off his outfit and into the small puddle of vomit he produced. Lochaven, next to Ravenwall, somberly nodded.

"I'm afraid it's true," said Lochaven. "The young woman gave her life for us all."

Cadfael pounded the earth with his bare fists, screaming with as much despair and rage as the ghosts he confronted. He sobbed heavy tears, and struggled to breathe.

Months had passed since the incident in the Banshees' Cave. Cadfael found himself in the courtyard of another nobleman, surrounded by a flock of young and fresh-faced entertainers. He was wearing his favourite leather jerkin studded with esoteric, artistic symbols while his motley crew of performers was clad in bright, form-fitting costumes of gold and purple. Many of their faces were painted in similar colours, and they smiled and laughed while juggling small coloured balls in the air.

Noblemen and women gathered around the troupe roared with laughter and delight. Cadfael stood in the centre of the celebration wordlessly and unmoving. His mind was too fixated on that single moment of loss and agony to feel any of the joy that was shared around him. In his heart, he yearned for the sweet, warm embrace of Philena. But he knew that would never come to him again.

Nearby, a juggler continued his act for some members of the nobility. The balls he tossed into the air flew overhead several feet and descended neatly into his hand. The short-haired, big-nosed, thin-bodied juggler bowed and smiled for his audience, who clapped with approval.

Then, with the balls still kept in his hand, they began to move on their own. The audience and even the juggler were taken aback. He kept his palm open all the while, and the balls began to rotate in his hand all by themselves, without the juggler even curling his fingers to manipulate them.

Then the balls began to float off his hand in midair and spin in circles over their heads at dizzying speeds. Gasps and shouts of surprise could be heard from all sides, such that every audience member and every performer looked on in astonishment. Even Cadfael was pulled out of his wallowing in despair to take notice of the strange occurrence. The balls spun around madly and travelled in more directions. One ball whizzed right by a nobleman's bald head, and another floated into a monk's robe. The hooded man yelped with surprise and lost control of his body. He flailed around wildly, trying to find what unknown force took hold of him. A single red ball popped up from under his hood and bounced off his head, rolling to the floor innocuously.

Soon the show took an even more unexpected turn. Audience members started to float in much the same way the balls did earlier. A large, portly noblewoman was lifted several feet off the ground, and then descended back down to her seat neatly. She gasped in shock, then roared in jovial laughter after being set down. A knight's helm was suddenly twisted around, such that his face was covered with blank metal. The knight flailed about trying to right himself.

Cadfael looked on at the madness all around him, and a smile slowly formed on his lips.

"Philly…?"

The scenario of people flying and knights flailing disappeared, replaced once again with the Mystic Theater. People in the audience were still laughing at the earlier scene, but they quickly came to their senses once the abrupt change took over.

"That, dear friends," stated Doctor Xoctarious, "is the terrible price to pay when trickery goes too far. Philena would not have dared to stain her honour, or that lovely blouse of hers, with blood. She forfeited her own life to the spirits, but her love for Cadfael was so strong that even the bleakest of damned spirits took notice. Her release was but conditional, and she followed her lover for as long as he lived, and they were together entwined in the bright, immaculate hereafter.

"Trickery in and of itself is not a sin against man, but one must exercise caution when doing so."

"And now, ladies and gentlemen, we are prepared to offer a complimentary catered meal for our intermission. The next show will commence in one hour. Please enjoy our complimentary buffet and return in one hour," said Doctor Xoctarius,

As the crowd headed for the lobby, Gabriel Crowell walked up to the stage to meet the doctor. Curious, Gabriel asked the doctor about how the illusions were performed thinking only of the doctor in the beginning as simply a museum curator with a gimmick. Yet, Gabriel saw from his own perception that the doctor and this theatre had something that was very special and rare. .

"Doctor, you have got a real treasure here, a true treasure if only life was as amazing as this place, and I don't think anyone would want to leave it," said Gabriel.

"Life is much more than what you see outside or inside this place. This world is full of miracles, like the way you see the stars shine at night, or when you hear the sweet melodies of the birds that sing at the breaking of a new day. Or the way the ocean and all its wonders of beautiful fish and marvellous creatures that God made when the world began. Oh my friend, such wonders are all around you, more than you could ever imagine," reflected Doctor Xoctarious.

"I guess," said Gabriel contemplating it all. "By the way, how did you do that, bear transformation trick earlier?" asked Gabriel inquisitively.

"A good magician never reveals his secrets; you'll have to find that out for yourself," he chuckled. Gabriel laughed in return. The doctor accompanied his dear friend to the feast where they would dine and drink with the other guest and enjoy themselves.

A few minutes later, Gabriel looked for the bathroom; unable to find it, he managed to stumble into an office off to a side, inside a large antique mirror stood. He very intrigued by this mirror, and he began to see something inside of it, and his curiosity was piqued.

He stepped into the room, closer to the mirror, but careful no one was aware of his snooping, when out of nowhere the mirror filled with light. He began to see images inside the mirror: white robed figures and a sprawling, golden city. It was a heavenly view, almost like one of the doctor's own "visions."

Doctor Xoctarious stood right behind him

"Please leave this room immediately. It would be most unpleasant if you stayed in here," said the doctor sternly.

"What is that mirror in there? I could have sworn that I saw something in it," said Gabriel.

"Gabriel, that's not meant for you. You would do well to stay out. Also, the bathrooms are on the left side hallway, clearly marked. Now, if you please," said Doctor Xoctarius firmly.

His curiosity was not satisfied, as he went back to the theatre for the next show.

Later, the festivities continued with the audience returning to the Mystic? Theater to continue the next presentation. The doctor before the next "vision" spoke up the crowd, with a simple question. "What is it to love another human being, another soul? Is it possible to truly fall in love?

"The answer to this is yes, of course, but can someone love again after he has lost everyone he has loved? Can that soul find hope or will his heart be trapped in the past of lost time?... Such is the case in our next story. I call this tale: 'Automaton.'"

AUTOMATON

Story by
Dominic R. Daniels
Written by
Dominic R. Daniels & Doug K. Owen

1

The Mystic Theater disappeared around the audience, and where the smooth white walls and spotlights once were, there was a city skyline unwrapping all around them. From where Gabriel sat, he noticed the familiar sights of the Sears Tower and the John Hancock Center, inferring that they were looking at the city of Chicago, but the similarities ended there. Several more skyscrapers towered over those familiar landmarks in all sorts of shapes and styles, from the massive, bulky buildings to thin, pyramid-shaped structures. This obviously was not the Chicago he was familiar with.

The scene shift to a penthouse in a high-rise building, overseeing the city. Leather sofas and high-backed armchairs occupied the spacious living room. An expensive landscape painting hung on the far left wall, overseeing the richly detailed wooden parquet-floor.

A man and a woman were both seated at a small mahogany table, both seated in luxurious captain's chairs with green leather trim. Each one dined upon juicy prime rib, succulent buttery lobster Thermidor, crisply steamed vegetables, cheesy baked potatoes, and aromatic white wine. Three candles shone brightly with a silver candelabrum in the centre of the table.

The man sat across from the woman, Matthew P. Livingston, a slim and lean figure in his mid-30s, with neatly-parted brown hair and thin-wired glasses over his grey eyes. He smiled at the woman across from between bites of meat and potato. The woman was his wife, Sarah, who was also 30 years of age. She had long and flowing reddish-brown hair draped down her back. Her body was well-curved and appealing, and her face was immaculately formed, with luminous green eyes and an amiable smile with fine white teeth.

"Mmm, this lobster turned out really good," remarked Matthew. "Better than our wedding reception."

"Do you like it?" asked Sarah. "I made it with some special cream sauce for you."

"Yeah, it's really nice."

Sarah gazed into Matthew's eyes sweetly. "Well, you're worth it."

"Hard to believe, isn't it?" Matthew said. "Two years, we've been married."

"Yes, two wonderful years," Sarah observed.

"I still remember what happened in the church the day we got married."

Sarah laughed. "Yeah, that was so silly. They thought you were a total klutz and they thought I was drunk. I slipped over my own dress, and you caught me!"

"Yes, but I did put on a good show, right? I caught you right then and there, and then kissed you in my arms!"

"And everyone was laughing hysterically!" she said. "I remember that Father Benedict couldn't even get through to the service, since he was giggling so much. He just asked, 'So, I take this as a yes from the both of you?' and without missing a beat, we both said yes."

"Yeah, that was pretty funny," Matthew remarked. "I still have the photos of that day. Your mother was so embarrassed, she passed out."

"It was worth it to see the expression on her face." She laughed and finished her glass of wine, then lounged at the table.

"Are you just about done?" she asked Matthew. He nodded silently, finishing off the last of his lobster and prime rib together.

After dinner, they took two glasses of amber-coloured dessert wine to the conservatory to the far left of the dining room. A wall-sized window provided a full view of the brightly-lit Chicago skyline against the solid night sky. From there, on a large and lavish sofa, they sat together admiring the view. Matthew savoured the cool springtime night air, the sweet sensation of the wine on his tongue, and his wife at his side. He placed a hand on her left knee and kissed her tenderly on the lips.

"How did I ever get so lucky to find you?" Matthew mused. "I love you so much."

"I love you too, Matthew," Sarah replied. She finished off her glass of wine and wrapped her arms around Matthew tenderly. She kissed him full on the lips and moved her hands up and down on his back sensually. Matthew started to breathe heavier; he could tell she was in the mood, and he was every bit willing to satisfy her.

With the glow of the distant city, providing their light, Matthew and Sarah laid down on the couch together, kissing and holding each other closely. Matthew's hands went underneath Sarah's blouse and started to lift it off of her body. Sarah responded by undoing Matthew's belt, and more clothes started to follow. Together, they spent a tender, blissful moment that they would both cherish forever.

The next day found them both in professional-looking lab coats, walking hand-in-hand in the massive foyer of a skyscraper. The stainless white walls reflected sunlight from the high windows above. Around them were other people in lab coats, some of whom had large metallic, cylinder-shaped plugs on the backs of their necks. Matthew and Sarah walked past them simply, smiling and nodding. They had long since grown accustomed to the presence of androids.

Matthew was hailed as a remarkable genius in many fields of experience; called by the press "The New Bill Gates of the Times," a title he seemed not to relish but would rather be engrossed in his research.

Under his guidance, Zecktroph Enterprises grew into a powerhouse of robotic research and manufacturing. It was thanks to Matthew's contributions and unbridled passion that robots had become common household items, and androids walked among the human population.

In this year of 2040, Zecktroph was poised to grow exponentially, far beyond what Matthew envisioned when he first started the company. As a young boy, he grew up a whiz kid, working with his father who was a mechanical engineer and inventor. Like Matthew himself, his father had a love and undying fascination of robots and mechanical marionettes. When Matthew has been just ten years old, he chose to dedicate his life to others in giving a contribution to mankind by way of robotic science. He was a passionate and kind young man with a zest for life and helping others, just like his father who he idolized and worked with designing obscure prosthetic apparatuses to help those who lost their limbs in the military.

The eager younger Livingstone wanted to follow his dad's footsteps to do the same. After graduating from MIT, he started out as an toymaker and in animatronics with the movie industry as a special effects and prop wizard in the early days of his work. Eventually, with the help of some investors, Zecktroph Enterprises became his brainchild, where he could share his dream of advanced robotics with the world. He owned most of the patents on the advanced androids as well as the household and industrial-grade robots, which made him a very rich man. Meeting Sarah came later, and his life was filled with contentment.

Nothing could be better for Matthew. He had everything he ever could have wanted: an enjoyable career designing advanced androids, a lavish home, and a loving wife. Even in his spare time, he was still designing small robots for himself or to donate to some of his friends. Everyone who knew him called him the "Father of Mechanical Minds." Some may have even accused him in the past of being a robot himself, given how long he can push himself at work, but he laughed it off, saying, "I just love what I do." He slept very little, especially when his mind was working so fast. Even Sarah knew that he would be very hard to control when his mind was set on something.

That was especially true in the board meeting today, when Matthew spoke to a large group of black-suit clad investors and executives.

"By now, ladies and gentlemen," spoke Matthew in the wide-open space of the lecture hall, "we have already answered some of science's greatest questions. We have already answered, 'Is it possible to create an artificial human being?' That answer is already right here sitting among us."

He gestured to a young man in a business suit sitting in the middle of one of the rows among the executives. This handsome young man had close-cropped brown hair, a thin frame and a subtle smile. On the back of his neck was one of the familiar plugs. He smiled slightly as the executives around him applauded.

"Androids, artificial sentient beings," Matthew continued, "are learning computers designed to absorb information and evolve self-consciously, just like a young child growing up into a fine adult. They are every bit as intricate, yet cohesive, as humans of mortal flesh and blood. They are self-thinking and self-feeling, just as much as ourselves."

The more applause came from the executives.

"The problem is no longer, 'Can we create an artificial life?' but rather, 'Can we prolong the artificial life?' As of now, the latest android models, for all their intricacies and advancements, are limited by their own power sources. A seven-year shelf life is simply not long enough for a person to learn everything that life is all about. Not to mention our customers would most certainly want their robots to last much longer.

"Therefore, ladies and gentlemen, I propose that we take our current project to the next level. The new fusion-energy reactors to be used with the latest models of androids will extend the lives of every android, and greatly benefit their human companions. With this new form of energy, both humankind and robot kind will benefit. By 2042, only two years from now, we expect to make these fusion-cell power sources standard for all android models and household-level robotic products."

"Mr. Livingston," one of the executives cut in from among the renewed burst of applause. "What is the point of extending the shelf-life of androids?"

"Reliability, of course, Mr. Reginald," Matthew responded promptly. "We did not get this far in pioneering robotics by being second-rate, and we do not intend to become second-rate at any time. The androids deserve longer lives, and humans deserve more time with them."

Another executive, a large bald man, stood up from among the group of executives. "Are you suggesting that you feel for the androids?"

"They do feel, sir," replied Matthew. "They *are* us, every bit as much full of life as you and me. Flesh and blood made through polymers and wiring. Then again, isn't the human body composed of the same thing when you think about it? Skin and sinew, those are polymers at the molecular level. Wiring? Every one of us has several hundred yards of nerves clustered into our bodies. Why are we so different from androids? Truth is, we're not."

"Then what do you propose we do with our current models?"

"Only that we extend their lives to the same degree as a human lifespan. When the advertisements talk about lifelong companionship, we mean it."

"And what about the social issues?" asked the bald executive.

Sarah picked up with her radiant voice filling the room. "We are providing an indispensable service to human beings who are longing to find a companion that will always be loyal to them. Many people in our modern society are not always fortunate and advantageous to be able to marry or to even develop close relationships with others. We are filling in that gap and that need in the world."

Some of the executives looked at Sarah almost enviously. It was no secret to anyone how strong their marriage remained even in the midst of their busy lives.

"I am speaking about androids that are given the capacity to become life mates. They can last a lifetime and be able to provide a need for nurturing and love for our clientele."

Sarah stood up and came to Matthew's side as the bald executive continued his line of questioning in front of the rest of the other executives.

"That's good intentions," said the bald executive. "But we can't force anyone to pick up an android. What if someone doesn't want that kind of companionship? What if even the robot doesn't want it?"

"We already have that resolved," Sarah said back, defending Matthew. "By developing a compatibility program with certain sensitive lines of code into a special microchip in each model, it will enable the android to seek the highest level of compatibility with whomever it comes in contact with."

"You mean that it could love someone?" the bald executive kept questioning him. "Absolutely, and wholeheartedly love someone?"

"In practical theory, yes," Sarah said.

"Not just in practical theory, actually," added Matthew. "We have a guest here among us today with some valuable information."

He gestured to the back of the room, where a stranger was seated quietly among the executives. He was a young man in his early-20s, far younger than Matthew or anyone else on the board. His face was slightly stout, and his black hair was slicked back. He wore a dark-grey business suit, different than the uniform black suits everyone else wore. He sat calmly and relaxed since he did not consider himself part of the board or any of its proceedings. He stretched out his limbs and let out a deep yawn.

"Andrew, would you mind coming up here to the front of the room please?" asked Matthew. Andrew did so with little hesitation, strolling casually down the small stairs on the side of the lecture hall past the gaze of all the executives.

"Can you turn around please?" Matthew kindly suggested. Andrew turned around slowly in a circle, showing off his front and back to everyone. Then Matthew turned to his audience.

"Ladies and gentlemen, would you think that our friend here is a human or an android?"

He was met with several suggestions from the executives saying he's obviously human, since he did not have the large plug on the back of his neck. Matthew grinned, expecting that answer.

"Actually," Matthew responded. "Andrew here is a prototype for the new android model. He runs on the very same fusion-chamber reactor that was just under discussion. As such, he doesn't need to plug in at all the way standard androids do, and there's nothing on his body to give him away as being an android."

"Even my own wife has yet to know that I am an android," Andrew added with a calm, nearly expressionless voice. Some of the executives went wide-eyed at this revelation.

"Yes, I am married," said Andrew, showing off a gold wedding band on the finger of his right hand. "Dr. Livingston made an excellent point about an android falling in love, and here is the proof. I have been happily married for approximately one year to a human female."

Mr. Reginald, one of the executives, was confused by this discovery. "If you're married, then how do you... well... procreate?" he asked, looking for the right words.

"That is still something of a challenge at this time," replied Andrew. "Though I am capable of stimulating a woman for physical pleasure, actual reproduction is still reserved for organic life forms."

"I'm sure we can get to that later," said Matthew.

That early evening found Matthew and Sarah together in bed. Their bedroom, like the conservatory, came with a wall-sized window that opened out over the Chicago scene. Their king-sized bed, with its soft mattress and smooth cream-white sheets of Egyptian cotton, offered a splendid view of the city in unrivalled comfort. Matthew rested down on the soft mattress next to his wife, letting his right hand caress her warm body. They were both still fully clothed, only just taking a moment to relax before it came time to sleep.

"The demonstration went really well today," said Matthew. "Andrew really impressed them."

"Just like we said," Sarah observed. "Lifelong companions. Just like us."

"Not everyone in the world is so fortunate to have someone like you and me, so here we are providing that experience to everyone."

"But those androids will never be as brilliant as you," Sarah said sweetly to her husband.

"Or as caring and beautiful as you," added Matthew. "I'll always be the brilliant mind, you've seen me to be, as long as you're there at my side."

"And I always will be at your side, as your muse, dear," said Sarah, with a loving embrace to him. "My brilliant mind."

"You're too kind, sweetheart," Matthew whispered."I wish this moment would last forever."

"I know, and I'm lucky I married you."

In the midst of their laying down together, Matthew began to stir and get up from the bed.

"Babe, where are you going?" asked Sarah.

"I just remembered that I need to head down and pick up some new power cells. The appliances have been acting sluggish again."

"What if I go instead?" Sarah suggested. "You've already done enough today as it is. I'll get the cells for you, and you can just get comfortable."

"Are you sure?" asked Matthew.

"Don't worry," Sarah said calmly. "I'll be fine."

She kissed Matthew sweetly on the lips, then grabbed her coat. Matthew laid back down on the bed alone. The last few rays of sunlight began to ebb over the city, and in response the towering skyscrapers pockmarked themselves with the lights. Each mono-lith became a checkerboard of light and darkness, twinkling in the ever-darkening sky. Above, the stars began showing themselves. Matthew started to doze off slightly while looking for the constella-tions Leo, Capricorn and Orion.

Four hours passed while he slept, and he was jolted awake by his phone ringing. The thin, wallet-sized device on his nightstand flashed to life, displaying a small holographic image of a yellow police badge symbol. Matthew grumbled as he was yanked out of a comfortable sleep, and lazily reached for the phone. His curiosity was piqued slightly seeing the police logo in the hologram that appeared.

"Matthew Livingston," he said as he pressed a small button to accept the call. An image of a bald, portly officer with overly pink cheeks appeared in the hologram that he held. His blue eyes in the image were kept turned down in a show of authority.

"Dr. Livingston, this is Sergeant Peterson, Chicago Police," the phone said with a low, stern voice. "We have news about your wife."

"Sarah?" asked Matthew with a sudden sense of trepidation, seeing as how she still has not yet come home. "What happened?"

"I hate to have to say this, but I've got bad news," resumed the officer. "There's been an accident. Her car had a malfunction and she crashed into the side of a building on 8th and Commonwealth."

"Where is Sarah? What hospital is she in?" Matthew asked fervently. "Is she alright?"

"I'm sorry, Doctor. Your wife is dead,"

Matthew froze, his eyes going wide and his breath coming out in short gasps. Every last part of his mind tried to absorb the information and then flatly refused to believe what he had just been told. *Impossible!* he thought to himself. *She can't be dead!*

"Doctor?" asked the officer over the phone. "I am very sorry but I had to inform you of the matter, especially to you of all people. I can refer you over to a grief counselling service if you want."

Matthew said nothing. His mind was reeling from the shock he had just sustained. Images of Sarah were already floating in his mind; her face was smiling and her eyes were bright. Then came the crushing realization that she was gone, never to return.

"Doctor?" asked the officer to the silent Matthew.

Six months had passed, and Matthew spiraled into the most severe state of depression. His entire life, everything that he had ever known and loved, had become unraveled and out of control. A stately funeral for Sarah had already long passed, with hundreds of black-clad mourners and Matthew so racked with sadness that his eulogy became little more than a disjointed series of sobs.

Weeks prior, the company that produced automatically-driven cars, seeing the malfunction that killed Sarah, issued a full recall of the cars and offered Matthew a paltry settlement, though he did not care about the money and had it donated to different charitable institutions; to him, his wife was worth more than all the wealth in the world, and his grief burdened his mind with the weight of shame his soul was crushed.

He started missing days at work, and he began to lose color in his face and had lost his appetite, losing weight as he became very thin. He lost interest in his work and mostly spent his days sitting in a motorized wheel chair with his own health, disintegrating rapidly from neglecting himself as he hid away in his self confined prison and penthouse from public life.

He began to abuse different psychiatric drugs to ease his sorrow, but it did not help take away his emotional anguish finally his muscles were starting to give out and his body was experience bouts of great spasms and pain; the doctors began to prescribe him morphine which only worsened Matthew's situation. The man that had once been hailed as a technological genius and legend by the worldwide media was reduced to nothing but a washed up wealthy drug fiend.

His despair did not go unnoticed by Zecktroph or the general public. Headlines on various newsfeeds kept coming up with new and inventive excuses for Matthew's disappearance from the public. The leadership of Zecktroph, after long deliberation, had placed the vice president in charge of the company until Matthew was able to return. But that time had yet to come.

There was a time when Matthew's penthouse was a place of joy and rapture. Matthew and Sarah would together throw lavish parties for friends, family and coworkers, and the halls would be filled with the sounds of pleasant conversation and festive music. The framed photographs of Matthew and Sarah together adorned every wall, reminding them both of the happy life they led.

Now, the halls were unbearably silent. The photos on the walls were stark reminders of the joy that Matthew had long since lost, never to regain again. There were times in which Matthew would quickly avert his gaze from any of the pictures on the walls just to avoid stirring that sense of longing. That fateful night had taken away more than just his beloved wife; it took his entire livelihood, his senses of purpose and direction, his very reason for being, all of his joy and wonder.

It was gone, leaving him as a decrepit wreck of a man resorting to injecting morphine into his body just to avoid feeling anything or caring about anything. Life was pointless. Nothing made sense anymore. For the first time in his life, and Matthew began to yearn for death. He just did not care anymore.

Another lonely night had come, and Matthew found himself seated on one of the plush sofas, hunched over a small pile of android parts on the wooden coffee table. Building small android toys became one of the very few ways he could pass the time, and it reminded him of that simple joy he felt in his early childhood, the love of creating robots that he once wielded.

It had been a very long time since he even gave any thought to androids or building them. His gnarled fingers struggled to fit the tiny metallic pieces into place, quaking uncontrollably. He sighed, and put the pieces of the half-finished robot on the table. *This was a waste of time*, he thought to himself. But then again, what good was his time anyway?

There was a knock on the front door, and Matthew struggled to get up from the sofa to answer it. The knocking was rhythmic and low in volume; whoever was on the other side was patient. Eventually Matthew reached the door to answer it, beholding a man with a slim build, a pointed nose and solid black eyes. A circular metal socket poked out through his neatly-groomed black hair on the back of his neck.

"Good evening, Dr. Livingston," said the man in a flat voice. "My given name is Bob, and I have been sent by Zecktroph Ent—"

"I know, Bob," Matthew cut him off with a grumble. "You were sent by Zecktroph to check up on me. You've been doing that for weeks now."

"It is only until we can formally assess that your condition has improved suitably." Bob stepped into the room with rigid, calculated steps, unlike the relaxed posture of a human.

An hour passed while they played chess together in the living room, with Matthew once again on the sofa and Bob seated in one of the high-backed chairs. After taking Matthew's bishop with a pawn, Bob glanced to his right of the chessboard to notice the small pile of android parts that had been swept to the side.

"We had been wondering if android production was still of any interest to you," Bob remarked. "Your move."

Matthew thought for a moment, and nudged a white rook forward one space, only to be taken by Bob's knight. "I tried," Matthew muttered. "But nothing's that simple anymore. I can't even make a toy model, my nerves in my hands are shot,"

"I had come to notice the tendency of grief to remove any interests one might possess," Bob observed. "In your case, the loss of Sarah, with whom you shared a deep emotional connection, was a catalyst creating these overwhelming feelings within you."

Matthew said nothing; he knew these feelings all too well.

"Feelings, however, even as overbearing as these, do tend to diminish gradually," Bob continued, sacking Matthew's remaining bishop with his black queen. "I believe the phrase is: time heals all wounds. Did I use that in the right context?"

"I think," said Matthew.

"Six months and one week have already passed since the accident. We both know that the accident can be attributed to nobody, not even Sarah and certainly not yourself."

"How do you know?" asked Matthew bitterly. "I said it was okay if she went on that errand! If I hadn't stopped her before she left…"

"There was never any way of anticipating the conditions leading to the outcome," Bob said to stop the Matthew's line of thought. "Nobody could have anticipated the car auto-driving system going into malfunction at that exact time or that exact place."

"But why?" asked Matthew. "Why did this happen to her? And why should this be happening to me? She never deserved to die!"

"Another common defence mechanism for humans in grief is to create a scenario which casts them as a victim of circumstance," Bob replied. "Some may take these events as a sort of carefully-devised plan by a deity, but those sentiments are unfounded. Much less is there any use in asking for any reason behind the events, as it is already established 'why' they happened."

"I already know!" Matthew stammered. "I miss her more than you can imagine! And here you are telling me the same thing over again that it wasn't my fault, that I'm not the victim here, but I've heard this before!"

"My only option is to repeat my advice until it is revealed that you are acknowledging and applying it. The main purpose of my visitations is to ascertain your condition at the behest of the company's leadership, until such time as when you are mentally and physically prepared to resume your role in Zecktroph's research and development sector."

Matthew simmered down in his outburst, exhaling deeply and staring at the chessboard. Very few of his white pieces were left, and his king was trapped in a corner, surrounded by Bob's queen, rook, and bishop.

"It's just... I don't know what to do anymore," Matthew whispered. "Nothing makes sense anymore without her."

"You invested a great deal of your energy building up a life that revolved around your wife and the hope that your circumstance would be a baseline for the rest of your life," Bob declared. "It is an historical fact that humans live a certain number of years, and then die due to a multitude of causes. There may even come a time in which I myself will cease to function, in which case I may simply be replaced with a new and upgraded model."

"Are you suggesting I look for someone else?" Matthew asked.

"The possibility of you locating a suitable companion is outside my computational range, especially the possibility of you locating someone with whom you can forge a new emotional connection as equally strong as it was with Sarah."

"Last week, I tried going to one of those dating service sites," Matthew muttered. "I got one message from a woman."

"That is a suitable place to begin," said Bob.

"She only wanted to get to know me because I'm rich. She kept going on about how wealthy and powerful I am, and how she'd always wanted to date someone important."

"It sounds like she is acting on impulses of vanity."

"They all are," said Matthew, nudging his king one space to the left.

"Dr. Livingston, there is still a great deal of information I lack regarding human interconnections," said Bob. "I will not know if another connection will be in store for you in the foreseeable future. But I am curious, especially seeing your incomplete android model to my right: is it possible for a human to emotionally bond with a machine in a similar regard?"

Matthew paused. Such a thought had never come across his mind.

"I couldn't," he replied. "You just said machines can be replaced, but I can't possibly replace Sarah and everything she ever was to me."

"My curiosity may have led me to a false conclusion, then," said Bob, moving his queen over a space. "Checkmate."

Matthew nodded, accepting his loss of the game.

"You lasted in the game for three more moves than last week's game," Bob remarked. "It is possible your mental acuity is beginning to increase. Perhaps if you cease your irregular doses of chemicals, your acuity may return to normal."

"What chemicals?" asked Matthew.

"You have been injecting yourself with high concentrations of morphine for the past month and a half. It would be to your benefit to cease these doses and permit your body some more healthy pursuits."

"I will, tomorrow," Matthew responded, getting up from the sofa.

"You have consistently responded by assuring me that you will begin taking these responsibilities 'tomorrow.' Remember that there are still investors and other figures that are dependent on your ability to recover and return to normal functions."

Bob got up from the chair and walked to the front door. He shook Matthew's hand in a cold, tight grip and walked out the door.

"You can anticipate my return next week at the same time," said Bob.

"I will. Good night, Bob."

"Good night, Dr. Livingston."

With that, Matthew shut the door and returned to the living room. He put away the chess set and returned to the half-done android model. The tiny, silvery pieces were still very difficult for him to work with, but Matthew was eventually able to snap them together in place. A small robotic torso was complete, and he added two spindly arms to its sides.

He looked through the pile of other miscellaneous pieces, finding the casing for the head. It was made from pink-coloured plastic, with a painted face and artificial yellow hair. Though it was not yet the piece he needed, Matthew held the little face in his hand and stared at it. The face looked almost like Sarah's. The more he stared at it, the more an idea began to take shape in his mind, coupled with Bob's previous notion about falling in love with an android.

He began to fall asleep at the table, hunched over the coffee table. Most of the small metallic pieces were off to the side, but one of them dug into Matthew's cheek as he slept. In his mind, he could see himself dancing a slow waltz with Sarah, as radiant and wondrous a sight as ever she was in life. Around them was a series of workbenches and android part in piles. They waltzed together over bundled wires and spent power cells, enraptured in each other's presence. Matthew felt none of the anguish that had consumed him; this was a perfect moment for him, dancing with his wife in a laboratory.

Sarah held Matthew's head close and kissed him romantically. Matthew held her in his arms and returned the kiss. He caressed the back of her body, his hand moving up and down the length of her back to the nape of her neck. There, his fingers ran over a small metal socket. Then Sarah's face began to change right before his eyes. Where the rosy cheeks, sparkling eyes and smiling mouth once were, there was a metallic face staring back at him. Matthew was not terrified, for the face still resembled Sarah, as if she had become a metal statue.

"I will always love you," said the metal face of Sarah. *"Even if we are worlds apart, I will always love you."*

Matthew awoke with a start. An android piece left a small rectangular-shaped indentation in his right cheek. His mind was reeling from the dream he recently had. What if Bob was right about people and machines having a connection to one another? What if he could make an android the he could love? What if he could bring Sarah back to life?

If the higher-ups at Zecktroph wanted to see a Matthew return to normal, then they would have been satisfied to see Matthew returning to the workshop in his home, creating detailed schematics of a new android model. Hours were spent poring over his holographic computer with various three-dimensional models of body parts and facial features. All the while, Matthew kept the small android face from the model kit on his desk, staring lifelessly at him while he worked.

The android parts were functional enough, as they came from recycled Mark I and Mark II designs, and the synthetic skin and facial features, tailored to Matthew's exact specifications, would be no problem either. Those he could acquire from Zecktroph's foundries.

However, for all the physical aspects of the android to replicate Sarah as much as possible, there was still a problem that gave Matthew pause for thought. Would this android have the same personality as Sarah once displayed? Would she remember all their little inside-jokes and names for each other? Or would she be a shell of her former self? He would need some way to ensure that this was as much Sarah as it could possibly be, without directly bringing her back from the grave.

But then again…

He drew out his cell phone and put in a call to the police department. The phone rang several times before he heard an answer or saw a face in the hologram emanating from his phone.

"Sergeant Peterson," said the voice on his phone.

"Good evening, Sergeant; this is Dr. Livingston," Matthew spoke into the phone.

"Dr. Livingston? It's been a while, hope you've been okay ever since, well, what happened a few months ago."

"I'm on the mend," said Matthew. "I was wondering what the laws are about exhuming bodies."

"What?" asked the sergeant. "Why would you want a body?"

"It's for research purposes, and I'd rather take this on legally. I'd like to have access to my wife's body if it's possible."

It took some effort on Matthew's part, but he finally got the sergeant to agree. The officer was still skeptical and more than a little unnerved by the doctor's request, but he saw no other way. Matthew was going through legal channels to get the body, and his request had to be granted. Matthew especially noted the extent of Zecktroph's wealth and influence, and suggested that one lone officer against a multi-national corporation would be an uphill battle.

Another restless night, and Matthew spent it in his workshop. Several workbenches were cluttered with android parts, and over to an operating table on the far end of the room, an android body in the form a woman lay dormant. Her skin was already applied to Matthew's specifications; the Zecktroph foundry did an exquisite job replicating Sarah's features, right down to the curve of her mouth.

Matthew dressed the android's body in one of Sarah's favourite blouses, with blue and white patterns. Another table next to it held the lifeless body of Sarah; the real and organic body that used to be Matthew's beloved wife. A mortician had done a job six months ago of cleaning her wounds and embalming her body. Her fatal wounds were entirely around her heart and lungs, so her brain was thankfully intact. Matthew had several metallic implants lodged carefully into the sides of her head, and each one connected to a tube that pumped nano-machines in her brain.

Those microscopic drones would travel through her brain and harvest data from the remaining neural material in her mind and would create a database of her memories, thoughts, and feelings. Thus, Matthew hoped, would be Sarah's essence be re-created, that he could place it inside the android. Sarah would live again.

"Here goes nothing," Matthew whispered, starting up his holographic computer. A series of windows opened in the holograms, prompting him to transfer metadata and activate the power cells in the new android. Without hesitation, Matthew selected "yes" to each one. The android was hard-coded and registered in to the national android database.

When the prompt came to give the android a name, he typed in one word: Clara. He chose this name carefully, as it sounded like "Sarah," but at the same time was different. He figured that if he was ever to come back to the public view, he had to keep up pretences. Clara would be his passage out of the spiral of depression. She would be his muse, his companion, his secret lover.

A short moment passed before the android next to Sarah's body began to stir and sit upright. Matthew's heart skipped a beat, seeing one Sarah still dead on a table, and another Sarah get up off from the table. Anticipation rose in his heart, and he could scarcely contain himself.

The android looked in Matthew's direction, and spoke with Sarah's voice.

"Where am I?" she asked, confused and looking around.

"You are here, in my home," said Matthew.

"Who are you?" she asked.

"My name is Matthew. Your name is Clara. I made you."

Clara looked puzzled, and turned to the inert body next to her, which was still splayed on the table with the devices implanted into her skull. She screamed in terror, and fled from the room. Matthew held out a hand to try and stop her, but she ran past him and out the door. Matthew ran after her as she bolted up the stairs and out the front door. She ran down the penthouse's hall and fled the entire building. Matthew stopped in the middle of the door frame, looking down the hall for any sign of Clara. It was hopeless; his creation had already fled.

There was only one thing for him to do.

The police station foyer was very spacious, and a hologram of an officer sat at a desk, a glowing image of a young man in a spotless blue uniform. He was speaking to a young, blond woman who was in a state of fear.

"Good evening Miss. How can I be of service?" asked the programmatic officer.

"Officer, I think someone is trying to kill me," Clara claimed, stricken with fear. "I just woke up in someone's house, and there was a dead body right next to me."

"What is your name, ma'am."

"My name? Uh… Clara," she said with some hesitation.

"Do you have a last name, ma'am?"

"I don't remember."

"Where were you when this happened?"

"I don't know! I was in a room in a building somewhere, and I ran out!"

"Miss, we cannot assist you without more information. I will call in one of my superiors to better assist you."

At that moment, Matthew stepped into the foyer, and instantly noticed Clara on the desk with the holographic officer.

"There you are!" he exclaimed. Clara recoiled in fear and pointed an accusatory finger at him.

"That's him!" she screamed loudly. "That's the man who kept me!"

The holographic officer looked at him, then turned to Clara, unsure of what was going on.

"Check her barcode," Matthew explained. "She's an android, Class 27 prototype."

"What are you talking about?" asked Clara.

"There's a data key at the tip of her left thumb. It's a scanable code. It has all the information. She's registered to me."

A small, square-shaped plate of metal appeared inlaid in the desk. The officer's hologram pointed to it and directed Clara to put her thumb there.

"Miss, please hold your left thumb onto the plate," the officer directed. She did so with hesitation, and a separate hologram appeared next to her thumb, with her picture, name and other information.

Name: Clara Livingston. Owner: Matthew P. Livingston. Registered model Class 27, Zecktroph Enterprises. Model systems number 010.

There was another technical jargon displayed in the hologram, but the proof of Clara's identity was clear. She took her thumb off the pressure plate, and the hologram with the information disappeared. She turned to Matthew, and nodded with her eyes closed.

"Alright, let's go back home," Matthew said calmly. Clara said nothing, instead going with him quietly in surrender.

Back at Matthew's home, Clara looked around the living room inquisitively, noticing the photographs of Matthew and Sarah.

"Who is she?" Clara asked.

"Sarah," Matthew explained. "It's you."

"But my name is Clara," she replied. "You just saw that at the station."

"No, it really is you. I created you using Sarah's memories. You *are* her. You're the same person. The only difference is your body."

Clara looked confused. "I don't know what you're talking about."

"Don't you remember anything? The past? Us?"

She shook her head.

"Hmm, maybe you should go into sleep mode for a few hours. Your memories may not have had time to fully synchronize with your neural relay system. I haven't done anything with organics before, so it might not be perfect just yet. It will take time to get used to."

That night was restless for Matthew. Clara was in a sleep-mode in the living room, leaving Matthew to sleep alone in the bedroom. His depression was slowly making a return, coupled with worry. What if the downloaded memories did not sync with Clara's mind at all? What if the nano-machines did not collect anything from her mind? What if Sarah's brain was already completely dead with nothing to collect in the first place? What if the entire project was just a waste of time? He thought in his mind what do with the android. He could not sell her, being registered to him, and she was a custom-built model. Who would even want to purchase a created android like her? It will be wrong to sell her.

"I'll probably just have to get used to her," he muttered. "And that'll be it."

Days passed, and Matthew was beginning to get accustomed to Clara. But she was not becoming accustomed to him in return. Every day was spent wondering who she was supposed to be, and what kind of person Sarah was.

Clara found Matthew working alone in his workshop, poring over a small android model. She approached her from behind and looked over his shoulder at what he was working on, seeing some backward-shaped legs and synthetic white and curly fur.

"You need something?" asked Matthew, not looking up from his work.

"What are you doing?" she asked.

"I'm building something for you," he responded. "It's not done yet. it's a surprise."

"What is it? What is it?" she prodded him repeatedly.

"It's not ready yet."

"Please?" she begged. Matthew smiled slightly and moved aside to show her the framework of a robotic puppy. The right leg was still not attached, but the overall framework was in place. The head and ears were attached, with its glass eyes inlaid in the metal frames.

"Sarah always wanted a poodle," Matthew explained as Clara looked at the incomplete model. "I thought you'd like it. But it's not done yet, and I still need to put the fur on."

She smiled. "This is for me?"

"Yes. Call it a welcome-home present."

"Thanks."

"You know, since you're here," said Matthew, "maybe you could stay as my guest for about a week. And after that, if you want to go, you can."

"Are you sure?" she asked. "I thought you made me?"

"I did, but I'm not going to force you to stay here. That would be wrong on my part. You're not a prisoner here, my dear, but I would not mind if you chose to stay,"

"I'll think about it," she replied, going upstairs to leave Matthew for his work. He resumed work on the small robotic poodle, completing the frame and installing it A.I. Construct. He thought about Clara as he made the puppy; the way she acted when she was trying to peek over his shoulder and beg to see the present reminded him so much of Sarah. Maybe the memories were starting to manifest after all. Only time would tell.

A few moments later, he went upstairs to the conservatory to find Clara looking out the window. The sunset over Chicago looked particularly radiant today, with clouds overhead filled with bright tints of orange, red and yellow far above the dark shapes of the city skyline. She then looked around the room at all the flower arrangements: the white tulips and the orange and purple dragons of paradise. A colourful Venus Flytrap opened its maw lazily and closed it shut.

"This place seems familiar," she muttered.

"I'd hoped it would," said Matthew as he entered the room. "Sarah used to love spending time in here, especially at sunset."

"What would you do together?"

"Oh, just talk. Sometimes we'd have tea together, and on occasion we'd even make love here."

"This seems like a strange place to do those things."

"Well, two people in their own home—it's quite common. You still don't remember very much. But it'll come back to you in time."

They sat down on the wooden bench together, facing the sunset among the plants. Matthew gently placed a hand on her shoulder.

"What do you want to talk about?" asked Clara.

"Do you remember anything?"

"I remember this room," she replied. "I feel like I've been here before."

"Anything about me?"

"I remember seeing you in the lab downstairs, and in that room with a large table. We were eating together."

"What did we have? We would cook together. I would prepare for you your favourite: braised prime rib, and you would make for me lobster Thermidor in a butter sauce," said Matthew.

"I remember now; you always were grateful to me," said Clara.

"Of course I am; I loved you. I still do, but this will take time to rebuild what was in the past," said Matthew.

"Is that why you built me?" asked Clara pensively.

"Yes," he admitted. "You were so precious to me, and I loved you with all my heart. How could I let the past go, what happiness we had together? Is it a sin to love someone that much?"

"I don't really know what love is."

"Would you like to learn?"

"I wouldn't mind," she responded.

The next day, Clara stood in the living room observing the framed photos on the walls. The wedding picture was on display, and various other pictures of Matthew and Sarah together on their honeymoon in Costa Rica, lounging on rolling green hills and posing with colourful exotic birds.

Inwardly, she felt something stir: a deep sense of connection to those moments captured in the photos. She thought about the wedding picture, and what that moment must have been like. Images started coming into her mind in fragments, like from a half-remembered dream.

She could faintly grasp what her wedding was like, especially that moment when Matthew caught her in his arms in front of the congregation. Another flashback appeared when she looked at one of the honeymoon pictures; she remembered swimming in a lagoon with Matthew under a waterfall. She pictured herself in a bright blue bikini and him in navy blue trunks, swimming together in the clear blue water on a sunny day. It was mildly warm, slightly breezy, and the waterfall was refreshing to swim underneath. She even remembered the sensation of small fish swimming against her legs in the water.

These memories and more flooded her mind, and her green eyes began to light up brightly.

"I remember...!"

Matthew came upstairs with the completed robotic poodle in his hands. Seeing Clara in the room, he brought the dog over to her. The dog delivered a small yelp of affection upon seeing Clara, and licked Matthew's hand lovingly with its artificial tongue.

"Matthew," Clara started. "I have to talk to you about something."

Matthew sat down the dog to let it scamper around the room, and turned to Clara. He had no idea what to expect, and after having known Clara this long, something important was bound to happen. He could sense a hint of sadness in Clara's robotic eyes.

"What's wrong?" he asked gently.

She said nothing at first, instead moving slowly right towards Matthew as he stood still. She caressed his cheek slightly, then moved her head forward to make their lips meet. Matthew was taken by surprise at first, but then realized what was going on, and returned the kiss. They both held each other, kissing and caressing. Clara pulled back slightly and looked into his eyes with a smile, the same smile that Matthew remembered so well from Sarah.

"I remember," she whispered. Matthew could scarcely believe it, let alone get a single word out to express his surprise and awe. He kissed her some more and held her passionately in his arms. As they made love in the living room, the golden rays of the afternoon sun shone through the overhead skylight upon them. The life that was denied Sarah, and the happiness that was denied Matthew, both had returned. "I'll always love you, " she whispered in his ear and could only smile in return to that gesture.

He had refound the love of his life, the most important person in his life and she found again the man of her dreams. Two lovers and matched minds of brilliance and passion, together again and that would be happy and together forever.

The passionate scene evaporated in an instant, and the Mystic Theater returned. The audience was mostly smiling with satisfaction, knowing that Matthew had found his peace.

Doctor Xoctarious took the stage and spoke once again. "The past may seem brighter now when you look upon it, but that is what it will always be is past. All that one can do is push forward, and create a brighter future for yourself and for those you love. Look forward, friends! Look ahead!

"And now, ladies and gentlemen, I invite you all to take a one hour intermission," Doctor Xoctarious announced. "Feel free to freshen up, explore the museum any more, or just take a moment to reflect on my stories."

Gabriel stifled a guffaw. Whoever this man was, he certainly did a lot of "inviting." Around him, people were shuffling for the exits and heading down the carpeted halls for the restrooms. Others simply remained in their seats to turn on their phones, taking selfies or checking their email. Gabriel remained seated; he did not need to use the restroom, and he had already seen his fill of the museum curiosities. Down near the stage, the doctor was speaking with a small group of people. Gabriel got up from his seat and moved down a few rows to investigate. Some of the interviewees were young men and women, with a very large bald man towering over them. Each of the interviewers held small recorders and prodded Doctor Xoctarious with questions.

"Mr. Grafton, I'm from *Entertainment Tonight*," said one reporter. "Can you tell us about those 'vision' things that you do? What kind of technology do you use?"

The doctor chuckled. "I use the same 'technology' as every storyteller has used since time immemorial. Strong characters, interesting situations, and messages worth imparting."

"Er, I meant the way you present them," the reporter corrected. "Is it holograms or VR or something?"

"I've never heard of those," replied the doctor. "The gadgets that people use these days are outside my own expertise. I can hardly even use my own iPhone that well."

Some of the reporters laughed. Another raised his hand and held his recorder near the doctor's face.

"Hi, I'm John from *LA Weekly*."

"Hello, John from *LA Weekly*," the doctor repeated with a laugh.

"My question is, have you ever worked with the major film studios before, or have you done any special effects work?"

"Never have, never will," the doctor responded simply. "I appreciate a good film as much as the next person, but those are becoming very difficult to find these days."

Another question came to the doctor, this one from the large man towering over the heads of the other reporters.

"Mr. Grafton, how much did this whole thing cost to build? And how much did it cost to produce your stories?"

"My good sir, that is not a relevant question," the doctor said, maintaining his composure. "I am only just here to illuminate and inspire. I have very little need of money, which is not what I can say for others in this day and age who fancy themselves as artists. Nowadays, what they call 'art' is nothing more than cheap knockoffs based on someone's old commissioned piece. It's produced in factories, millions of times over, and consumed for a passing, ephemeral thrill, only to repeat *ad nauseum*. Though I do wish them all the very best at their jobs, I only wish that more care was taken into the very purpose of their arts."

"Purpose?" asked the bald reporter.

"Yes, purpose. If a studio is going to create a two-hour long feature film with a budget that dwarfs the entire treasuries of nations just for the sole purpose of entertaining teenagers on a Friday night out, what does that accomplish for the world? Well, aside from giving them a fetish for gunplay and fake-looking monsters, anyway?"

"So what's the purpose of your movies, then?" asked the fat reporter.

"My purpose is to reveal truths about the human experience, and if I'm doing anything right, to elevate my audience to a higher form of thought. The need of my Mystic Theater could not have been greater since the turn of the century."

"So—your theatre was around at the turn of the century?" asked the fat man. The doctor paused, and smiled.

"I've been at this for so long, time is starting to blur together."

Gabriel listened in on the conversation from afar, which left him with more questions than before. The doctor expertly dodged some hard questions that would have cornered anyone in the business, and he showed a clear disdain for the industry. Anyone who fancied themselves as an entertainer ranting against the entertainment business was either so well-off that he would not even need the money, or he was completely out of his mind.

Furthermore, if those interviews got published, the doctor would not even have a future in the entertainment at all; even Gabriel knew better than to publicly criticize a multi-billion dollar industry, especially if he, like the doctor, intended to work in it.

But there was something to the doctor that still perplexed him to no end. The mirror in his office was curious enough, but remembering the things that he saw in the museum also gave him pause. Things like that, to him, simply should not even exist. Either those bones and wisps of light were all elaborate props made from plaster and illusions, or there was something else here.

Near the end of the hour, the rest of the audience started filing back into the theatre, locating their seats and relaxing. Around them, the toll of a deep, metallic bell reverberated through the air. The audience hushed in anticipation, and the doctor took the stage once again. Applause broke out among the audience, and the doctor raised a gloved hand over his head to try and calm them down. The applause slowly petered out, and the room was silent.

The doctor looked around the auditorium with his hands behind his back; it looked like everyone was back in their place. He loved when an audience was punctual; it meant that they were getting heavily invested in his stories and were eagerly coming back for more. He figured now would be a good time to take a quick peek into their thoughts.

From one corner of the room, he looked into the mind of a young woman who was getting over the loss of her boyfriend, and seeing the visions was a great help to her. The doctor stifled a grin, knowing that he was truly making a difference in her life.

In the centre of the auditorium, near the middle of the fourth row, was the CEO of a large software company. Xoctarious centred his gaze on this man: middle-aged, short blond hair, a pointed nose, and an impeccable business suit. Inwardly, Xoctarious peered through his mind and almost regretted what he saw. This man was a consummate user of people; he built a multibillion dollar empire upon the sweat and tears of talented software writers, while he himself didn't know a single line of code. He placed immense pressure on those associates that were more honest than him, strapping them with endless overtime hours with little pay, while he himself reaped the fruits of their labour by going to fancy parties and special events, such as tonight's showing at the Mystic Theater.

"The play's the thing," he sighed inwardly. *"Wherein I'll catch the conscience of the king."* This particular line from <u>Hamlet</u> suddenly sprang to mind, and he would indeed bring a performance to make the CEO question his values and confront the evil in his own heart.

The doctor outstretched his left arm in front of him, and a thin black ribbon shot out of his sleeve. It began twirling and snaking into the air, as if held on by an invisible rope. The ribbon rippled in the air as it spiraled around over the heads of the audience, similar to the phoenix trick from earlier.

After the ribbon circled the theatre twice, it rose up over the main stage and started twisting into a shape. From where Gabriel saw it, the ribbon was forming the shape of a person, but with a lot more girth. The ribbon twisted around itself, so that the shape of the person became three-dimensional, as if there was a real person all wrapped up in the ribbon. It started floating down to the stage, and the ribbon-figure grew bulks on its body that resembled plates of armour, and a curved helmet on its head. The two prongs of a crest popped up on the front of its helm.

A samurai? Gabriel thought to himself, seeing the ribbon-figure start to walk about the stage. It moved its right arm over its body, and drew out a black-ribbon katana over its head. The figure of ribbon then started slicing through the air around it in a show of martial prowess. The audience reflexively made "ooh" and "aah" sounds, watching the ribbon-samurai slash all around it, with the doctor standing nearby. In one motion, the samurai pointed its black ribbon blade at the doctor himself, and made a move that would have impaled the doctor right in the chest. Some audience members clutched their seat rests tightly in trepidation.

However, the doctor grabbed the ribbon blade with one hand and yanked it upwards. Instantly, the entire samurai figure became unraveled, and all that remained was a long, loose strand of black ribbon in the doctor's hand. The rest of the ribbon was splayed out all over the stage in front of him, with some draping off the side of the stage. The doctor tugged the ribbon, and the entire strand slipped into his sleeve, as if pulled with magnetism. The doctor took a bow to some loud accolades from the audience.

"Thank you," he said as the cheering and clapping died down. "And now, dear friends, as you may be guessing, our next vision sets its sights in the realm of the Shogunate and the *Shinobi*, in the year 1473. It is a tale of lost love, retribution, and dire consequences. My, friends, welcome to the Sengoku period, to the tale I call: 'Feudal.'"

FEUDAL

Story by Doug K. Owen
Written by Doug K. Owen

All around the audience, the Mystic Theater disappeared, replaced in an instant with a wide street paved with gravel. Lining the street are rows of thin wooden houses with tall, dark-tiled triangular roofs, sliding doors and rooms, open porches. Far in the distance, towering overhead and shrouded in clouds and lit by the setting sun, was the white-capped summit of Mount Fuji.

Here and there, between the street and the houses were large, thin trees which were shedding pink and red petals from their branches to the ground. A young woman was sweeping some of the fallen petals off of the porch of the house on the street corner. She was young, and wore a red cotton kimono with a red flower in her black hair. The door to the house slid open, revealing a middle-aged man whose face showed several age lines around his forehead and around his mouth. He wore a dark blue cotton robe and a black skirt.

"Omitsu, the travellers might be here soon," said the man to the sweeping woman. "I'll be at the counter inside when you're done."

The woman, Omitsu, swept away a small pile of petals off to a side.

"There's not much left, Matsuzo. I should be done before anyone arrives."

Omitsu went to finishing off the sweeping, while Matsuzo went inside the house. It was an inn that he and his wife ran together. A relatively simple place, the *kitchen-yado* provided a room and firewood for travellers hoping to stay the night or to prepare their own meals. Matsuzo had heard of some of the other large *hatago* inns over in the centre of Edo, which provided more room space and their own meal service, but here on the outskirts of Edo there was not much need for extras. Matsuzo's inn usually only catered to travels bards and holy men on pilgrimages to the towering Mount Fuji in the distance. Matsuzo prided himself on charging a decent rate for travellers, just enough that nobody would argue with him, given what he offered.

Matsuzo sat at a small desk on darker wood than what the rest of the room was built from. The room for guests was freshly swept, and the mattress, made from hemp and cotton, was newly cleaned. The woven grass mats set over the floor felt pleasant under Matsuzo's feet. The walls of thinly-woven bamboo were white and spotless. Matsuzo looked around his inn and smiled. Any traveller would be certain to find comfort here.

Sure enough, a man entered the inn, with Omitsu bowing pleasantly near him. The man, dressed in a flowing white silk robe and bald except for a tightly-woven top knot of black hair on his head, removed his sandals at the door and entered. Matsuzo bowed at the desk as the man approached. At a closer distance, Matsuzo could see a sense of deep longing in the man's face, as if he had recently suffered a great loss. There was redness in the whites of his eyes, and his face was curled down in a frown.

"Welcome, good sir," said Matsuzo courteously. "Are you interested in staying the night here in our *kitchen-yado?*"

"As long as there aren't any of Yorisama's thugs here," the man grumbled.

"Beg your pardon?" asked Matsuzo. "I've never heard that name before."

"You haven't gone abroad very much, have you?" remarked the man, leaning tiredly on the counter. "Worrisome is that shogun who's been terrorizing the lands east of here. They've been raiding every village that they come across. I barely made it out with my life."

Matsuzo listened with rapt attention, but he genuinely felt sorry for the man. "You have my sympathies, friend. You may stay here as long as you wish. May I take your name for the registry?"

"Ichiro."

Matsuzo inscribed the name in his registry book on the counter, seeing the man still filled with dread and regret.

"Ordinarily, we charge ten pieces of copper for one night, but in your current situation, I am prepared to make it five per night for you," said Matsuzo.

"Sounds reasonable," muttered Ichiro, reaching into his pocket to provide five small faded copper coins, each one with a square-shaped hole in the middle. The coins fell onto the counter top with a small, musical jangle, and Matsuzo swept them up with the palm of his hand to collect them.

"The room is over there," explained Matsuzo, pointing to his left to the wall where a door was left ajar. "You'll find all the basic necessities there. If you ever need anything, I and my wife Omitsu will not be far."

"Thank you very much," Ichiro said with some relief in his voice. He bowed, and Matsuzo returned the bow. As Ichiro went into the guest room, Matsuzo peered outside to find Omitsu finishing with the sweeping. Several other people were coming down the gravel road, and one of them stopped at the door pensively. He was younger than Ichiro by the looks of him, and black hair was wild and untidy. His blue *Haori* robe was stained with dirt and small bits of plant matter.

"Can I help you?" asked Matsuzo from the door.

"Do you have a room I can rent?" asked the young man. Matsuzo shook his head regretfully.

"Sorry, we're full."

"Do you of any place nearby that might be open?"

"You could try some of the other inns down the road," Matsuzo explained, pointing down the road to his right. "But they may charge steep prices, and in more than just copper."

"Anything to keep me out of Yorisama's gaze," replied the young man, walking with the other people down the road.

As Matsuzo walked back into his inn, he wondered who this Yorisama is, and why everyone was so afraid of him. All his life he had rarely even seen a samurai, and never a matchlock rifle. The presence of a samurai was highly uncommon here in this part of Edo, and Matsuzo did not have the spacious rooms or accommodations that they were known to demand. He had no stables for their horses, and no places to prepare meals for them— and he had heard stories before about their voracious appetites.

Matsuzo went back to his desk as Omitsu re-entered.

"Did you see all those people outside?" asked Omitsu.

"I have. They look like refugees," answered Matsuzo. "I'd heard someone named Yorisama is stirring up trouble afar."

"We'll be alright," Omitsu mused. "Samurai wouldn't have much need for a *kitchen-yado*."

"All the better for us never to have started one in the first place," Matsuzo remarked with a hint of a grin.

Matsuzo awoke that night to the sounds of screams. He jolted upright from off his small mattress and looked around his empty, darkened room. From through the thin bamboo wall, he could see some bright orange lights, and dark figures moving fast around. The screams continued all around him, and he quickly pulled on a robe and fled from his bedroom. Omitsu was nowhere to be found in the dark inn, but he could be certain Omitsu's voice was among the screams that he heard.

His heart pounded quickly in panic, and sweat dripped down his brow. He searched every room in the inn; the guest room, the foyer, the closets, and everywhere in between. The inn was desolate. Matsuzo went to the foyer of the inn, and opened the door just a crack. It was close enough that nobody outside would notice, but just open enough that he could peer through the narrow slit.

Outside, the village had fallen into chaos. Several homes and trees were set on fire, which burned brightly and furiously in the night. Several armoured horsemen careened down the path, armed with curved swords and long pole-arm weapons, with blades that shone brightly in the light from the fires. People such as the young man from earlier that day were found fleeing from the marauding warriors, only to be brutally cut down in their path.

Matsuzo recoiled in terror as one samurai in bulky armour and with long horns on his black metallic helmet sliced through a peasant with a long blade mounted on a pole. The shrieking peasant fell motionless with a ragged gash running diagonally down his back. The gravel underneath him was drowned in a crimson pool that spread around his lifeless body.

Other scenes similar to that display of carnage played out all around the village. The relentless samurai went unchallenged through the village, burning houses with torches and carving through any man in their way. Matsuzo also saw several young women being bound by the wrists by four armoured samurai footmen. Among them were young women, geishas captured from the richer inns, and—Omitsu!

Against all better judgment, Matsuzo tore the door open and charged selflessly into the fray. The house across from his inn was consumed with flames, stinging his eyes. Still, he kept going, running headlong towards Omitsu's four samurai captors. In a rush, Matsuzo grabbed a handful of gravel from the ground, and tossed it into the eyes of a samurai. His ceramic mask, which was moulded in a vicious snarl, took most of the gravel, but some got into his eyes. He doubled over with his eyes full of tears and dust, and Matsuzo reached for his sheathed sword. He pulled out the long, shiny weapon from the downed samurai's scabbard, and he plunged it tip-first into the exposed throat of the downed samurai. The downed warrior convulsed and gurgled in his own blood oozing out from his wound.

Three other samurai encircled Matsuzo, and he pulled the sword out of the warrior's corpse and began swinging it around frantically. The three samurai kept their distance from Matsuzo, while other armour-clad invaders still kept the women, including Omitsu, bound and under control.

Across the road, a samurai in solid black armour looked down from his muscular black hairs at the scene that unfolded near him. Beneath the tall, pointed crescent-shaped crest in the centre of his helmet, and above the moulded, snarling mask over his lower face, he looked with a cold stare at the fight his samurai subordinates were now engaged. A peasant innkeeper had gotten the best of one of his fighters, and stolen his sword, which he was now swinging around undisciplined and unfettered at some of his other underlings. The other three samurai unsheathed their own weapons and took defensive stances, encircling the wild man and leaving their captive women thrown on the ground. One particular young woman, dressed in a red kimono and with a thin, youthful face, went wide-eyed in terror as she saw from the ground what the wild man was doing.

Matsuzo kept swinging the stolen katana all around him, daring the samurai that surrounded him to a fight. The samurai kept their distance and their swords held in front of them. Every so often, one of their blades would sound off with a metallic *clang* off of Matsuzo's sword. Behind him, the larger samurai in black armour rode on horseback right behind him a few paces. The samurai stepped back, and Matsuzo looked behind him in fright. The black-armoured warrior looked down over him like a giant, and his horse let out a slight snarl.

Matsuzo readied his sword near his face, and stepped in to strike. But the black-armoured warrior flicked his sword out of his hands in one expert swipe with his own sword, and pummeled Matsuzo's scar on the back of his head with an armoured fist. Matsuzo collapsed lifelessly to the ground as Omitsu screamed in shock. That sound rang in Matsuzo's ears as the world around him faded into blackness as the sudden and extremely sharp pain in his head consumed his every sense.

Matsuzo awoke on his back. His vision was still blurry, and his head was still engulfed in agony from the attack. Sunlight from a small window overhead poured harshly into his face, stinging his eyes. The rough texture of the stone floor that he laid upon was digging into his back. Matsuzo tried to move over, out of the sunlight and onto a slightly smoother part of the floor, but the pain in his skull seemed to multiply with each movement he made. Therefore, it was no small effort on his part to shift his position.

Matsuzo cringed and hissed in pain as he moved his fragile, agonized body a few inches to the right, away from the patch of sunlight and into a cooler part of the room. At this point, he was able to get a glimpse of his surroundings: nothing more than a small, square-shaped room with a low ceiling. The walls and ceiling were built from packed earth with wooden frames. Small clumps of straw littered the floor on which Matsuzo lay. One single door was locked in the wall opposite from where he lay.

"Did you sleep well?" asked a voice across the room to his left. Matsuzo looked around, still on the floor, not finding the source of the voice. A moment later, a man walked into the bright rays of sunlight and stood over him. He was younger than Matsuzo, about twenty years of age. His black hair was close-cropped, and his grey eyes darted around the room with a sharp gaze. He wore a simple black robe tied with a sash around his waist, and a white cotton *hakama* skirt.

Matsuzo grumbled in pain. "My head hurts," he muttered.

"You should take some more time to rest," said the stranger. "We'll be leaving soon."

"Where are we?" Matsuzo asked.

"Samurai prison," he answered simply. "I'd imagine Yorisama's holding us here before we get conscripted into his army, or executed—whichever he's in the mood for."

Matsuzo was confused by this young man. It was not the fact that they were both imprisoned by the samurai together, but rather the fact that he found no hint of fear or even hesitation in the young man's voice when he spoke about being in the prison, or their possible fates.

"They wouldn't dare!" Matsuzo yelped, trembling.

"You obviously don't know Yorisama very well," the young man replied, still maintaining his stoic attitude.

"Why aren't you afraid?" Matsuzo questioned him. "They could come for us at any moment!"

The young man scoffed. "The samurai are fools. I've dealt with them before."

"Who are you?" asked Matsuzo.

"Ryo," he answered simply. "I was a farmer."

"Did Yorisama raid your village?"

"Plenty," Ryo stated. "They killed half of my family before my eyes, and threw me in here. The rest of them— I don't know where they are."

"Well, I hope you find them soon," Matsuzo remarked, still motionless on the stone floor. He found that not moving his head at all was the best way to keep the pain at bay until it diminished. "When they arrived at my village, they took my wife."

"Yorisama tends to do that as well," Ryo commented. "He turns captured men into his soldiers, and captured women into his concubines."

"Concubines?" Matsuzo repeated in a terrified whisper. "Omitsu!"

He instantly pulled himself up off the floor, propping himself up. But the pain in his skull came back with a vengeance, and he screamed in shock. Ryo came to his side while Matsuzo clasped his injured head.

"Calm down," Ryo whispered. "The guards don't like people shouting in here. They're usually the first to die."

Matsuzo stopped screaming instantly. While he still cradled his painfully throbbing head, Ryo looked around some of the straw piles on the ground. He took some of the small, thin strands and checked each one closely, discarding some as if they did not interest him enough.

"What are you doing?" asked Matsuzo. Ryo shushed him without even glancing in his direction, still picking at the straw. Matsuzo said nothing as Ryo checked one particular piece of straw and pinched its end several times to form a point. He took the pointed straw to the door and jammed it into the door crack. Ryo took his time wiggling the sharpened straw up and down the door jamb until he found something solid behind it. After some more finessing, Matsuzo heard a faint *thump* behind the door, and it instantly swung open. Ryo stood by and gloated with Matsuzo frozen in disbelief.

"Time to go," said Ryo, pulling Matsuzo to his feet. Matsuzo hissed in pain, but it was beginning to subside. He stumbled to his feet and held onto the earthen walls to balance himself. Ryo looked down the halls outside their cell, finding two armoured samurai with their backs turned. The sentries looked the other way down the hall, assuming nobody would be approaching from behind. Ryo proved them wrong and crept up silently behind them.

Upon approaching, he filled them with a sweeping leg kick and unsheathed one of their swords. Taking this sword, he stabbed them both in very rapid succession. From the doorway of the cell, Matsuzo looked in astonishment. The guards were dead before he even had time to fully grasp the situation. All he saw was Ryo stands over the armoured corpses with a bloodstained katana, looking down the hall back at Matsuzo, and gesturing with a head tilt to come with him.

Matsuzo stepped out of the hallway, looking around frantically down the hall. Seeing nobody else coming, he determined it was safe to follow his new friend. But something gave Ryo pause before they could leave the prison.

"There might be others here too," he muttered, still standing over the dead guards. "Check the other doors in the hall."

"We can't stay around here!" Matsuzo protested. "I need to find Omitsu!"

"There are other people who probably want to find their wives as well, old man. We're not going anywhere until they're all free."

Matsuzo tried to plead, but he saw no other option. More guards could come at any moment, and Ryo was still the one with the sword. Hesitantly, he checked each of the doors in the small, earthen hallway. Most of them, he could unlock from outside using Ryo's sharpened straw, and they each held prisoners from Matsuzo's village. Matsuzo tried to calm them down and keep them silent upon rescuing them, and soon the hall was filled with people Matsuzo saved. They each turned to Ryo at the end of the hall, over the bodies of the dead samurai as Matsuzo checked the last room, which was nothing more than a supply closet.

"There's a forest not too far from here," Ryo explained to the group. "We can hide there once I'm done with the guards if there are any left. Just leave them all to me."

With the sword in hand, Ryo walked out of the hallway to the right, and out the front door leading to a grassy field. The several unarmoured samurai was patrolling the area, each one clad in fine white silk robes that made them easy to spot among the green grass and the cloudless morning sky. They walked casually with their swords at their sides, probably bored with the work. From inside the house, Matsuzo and the other prisoners watched with awe as Ryo crept up behind each guard and ran them through their chests with the sword. Most of them barely even screamed when they were killed, and none of them even noticed when their comrades were dead until Ryo's blade found its mark in their own backs. Ryo made short work of the sentries, littering the field with corpses. Their white robes were stained red, and blood was pooling up in the grass.

"Let's move!" Ryo announced.

The forest was vast, and the narrow dirt trail snaked around the tall, round birch trees constantly. Sometimes there was no trail at all, and Matsuzo found himself stepping over massive roots jutting from the ground. He and the company of prisoners followed Ryo, who seemed to be the only one who knew his way around the forest.

"Where are we going?" asked Matsuzo, exhausted from the hike.

"*Hinansho,*" Ryo replied. "A safe place."

Crossing over a small hill, Matsuzo and the prisoners found a small clearing in the woods. A small ramshackle house was built from straw and wood in one edge of the clearing, and there was plenty of space in the circle-shaped area.

"You knew about this place all along?" asked Matsuzo incredulously.

Ryo nodded. "It's my other home. Nobody knows about this place, nobody will bother us here."

The refugees from Yorisama's prison looked around the area and sat down to relax. The trek from the prison through the forest left them all drained and eager for some rest.

"I don't suppose you know where we can find some food?" asked one of the refugees. Ryo looked to his small hut and opened the door.

"I should still have some rice and water here," answered Ryo. "If someone can get a fire going, we can rest here."

Night came quickly, and Matsuzo's fellow villagers were lounging by the fire pit in the centre of the clearing. Matsuzo looked around the group, finding everyone content to be free, but still apprehensive about their fate. Two wrinkled old men were still eating a bowl of rice each, and the others were sleeping on the dusty ground, looking up at the stars.

Matsuzo glanced up at the night sky, and found the scene quite enticing. Between the trees, Matsuzo could see the wide expanse of the starry sky unfold above him, the distant and the magnificent cosmos in their array. Much as he would have loved to savour the moment to lay down and rest with his friends beneath that wondrous sky, he had other matters to tend to.

"What now?" asked one of the refugees, the old man who just finished his bowl of rice. "Do we spend the rest of our lives hiding in the woods?"

"Well, we can't go back home," answered a young man near him. "Not that we have much to come back to, anyway. The samurai probably destroyed the entire village by now."

"We should band together and stop them!" came a voice from among the group, followed by some shouts of assent.

"Let's make those samurai pay!"

"Death to Yorisama!"

Matsuzo escaped the growing throng of angry villagers and went to find Ryo. He found Ryo inside the hut, seated on a small log and toying with a long piece of rope and a small farming sickle. The walls were bare, and only a small window above Ryo's head, let in the fresh night breeze. A shelf on the right-side wall held some miscellaneous wood and metal tools.

"How long are we going to stay here?" Matsuzo asked.

"You know, you've never really introduced yourself to me yet," Ryo mused. "I've taken you to my hideout, and I still don't know your name."

"My name is Matsuzo," he replied. "I was an innkeeper on the outskirts of Edo."

"And you had a wife, Omitsu, until she was taken by Yorisama, right?"

"What do you mean, 'had' a wife?" Matsuzo demanded. "Omitsu may still be alive, and we're wasting our time hiding in the forest!"

"Patience," Ryo halted him, going back to his rope and sickle. Matsuzo was starting to lose his temper, and stormed into the house to stand right over Ryo.

"We have to go!" Matsuzo growled. "Now!"

Ryo said nothing, and in one movement he flicked the end of the rope towards Matsuzo. It wrapped itself neatly around his right leg, and with a hard tug, he pulled Matsuzo off his feet. Matsuzo crashed to the ground, dazed and surprised to find Ryo standing over him with the curved sickle blade pointed at his neck.

"People who talk back to a *Shinobi* don't live long enough to regret it."

"*Shinobi?*" asked Matsuzo, not daring to struggle on the ground with Ryo's weapon pointed at him. Ryo looked down at Matsuzo with a piercing gaze every bit as sharp as the sickle blade.

"I grew up learning the art of *Ninjutsu*, the Eighteen Disciplines," Ryo explained. "There's still much for me to learn, but I'm quite certain I can overpower you if I wanted to. Now, are we going to have any more trouble?"

Matsuzo shut his eyes and shook his head. Ryo nodded, and withdrew his weapon. Matsuzo exhaled with relief and pulled his back off the floor, still sitting down. He saw Ryo set down the sickle and the rope on the shelf on the far wall, and he picked up a small length of bamboo from the shelf.

"The samurai never let us keep weapons," Ryo explained. "They thought we'd all rise up against them. Those dimwits never would've known, we had weapons all along."

He held the end of the bamboo to his lips, and pointed the other end at Matsuzo, then at the wall directly behind him. Ryo gave a quick but forceful blow, and a single dart bolted out of the bamboo, sticking into the earthen wall to the right of Matsuzo's head, missing it by inches. Matsuzo gasped in surprise, then turned to Ryo, who withdrew the blowgun from his lips. After a moment, a thought crossed Matsuzo's mind, once he had time to properly recover from the shock of being threatened by a *Shinobi*.

"Can you teach us?" he asked. "The people out there, I mean."

"I heard them outside. They're rowdy, but I'll do what I can."

Matsuzo pulled himself onto his feet. "Can you help me rescue my wife?"

Ryo said nothing, instead going back to his rope and sickle, tying a stronger braid around the sickle's end. Matsuzo stamped his foot impatiently.

"Ryo! I asked you a question!"

"One thing at a time," the ninja muttered.

In the distant hills, overlooking a vast, lush forest, there stood the imposing Yorisama Castle. A massive structure of black and grey towering over the treetops, the castle was comprised of five levels, each with flat-square-shaped floors and tall, triangular roofs above each floor. The entire structure was a concentric series of those flat floors and tall roofs, one on top of the other, all surrounded by a high, slanted wall of stone and plaster, guarded by armed sentries.

At the very top of this colossal, forbidding castle, was Yorisama's sanctum. The room was mostly empty except for a few wooden chests full of supplies, a soft mattress in the centre of the room, and several candles on pedestals in every corner. The light from the candles illuminated the fine wooden floor and rafters, as well as the gruesome murals of warriors and creatures on the walls. Most of the murals depicted armoured warriors fighting with leering, horned *any* demons with hulking, muscular bodies painted in livid red and with piercing yellow eyes. The flickering light from the candles made the painted *one* look even more frightening, as if the fanged, horned faces were alive within the walls.

A door slid open, and into the room, walked a tall, middle-aged man in large black pants, a black kimono and a flowing red silk *kamishimo*; a jacket over the kimono with wide, pointed shoulders jutting over his arms. The man stroked the left side of his thin black moustache, the light from the candles shining off his mostly bald head. His eyes were thin slits, looking with a forbidding, deadly gas. His hand went from his moustache to the hilt of the katana resting on the side of his hip.

Behind him, several women were dragged into the room by samurai captors. Each woman was bound around the wrists with rope, and their kimonos were torn and dirtied. Among the captive women was Omitsu, whose hair was unkempt and her kimono torn in several places. The samurai pulled the women to the far end of the room, and bowed before the man with the piercing stare.

"These are the best women we've taken, Master Yorisama," said one of the bowing samurai. Yorisama gave him a slight, silent nod, and motioned for them to be dismissed. The samurai walked out of the room, keeping their heads bowed before Yorisama. The women stood paralysed with fear, at the mercy of the brutal, unmerciful warlord.

Yorisama looked over each of the captive women, and stopped in front of Omitsu, who had her gaze pointed down. With slender fingers, Yorisama grasped Omitsu's cheeks and held her head up, looking into her eyes. His grip was strong as steel, and as cold, upon Omitsu's face. Omitsu dared not move, frozen in terror. The warlord's hand, then moved to the ropes around her wrists, and pulled her over to the mattress in the centre of the room.

"Do you know who I am?" Yorisama drawled coolly to the woman on his mattress. She nodded silently, quivering. He stood over her, looking down upon her like a long-sought trophy.

"I am the ruler of this domain, and the most powerful man you will ever know," Yorisama explained in his icy tone. "I command legions of the finest warriors ever to walk the earth. I had more gold than even the Emperor could ever hope to collect, and more power than the gods. I expect you to satisfy me."

Yorisama crouched down in front of Omitsu, neatly caressing her head and shoulders. Omitsu shuddered at his touch, but Yorisama held her in place on the mattress. He then shoved her down on her back upon the mattress, and crawled over her, his eyes flashing with lust. He grabbed Omitsu's still-bound wrists with one hand, and felt up her body with the other. Omitsu struggled bitterly, throwing Yorisama off of her. The shogun rolled off to a side from the force of her throw, then stood up over her with a look of fury. He unsheathed his katana and pointed it at Omitsu's face, right between her eyes. The other women in the room looked at the scene in horror.

"I'd hate to kill someone as beautiful as you," Yorisama growled. "I'll make you learn to serve me."

He sheathed his sword, and Omitsu sighed slightly, thinking that she would be spared. Instead, Yorisama slapped her across the face, sending her collapsing into the mattress. Some of the other women yelped in shock, and Yorisama turned to them with the same furious expression.

"All of you!" he bellowed to the captives. "You will all come to serve me!"

In the castle's paved courtyard, a black-armoured samurai general found himself surrounded by five kimono-clad swordsmen.

The figure in the thick black armour stood stalwart and unmoving, his armoured hand clasped around the hilt of his katana. The other men around him steadied themselves, ready to strike.

One of the young men behind the armoured warrior raised his sword and ran towards the samurai general, bellowing a war cry. He was the first to have the general's blade rammed through his chest, and his war cry tapered off into a gurgling, blood-choked death rattle. His lifeless body slid off the general's sword and collapsed onto the paved stone ground.

Another swordsman advanced to the general with two horizontal slashes, which were both deflected with ease. The general parried his sword out of the way, leaving his silk-clad chest open to attack, which he did, and another bloodied corpse was left on the ground. A third fighter tried to attack from the side, but the general was not off-guard. His attack was deflected, and the general sliced into his chest, cutting his torso off from his hips and legs. Blood and intestines spilled out of the fighter's torso onto the ground, and his scream was silenced with a gurgle.

The fourth warrior had his blade parried to a side, and lost his head to the general's sword. That left only the fifth man alive, who trembled in terror seeing the fates of his comrades. He threw down his sword and bowed before the general.

"At least you know when to quit," the general muttered beneath his scowling mask.

"Yes, Master Tokubei," whispered the survivor.

The general shoved the survivor's shoulder with the hilt of his sword. "Go find me some better sparring partners!" he demanded.

Daylight was quickly slipping away as the sun was setting over the forest, and very little light was left by which Matsuzo and the villagers could see. Matsuzo grumbled and wiped sweat off of his brow. A mosquito-bite on the back of his neck was becoming a bothersome, itchy burden, but he still needed to stay in formation with the rest of the villagers. He hefted his length of bamboo and assumed the stance that Ryo taught him again. Ryo himself was pacing around the orderly lines that the villagers formed, side by side, each armed with a bamboo stick held like a sword. As their trainer, Ryo corrected their stances and showed them proper sword techniques.

"Hold it out farther," he instructed one of the villagers, a young man with a bowl-cut hairstyle. "Let the sword become not just a tool, but an extension of your body. Make those downward slashes more fluid, and keep your balance."

On Ryo's commands, Matsuzo struggled to keep up information with the rest of the students, trying to mimic their moves with upward and downward slices and parries. He constantly kept shuffling his feet and wobbling, trying to hold his training sword in the same stance as everyone else around him. On one occasion, his stance was so wide that he went off-balance and fell to the dusty ground. Ryo and the other students looked silently and surprised as he pulled himself to his feet and tried to re-assume the stance.

"Your form's too rigid, Matsuzo," Ryo told him. "Bend your knees some more, and lean in slightly. You'll stay balanced that way."

Matsuzo grumbled. "How long am I supposed to keep this up?"

"As long as it takes. Keep going."

With the bamboo sword in hand, Matsuzo exhaled a slow breath to try and steady his nerves. He assumed the stance and held the weapon close and upright at the ready. He looked ahead, and clenched his grip on the branch.

"Try two downward slices," Ryo suggested calmly. On command, Matsuzo stepped forward, swinging the stick in a diagonal motion, as if he was chopping through an invisible opponent. Ryo stood in a side observing his movements, and he shook his head in disapproval at Matsuzo's harried, unfocused moves.

"You need to focus on where your weapon is going, and how you're going to defend your own body with it," Ryo remarked, seeing where Matsuzo's sword was pointed in relation to the foot that Matsuzo was balancing on in front of him. "If that was a real sword, you may have cut through your own front leg."

Matsuzo was clearly getting impatient. "Ryo, I've been at this for hours! When are we going to save my wife?!"

"Patience, old man," Ryo responded simply. "If you really want to go up against samurai, these are the moves that will save your life. Now take the stance and try again."

"I've had enough!" Matsuzo shouted, throwing down his weapon. "I already know how to use a sword! I killed one of them in my village before!"

"That might be good enough for the samurai grunts, but what if you're up against Tokubei?" asked Ryo.

"Who's Tokubei?"

"He's the *daimyo* to Yorisama," Ryo explained. "His general. The samurai takes orders from him, and he only answers to the shogun. He's a monster."

"I've already got enough experience; I could take him!" Matsuzo declared.

"Can you?" Ryo asked incredulously, borrowing a bamboo sword from a nearby student. "Then let's see how. On your guard!"

Matsuzo picked up his sword and assumed the fighting stance, while Ryo in front of him did the same, staring him down with an icy look in his eyes. The other students stood back, all watching the two combatants about to fight, their anticipation collectively running high. Most of the students expected Ryo to easily win, but some inwardly hoped for Matsuzo to at least hold his ground. Matsuzo's pulse beat like a rapidly-pounded *Taiko* drum.

"*Hyah!*" Ryo shouted, and advanced on Matsuzo. The innkeeper wiggled his sword out in front of him trying to contact Ryo's weapon, but Ryo sidestepped around him and put his weapon right to the side of Matsuzo's neck, stopping short of tapping him. Matsuzo spun around wildly, pushing Ryo's sword out of the way with his own weapon, and brought his own sword up for a downward slash. Ryo in turn jabbed him once in the belly, and sidestepped around Matsuzo's downward slide. From there, Matsuzo kept repeating the same downward-slash move over and over, even when Ryo was standing a foot away from his reach. The *Shinobi* nonchalantly tapped Matsuzo's sword out of the way and delivered him several more jabs to his chest and his back.

"If this was real combat, you would've been dead several times over," Ryo muttered. "Do you still want to go against Yorisama now?"

"That wasn't fair!" Matsuzo complained.

"Your enemy won't hold back, old man. Neither will I."

"Stop calling me that!" Matsuzo bellowed in rage, charging at Ryo. He swung his sword around wildly, growling and shouting with every move, desperate to land one blow on Ryo. In response, Ryo expertly dodged and parried each move with barely a flicker of expression on his face, contrary to Matsuzo's enraged countenance. Ryo dodged out of the way of Matsuzo's bamboo sword when he swung it downwards, and Matsuzo lost his balance, falling face down into the ground.

"Are you quite finished?" asked Ryo, standing over the defeated innkeeper. Matsuzo pulled himself off the ground, trembling and breathing heavily. Sweat poured down his dust-covered brow, and he dropped his sword.

"Mastering the physical takes time, Matsuzo," Ryo explained.

"I don't have any time!" Matsuzo protested hoarsely. "Omitsu could be dead by now for all I know, and you're holding me back!"

"You still think you're ready?" Ryo asked incredulously.

Matsuzo paused, still feeling the pain all over his body from Ryo's jabs and the tumble he took to the ground. He sighed deeply and turned his gaze down.

"I'm not ready," he admitted. "But I need to be. It's the only way I'll ever save my wife."

"Hmm..." Ryo pondered aloud. He turned to his students, all of whom stood with apathy, trying to comprehend the scene that just played out before them. Some of them were trembling in fear, hoping that they would not be next to fight Ryo and face a defeat as certain as Matsuzo's.

"Perhaps someone I know can help you."

A day later, Matsuzo found himself regretting the decision to go with Ryo to find the mysterious person he mentioned. At midday, Ryo led him far from his hideout eastwards, through an endless bamboo forest. Thin, green stalks towering over their heads stood in mess all around them, blocking any path. Ryo led him through narrow passes between the trees, bending them slightly to form a space for them to pass through. The terrain was more uneven and treacherous than it was near Ryo's hideout, such that Matsuzo found himself having to climb several hills that were slightly as tall as himself. Ryo had to pull him up over some of the hills.

"Who is this person you mentioned?" asked Matsuzo, passing through some more bamboo trees.

"Heishiro," Ryo answered. "He lives in a house in the Sakuragaoka forest. He taught me everything that I know."

As if on cue, they came to a clearing in the middle of the bamboo forest. A barren hillside, covered with dead leaves, rose up to meet them. Several steps to the left, there was a small house made from wooden planks lying against the hillside. The house looked slightly larger than Ryo's hideout, and less stable. The planks making up the walls of the house looked as though a slight breeze could collapse the entire house, and the thatched-straw roof would flatten whatever was inside. Matsuzo felt his spirits lift, and started for the house, but Ryo promptly stopped him with a hand on his shoulder.

"A word to the wise, Matsuzo," Ryo warned him. "Do not make him cross. It might just be the last thing you ever do."

Matsuzo sucked in a breath, gathering up his courage, and walked alone into the house. Inside, several candles in the corners of the room illuminated wooden chests and several mounted wooden stands holding sets of well-polished katanas, each with differently coloured hilts and scabbards. At the far wall of the room, there was an old man seated cross-legged, his eyes closed and his face devoid of feeling. His face was more wrinkled than Matsuzo's, and he wore a spotless white *hare* and *hakama*. His head was shaved bald, and his face was beardless, a face that had seen countless years of battle and was now more than weary.

"Are you Heishiro?" Matsuzo asked. No response came from the old man, who was still silent.

"Ryo sent me here," Matsuzo insisted. "I was told you were a master."

No response.

"Listen, my wife was captured by Yorisama! I need your help to save her!"

The old man said nothing as he stood upright and walked several paces forward. Matsuzo stood off to a side to let him pass, and the old man turned to one of the swords on display. He raised a trembling, gnarled hand to a long katana in its sheath and wrapped his wrinkled, bony fingers around it. Matsuzo watched in dismay as he could barely even lift the sword out of the display.

"What is this, a joke?!" Matsuzo stammered, losing his temper. "*This* is the man who trained Ryo?"

Matsuzo turned for the door, but was stopped by the unmistakable sound of a sword being unsheathed, and the feeling of a sharp, cold strip of steel against the side of his neck. Matsuzo froze in terror, his breath coming out in short gasps.

"Don't move," uttered a stern voice behind him. The old man pointing the katana at his neck slowly moved around Matsuzo, who held perfectly still. His weapon was still trained squarely on Matsuzo's neck. When he came right before Matsuzo, the innkeeper was confused; this was certainly not the same old man that could not even pick up a sword, but rather a much younger man with a mane of wild black hair, and large bulging muscles, and a sharp, scornful look in his dark brown eyes. Nowhere in his face or body was there a trace of greyness or wrinkling.

"Heishiro?" Matsuzo whispered. The man with the sword nodded slightly, keeping his steely gaze skyward upon the intruder in his home.

"I can change my guise, as I need to," Heishiro explained. "You have come here seeking to master the physical, yet you have no balance, no fortitude, and no insight."

"I can learn quickly," Matsuzo shot back, hiding an offended tone, which was not lost on Heishiro. The man withdrew his blade, and stepped outside of the house. From several feet out of the door frame, Heishiro gestured for Matsuzo to take one of the swords. Matsuzo picked a katana in a fine jade scabbard with black cotton bands around the hilt. He unsheathed the sword, exposing the curved, shiny grey blade with the triangular tempering pattern running along the sharpened edge.

Matsuzo hesitantly stepped out of the house with the sword, facing Heishiro in the clearing between the forest and the hillside. He sucked in a breath and tried to steady himself, remembering everything that Ryo tried to teach him before. He held the sword up and took a ready stance, spreading his feet apart and bending his knees slightly, looking right ahead at Heishiro.

Heishiro charged at him very suddenly, such that Matsuzo was taken completely by surprise. Heishiro's weapon sprung at Matsuzo from the left side, about to slice into his body. Matsuzo tried to block the strike, but it was so strong that his sword fell out of his hands as the two blades impacted on one another. The loud clang echoed through the forest, and Matsuzo's blade disturbed the cover of dead leaves on the ground as it fell. The two combatants stood against each other, unmoving. The Heishiro's blade was right against Matsuzo's side, not leaving a scratch on him, but it did cut through his robe.

"Learn quickly, you said?" Heishiro grumbled. "How's THIS for learning quickly?"

As suddenly as he attacked, Heishiro held a flat palm onto Matsuzo's forehead, pressing into his skull. Matsuzo stood rigid as a surge of energy flashed into his body from where Heishiro pressed onto his head. His body began trembling violently and uncontrollably. The sensation only lasted a few minutes, and then Heishiro withdrew his hand. Matsuzo fell to his knees on the leaf-covered ground, trying to catch his breath and recover from what came over him.

"Pick up the sword!" Heishiro commanded. Matsuzo did so without hesitation, then pulled himself to his feet. Surprisingly, his movement felt a bit quicker. He flexed his right arm, and felt that the movement was slightly stronger and faster than before. He felt refreshed and lighter, as if he had woken up inside a younger body.

"Attack me!" ordered the master. Matsuzo assumed a ready stance, and mustered his strength. He steadied his breathing and his pulse, which was much easier for him to do this time. He sprang forth against Heishiro, controlling his sword in every slash and parry. Heishiro deflected every move in the fight, but his attacks never went near Matsuzo's body; the innkeeper was suddenly highly adept in combat, and he blocked all of them with finesse and poise. Inwardly, Matsuzo was surprised at how well he was able to command his body and control his sword, but he had to remain steadfast in the battle.

Matsuzo knocked the katana out of Heishiro's hands, and held the tip of his own blade right to the master's neck.

"Yield!" demanded Matsuzo. The Heishiro's face was still contorted in scorn.

"I have just given you the gift of control," Heishiro growled. "But you lack the most important aspects of combat. Thus, you must learn in time."

Matsuzo scoffed and withdrew his blade.

"I have only given you this gift because I too seek the destruction of Yorisama," Heishiro explained. "And as a favour to Ryo."

Matsuzo walked away from the master without another word. Heishiro was silent as the ingrate walked back into the forest without even a bow or a word of thanks, taking the jade-cased sword.

The trek back to Ryo's *hinansho* took more time than Matsuzo would have expected. Ryo had left him in the forest of Sakuragaoka to tend to the villagers, but Matsuzo found his way through the bamboo forest with little difficulty. Most of the landmarks they passed, such as the certain hills or the trees that formed narrow passes that he had previously traversed with his ninja friend. The sun was beginning to set over the deep, lush forest when Matsuzo heard a rustling among the vegetation. He stopped still and listened.

All around him, there was nothing but the sound of a soft breeze disturbing the falling leaves from the trees, and blowing around some of the dead leaves from the ground. But there was something else out there, something that was not natural, and something that was watching Matsuzo's every move. His hand reached for the hilt of his katana.

"HYAAAAH!"

An armoured samurai rushed from among the trees, making a beeline for Matsuzo. In the afternoon light from among the green and tan tree stalks, his dark grey armour and crested helm made him easily stand out. Without hesitating, Matsuzo clashed his katana's edge against that of the samurai's own sword. Again, the samurai tried to attack him, only to have Matsuzo cleanly deflect his sword away. With the samurai momentarily defenceless, Matsuzo took initiative and plunged the tip of his sword into the exposed neck of the samurai. Between his large helmet and moulded, leering face mask, the samurai's eyes went wide with disbelief, then rolled back in their sockets as he died. When his enemy fell, Matsuzo looked around for any others who may have come with him. Seeing no one else, he turned to the dead samurai on the ground. Blood was trickling from the wound in his throat and pouring over the dead leaves.

Ryo stood on the edge of the clearing near his hideout, training the villagers. Their form was getting noticeably better as Ryo directed them in mock combat against one another. Ryo smiled as the villagers practiced attacking and defending with their wooden practice swords. The air was filled with the sounds of the sticks clashing against each other and Ryo's word of encouragement.

"You're remembering what I told you about keeping your balance," Ryo remarked as he watched two students spar against each other. "Very good form."

Over the hillside, Matsuzo marched into the clearing. A katana in a jade scabbard was tied to his waist. The villagers were clearly surprised by his return, and bowed before him silently. Ryo was equally as stunned, but he did not bow.

"I see that Heishiro resorted to the easy way of training you, right?" Ryo observed. "And you certainly look the part."

"We make for Yorisama's lair tomorrow evening!" Matsuzo declared.

"I appreciate your enthusiasm, but we're still not ready," said Ryo.

"No excuses!" Matsuzo bellowed. "Tomorrow, we attack!"

In the waning light of the sunset, Yorisama Castle looked even more forbidding in its grandeur than ever. Against the backdrop of a sky alight with bright, harsh streaks of yellow and orange, the massive fortress loomed over Matsuzo and his companions like an angry deity, daring them to come forward on their mission. From their hiding spot on a hillside surrounded by trees, Matsuzo could see the torches being lit along the wall's perimeter, and several sentries on patrol, armed with a pole-arm weapons with long blades at their tips, as well as swords on their waists.

"What do you see?" asked Ryo nearby. He was clad in a form-fitting black suit, with a mask that covered all but his eyes. His ankles were wrapped in black bands of cloth, and his feet were covered with *tube* socks. He carried a rope slung over his shoulder and several tools and weapons in pouches on his waist. A sheathed sword was held on his back.

"Only a few sentries along the wall," Matsuzo relayed. "I don't see any archers. They just have swords and *naginatas*."

Ryo checked some equipment in a small pouch on his waist while listening. "He probably never expected an attack on his castle. Typical of Yorisama."

Matsuzo turned to his company of villagers behind him. "You all remember the plan," he announced. "Ryo and I will scale the walls and make for the sanctum. The rest of you will draw the samurai out of the castle and away from us."

One of the villagers, a man younger than Ryo, stood forward with a question.

"Matsuzo, we can't fight them!" he protested. "All we have are bamboo sticks to fight with!"

"You don't need to fight them, just distract them," Matsuzo corrected the young man. "You can either run or just throw stones at them, whatever works."

"If you do find yourselves in combat against the samurai," Ryo added. "Their armour is weakest at the base of their necks. A good job there should do the trick."

"Enough!" Matsuzo barked. "Everyone gets into formation! The main gate is down the hill and to the left. Start enough of a riot there and draw them out."

The villagers reluctantly followed a narrow trail down the hillside, circling around the area where Yorisama's lair stood, leaving only the innkeeper and the ninja.

"Are you sure about this?" asked Ryo.

"I've never been so sure in my life," Matsuzo answered with confidence, gripping the hilt of his katana. "Let's move."

They silently crept down the hillside opposite where the villagers went, and moved among the trees towards the outer wall of the castle, which seemed much taller now that they were both right up against it instead of surveying the scene from above. Ryo took the rope off of his shoulder and attached a grappling hook to one end. As he did so, Matsuzo kept a watch for guards on the ground. He could hear in the distance the sounds of shouting; the villagers must be doing their job by now. He tried to steady his breathing and his heartbeat, using the new skills that he picked up from Heishiro, and wondered whether or not he would be able to kill any samurai tonight.

Ryo threw the grappling hook up over the side of the wall, and it snagged on the edge of the stone wall just above the wooden walkway. Ryo tugged on the rope to ensure its stability, and gripped it with both hands, pulling himself up. He put his feet to the wall and steadily headed up the rope. Every grip and step on his way up was smooth and precise. Matsuzo came up the rope right behind him, calling on every ounce of his newfound powers to keep his balance and not give in to panic at the realization of how far above the ground he was. He willed himself to keep his gaze above him on his way up the wall.

Strangely, the walkway was deserted by the time they reached the top. Ryo readied his rope-tied sickle, looking around for anyone to attack. From the top of the wall, Ryo spotted some movement on the hillside near the castle's main gate. Sunlight was quickly fading, but he could discern the figures of men in white *Haori* robes massing at the gate. The villagers had the attention of the samurai, and the gates were already open to let several of Yorisama's armoured warriors through. Ryo looked in dismay as many of the villagers were quickly sliced apart at the edges of samurai swords.

"Matsuzo, you damn fool!" he cursed under his breath.

"They're doing their job, and now it's time for us to do ours," Matsuzo hissed, easily hearing what Ryo said.

They crossed the walkway around the walls together, entering a tall guard tower at the corner. The open door led into a small, square-shaped room, where two guards had very little time to react to the intruders that entered. Ryo spun his rope with the sickle-tied end out and lashed it out against the guards like a whip. The sickle blade sliced neatly through the guards' necks, spilling massive torrents of blood onto the floor as they fell.

Past the guard tower and further down another side of the wall, and the castle's side entrance was coming up fast. Four guards charged at Ryo down the walkway, pointing the long, curved blades of their *naginatas* at him. Ryo easily swept away the weapons of the first two guards with a flick of his rope-tied sickle to wrap around the shafts of their staffs and yanking them out of their hands, sending their polearm weapons clattering down below to the ground. With another flick of his weapon, he slashed across the face of one guard, cutting a crimson gash from his right cheek across the bridge of his nose and through his left eye. The wounded, blinded guard recoiled in agony, and fell off the walkway.

Another guard was sliced through the chest with the airborne sickle, and his lifeless body collapsed in a spreading pool of blood that dripped off the edges of the walkway, his dead eyes staring upwards. The two remaining guards charged with their weapons out, and Ryo drew out from a pouch on his waist a small metallic throwing star with four long, pointed edges. He threw the metal star right into the face of one guard, and another into the left forearm of the other guard. The guard with the wounded arm dropped his polearm weapon and gripped his bleeding arm with the metal star stuck in it, shrieking in agony. He lost his footing on the walkway, and fell face down on the ground below.

Matsuzo walked over the bleeding corpses on the wall, heading for the castle's entrance.

"I'll take the next guards we find," Matsuzo insisted, spiteful over Ryo's easy handling of the assailants they encountered.

Yorisama was furious at the news he was delivered by a lowly chamberlain. This insufferable slave, with an untidy black robe, a short topknot of hair, and a pointed nose, had dared to tell him that his castle was under attack by a rabble-rousing squad of peasants. After thoroughly berating the chamberlain for delivering such ill-timed news, he ordered every available samurai down to the gate to quell the uprising and to leave no survivors. His temper only got worse when he was told that the peasants were adept at using bamboo sticks as effective weapons.

"How could peasants with sticks overcome the finest warriors in Edo?!" the shogun roared. "Route them around the area and kill the lot of them! I want to be walking over their corpses by sunup!"

The chamberlain hustled out of the sanctum, keeping his head low before the shogun. Yorisama then turned to his fully-armoured *daimyo*.

"And you," he started, looking sourly at Tokubei. "I don't see how useful you are if all you're going to do is just stand there!"

"I shall defend you to the death, my lord," Tokubei growled under his moulded mask of a fanged snarl. "Not even the gods will get past my blade; those peasants will not stand a chance."

"See that they don't!" Yorisama demanded. Without another word, Tokubei bowed, and exited the room, standing guard outside the closed sliding door. That left Yorisama to the woman on his mattress: the freshly-cleaned and clothed Omitsu, garbed in a splendid kimono of red silk.

"When this rabble is over," Yorisama whispered coolly in her ear. "We can properly enjoy each other's company."

Omitsu barely even flinched at his voice.

Outside the room, in the castle's halls, the *daimyo* stood guard. The wooden halls and white plaster walls were bare, save only for two tall, metallic oil lamps in the hall's corners, providing enough light for Tokubei to see anyone coming through the single door on the opposite end of the hall. It was with some ease that he saw the slender, black-clad figure running down the hall right towards him, wielding a short sword that he pulled from a scabbard of his back. This meagre assailant was no match for his brute strength, as all it took was one powerful blow from his iron-covered fist right in his face to knock him to the floor, and one stab from Tokubei's own sword to kill him and stop any threat to the shogun. These peasants were starting to get bolder, to be able to come this far into the castle.

Down the hall, another armed person entered, looking dismayed over the loss of his ninja friend.

"Ryo!" he yelped, seeing the body under Tokubei's blade. With little time to mourn the dead, he faced Tokubei and unsheathed his sword, assuming a ready stance. Tokubei grunted in dismissal; a well-trained *Shinobi* died at his hand; how could a peasant fare against him?

Matsuzo charged at him and struck hard against Tokubei's decorated Chestplate, resuming his stance right behind the hulking, armoured warlord. Tokubei spun around, and clashed swords with Matsuzo, matching his every move with brutal, uncontrolled rage. With every clang and ring the crashing swords made against each other, Matsuzo held his ground. The armoured behemoth still had not laid a scratch on his body, but his face was beaded with sweat, and his hair was loose and untidy. Matsuzo's eyes were filled with determination, whereas Tokubei stared down with unbridled anger.

Tokubei made another charge at Matsuzo, holding his sword over his head, willing for a downward slice through Matsuzo. In an instant, Matsuzo crouched down slightly and sliced Tokubei across his chest, right where his armour plate ended. Tokubei fell lifelessly behind Matsuzo.

Without any other obstructions, Matsuzo headed for the sanctum and pulled the door open. Inside the room with the gaudy murals of warriors and *any* demons, all he could see where the two figures on a silk-laden mattress in the centre of the room. One of them was a man with a thin moustache and a self-righteous look about him, and the other was none other than Omitsu.

Yorisama looked up from Omitsu at the swordsman in the room with an expression of shock and disbelief. He had no time to get out a single word, as all it took was a quick slice from Matsuzo's sword to sever his head from his shoulders. The shogun's blood spilled in a torrent from his headless body all over the floor at Matsuzo's feet. On the mattress, Omitsu lay in shock. Her husband had returned, just as she knew he would, but she never expected him to come with a killer instinct.

"I knew you'd come back for me, Matsuzo!" Omitsu said happily.

"I did come back for you," Matsuzo growled. "And this is how you repay me? By bedding the shogun?!"

Without hesitation, he stuck the sword through Omitsu's heart. His wife slipped back onto the silk mattress with a frozen expression of regret on her dead face. Behind Matsuzo, several guards entered the room with their swords drawn. Upon seeing the severed head of Yorisama, they prepared to strike at his assassin.

That is, until Matsuzo unsheathed the sword from Yorisama's corpse. The guards stepped back in fear of seeing the assassin holding two blades, one of which was taken from the shogun.

"Would you dare to attack me?" asked Matsuzo, tauntingly. "Your master is dead. Now, you can either serve me, or become *raining* for the rest of your life. What will it be?"

The guards were speechless. Facing the man would be suicide, but the prospect of becoming unemployed warriors would be a worse fate indeed. They hesitantly bowed before Matsuzo.

The cherry blossom trees were shedding their small, pink petals on a paved street and the wooden roofs of the long houses lining the street on a cloudless day. On the street corner, a travelling man in a dark blue *Haori* entered the village inn, greeted by a jovial-looking man at the desk with portly cheeks and a well-kept top knot of hair.

"Welcome!" the innkeeper said forcefully. "What brings you to our humble inn?"

"I just need somewhere safe to stay," the traveller whispered. "The samurai have been getting more aggressive this whole year."

"Is that shogun stirring up trouble again?" asked the innkeeper. "The one called Matsuzo?"

"Yes," the man muttered. "Not even under Yorisama has been they ever this act, or this brutal."

"You have my sympathies, friend," said the innkeeper. "Many of us were trained by the very man who knew Matsuzo. We should be able to keep you safe here."

"I've heard the stories about his rise to power," the traveller said to the innkeeper. "They say he used everyone as stepping stones to become a shotgun. The ninja, the hermit, the people from Edo... has that man no shame?"

At the apex of the newly-refurbished Matsuzo Castle, the new shogun, clad in an impeccable black and green kimono and *kamashimo* stood on a balcony overlooking the courtyard. Several of his armoured samurai stood in a rigid, disciplined formation while one of his raiding parties returned through the castle gates with a fresh group of conscripts and concubines. From above, Matsuzo could almost hear their desperate cries for mercy getting quickly silenced by their armed captors. He smiled slightly; everything was working out splendidly for him. The death of Yorisama seemed like a lifetime ago for him, though only a year had passed. Now, the humble innkeeper was living in godlike luxury, surrounded by wealth, women and warriors.

Night descended over the castle like a black shroud, and Matsuzo retreated to his sanctum, resting on a lavish mattress covered in fine, smooth silk. Outstretched on the mattress, he allowed himself to fall into a peaceful slumber.

Above him in the rafters, a lone figure clad in black watched him carefully, unseen and unnoticed. Several minutes passed as the ninja in the ceiling watched the shogun fall asleep on his silk-covered bed, resting on his back all the while. The ninja maneuvered over to a hanging wooden beam in the ceiling, directly above the sleeping shogun.

From out of a pouch on his hip, he drew a spool of thin black wire, which he unraveled downwards until the thin strand was pointed down at Matsuzo's mouth. He held the spool steady, keeping the end of the string right where he needed it to be, and then produced from another pouch a bottle of a clear liquid. He poured a small amount of the liquid onto the string, letting the tiny drops cascade their way down the string towards Matsuzo's mouth. Two drops fell off the end of the string, directly onto Matsuzo's lips. Instinctively, he licked his lips, tasting the liquid.

The ninja rolled the spool in his hands back up, just as the poison was taking its effect on the shogun. Matsuzo started moaning and convulsing on his bed. His stifled moans became louder, and his movements more frenzied, until he went stiff and rigid.

The new shogun was dead.

The shogun's sanctum disappeared, and the Mystic Theater materialized in its place. Where the dying shogun once lay, Doctor Xoctarious stood on stage before the audience. Somewhere in the middle of the audience, the software company executive was sweating profusely.

"You know," started the doctor, "I was approached once several years ago by a Spanish noble lady. Her name was Señora Morella, and she asked me what her future held. I simply told her not to worry about the future, but instead to open her mind to the experience of being alive. There is more to life than obsessing over your career, I told her.

"However, she did not take my advice. Instead, she obsessed more than ever at her career, whatever it may have been. When last I heard her name, she was one of the world's wealthiest, as well as one of the world's loneliest. She pursued with a single mind all those riches and titles, but she forgot to enjoy everything else that life had to offer. She died rich, but friendless."

Gabriel Crowell sat in the audience reflecting on the good doctor's message, recollecting when he first met Philip Grafton at the museum exhibition in Prague. At the time, Gabriel was suffering from a severe case of writer's block, unable to self publish a book in a long time, so he travelled to Prague seeking inspiration. He found the museum exhibit on esoteric and occult artifacts, which even included an ancient stone Golem, and met Grafton there. They talked a bit in the exhibit hall about his interest in the unknown, the supernatural, and what science and society still has yet to understand about the world.

From there, after the trip, Gabriel would converse with Grafton over email or instant messengers. Grafton would hear out Gabriel's problems with his professional life and his hopeless love life and having difficulty finding women, and Grafton would advise him on such matters. Gabriel was spellbound about how carefree Grafton, this unusual older man, usually acted. It was not until they met again later in his exhibit that he saw a different side to Grafton as a showman, that he ran the "Mystic Theater of Doctor Xoctarious."

Gabriel told the doctor that during that "vision," as he took to calling them, he dared to reach out his hand and he could almost feel the elements which came about in each story that was told. Maybe Grafton used stage actors in conjunction with projection systems or holograms? But the doctor's lips were sealed unless he chose to reveal such secrets, as he smiled with mild pride.

Gabriel's instincts were sharp like a surgeon's knife, and he was on to him; soon he would uncover this enigmatic man's secret. But the doctor had already given him an answer when he asked the same repetitive question, even when he met him for the first time in Europe and the answer was this: "The only way to uncover the secrets is to find out what you want with them. It is not to be taken, but given, and there is a price. It must be earned," remembered Gabriel, in his thoughts.

One last intermission was called, and audience dismissed themselves for drinks. A band was also playing at the doctor's request. But Gabriel stayed in the empty theatre with Xoctarious; he had become fully suspicious of the man himself.

"You're not all you appear to be, are you, Philip?" questioned Gabriel

"Part of being a showman is to adopt a certain guise; everyone knows that," said Xoctarius duplicitously.

"But what kind of man are you, really?" pressed Gabriel

The doctor sighed. "May I ask you a question first? Are you truly happy in your life?"

Gabriel was confused. "I don't know, maybe. Maybe not," he sighed. "The truth is that I am very lonely. So the answer would be no," Said Gabriel honestly; he wanted to deny that truth dearly, but the reality he knew too well that he could not run away from his struggling aspirations as a writer anymore.

"I feel the same way sometimes. Over the years, I've seen people come and go, and some I wish that they would stay with me longer than they have. I've heard more goodbyes than I've said hellos. A sad, lonely existence, even for a man such as myself," pondered the good doctor.

"Not very good with people?"

"Not especially, no. Even with everything I've ever accomplished in this theatre, sometimes it seems difficult to get through to help a human being achieve their ultimate potential; that rare, precious spark which drives mankind to fulfil their divine purpose, even personal dreams, I suppose... It would take centuries to change the hearts of men, completely."

"Centuries?" said Gabriel, off guard by the doctor's statement.

"Hmm. And I've tried, too hard sometimes,"

But Gabriel caught on, intuitively. "What do you mean you've tried?"

The doctor was stunned slightly. "I guess I should say no more."

"No, go on. There's something about you."

"I shouldn't," said the doctor, but Gabriel insisted strongly.

"I already saw your mirror, Doctor Xoctarious, Philip Grafton, or whomever you are,"

The doctor shook his head in mild yet friendly defiance, smiling subtly.

"There's too much to tell, and you wouldn't believe me anyway, much less understand. All you need to know is that I am more than I appear. If you remember the last story, you'd do well not to go chasing after things you'd be better off not knowing."

Gabriel felt shot down. "I'm sorry," he said regretfully.

"Don't worry," said the doctor calmly. "You're still a good friend, and a decent human being, for that matter. I do wish I knew more people like you. You have sensible qualities about you, my young friend,"

"Such as?" asked Gabriel.

"Humility for one thing, that is a very rare quality to find in a human being in these strange times,"

"Thank you, Phillip," complemented Gabriel.

"You're welcome. We best be heading back. It's time for the grand finale, and you may want to take your seat; you will enjoy it. I gurantee it," Said the doctor as the crowd was being ushered by attendants back to their seats for the evening's final performance.

The audience reassembled, with Xoctarious readying the final act of the show.

"Ladies and gentlemen: this, I'm afraid, this is the final vision that I will present to you all this evening. Over the course of these short hours, we have travelled together through realms beyond history and legend, through the wonders of imagination. Now, the grand dénouement is upon us, where I will personally be your guide. Some of you may be driven to wonder about my very nature, and I do not blame you for such curiousity. Here is a story from my own past, one of many lives I've lived. "Please come with me to the very cradle of civilization, to the year 1764 B.C., in the region known as Mesopotamia in ancient Babylon. Now, here I present the tale known as 'Forbidden.'"

FORBIDDEN

Story by
Dominic R. Daniels & Doug K. Owen
Written by
Dominic R. Daniels & Doug K. Owen

.

With a wave of his hand, the lights in the Mystic Theater petered out, and the great auditorium was cast in absolute darkness, such that every member of the audience was sightless. Gabriel squirmed in his seat; darkness made him uneasy, and this was a very dense shadow that he found himself seated in, a complete absence of light. For a moment, he thought his eyes had failed him, and tried to raise a hand in front of his face to reassure himself, but he saw none of his own fingers. He started to panic, his breath coming out in gasps and sweat rolling down his forehead.

Then, in a slow turn, a bright sun shone overhead in a cloudless blue sky. Where the walls and floor of the Mystic Theater once were, there was an expanse of a rocky, arid desert. A hot wind blew unrelentingly at the audience, kicking up small clouds of dust and pebbles, from which the audience had to shield themselves. The rock-strewn terrain shone harshly in the desert sun as the waves of the intense heat rose from the ground, distorting the audience's vision. As glad as he was to get out of the darkness, Gabriel was not fond of the new setting. He wiped dirty sweat off of his forehead as the wind started to die down, leaving only the viciously hot water for them to contend with.

Their seats started to move forward, as if there were high-powered motors attached to every seat in the auditorium. Together as one, the audience lurched forward quickly, such that Gabriel gripped onto his armrests tightly, like riding in a speeding roller coaster without a seatbelt. He could hear some harried screams

coming from other theatre attendees around him. While his frenzied mind tried to comprehend everything around him, a part of
him hoped desperately that Doctor Xoctarius would hold true to
his promise not to let any harm come to anyone in his audience.

The scene changed to a rugged, hilly terrain in the desert. The
sun was dipping down beneath the horizon, casting the last few rays
of light into the sky. The cloudy wisps caught these beams, turning
them bright orange and violet against the field of darkening blue
that was the sky. Below, an army stood at attention: thousands of
armoured, well-disciplined soldiers, endless as if the roaring waves
of the great oceans during a storm, to let loose the beastly savagery
of war.

Several paces before the front ranks, a rider on a strong, pale
horse rode to the centre of the ranks. The rider was young, with
long locks of auburn hair and a short moustache and beard. He
wore a gleaming iron breastplate, adorned with bronze beneath a
linen tunic, and a bronze-studded helmet on his head. His feet were
wrapped in leather sandals. He drew from two scabbards on either
side of his waist a pair of shiny bronze swords, waving them over his
head to rally his troops. The ranks of the soldiers shouted proudly
in the presence of their esteemed general.

"The Assyrians approach!" the general shouted over the din of
his soldiers. "Stand united, defend your brothers' flanks, and don't
let any of them past you!"

The soldiers kept a tight grip on their spears and shields, facing
straight ahead, ready to face any enemy force that awaited them.
They stood fearless and unwavering, like perching hawks before
the attack.

"In this life," the general shouted, "every man is given just but
one chance for greatness! He who gains it is remembered for all
eternity! So make this day your day to find greatness, and it shall be
yours for the taking!"

The general on horseback charged forth into the desert, followed by his troops. Ahead of them was an army that stretched across

the horizon, every bit as determined and strong as the Babylonians. The Assyrian force began their charge, wielding bronze-tipped spears and swords and shouting outlandish war cries. In the centre of the desert, the two sides crashed into one another in a cacophonous mass slaughter. Swords were thrust deep into the bodies of enemies, and blood spurted in torrents onto the rocky gulch. Heads were cleaved off from shoulders, rolling onto the ground amid other fallen bodies.

Overhead, a storm of fiery arrows pierced the sky and impacted deep into the Assyrian ranks. Those soldiers unfortunate enough to be caught in their warpath fell with the flaming missiles lodged right through their armour plates, screaming in agony as they died.

The general rode headlong into the chaos, sending his dual swords into Assyrian skulls and necks, his every motion calculated and rehearsed. His horse's hooves splashed in puddles of blood on the ground and trampled over corpses. His gaze was as cold and unrelenting as the bloodied blades he wielded against his foes, slashing and thrusting through them.

"General Daresh!" came a voice from among the battle. The general steered his horse around to find one of his commanders in the fray, carving into an Assyrian soldier.

"We've almost routed them!" called out the Babylonian soldier to his superior officer. Daresh on his horse turned to face the ever-charging enemy hordes still coming at his army.

"Send them in!" Daresh commanded. "Go for the kill!"

Deep in the Assyrian ranks, the general Daresh had a surprise coming from his enemies. A team of two chariots charged against the Assyrians' left side, but these were no ordinary chariots. Pulled by teams of six muscular, lightly-armoured, multi-coloured feather-adorned stallions each, these iron-clad attack chariots rode in teams of two, each with a net of chains between them. The chained nets held arrays of small, sharp caltrops that carved into Assyrian flesh as they rode headlong into the battle. These attack pairs funneled several Assyrian fighters into their metallic traps, ripping into their bodies, adding more corpses to the burgeoning corpse piles. Their screams mixed with the sounds of fury from their Babylonian conquerors.

Eventually, Daresh and his forces carved a swath through the Assyrians, reaching the encampment of their generals. Tents with linen sheets stood erect with split logs and thick branches around several burning fire pits in the ground. Their occupants were taken by surprise by the encroaching Babylonians, and hastily armed themselves, only to be quickly cut down by Babylonian blades. Daresh dismounted from his horse and entered one of the tents, finding only chests filled with silver coins and unused weapons.

"Take everything!" he commanded, looking over the rightfully-gained spoils that lay before him. Some of his soldiers proceeded to plunder the tents, carting off several chests of gold, silver, and supplies. Daresh darted into another, larger tent, finding a wide open space inside, lined with tables bearing maps and diagrams, as well as several chests with weapons and gold. On the far end of the tent, Daresh found a woman chained to a pole. She was clad in a gracefully smooth orange tunic and had metal bracelets and anklets on her limbs. Among her long, flowing red hair, she wore a golden headdress with a disc-shaped crest embedded in the centre. Her electric blue eyes flashed with fear at Daresh's approach, and she recoiled away from him.

"Get away from me!" she screamed. Daresh moved closer in curiosity, raising a hand towards her to try and placate her, but the woman snapped at him, biting at his hand. Daresh pulled his hand back with a jolt of pain, finding some teeth marks on his skin. He sighed and stared down at the woman.

"I'm not here to hurt you," Daresh explained. "The Assyrians have been dealt with. I assume they're holding you as a captive?"

"They said they were keeping me until they won the war against Babylon," she explained. Daresh shook his head.

"Well, it seems they were wrong in that regard," said Daresh. "I am Daresh, general of the royal army of Babylon and a servant of the exalted King Hammurabi. If you come with me, I will assure you that no harm befall upon you. What shall I call you?"

"Tamira," she answered simply. "I am the princess of Larsa."

"Larsa?" asked Daresh. "My city is an ally of yours! I'm sure you will be welcomed in our courts."

Daresh crouched next to Tamira and undid the ropes binding her to the pole. She relaxed her posture and touched her wrists, feeling the rope imprints in her skin.

"The Assyrians have been slaughtered," Daresh explained. "We will ride back to Babylon, and then you will be escorted safely back to Larsa."

Tamira nodded, and took Daresh's hand.

Past the arid, parched desert, the walls of Babylon loomed high above the ground, the earthen tones of the clay bricks almost blending into the desert itself. Armed sentries stood atop the walls spotted the returning army and blew on a horn to signal their return. The blares of the horns echoed over the massive, sprawling city of Babylon. Patches of green fields were tended by farmers and slaves, and a bustling marketplace was crowded with buyers and sellers. Clad in several shades of coloured linen, those commoners felt a tinge of excitement among themselves. Their warriors were returning triumphant from the field of battle against the distant, brutish Assyrian raiders.

In the centre of the city, the sacred Ziggurat towered high above the ground, a monolithic tower with sloped edges and inset cylindrical rings one atop the other. The priests in the tower and the surrounding grounds heard the blaring horns and prepared their prayers to the deity Marduk in recognition of Babylon's victory.

Beyond there, Daresh led his army to the grand palace, a colossus of stone towers, banked walls decorated with intricate patterns, and gracefully-designed gardens. Sunlight poured into the opulent throne room where Daresh entered with Tamira and some of his commanders at his side. Several guards were posted at intervals around the room, where large stone columns upheld the slotted ceiling. Linen banners of white and gold hanging from the ceiling swayed gently in the breeze that flowed from the ceiling slats.

Across the room, on a raised dais inlaid with emerald-green tiles, there sat on an ornately-carved wooden throne a man with a long black beard and an immaculate robe of black silk trimmed with gold. Atop his long black hair was a golden crown inlaid with emeralds. His luminous brown eyes sparkled as Daresh entered the chamber.

"Welcome, Daresh!" the king said jovially as Daresh and his company bowed before him. "What news do you bring from the field of battle?"

"Wise King Hammurabi," Daresh addressed the monarch,. "the Assyrians have been thoroughly beaten and humiliated! It will be years before they could mount another attack on us again."

"Excellent!" Hammurabi declared, clapping his hands together. His gaze, then turned to Tamira at Daresh's side.

"And who might this fine young woman be?" he asked. Tamira bowed before the king and pulled in a breath, standing confidently among the royals.

"I am Tamira, princess of Larsa," she addressed herself. "Your majesty's general Daresh has freed me from the Assyrian's grasp, and here I stand before Your Highness."

"A fellow royal!" said Hammurabi excitedly. "My dear, you are most welcome in our fair city and in my palace!"

He turned to some of his stewards near the platform and motioned for them to come forth. The leather-clad servants stepped forward meekly, and the king motioned towards Tamira.

"Stewards, please prepare a room for our esteemed guest and bring her the finest silks to wear. Also prepare a bath and a feast for the lady as well! Tonight, we celebrate our victory and rescue of our ally's princess!"

Tamira bowed. "Your Highness, you are most gracious," she said.

"Daresh, the princess shall be in your charge until my envoy returns from Larsa with the news of her rescue, give her a tour of our kingdom and make her feel welcome. I am sure she is exhausted from her capture," the king declared in the general. Daresh placed his clasped fist over his heart and bowed slightly in salute to the king.

"Sire," saluted Daresh respectfully bowing to the king then taking his leave with Tamria.

"Come with me, and I will show around," said Daresh to Tamira.

Tamira bowed to the brave general and she followed him as he escorted her to the enclosed royal bath house that was located in the lower outer courtyards of the palace near the lush green gardens which was laden with date and fig trees including an assortment of the most rarest of species of Nile lily flowers imported as seedlings from Thebes in Egypt and grown to perfection with exalted colors of orange and shades of indigo blues, white and pleasant tones of violet filled with a sweet fragrance as the petals were soft to the touch.

As Tamira and Daresh entered into the bath house they noticed that the walls of this chamber were layered with finest decorated patterns of insignias and images of lions and eagles that were designed by Babylon's chief artist and stone masons, four large hand carved marble pillars were placed around the ritual bathing pool with a statue of winged lions standing guard on each side to protect the bather that was to enter the pool. The room was lit with an altar with white candles and brass braziers that burned wisps of musk scented incense to give a relaxing experience to both the mind and body.

Two young female stewards dressed in humble robes which were dyed beige coloured cotton, with two additional female stewards who were already preparing the large bathing pool with warm water, not too hot, but comfortable enough to sit in and rest for a spell, as they poured in the vat of soapy waters, bourbon rose petals and a honey potion infused with herbs of mint and eucalyptus with a dash of dead sea salt to give a delicate balance to the bath and act as special cleaning agent to preserve the smoothness of the skin.

Tameria was impressed by the beauty of this bathing chamber; Daresh carved a polite smile around his lips.

"My lady, I am sure you will find everything here very comfortable; now, if you need anything, these gentle creatures will attend to you. If you will excuse me," he murmured.

"I must prepare myself for this evening," said Daresh

"But of course. Thank you, General; I will see you later then," said Tamira.

"Enjoy your bath, your Highness," said Daresh smiling, leaving the four servant maidens to take on Tamira's needs.

Daresh proceeded to his chamber that was just down the grand hallway, opposite from Tamira's room, and he bathed himself in his private chambers. Then he dried off and dressed himself in his undergarments and a nobleman's robes embodied with gold and hazel fabrics and a browned beaded leaden copper sash with his evening reed sandals and a large black-pearl ring, encrusted with gold that he placed on his right ring finger.

He he put on his cape with a large amulet made of the stone tiger's eye, and he removing a small jade bottle of perfume from his jewelry box. He pulled off the cork lid and anointed his face with a few drops, and then headed off from his room to speak with the king before the feast.

But his Majesty was not present in the throne room. Daresh was directed by the palace guard to find the king resting in his study, sitting down and drinking a small goblet of choice wine while reviewing a matter of state that had been on his mind for quite some time.

Hammurabi sat in a chair made of bronze next to a simple table carved from cedar trees that polished and shaped sublimely, with a scroll with writing on it that had been scrawled by his committee of princes about a separate kingdom that they perceived would be trouble if he did not take action to bring a resolve to.

Though the king was well pleased with his victory over the Assyrians, he was still concerned for the growth and expansion of the empire as well as for the protection of his people in Babylon. During these days, his country was currently warring with Elam, and he felt in his heart that his kingdom needed to build better defenses and improve it sciences in the field of advanced weaponry and objective military strategy to prevent incoming raids from his enemies.

Though the mighty Hammurabi was a very powerful man, he was not a fool, and he was not prideful enough to let his enemies take advantage of him, even for a brief moment. A smack of pride could bring down the strongest of dynasties, and he did not wish that particular weakness to become his, but there was more to it than that; he also he valued his people's opinion.

What would they, the Babylonians, say of his great name in the years that would follow? How would his people see their king? Would he be known in his future fame as: The warrior, the scholar, the lawgiver or the tyrant? These questions he thought in his mind, they bothered him time and time again. He seldom slept at night with these disturbing thoughts in his mind, but the important concern that mattered to the king at that moment was the glory and greatness of Babylon, the center of human civilization, seat of the world's power and innovation.

Few men in his position were fortunate enough to be a sovereign of a nation, so he decided to be cautious of any future alliances he would make. In these blood thirsty days, the earth was not fully civilized; only the strong and wise would survive. The arrogant and conceited would die.

King Hammurabi heard footsteps at the entrance of his study, and he slowly raised his eyes from the parchment he was reading and noticed Daresh in the entry way.

"Daresh, come here please; I need to confide in someone. I am deeply... troubled," said the king restlessly. His jovial side was replaced by sternness as he showed his true colors.

"Highness," said Daresh as he entered the king's study and bowed.

"Please do not humble yourself before me," said the king. "Daresh, let's now talk... as regular men, speak to each other. As friends," said the king. "Tell me General; why are we at war with Elam, the Barbarians, and what other demons in flesh that the gods have cursed us with?" said Hammurabi, meekly, with a hint of sarcasm.

"For the greatness of your Empire, sire," said Daresh.

"Greatness, mmm... Well, what truly is greatness? I wonder ... Oh, what my people and nations will do for greatness, and they are much opinionated these days, my old friend," reflected the king sadly.

"Why do you feel sorrow?" asked Daresh, surprised by the king's remarks.

"I am tired," said the king burying his face in his palms, a look of self hatred in his own heart as he rubbed his head. His anger was splitting his mind apart as he removed his hands placing them on his lap.

"I am tired of the killing and fighting with our neighboring kingdoms; they attack us and we slaughter them and their children in the night, and for what ? Wealth? Power? ...The way of fools. ... There is more to life than pleasure and power," said the king.

"Do you mean to say that we are fighting for nothing, Your Highness?" questioned Daresh seriously. This disturbed him greatly as he was loyal to the empire but did not want his soldiers to fight for nothing. It made him feel if anything, empty and a little sad.

"Nothing ... nothing... Yes, it is for nothing... It is all for total stupidity and foolishness," said the king sadly.

"Then what do you want of me, Highness?" said Daresh.

"I want you to send word to Elam to set up negations to establish peace. Our kingdoms have more than enough in resources and gold to go around; this war grows colder and more futile each day. As much as I desire glory for our people, I do not wish to go down in future histories as an evil king. When it is over, no good will come of it," said the king.

"And if they refuse your council and continue to fight us, sire?" asked Daresh.

"Then we have no choice but to destroy them and their brood as well. My soul is gravely troubled. In dreams, the gods speak to me with thunderous voices of displeasure, and I see winged creatures so wondrous, theirs eyes sparkle like the stars and faces that glow brighter than the glistening of the moon, yet they appear as if they were men and yet... I hear a god who is different among all the others, a strange tender voice, a voice of compassion, a deep bond I feel when I hear him, as if I have never heard by any being ever before in all my days, he tells me in my heart: ' *Make peace with thy enemies or disaster shall come upon your people in generations to follow...*'

"I am afraid when I hear this god's voice. He comes to me, speaking in my mind at the rising of the rays of the dawn, and in my dreams when I lie down to sleep, and night visions of terror befall me," said the king. "Do you believe in dreams, my friend?" asked the king.

"Dreams, your majesty, are the business of the wise ones, but I will pray to my god, for you. If that would give you peace, it may be him in heaven that is sending you a message," said Daresh.

"Yes, you have told me of your ancestral decent; your god, the god with no name," said the king.

"Indeed. I have," said Daresh.

"Pray to your god then for me. It seems he has given you much favor with me and the kingdom. Perhaps if we listen to his words, we will make peace and this evil war will end," said the king.

The king's words lingered in Daresh's mind as he made his way back to his chamber, through the maze of open, spacious hallways lined with smooth stone columns. Night had since fallen, and the oil torches in the halls and in his chamber were already lit by the stewards, casting a golden glow over the stone walls and wooden furniture. A light breeze blew in from the open window at the end of the room, right in the middle of the wall. A thin linen curtain danced in the breeze that Daresh moved to a side. He then sat down on a large, luxurious mattress stuffed with ostrich feathers and coated with rich, soft fabric of dark red.

Daresh exhaled and pondered the king's words. He had become weary of war, and worried how future generations would remember him. Would Babylon still prosper long after he passed from this earth? Would Daresh's children and grandchildren remember him as a noble, honourable commander, or as a brutal despot bent on conquering other lands?

This question was especially difficult for Daresh to answer, seeing as how he himself carried out Hammurabi's will on the battlefield. Every life he had taken, every soldier that fell by his swords, all of them were only to serve his king and his mighty empire. Never once had he dared to question his king or his own motives. If Hammurabi was going to send him on a mission to sow peace, then that is what he will do, even if his sole occupation for several years had been the opposite.

A steward in a red robe and sash entered Daresh's chamber, bringing a rolled-up scroll of papyrus. Daresh lazily motioned for him to enter, and he handed the scroll to the general, bowing low to the ground.

"Esteemed general, the king wishes for you to read these instructions for the trip to Elam," said the steward.

"It shall be done," replied Daresh. "Please tell the king that his general shall comply."

"Yes, general," the steward said, exiting the room.

"Steward?" asked Daresh before the steward could reach the curtain. He turned around quickly to face him again.

"Where is the princess Tamira?" Daresh asked.

"She slumbers in the guest quarters, general," the steward responded.

"Well, I won't be one to wake her then," the general mused. "Please write a message for her that matters of state have come up, and I shall be seeing her again very soon."

"With all haste, general."

The steward exited the room, leaving Daresh alone in the opulent room. He collapsed on his back onto the mattress and unrolled the scroll. The wedge-shaped cuneiform letters in black ink on the light tan scroll detailed instructions for Daresh and his company on their trip to Elam, to the east of the Persian Gulf. The cool breeze caressed his brow as he read the message, and inwardly he wondered about Tamira and how she was enjoying her time at the palace. They were to leave the palace by dawn tomorrow, which would not afford him any time to properly bid her farewell before the journey, and it would be several weeks until they returned to Babylon.

He read and reread the scroll, and started to feel very drowsy. His eyelids started to fall over his eyes, as if they were weighted with lead. The weary general lay down on his back on the mattress and allowed fatigue to overcome him. He drifted out of consciousness, and into the realm of dreams. If the gods were to deliver him a message as they did for Hammurabi, then this would be the place for it to happen.

The night sky was beginning to show the first faint traces of light from a newly-rising sun by the time Daresh stirred from his slumber and garbed himself in full battle regalia. His armour was clean and polished, his cotton tunic was spotless, and his sandals were wrapped tightly on his feet. The twin bronze blades in their leather scabbards at his belt, were clean and sharp. The soldiers that were gathered in the palace courtyard were all similarly geared, ready for his command. They stood in rigid formations by the time Daresh exited the front gate of the palace. A steward brought his pale horse to him, with a saddle mounted on its back. As Daresh mounted his horse, he turned to his army and spoke.

"My brothers, our illustrious king command us to ride forth to the east, to Elam. There, we are to arrive not as warmongers, but as friends. Our king commands us to establish negotiations for an alliance, and we are to offer tribute. If, for any reason they dare refuse, then we are to defend our great empire."

With that, he rode away from the palace and out through the city gates. His army and several caravans of supplies joined him on his trek through the desert. Camels and horses pulled sturdy wooden carts loaded with food and water for the troops and several casks of gold, silver, wine, oil and other precious cargo as a token offering for the Elamites. Whether they would accept the offer, Daresh could not say.

From above, Tamira stood on a balcony overlooking the eastern quarter of the city. The sunrise was bright and glorious over the tall Ziggurat in the distance and the tiny buildings below it. Tamira marveled at the rays of light spilling over the dark indigo sky, forcing the darkness to flight. Deep in her heart, she preferred it to be dark; the sunlight was already beginning to sting her eyes. She turned away from the sunrise and walked through her guest quarters, down the palace halls, and rounding a corner to the royal aviary.

The mesh walls and ceiling allowed the first few rays of sunlight to offer some scant illumination, and several birds of all different colours and sizes stood perched on a scaffold around the walls. Tamira shut the door behind her, and reached for the nearest large, yellow-eyed falcon.

The journey to Elam lasted several days, and Daresh felt weary by the time they entered the court of the Elamites. The city walls were taller, bulkier and less decorated than the fortifications at Babylon. Daresh on horseback looked with awe at the tall, pointed guard towers dotting the city walls, and their own Ziggurat that pierced the sky. Past the bustling markets and well-kept farmlands, Daresh and his company beheld a splendid palace lined with tall stone monoliths and guarded by a large company of armoured soldiers. Daresh dismounted, and commanded his troops and envoys to follow him into the palace.

The guards at the palace's heavy, polished wooden front gate were taken aback by the presence of a contingent of Babylonian soldiers, and they quickly unsheathed their swords, ready to strike.

Daresh, walking up the steps to the palace, kept his own weapons in their scabbards, and he bowed lightly to the sentries.

"I come with an envoy from Babylon and a token to the exalted king of the Elamites, Siwe-Palar-Khuppak. His Exaltedness is expecting us." Behind him, his envoy opened a chest from one of the carts in his caravan. The guards were easily entranced by the glittering pile of gold and silver coins inside.

The guards obediently sheathed their swords and stepped aside, allowing Daresh and his companions to enter. As Daresh walked by them, he glimpsed a hint of a sneer from one of the guards. Down a wide, spacious hall, the throne room of the Elamite king reminded Daresh faintly of home, with its thick alabaster columns and breeze swaying in from the vaulted ceiling. As Hammurabi's throne room featured soft earthen tones and graceful green tiles on his dais, the lord of the Elamites surrounded himself with bronze statues of warriors and deities, and nearly every last inch of the walls was decorated with stylized murals, mounted weapons from battles past, and hanging tapestries.

The king himself was seated on a throne carved of polished white and red alabaster stone, inlaid with gold and carved with intricate designs. Siwe-Palar-Khuppak himself had a short brown beard and a stern countenance, garbed in shiny golden armour and a red cape. Black sandals were wrapped tightly around his feet. A golden sword was sheathed and sitting right by his throne where he could easily reach it.

Daresh entered the throne room with his envoys and bowed low before the Elamite king. Upon his approach, the king instantly was overcome with rage, and got up from his throne with clenched fists.

"Guards, who are these intruders? How dare you allow them into my presence!"

"Noble Siwe-Palar-Khuppak, most honoured king of the Elamites, I am General Daresh of Babylon, and I come before your greatness to offer a token of alliance between our great kingdoms."

"You flatter us with your presence, sir, but I need no tribute!" the king declared. "My wealth exceeds far beyond that of Babylon and even Egypt! Go back and tell King Hammurabi that his emissary's presence is not welcome here! Leave now with your men, or my soldiers shall kill you right here in my presence!"

"Your Majesty, if I may…" Daresh tried to plead, but was quickly cut off by the king's terse warning.

"Leave. Now."

There was nothing Daresh could say to the king's stern warning, so he hesitantly turned his back on the king after a slight bow, and left with his troops and envoys.

Daresh's heart was weighted with dismay on their trip back into the desert, westward to Babylon. For the first time he had ever known, he had failed the word of his king and an alliance between the two kingdoms was out of reach. What kind of despot was this Siwe-Palar-Khuppak, who refused a substantial offer and the promise of a lasting peace with a strong nation?

More than the political ramifications, Daresh found himself thinking more about Tamira, safe in the guest quarters of the palace. Inwardly, he yearned to see her again, and to share some private, undisturbed time with that alluring princess. After he had to bear the ill news to Hammurabi, who would doubtlessly be dismayed, he could ask for some time alone with their guest, if he would oblige.

"General?" asked one of Daresh's commanders walking at his side, fully-armoured and carrying a long spear and tall, wooden shield.

"Commander Amstet," Daresh addressed him.

"His Exaltedness will surely be displeased," Amstet said to the horseback general.

"Our king is a wise man, Amstet. I'm sure he will understand none of this is our fault."

"And what of the Elamite king?" asked Amstet.

"That young king is very foolish. If he doesn't ruin his own kingdom first, we'll surely ruin his."

Just then, a young scout ran hastily to the front of the column to the commander and the general. Daresh gestured for him to calm down, and the scout tried to catch his harried breath, his whole body trembling violently.

"General…!" the scout wheezed. "An Elamite army has followed us!"

"Elam sent their army after us?" Daresh asked in surprise. The scout nodded, and Daresh steered his horse around to survey the desert they had already traversed. Over a nearby sand dune, Daresh could see hundreds of armoured elements with long spears on their trail, as well as several horses-mounted cavalrymen and officers.

"The Elamites are on our flank!" Daresh shouted to his soldiers. "Turn and face them! Lock your shields and ready yourselves! Go now!"

His soldiers did so, obedient and courageous in the face of the battle to come. The envoys retreated into their carts to protect their precious, unspent cargo while the soldiers rushed into their formations to face the elements above on the hilltop. It was not long before the elemental rushed down the hillside like a tidal wave of spears, horses and armour. War cries echoed over the desert from the Elamites, every one of their soldiers charging forth towards Daresh's army in sheer fury, ready to kill anyone in their way.

The first few lines of the warring armies collided in a great clash, and the orderly lines of soldiers broke into chaos. Babylonians and Elamites plunged swords and lances into one another's body. Cascades of blood spilled from falling corpses and severed heads, staining the desert crimson. The air was dense with the cries of warring soldiers and screams of pain and death.

Amid the chaos of battle, Daresh rode among his comrades with his twin swords out and slicing through Elamite flesh. All the while he tried to maintain his martial poise and well-ingrained training, but the sight of his soldiers getting killed broke his demeanour. Soon, the ordinarily methodical and calculating general Daresh became a hurricane of unbridled rage, slashing through every enemy soldier in his path. As Elam's ranks started to thin, Daresh tossed one of his bloodstained bronze swords several yards, plunging tip-first into the face of an Elamite straggler, who promptly fell down dead.

Daresh tried to steady himself, breathing the fury out of his lungs as the battle ended, and the last of the elements was killed. Still on horseback, he travelled over the battlefield, over the corpses of his brothers in arms. Every dead Babylonian was a shame he would have to bear for the rest of his life, and it was taking a heavy toll on him.

King Hammurabi was surprised by the entrance of a bruised and bloodied Daresh in his throne room several days later. Only a handful of soldiers came back with him, and the treasure-carting caravans were left untouched.

"Noble King Hammurabi," Daresh said with a bow, trying to mask the pain in his voice. "Regretfully, I bring troubled news."

"Speak plainly," Hammurabi prompted him.

"The Elamite king has rejected our offer and attacked our troops. He sent a garrison after us as we were leaving. We had no choice but to fight back and kill them all. The caravans were left untouched and the treasure is still yours."

"I care not about the treasure, General," Hammurabi replied. "You are right to think me disappointed, but I believe this is not any fault of yours."

Hammurabi shifted in his throne, lost in thought. "Something is wrong. Why would Siwe-Palar-Khuppak turn down my offer?"

"Sire?" asked Daresh. The king wearily rubbed his forehead, clearly disappointed.

"Leave me at once, General," the king commanded sternly. Without another word, he did so, retreating to his private quarters. The night breeze wrapped around him as he entered, but his frustrations overrode his senses as he took off his armour and cleaned his bloodied hands and face with a water-filled basin near the door. His breathing was still heavy and his fists were balled up. He was so intoxicated with the rage directed at himself, that he almost missed the figure on his mattress.

"Tamira?" Daresh asked. "What are you doing here?"

"Waiting for you," Tamira answered. "Your Highness."

"Don't call me that," Daresh muttered.

"I can see you're quite tense," said Tamira.

"I lost many good men today."

"Then let me put you at ease," she said teasingly, uncovering her bare shoulder and some of her right breast. Daresh understood instantly what she meant, and he walked to the mattress, crawling slowly over her. He looked deeply into her luminous blue eyes and kissed her on the lips.

The rest of the evening devolved into a passionate display for the two lovers, their two bodies entwined together in vigorous motion. The weary general caressed the princess's tender flesh and felt all his cares vanish in an instant. He pressed into her body, showing great energy to please Tamira.

Hours passed, and the two lay together on the bedding through the night. Daresh and Tamira covered themselves with soft silk covers, keeping each other close. Tamira had been already fast asleep in his arms, and Daresh drifted into a peaceful slumber at her side.

The battle raged all around Daresh as he surveyed the scene. In a distant desert lined with gnarled, jagged trees, two opposing armies fought to the death against one another. Daresh's heart was filled with that familiar sense of regret and despair, watching his own people die before his eyes and powerless to stop them. He unsheathed his swords and charged headlong into the fray, parrying an enemy blade that was meant for one of his own soldiers.

Daresh clashed swords with the masked, armoured enemy soldier, struggling to parry his oncoming blows from the enemy's massive broadsword. In an instant, Daresh deflected the enemy's blade and plunged one of his own swords into his assailant's stomach, through the slits in his armour plate. The enemy gurgled blood underneath the helmet that masked his face, and Daresh pulled away his helmet to look upon the face of his enemy. Instantly, his hand let go of the sword's hilt, and he winced back in terror with eyes gone wide and a blanched face.

The enemy he just stabbed… was Tamira.

Daresh awoke with a sudden scream, jolting upright in his bed and gripping his forehead. Sweat beaded on his brow, and his breathing was fast and laboured. His heart pounded like a war drum with such fervour that it beat rang in his ears. He looked around his quarters, trying to ground himself in reality. Whatever battle that was, it was not any one that he himself endured. What enemy he was facing, he could not name; it was not an Assyrian or Elamite that he faced. Tamira herself stirred awake at his side, alive and well.

"Daresh? What's wrong?" she asked.

Daresh tried to steady himself. "A horrible dream," he responded.

"What did you dream?" asked the princess.

"I don't believe you'd want to hear it."

"I specialize in dreams, Daresh."

"What do you mean?" asked the general.

"Maybe the gods are sending you a message. Tell me what you saw."

"I saw…" Daresh started, trying to find the right words. "I saw us on a field of battle. You and I were dressed in armour, we drew swords… I killed you."

"I know you would never do that," Tamira observed.

"Of course I wouldn't, especially a woman of your status."

"Is that all I am to you? A lady of status?"

"No," Daresh answered. "You're a very passionate woman."

"You mean a lover?" she asked.

"Yes."

"So why should this game end now?" asked Tamira seductively. Daresh shrugged slightly.

THE MYSTIC THEATER OF DOCTOR XOCTARIUS: VOL. 1-2

"If we're discovered…"

Tamira held a finger to his lips to silence him. "But we won't be," she corrected him. She planted another kiss on Daresh's lips to put him at ease.

They spent the rest of the day remaining in Daresh's quarters, continuing to make love. They rested in between sessions to dine together on a small feast brought by the servants. Roasted quail, fruit and fine wine were brought to his quarters for them to share.

A day passed, and the morning found them both together in a palace lounge. Together they sat on fine wooden chairs in the spacious, breezy room, having a light breakfast and enjoying each other's company. A sudden intrusion from two finely-dressed men broke the mood. Daresh stood up to face the strangers, ready to call for the guards.

"My lady," said the first man to Tamira, who also turned to face him.

"Ambassador Kemosh," Tamira said with surprise. "To what do I owe your visit?"

"Your Majesty, I've been sent by your father, the king, to escort you home. We have prepared a full caravan and are ready to leave."

Tamira scoffed. "I did not ask any of you to come, and I am not yet ready to depart."

Kemosh stood defiant. "Your Highness, please be sensible. Your father's orders must be obeyed," he said sternly.

"By whom? You?" Tamira shot back. "I will be your future queen, and I make it my business to come and go when I please!"

"With all respect, Your Majesty, you are not yet on your father's throne."

Daresh stood to intervene. "What's the problem?" he asked.

"The problem, General," said Tamira, "is that these palace dogs want their seer back. I grow tired of speaking in tongues and casting spells for my father and his court of fools! I am not a slave!"

"Your Highness, please!" Kemosh pleaded. "Your father needs you to interpret the gods' messages for him! He is deeply concerned about stately matters!"

"I do not care what he is concerned about!" Tamira shot back. "For twenty-seven years I have been kept locked away behind iron doors! I will interpret the king's omens no longer! Leave me, or I will have you put to death!"

The Larsan soldiers instinctively unsheathed their swords and pointed them right at Tamira. Two of their companies approached and grabbed her by the arms. She struggled bitterly against their firm, unwavering grips as they started hauling her out of the room. One of the guards suddenly had the point of a bronze blade thrust through his back and out through his chest, sending spurts and ribbons of blood into the air and painting the floor a grisly scarlet.

The blade was held by Daresh. He pulled it out of the dead guard and proceed to slash at the other guards, sending their bodies collapsing to the ground. Tamira broke free from the grasp of the remaining soldier and pulled his own sword away, stabbing him in the chest. It was not long before Daresh and Tamira were the only ones standing among the corpses in the room. Daresh's battle instincts subsided, and he realized in horror at what he had just done.

"Tamira, we have to go! Now!" he hissed through a clenched jaw. Together they fled the scene and out of the palace grounds. They each took a horse from the nearby stables and mounted up, galloping quickly out of the city and into the desert. Together they raced into the wilderness, leaving everything behind, unsure of where to go or what to do. All they had were the weapons they used to slaughter the Larsans.

A day passed as the two wandered on horseback in the desert, countless miles away from Babylon. Their stomachs were growling unrelentingly, and their throats and mouths were parched. The horses they rode on were not faring much better, as they were getting wobbly and difficult to control. The brutal desert sun bore down on them, sapping away their strength, and the hot desert winds blew stinging dust in their eyes. They were at nature's mercy in an unforgiving, inhospitable landscape, from which there would surely be no escape. If they did not find water or food soon, they would certainly die.

The horses they rode upon succumbed to the heat and exhaustion, collapsing under the weight of their riders and fell into the desert sand lifeless, leaving Tamira and her lover to continue their journey on foot. Daresh held her close to try and shelter her from the dusty wind, holding a hand in front of his own face to protect his eyes. Among the dense dust, he could faintly discern the shapes of people in the distance. His spirits lifted slightly at what may be a fleeting hope of redemption. At his side, Tamira was beginning to collapse. Daresh picked up her body in his arms and stumbled towards the people in the distance among the raging winds.

"Help!" he croaked with a parched throat. "Help us!" He could not tell how loud he shouted or even what he sounded like as he trudged through the dust storm towards the people. Getting closer, he could see carts and horses among the people. Some of them ran over towards Daresh and Tamira, just as his eyesight was beginning to go dim. His legs gave out beneath him, and he fell to the ground with the woman in his arms.

Daresh reopened his eyes that night, still feeling weak and paralysed. He found himself lying down on his back in a tent made from a large red linen sheet, propped up with thick tree branches. His eyes struggled to adjust to the light, barely discerning a dark figure standing over him with a clay jar full of clear, clean water. The unknown figure held the jar to his lips and propped his head up, allowing him to drink. The water flowing into his mouth and down his dry, scorched throat felt like a current of rejuvenation flowing right into his body. He exhaled with relief, feeling much better with each sip of water.

"Keep drinking," said a voice over him, coming from the unknown person. Daresh could faintly tell that the voice was female.

"Thank you," Daresh whispered in a hoarse voice. The figure in the dark silenced him, and pressed the jar to his lips.

"Save your strength," the voice whispered again. "Drink."

Daresh kept taking sips of water, then he closed his eyes again. He could still not move, and the figure got up from over him.

"Take some rest, traveller," the voice bade him. "Rest until you are ready to move again."

When Daresh awoke again, he was outside in another night, splayed on a linen sheet on the desert ground. The cool night air caressed his brow gently, a stark contrast to the punishing hot winds he endured before. He heard voices around him, filled with happiness. Daresh tried to move, and through no small effort he hoisted himself up, propping himself up in a sitting position to look around. Tents were pitched nearby, and several people were seated around a roaring campfire, the light of which stung his eyes almost as much as the earlier dust storm. To his side, Tamira was asleep. Daresh felt a tinge of worry creep up in his heart, and looked carefully at her. She was still breathing, and she was stirring slightly in her sleep.

"She'll be fine," said a voice over him. Daresh turned around to behold, a woman standing over them. She was a tall woman, dressed in a dark brown linen robe with a tan shawl wrapped around her head. She smiled and knelt down at Daresh's side.

"Where are we?" asked Daresh, his voice still hoarse.

"We're still in the desert, if anything else," she replied lightly. "You're a long way from home, general Daresh."

"How did you know my name?"

The woman laughed. "Your reputation precedes you. You were very fortunate that we found you in the desert, else you both would have died."

"What is your name?" he asked.

"My name is Rahab. I am the mistress of this caravan. We are with my family now, and we will take care of you until you're both fit to travel. Who is your companion?"

Daresh paused, trying to find a suitable alibi, then spoke. "Her name is Atarah, and she's my cousin. We were on our way to Judah, my father's home is there, and I have business there with my family."

"That's convenient," said Rahab. "That's where we're all headed. You can travel with us, then!"

Next to Daresh, Tamira awoke. She looked around in surprise, much as Daresh did before, and her eyes met with Rahab's.

"Where am I?" she asked.

"Cousin, don't you remember?" Daresh asked her, nudging her slightly. "We were on our way to Judah, and we were robbed by bandits on our way."

Tamira was speechless, then caught on with his ruse. "Oh, now I remember," she responded, returning the nudge to Daresh.

"Excellent," said Rahab. "We can take you to Samaria in northern Judah, and from there you should be able to carry yourselves where you need to go."

"Samaria will be fine," Daresh replied. "Sorry, but we don't have much in the way of money to repay you."

"What about some of my jewellery?" Tamira cut in, revealing her silver bracelets and an amulet she wore beneath her shawl. Rahab looked over the items curiously, then smiled.

"That should be more than enough, my lady," Rahab explained. "I will instruct the members of my family prepare some food and water for you both for the rest of your journey. Should you decide to part ways from us sooner, we will provide two camels for you as well?"

Daresh shook hands with her, still trying to get used to moving again.

Three weeks passed on their journey with the caravan through the desert. They each rode on the backs of camels, shaded with linen sheets from the desert sun. Every so often, the caravan would stop to rest or to resupply at a nearby village. At one point, Daresh overheard some conversation between Rahab and a trader she dealt with at a small village.

"You drive a hard bargain, Rahab," said the trader, an old man.

"It's for my family, Amir," Rahab responded. "Dates, locusts, figs, and a barrel of water."

"You haven't heard of the fugitives from Babylon, have you?" Amir asked.

"Fugitives?"

"The royals are offering two thousand shekels for the capture of a Larsan princess and a Babylonian ex-general. They say there was a massacre in Babylon, probably some political strife. Now there's talk of war."

"With Babylon or Larsa?" asked Rahab.

"Both. Babylon and Larsa have been getting at each other's throats since then. I'd imagine the return of those two might be worth more than what they're offering."

Rahab concluded her business with Amir, and left the village. By the time they were out of earshot, Rahab rode next to Daresh, making doubly sure nobody in the passed village could see or hear them.

"Did you hear any of that?" she asked.

"Every word," he replied.

"Daresh, they want your head," said Rahab. "You know I could easily give you up if I wanted."

"Please don't," he pleaded. "As soon as we get to Samaria, I can double the reward money to four thousand."

"So be it," she agreed.

Time passed, and the caravan manoeuvred through a mountain pass into the Canaanite territories. Other caravans passing by were becoming more numerous, and there were more opportunities for Rahab to conduct trade to benefit her family and her guests. With each caravan that passed, Daresh grew suspicious; Rahab was also given several opportunities to betray them. One morning, when he met eyes with some of the other traders, they instantly winced back in fear and fell to the ground in fervent, harried prayers, chanting slow, unknown hymns in their native dialects. Daresh passed them by with the rest of the caravan, leaving the Canaanites to pray.

"Daresh, we need to get away from these people," Tamira whispered to him. "I don't trust that woman Rahab."

"I gave her my word," Daresh replied. "I will pay her when we reach Samaria."

"I saw it in a vision," she explained. "Rahab will sell us out to the Babylonians. They will kill you on sight and drag me back to Larsa in chains. I already know it's going to happen."

Daresh sighed, then nodded in agreement. "Fine. We'll leave tonight after everyone else is asleep."

The evening crept up on the caravan as they traversed the hilly desert. The camels that Daresh and Tamira were riding were both stocked with some food and water in pouches on the camel saddles, and Daresh found out where Rahab kept her money purse, in case they needed to steal any for the rest of their journey.

As the sun started to descend towards the western horizon, the caravan abruptly stopped. From where they were in the caravan row, Daresh could not see why they stopped until several familiar-looking soldiers walked down the row talking to some of the caravan members. Daresh froze with fear; those were Babylonian soldiers, and there was no doubt in his mind that they would instantly recognize him and Tamira if they found them.

Without warning, Daresh steered his camel out of the caravan row and darted to the north, out into the wild with Tamira quick to follow. The nearby soldiers were surprised by this sudden move, and turned to Rahab, who instantly went into a conniption, shouting and pointing in their direction.

"It's them!" she shouted, enraged. "Those are the two you've been looking for! The princess and the general, those backstabbing jackals!"

The soldiers alerted the rest of their patrol, and mounted up to pursue Daresh and Tamira. The two fugitives rode their camels hard and fast into the desert, desperate to stay clear of the soldiers who almost recognized them. Daresh did not dare to look behind them, staying fast on course with his lover as far from them as possible. They rode over steep hills and down into deep valleys, and the sun was dipping down below the horizon; daylight was receding as fast as they rode.

After charging into a low valley surrounded by hills, Daresh reared his camel and came to a stop with Tamira at his side. He looked behind him, neither seeing, nor hearing any sign of ever having been followed. The Babylonians may have lost their trail. Daresh heaved a deep sigh of relief, and dismounted from his camel, then helped Tamira down to the ground. They embraced each other tightly and shared a kiss.

"We're safe now, my love," Daresh whispered, holding her close. "They won't find us out here, not this deep in the hills."

When night fell, the two slept together next to a small campfire. Their camels slept off to a side of the valley, their saddles removed to give them some respite. Daresh was fast asleep, but Tamira was wide awake. Being free from the Babylonians' grasp was enough of a blessing for her, as was the prospect of open war being declared among the nations, from which she would be far enough away not to be suspected about it. If anything, her plans were proceeding nicely. However, something was making her feel uneasy about the whole endeavour, some unforeseen complication that if left unchecked, would make things very difficult for her to accomplish.

She turned to the sleeping Daresh next to her, and realized what just happened. Tamira had committed a terrible mistake by getting involved romantically with him. This was not part of her plan, and it would threaten to undo everything she had worked to achieve.

Daresh opened his eyes, and found Tamira restless at his side. He got up and gave her a light embrace.

"Is something troubling you, my lady?" asked Daresh. Before she could answer, the unmistakable sound of footsteps could be heard over the hills surrounding the valley where they were camped. In the light of the campfire, Daresh could discern the shapes of soldiers armed with spears and shields, just like the ones he commanded back at Babylon, in what seemed like a lifetime ago even if it was only just a few weeks since they fled from the city.

"There they are!" shouted the voice of Rahab from among the soldiers. "You've found your prize, Babylonians, and that's two thousand shekels you owe me!"

"There's nowhere left for you to flee, Daresh and Princess Tamira!" came a different voice, a booming and powerful voice from a massive, muscular new Babylonian general in full armour, hefting a broadsword. "Surrender now, or we will attack!"

"Never!" Daresh shot back, reaching for his twin swords, leaving Tamira unprotected for a fleeting moment. When he returned with his armaments, Tamira went into violent, painful convulsions. She fell to the ground in spasms, her muscles going painfully tight and her skin losing its colour.

"Tamira?" asked Daresh, kneeling over her. She quickly turned to Daresh with a painful, enraged look upon her face and shrieked at Daresh with a loud, shrill scream, such as which Daresh had never seen or heard before. He recoiled in fright and covered his ears to stop the piercing scream from echoing in his mind as Tamira started to change shape. Her eyes that were once sparkling blue were now a livid yellow, and her mouth was full of sharp, animalistic fangs. Two curved horns sprouted from her forehead, as did a pair of black leathery wings from out of her shoulder blades. Claws grew on the tips of her fingers and toes, glinting in the campfire's light. All around the valley, the soldiers dropped their weapons and all of them, including Rahab clasped onto their ears, petrified by the creature's screaming.

The thing that was Tamira spread its wings and flew into the air, shrieking all the while. From below, Daresh witnessed in horror as it dived down upon the troops with its claws out, slicing into them all indiscriminately. Their dying screams mixed with the shrill cry of the bloodthirsty demon, which never stopped its vicious, frenzied assault.

Even Rahab was not spared the creature's wrath, and her throat was ripped open, blood gushing in thick torrents from her gaping wound. In the middle of the harrowing scene, Daresh was left alone, made to watch in sheer terror at what unfolded around him. Everywhere he looked, he saw death and dismemberment, and like in his dream, he was powerless to change anything about it all.

The only thing left for him to do was to fall to his knees and beg for guidance from on high. As the creature finished its slaughter and drinking deeply of the blood of its final kill, it saw Daresh drop the ground as he began to pray on his knees in the middle of the valley. It flew down to the ground and changed shape; the wings and horns receding back into its body, and the sickly grey skin and yellow eyes were replaced with a youthful russet skin and electric blue eyes. What was once a murderous demon returned asthe princess Tamira, and she walked down into the valley. Daresh looked up from his prayers, and saw Tamira looking down at him. Every last emotion he felt railed against the dark reality that he just witnessed; the love of his life had turned into a murdering, marauding creature of darkness.

From above, a cascade of pure white light, brighter than the sun, broke over Daresh. Tamira shielded her eyes from the light, and Daresh looked up to find its source. A powerful voice echoed in the night from above.

"SHE IS OF SATAN," said the voice from above. "SHE HAS SET THE NATIONS AGAINST EACH OTHER WITH HER DECEIT. YOU MUST SMITE HER."

"My lord," Daresh cried out, looking for the light in the sky. "Have mercy upon her! I love her!"

"SHE IS AN ABOMINATION," replied the heavenly deity. "SHE WAS SENT BY THE MOST UNCLEAN ONE TO CORRUPT, AND DESTROY MY CREATION. YOU, AS MY ANGEL OF DEATH, MUST CAST HER INTO OBLIVION."

"What if she could repent?" Daresh pleaded. "Could she be saved?"

"IT IS NOT IN THEIR NATURE TO DO SO. MY LAWS MUST BE UPHELD."

"If I redeem her, will I be no different than the Fallen One?"

"YOU MUST BANISH HER TO THE PIT. TO REFUSE IS TO SERVE THE ENEMY. DO NOT DEFY ME."

Daresh bowed his head in reverence and unsheathed one of his swords. "Yes, lord. I shall obey."

As quickly as Tamira changed form, so too did Daresh. Standing in the column of celestial light, a pair of white, feathery wings shot out from his back. His armour, which was once a mere rough iron, transformed into a shiny, polished alloy more finely wrought than any to be found on Earth. In his hands, a tall scythe with a golden handle and a silver curved blade materialized in his hands. He became more than the Babylonian general Daresh; he was now Azrael, the legendary Angel of Death, sent by the Most High to do His will in the mortal world. What's that now meant to be to smite this demon that plagued the world.

"I know who you are, Tamira," Daresh said sternly.

"You wouldn't kill me, would you?" Tamira asked seductively. "After everything we've done together?"

"It is what I must do. You have set nations at war with each other, and this is the price to pay. It is not my choice to make." He stepped out of the column of light and towards Tamira, hefting the scythe in his hands. Tamira stepped back, trembling.

"Are we so different?" she pleaded. "We all have our masters, yet here we are. I would trade it all away for a chance to spend eternity with you. If you kill me, what will be left for you except the endless years of an eternal life filled with loneliness and regret?"

Daresh's hands quivered, and the scythe was starting to feel heavy. He froze for an instant, unsure of what to do. Tamira gave her a smile and a nod, thinking that she had finally put him in his place.

But Daresh shook his head and stepped forward with his heavenly weapon. "No," he stammered. "I have my duty."

With that, he grasped the golden scythe handle, and assumed a ready stance. His face was filled with the deepest pain as he readied his weapon.

"Forgive me," he whispered.

The blade sliced through the night air, finding its mark right in Tamira's heart and piercing her chest. The blade sank into her flesh and popped out of her back. Where there would be blood falling from the wound, there were bright beams of pale yellow light spilling from her body, lighting up the shadowy corner of the valley. Tamira screamed as the light poured out of her, and Daresh pulled the blade from her open wound. Tamira fell to her knees, dying.

Daresh dropped the scythe and hastened to cradle her body, heartbroken. Tears welled up in his eyes and dripped down his face. Tamira's eyes were wide, and the blue glow that he saw in her while alive was beginning to ebb away.

"I love you," he whispered.

"I love you too," she replied. Daresh leaned over her, and they shared one final kiss before her body disintegrated into gray ashes scattering in the breeze. Daresh was left with nothing but a handful of these ashes, and he fell to his knees weeping for his lost love as streams of tears flowed down his hot cheeks. The white wings on his back folded over his body, as if trying to hide him from the entire world, and from the God of all life, everlasting.

"YOU HAVE DONE MY WILL, AZRAEL," said the Lord above. "YOU WILL BE REWARDED IN THE ETERNAL KINGDOM."

"My Maker, and my God," cried the angel. "Please, I beg of you, my lord, grant me peace. All I have ever yearned for was just taken from me."

"THIS TOO SHALL PASS."

The Angel of Death remained kneeling in the valley among the corpses of the Babylonian soldiers and the caravan leader, all of whom were left eviscerated in the desert. The ashes of the creature that was once Tamira blew over the bodies in the wind. From out of the angel's tear-filled eyes, he could see faint wisps of white light flowing from each body, ascending over their former homes and floating upwards to the heavens.

Seeing this, the angel knew what he had to do. This was his purpose, the one task he was suited for and would continue to execute for all the ages. He picked himself up off the ground and took the scythe in his hands. The angel exhaled a deep sigh, and wiped away his tears. His wings outstretched, and he flew up off the ground into the night sky, surrounded by the spirits of the dead.

The desert disappeared, as did the bodies and spirits. In its place, the Mystic Theater returned. The audience was altogether silent and wide-eyed. Gabriel especially felt every sense of fear, longing and regret that the angel had fallen. All the while, he knew that the Babylonian general who fell in love the princess turned demon looked staggeringly familiar.

Onstage, Doctor Xoctarius stood alone, his gaze turned down and a hint of a teardrop could be seen on his face. From there, Gabriel knew that it was him all along. Doctor Xoctarius himself *was* the Babylonian general, and the Angel of Death.

"Was that really you?" asked one theatre attendee in a whisper. "Are you an angel?"

"Are you going to kill us?" asked another.

"Do you know God?"

"Can you tell us the future?"

The doctor kept his gaze low, and he waved a hand over his head to silence the voices around him.

"My purpose," he stated, with a voice that was surely strained from emotion, "iss to bring souls to a higher state. I can do no more than that. All I have done here tonight was for the benefit of mankind, to inspire a higher state of thinking and being within all of you. I work for no selfish ends, and I offer no selfish ideas. All I come to bring to you is wisdom.

"What you have seen and felt tonight is entirely yours to contemplate, how you do so is entirely yours. Will you, as I hope, strive for greater heights and greater standards? Or will you be the same as you were yesterday and the days before that? As I have done in all times before, I offer you a chance to find redemption. Whether you will take, it is yours to decide."

The doctor waved his hand over his head again, and the Mystic Theater disappeared once more. However, there was no other vision to be shared, no other distant place to be explored. The Mystic Theater was gone, and the entire audience was left standing in a vacant lot in the middle of Los Angeles in the present day, exactly where they were when they first entered the theatre.

The doctor himself was nowhere to be found. Everyone looked around, puzzled as to what just happened, as if they had just awoken from a vague dream. There were no words, just faint gasps of alarm, then the realization that the trip was over. All that was left now were their lives to which they had to return, but the memories of the visions imparted by the doctor remained with every one of them.

Gabriel shared in their collective bewilderment, pondering every vision with the intent that the doctor had promised; the idea that life was worth living in this great existence that man calls the ultimate adventure, to live and explore the meaning of life, that the future is what is we make of it, that trickery and domineering human behavior in the choices we make will only lead to disaster, and that certain secrets that exist should never be seen or wielded by anyone who cannot hope to control them. All these ideas stayed with him as he walked down the sidewalk through the decrepit city, as he boarded the nearest metro bus and headed back to the museum where his car was parked.

His red sedan sat in the same spot where he left it. The parking lot was deserted, and the only light by which he could see was from a bright street lamp overhead casting pale orange light over the concrete parking lot. The visions presented by Doctor Xoctarius stayed in his mind as he fumbled for the keys in his pocket and unlocked the car door.

Getting in, he exhaled a breath to try and steady himself, as if he had just gotten off of a roller coaster. He tried to slow down his heartbeat and regain his bearings before turning on the ignition. The car's engine roared to life, and he turned on the headlights before putting the car in reverse to exit the parking lot.

"Was it all a dream?" he asked to himself, still dwelling on the imagery that he saw earlier in the Mystic Theater. "Maybe it was."

"No," came a voice in response. "I did it for you, Gabriel."

Gabriel recoiled in shock from the unexpected response, and even less expected was the presence of Philip Grafton, also known as Doctor Xoctarius, seated in the front passenger seat of his car. His Doctor Xoctarius costume was gone, replaced with the impeccable business suit and ascot that he wore when they first met in the museum.

"Am I..." Gabriel stuttered, lost for the right words. "Am I going to die?"

"No, it's not your time; not yet," the angel responded.

"Then why are you here?"

"There are many other stories to tell, and I could use your help, my friend."

Gabriel could not believe this any more than the visions he beheld in the Mystic Theater.

"You really are an angel..." he breathed.

The angel stretched his arms casually. "I always have been and always will be, my friend."

"I've never had a friend like you," said Gabriel.

"I've always been at your side, Gabriel. Before you were even born, I've was there to protect you."

"The Angel of Death was sent to protect me, by God in Heaven?"

"Yes. Is that so hard to imagine? I do what is needed of me, just as I did back at Babylon. We have a long road ahead of us, and it only gets better from here."

"Where are we going?"

"Don't worry; I will guide you. You shall see,"

Gabriel drove his car out of the parking lot and onto the darkened, deserted street. With his passenger, he felt ready to face anything that was yet to come. Full of confidence and courage, Gabriel would stay at the angel's side and the angel at his side, ready to embark on a new adventure as they proceeded to drive through the city toward a strange looking dark tunnel on the nearby freeway, which filled with otherworldly white light with time itself fading into the future unknown.

...... To Be Concluded

www.ingramcontent.com/pod-product-compliance
Lightning Source LLC
Chambersburg PA
CBHW051431260626
47162CB00001B/40